I0690000

Reborn a Hero: Asher Merrick

By Solomon Ignis

GLOWSTONE PUBLISHING

Copyright © 2021 by Glowstone Publishing

All rights reserved

ISBN - 979-8-9862795-1-0

Dedicated to me.

Thanks for finally shutting the hell up and writing a book.

Acknowledgements

Thank you to my wife for supporting my dreams and encouraging me to write whatever I want and go for broke.

Thank you **_linakkuma** for the cover art, you did an amazing job. **Giznizzle**, you also did wonderful work on the promotional material.

Big thank you for interior art by **GhostCollectiveArt**, **ScapeFiend**, and **MacTeg**. You all did a wonderful job, and turned a dream into reality.

Thank you **Lady**, **Penny**, and **Aife** for helping bring the trio to life.

Thanks to my editors **Carry** and **Frances**. Y'all made magic happen.

And a quick shoutout to */r/HaremFantasyNovels* and the Facebook group *Harem Lit* for continuously adding to my reading list. I hope this book can join some of your reading lists as well.

Lastly, a special thank you to the first person who made fan art of anything I ever did: **Zee**. You have no idea how cool that made me feel.

Table of Contents

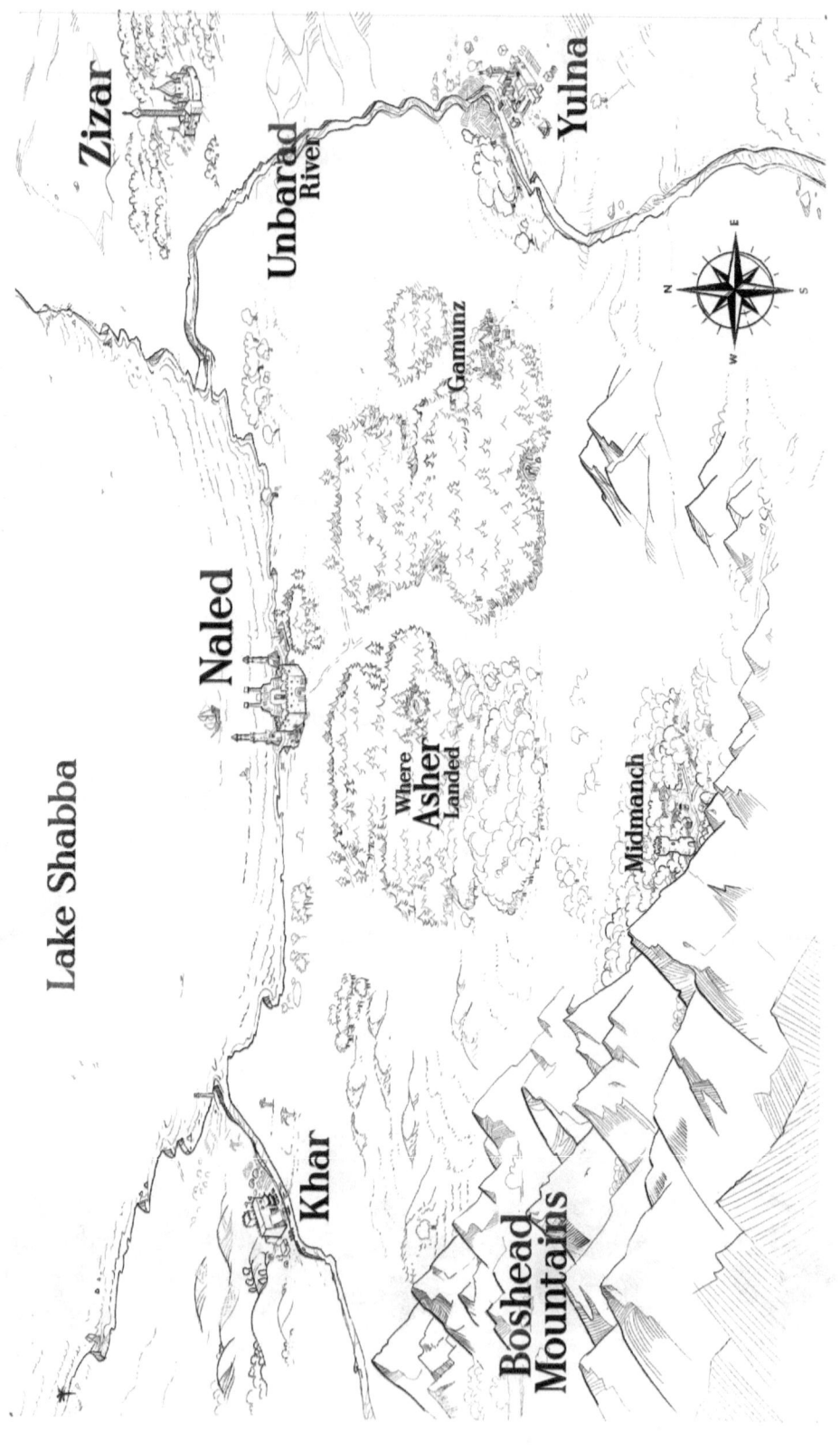

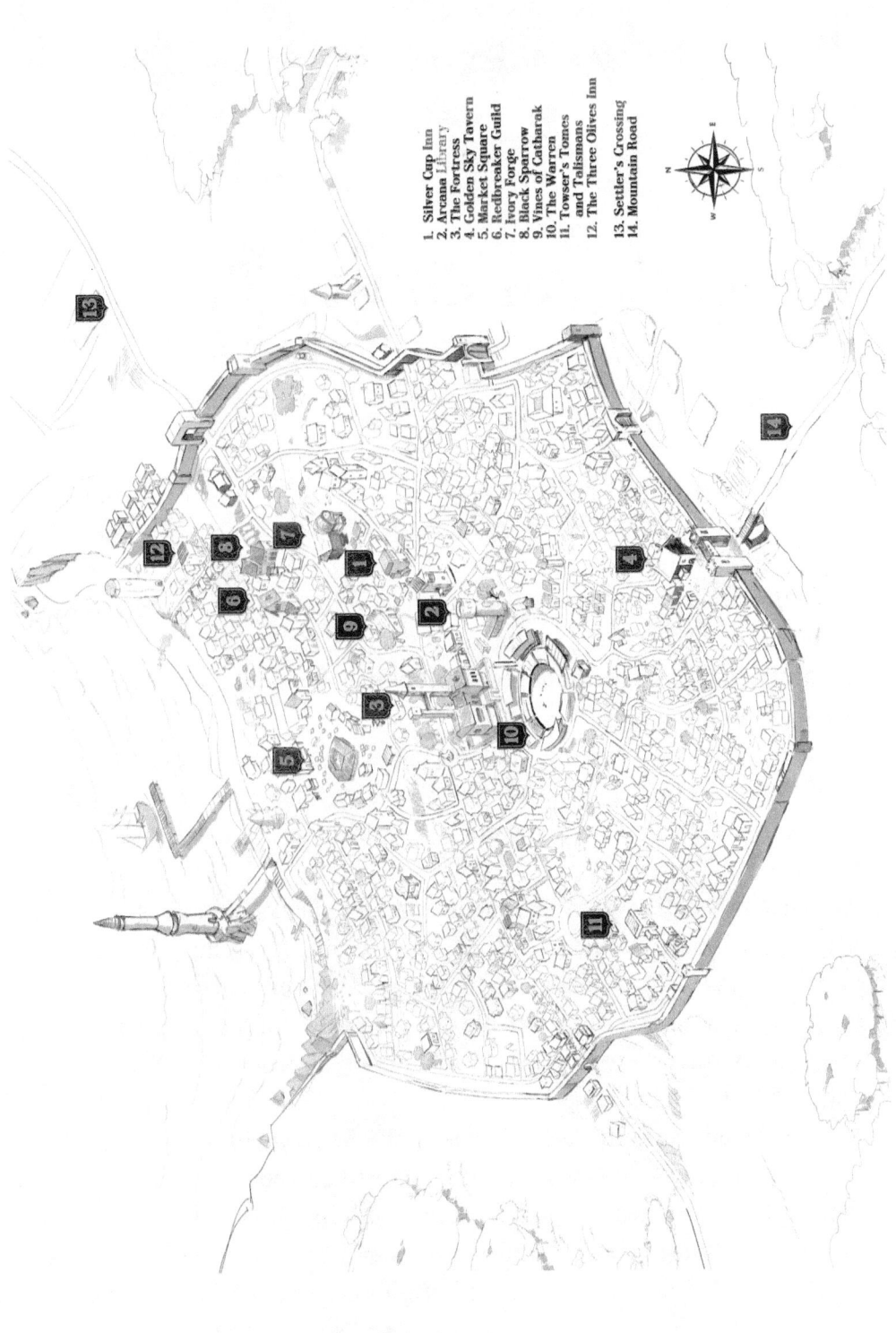

1. Silver Cup Inn
2. Arcana Library
3. The Fortress
4. Golden Sky Tavern
5. Market Square
6. Redbreaker Guild
7. Ivory Forge
8. Black Sparrow
9. Vines of Catharak
10. The Warren
11. Towser's Tomes and Talismans
12. The Three Olives Inn

13. Settler's Crossing
14. Mountain Road

Death: An Empty Thing

Chapter 1

You never know when your last day is. You never know why it will be your last day. And I can say for certain, you don't know what comes after. I certainly didn't. But I was about to find out...

The familiar sounds of twenty-somethings rummaging for fake IDs at the door, disappointing local sports on grainy television screens and the faint smell of vomit behind the building brought me back to the glory days of about six months ago.

"So then, Old man Emerson is smacking his monitor saying it ate his emails" I giggled to Anastasia 'Annie' Evans, my day-one friend from college. She fished for her cherry out of her drink as she laughed along with me.

"Because he's a dinosaur." she chimed in, her cheeks red as roses.

"Right!?" I shouted while polishing off my drink. "And he looks at me and says 'Asher! Get this thing to give me back my email now!'" I scrunched my nose and did a terrible impersonation of the old geezer.

"And quit putting your money in that damned electro-dollar! Gold and silver, Asher! Gold and silver!"

Annie snorted while she laughed and threw her head back in a cackle. We were at Shanny's, the local uni bar that we had spent too many nights at during college when we should have been studying. I was two shots of Jack and a pitcher of deep, while Annie was on her fourth or fifth old-fashioned. Her pale, freckled face always burned bright red when she was drunk.

After a moment, our laughter died down and we looked at each other.

1

She looked stunning. Her steel gray eyes always made me feel lost when I looked at her. It was like they could grab me and demand my attention. She smelled like lavender, which mixed well with the whiskey and cherries on her breath. I could never tell what was on her mind, even four years later, whenever I looked at her.

It's not like my attraction to her was ever a secret, but I always did my best to keep things strictly platonic. But after not seeing my best friend for six months, she looked... different. She looked... serious.

"Asher, can I ask you something?" She moved her hand to mine, and I felt a lump form in the back of my throat.

"Uh, yeah, sure." My feet shifted uncomfortably.

"What happened to you? One day, you're set to take on the world, and the next, you're working the counter at a pawnshop."

"Just wanted something easy, I guess. Didn't need the money," I said with a shrug.

"Is that right?" Annie asked. "You hit big on some coins and decided to turn into a recluse?"

"I wouldn't know if recluse is the right word," I protested. "Besides, with this thumb drive, I can sell my crypto safely and securely. No online wallet. No need for a third party."

Annie just rolled her eyes and looked at the thumb drive contemptuously. She turned her eyes back to me and gave me a long, serious look.

"You've got all this money. You could do anything. Be anywhere. The whole world is open for you to do everything. Why aren't you doing anything?"

Ever the queen of eloquence, old Anastasia Evans. I pulled back slightly and gazed off at a whole lot of nothing on the walls, placing the drive back in my pocket. My head buzzed like the neon signs plastering the walls.

"I mean…"

I couldn't say anything. The words were all stuck on my tongue. I looked back at her glumly. She really should have been a police officer or something with how good an interrogator she is. It was like I was a mouse getting batted around, and she was ready to go in for the kill.

"You really don't have an answer, do you?"

I crossed my arms on the sticky bar and slumped over. Try as I might, I didn't have an answer. Here I was, six months out of college, working as a desk jockey at a local pawnshop. I wasn't working in my field. I hadn't bothered going for internships. But, I didn't really need to. I really had sold a bunch of crypto I'd bought in college and lived comfortably. Lonely, but comfortably.

"Dunno," I finally said in defeat. "I just wanted a job where I could..."

"Where you could what?" Annie pressed.

"I don't know!" I shouted, putting my face right in hers.

The bar got awkwardly quiet for just a moment as I felt dozens of eyeballs burning through me. Despite my sudden invasion of her personal space, she didn't flinch. She just stared at me with those eyes, piercing me like a knife to the chest. I looked away and leaned back.

"Sorry."

She just rolled her eyes and sighed.

"It's fine, Ash, I just think you have so much potential that you're afraid to use," She said shaking my shoulder. "I mean, seriously, this is probably the first time you've gotten out of that apartment since we graduated."

Her remark was more accurate than she realized. The pained expression on my face bore witness to its accuracy. Her eyes widened and she brought her hand to her mouth.

"Oh no," she said. "I was just... I was joking. I wasn't trying to insinuate..."

"Nah..." I sighed. "You're right. Just like in college, you're the only thing that ever got me to leave my bedroom. If I'm not at work, I'm just in my apartment. By myself. No roommates, no family, not even a cat or a gerbil."

"Ash," She put her hand above her mouth and leaned in closely. "I-I'm so sorry. I shouldn't have ever said that. And I should have texted you sooner, or came to see you or-"

Before she could finish, our heart-to-heart was interrupted. I saw their garbled reflection in my empty beer glass. Turning around I saw a sleazy figure in a green jacket with some obscure metal band shirts underneath. He looked like he fell out of the ugly tree and was hit by every branch on the way down. And then the tree tipped over and fell on him after his fat ass caused a shockwave on landing.

"Hey, there sweet cheeks," His hair was slicked back in a greasy black ponytail with a widow's peak sharp enough to gouge your eyes out.

3

"Why don't you get rid of that sad sack and get with a reeaalll man," He punctuated the remark by putting his hands in his pocket and pushing out his waist.

Annie looks like she was about to throw up. Her red cheeks had gone completely pale. Well, paler than she originally was. That boiled egg-type of pale that your skin gets if you have a bad fever or something. She tried to say something, by she couldn't get the words out as the bastard grinned.

The way he looked at her was like a bloated crocodile. He managed to sweat in an unheated bar in the middle of fall. And the only smell my nose could sense was whatever he rolled around in before walking inside the bar. I really didn't like this guy. I balled my fists in anger.

"Hey, walrus," I chided him, leaning towards his face. "If you're going to try to find something to screw, why don't you headed back to the Arctic Circle? Or why don't you go back to the gloryhole your mom conceived you in."

His face turned a disgusting shade of purple at my comment. "The hell you say to me?" He whispered at first.

Annie tried to intervene, "He didn't mean any-"

"The FUCK did you say to me, you little shit!?"

My grey eyes blinked out of unison as I looked him in his beady, little brown dots.

"I said that you should stop interrupting her. Now, fuck off."

In a flash, my head was slammed onto the bar top. Luckily, he missed smashing me into my glass. Unfortunately, Shanny's bartop was an authentic slab of black oakwood. The side of my face throbbed in pain as I saw a few splotches in my vision. The sounds of other conversations stopped abruptly.

'Yeah!" The greasy bastard shouted, "Not so fucking funny now, are ya? You little ginger prick."

"Shit," I grunted in pain as he grabbed me by the hair.

"Asher!" Annie screamed.

I blinked several times and my vision cleared, along with my head. Luckily, my senses were thoroughly dulled by the alcohol in my system. It was probably the liquid courage in my liver, but suddenly, I felt 6'6" and 275 pounds.

I looked back and mule-kicked him in the gut. He stumbled back into a

4

wall, and I leapt out of my seat. Too drunk, inexperienced, and downright clumsy to punch, I launched myself at him and landed headfirst on his nose.

You could hear the sickening crunch as it broke, and he swore loudly. I bounced back from the impact and felt a droplet of blood on my forehead. He swung with his free hand and was too fast for me to dodge.

I went careening back into the bar. My ribs caught the edge and plunged the air out of me. With a shout of adrenaline, I grabbed the basket of fries Annie and I had nearly finished and slung it back at the bastard.

It didn't do any damage, but the surprise of it gave me an opening. I roared before drunkenly charging back into my pudgy adversary, swinging like a madman. Both of us landed shots at each other's stomachs and faces in a scrum at the corner of the bar. One thing was for sure, this fat fuck could punch really hard. Luckily, I was as stubborn as he was stupid, fat, and ugly.

A group of bar patrons grabbed us and tried to keep us separated. We both shouted obscenities and insults at each other along with insinuations about the other's various female family members. Annie fought through the crowd and pulled me back from the fight. The bartender kicked him out as the crowd sent him on his way.

The cumulative impact of all his punches seeped into my nerve endings. I slumped back down onto the bar for a minute. I was groaning in pain when the bartender snapped her fingers for my attention.

"No fighting, Asher, you know the rules. You too, Annie."

"She didn't do anything," I protested, grabbing my ribs.

The bartender just shook shaking her head, "Both of you, get out. I don't want any more trouble in here tonight."

"Never took you as a fighter," Annie said softly, wrapping an arm around my shoulder.

"Life is full of surprises," I mumbled.

The bartender was about to say something, but Annie just slapped a couple of twenties on the bar and got out of her seat. Annie and I left the bar that was home to many college memories and my last taste of Earth.

As we walked down the street, she fretted over the lump on my cheek. I tried to assure her it was nothing. By this point, it was well past midnight and both our cars stayed at the bar for the evening.

"You sure you don't mind walking?" I asked while struggling to catch my breath thanks to my bruised ribs.

"Nah, there's a bus that runs super late for all the college kids. I live just off campus anyways. Are you sure *you* don't mind walking?" She chided me lightly. I just snorted in protest, and we kept on walking.

"Thanks for sticking up to that creep, by the way. I never thought in a million years you'd ever fight someone like that. Or at all, in real life, at least."

Ignoring the doublespeak of her compliments, I just shrugged my shoulders. "I didn't either, to be honest. But I saw that guy and snapped." I winced as one of my bruises flared up. I looked back at her.

"I just didn't want you to get hurt. I know you can take care of yourself, of course. You've been doing a great job with that. It's just..."

"It's just...?" Annie looked at me, her head cocked slightly.

I put an arm behind my head and dragged my foot across the ground. My cheeks burned brightly as I mustered up the words.

"It's just that, I wanted to protect you. I didn't want to see anything bad happen to you. "

Annie just looked at me for a moment and said nothing. Her eyes just fixated. As we walked through the gentrified neighborhood, I was assaulted with a tidal wave of memories.

Over on that fence was where we found a stray cat and walked across the city to return it to its owners. That basketball court was where I nearly got in a fight with a bunch of middle schoolers over what constitutes traveling in basketball... That bookstore was where we would buy weed from our dealers at a discount for good grades.

"We sure had some good times, eh Annie?" I chuckled.

Annie looked down at the ground and said nothing for a block. I heard a cat knock over a trash can about a block away as we waited for the crosswalk across from my apartment. When I looked back over to her, there were tears on her face.

"I wish it never had to end, Asher. I'm so sorry for everything," She let out a small sob. "I wish this night'd never end." Her face held a morose smile. It was the same kind she had when she told me stories about her dog Benedict after he died.

A weird sensation crept up in my stomach as I looked at Annie. I felt all wiggly and nervous. Those damn butterflies had made their way into my stomach. She took a step closer to me. A little too close for comfort.

I could count the freckles on her face now. I could see the movement in the nostrils of her little nose. I could see how well the red complimented her from the stoplight. My heart was beating faster now than during the bar fight.

A breeze rolled through the street picking up leaves.

"Doesn't really have to end, Annie." I whispered. "I always figured you and me would take on the whole world anyways. You know, as friends?"

She took another step closer. I could feel her chest gently pressed against mine. Her slender hand slowly traced its way along my arm and cupped my face.

"Doesn't have to be as friends, Ash." her smile was soft as silk, and her lips looked sweeter than candy.

A harsh, familiar voice cut in on our moment. "Ain't that cute."

Both of us turned at the voice. It was the asshole from the bar. He was covered in bruises and held his arm in his jacket. Instinctively, I pushed Annie behind me, trying to protect her. The fat fuck just smiled with a big dopey grin.

"Look at this here, knight in shinin' armor." He said mockingly.

"Leave." I said, ignoring the bruises he'd covered me with. "Before I call the cops."

He pulled his hand out of his jacket, revealing a pistol. "Cops ain't gonna be here in time, Crypto Boy."

My heart dropped instantly as he pointed the barrel towards me. Annie let out a small yelp, but was frozen in fear. I couldn't move either. I was too far to grab the gun. He was too close to miss. I quickly put my hands up.

"Easy, man," I said slowly. "It doesn't have to be like this."

"Oh, it doesn't?" He said lightly. "Got a nice thumb drive with a million reasons for me to keep you alive, right?"

"You were listening in at the bar?" I asked, trying to keep his attention on me. "About the money?"

"Oh yeah." He laughed. "Really easy though when she had you hanging on her every word. Good job by the way, sweetheart."

He looked past me and smiled at Annie. I looked behind her and noticed she was eerily calm. She didn't even have her arms raised. She just stood

7

there, staring back at the man with this peculiar look on her face.

"How much does it got on it?" He asked, arching an eyebrow.

Before I could answer, Annie answered with her phone in hand. "$1.8 million." She said, emotionlessly.

I whipped around and saw that she was a good ten steps away from me now. She had the USB drive connected to her phone. More importantly, she had a gun in her hand. A little snub-nosed revolver.

And it was pointed at me.

"Annie!" I shouted, tears stinging the sides of my eyes. "What the fuck?!"

The bastard cackled like a hyena. "Oooooh, I think you broke the little shit's heart."

She ignored his remarks and looked at me, tears on her face as well.

"Stay still, Asher."

Bang!

I closed my eyes and flinched, but I didn't feel the bullet's wrath. I opened my eyes and saw her gun smoking at the end. She was looking past me, and I saw what she'd done. The fucker was lying on the ground with a bullet in the chest. His eyes quickly glazed over as he said his final words. "Traitor fucking bitch."

Oh, thank fucking God. I ran over and kicked the gun away from him. Even if he was dead, I didn't want to take a chance.

"Why didn't you run when he pulled out the gun?" Annie asked as I stood over him. "Why didn't you run?" Her voice sounded broken.

"I was afraid he'd hurt you," I said, my mind still racing as I searched for my phone to call the police. It sounded like she was crying. "Couldn't let that happen."

"That's really stupid," Annie said softly

Even in a moment like this, she had a way with words. I gave a humorous breath out my nose.

"Yeah," I said quietly. "Pretty stupid."

"Asher," Annie said, in a full-on cry. "Don't turn around."

Wait. What? Why was Annie crying? Why would she say that?

"Don't turn around!" She screamed.

Ignoring her request, I slowly turned and faced her. And when I did, I saw what I didn't want to see. What I knew I was going to see. What I desperately hoped I wouldn't see. The kind of thing you thought was only possible on the television. The thing that shreds your heart to pieces.

Annie was pointing the gun straight at me. Right at my chest. Her face was bright red, like the morning sun.

Tears flowed like a river down her face. She was sobbing uncontrollably. Her hands shook violently as she held one finger on the trigger. She looked at me, but she couldn't bear to look me in the eyes. But for me? I couldn't look anywhere else. I couldn't look away. I couldn't look at her hands. I couldn't even look at the gun. I could only look her in the eyes.

"Anastasia," I said slowly, putting my hands up.in front of me. "Please, don't-"

Bang! Bang!

She shot me. Twice. And I died before I hit the ground.

The skyward beast let out a mighty roar to the heavens. as it bellowed, sparks and flames sprouted from its maw...

Chapter 2

Death sucks. Really captivating analysis, I know. But I never did appreciate just how bad death was while living. And right now, I wasn't living. I was dying. I could see an echo of the world spinning, as I fell to the ground. Only, it was as if my body had kept moving.

I had died before I hit the ground. My last view of the world was a flickering streetlamp, and a few twinkling stars as I fell.

For however long death was, seconds, hours, years, or millenia, my consciousness experienced it for a split second. The flickering light and wind rushing past suddenly changed into a bright blue light. It rushed past me as I continued to fall further and further down. It didn't make sense. I shouldn't have been experiencing anything. I was dead. I experienced what it was like to go through the Veil.

But here I was. Falling into a whole different kind of abyss. As wind rushed past my ears. I strained my neck and looked downward. A small white circle began to grow. As I fell faster and faster, my eyes strained, and I pushed my hands in front of me.

"Aaaaahhhhh!" I screamed out in terror.

Right before I hit the ground, I jolted to a stop. About two feet from the ground, my inertia was ultimately arrested as if all acceleration just disappeared.

"Well, it's about time I got my hands on you," a disembodied voice chortled. The voice filled the whole space around me, or maybe it was in my head. Probably both, to be honest.

"What?" I said to nobody in particular, stepping down onto the circle. The surface was hard, but felt as if it was floating. Tiny echoes emanated from my steps.

"Don't look so surprised now," the voice said. This time it sounded as if it came from right behind me.

I turned around and saw the person speaking to me. He was tall, with a narrow face and lips. His eyes looked too big for his face, but he emanated a good-natured aura. I stepped closer to him and saw that his eyes were colored like a rainbow, swirling around in a turbulent flow behind his golden pupils. His clothes reminded me of a beggar's.

"Huh," I said to myself.

He smiled and revealed a few chipped teeth in an otherwise perfectly white set. His presence was unlike anything I had ever experienced in my life.

"Asher," he said with a warm voice. "You were quite hard to track down, you know."

He wrapped an arm around my shoulders and gently pushed me to walk alongside him. The white circle extended out, words forming a road just a few feet ahead of his steps. I looked back and saw that the circle had disappeared.

"Did you try checking the morgue?" I asked, fighting the lump in my throat to speak.

The man laughed heartily at my sardonic response. I couldn't bear to join him but did crack a bitter grin. He looked at me and stopped laughing. Replacing his amusement was a look of sadness.

11

"Yes, that wouldn't have been a bad place to look," he admitted. "When I found out about you, and what happened it tore me to pieces. It was a tragedy."

His words stung like thorns on sunburnt skin. I looked away and scowled at the memory. Being dead gives you a weird way of processing things. Annie killed me for my money. She didn't even need to kill me, really. She had to know I'd have given her the money.

"Well, it's a bit more complicated than that, Asher," he said with a knowing look. He read my look of surprise and put a hand up. "Sorry! I didn't mean to read your mind."

"Read my mind?" I shouted, "What the—" I tried to push myself away from him, but I was the only one who moved. My feet slid frictionlessly across the white light and created a small branch from the road.

I looked down and saw the faint blue void in all directions. This had to be a dream. All of this had to be some messed-up dream. It didn't matter how long I was "dead." This had to just be some weird dream.

I touched my face several times and pinched myself. The man looked at me in concern but didn't come any closer. My pulse was starting to go out of control. That fight or flight sensation was back again. Only this time, I had no desire to fight. His aura was so intimidating that I'd rather...

"Asher, no!" he shouted as I leapt off the platform. I had no idea what was going on, but I did not want to stick around and find out.

Something strange happened when I tried to make my escape. I fell for a few seconds, only to land on the exact point I had jumped from. The weird old man was right in front of me still. I looked up and didn't see anything. I looked down the side, and there was nothing there either.

The Old Man had a cockeyed smile on his face. Panicking, I jumped again, looking straight down. As I did, I saw my feet plunge into the depths below. But after a few seconds, I saw the platforms and him again. I landed exactly where I had jumped off, soft as a feather. The Old Man started to laugh.

"Asher, please, I mean no disrespect with my words. But if you keep trying that, we'll be here a long time. Please, dear boy, just come closer."

Fighting literally every instinct inside of me, I walked back towards him. My body felt fidgety and desperate to run away but I stayed still.

"Who are you? What is this place? Why am I here?"

After a moment's contemplation, the man looked at me and spoke.

"I am Gathos, and I am the god of the lost, homeless, and needy in my realm, known as Echo Veil. I have been looking for somebody special to bring there."

"Bullshit," I deadpanned. "Prove it."

"As you wish," he said with a wave.

As he waved his hands, I saw a familiar site appear in a small circular portal. It was the spot right in front of my apartment where I'd been shot. There were two figures there, it was Annie and myself. She was running away from the scene of the crime where I laid dead in the streets.

I looked at Gathos, and he pointed me back to the portal. The view became a bird's eye view, growing higher and higher. I could suddenly see the whole neighborhood. Then the city. The state... The world.

"Earth," He said quietly, "is but one of many places."

With another wave of his hand, the portal's view grew wider and wider showing the solar system, the galaxy, and so on. My mind struggled to grasp the idea of something so large in conjunction with my whole life. My entire existence reduced to less than a speck of dust in a moment.

"And the dead wind up here," Gathos said, showing the universe begin to shift and melt into a gray fog. "Echos of their former lives, drifting in infinity."

The portal showed a blueish-black expanse covered in a dense white fog. It produced an eerie sound, like a gargantuan harmony of voices. I stared at the fog, concentrating as its warbling tune sent a chill down my spine. As I concentrated, I realized that the source of the noise was the fog itself. But I got the distinct feeling it wasn't fog. It was...

"Souls of the dead," Gathos nodded, finishing my thought for me. "You are right there."

He pointed to no spot in particular, and gently reached into the portal. The fog dispersed around him, save for a small speck of dust that remained in place. Pinching his fingers around the speck, I felt an odd sensation, as if I'd just been picked up. He lifted the speck up and I started to float in the air.

"Proof enough?" he asked with a mischievous smile, putting down the speck.

"No," I protested. "But I'm not going to give you any more rhetorical

13

conditionals."

"Fair enough," he mused. "And I must say, that was a two dollar phrase if I ever heard one."

I laughed nervously.

"So..." I started. "You're a god from a different dimension basically, and you're looking for somebody special."

"Yes."

"And rather than go find somebody in this place, you decided to grave-rob my soul and bring me there."

"A bit tactless, but accurate."

His matter-of-fact tone confounded me—the situation seemed so fantastical and ridiculous. It also raised one important question.

"Why me?"

That one had him stumped. He got ready to say something but closed his mouth. He put his hand to his chin and thought for a moment. He rubbed his fingers along his bald face as he chewed on his words.

"Honestly," he said while still rubbing his chin. "I don't have a good answer for you. But they say that God works in mysterious ways where you are from. And it's true in Echo Veil, too—the gods do work in mysterious ways."

I looked at him and sighed at his unsatisfactory response. He couldn't seem to answer the essential parts of my questions. Or he simply chose not to. Well, I suppose I couldn't complain about my situation. I figured it was still trillions of times better than just being dead for the rest of eternity.

"Okay," I said warily. "What do you want me to do?"

Gathos' eyes lit up like a child on Christmas. His teeth shone brightly as he cackled with excitement. Grabbing both of my shoulders, he hooted and hollered for a moment before calming himself down. Still holding me by the shoulders, he looked me in the eyes.

"There are many down in Echo Veil who are lost. Lost in ways that they are not even aware of. It is my job to shepherd the lost, but am powerless to do so as of now."

I looked at him funny. "How can a god be powerless?"

Gathos squeezed my shoulders and with a pained expression. "It can happen when other gods conspire against another. Not all gods are the same. Some wish to commit great evil and will stop at nothing to achieve

14

their goals."

The thought of a cabal of evil gods conspiring against one another was terrifying.

"So, I go down there, and save the lost for you?"

Gathos nodded vigorously. "Yes, Asher. Save those lost on their journey in life."

"Right," I said, unsure of what he meant. "But everybody is lost in their life. I mean... how will I know who I'm supposed to be saving?"

Gathos chuckled and smiled at me like a favorite grandparent. "A sharp young man like you will know."

I stared at him blankly while his eyes shimmered like sunlight refracting through water droplets. Gathos' enthusiasm radiated like the sun, burning my face.

"Okay... but, what if I fail? What if... I die?" I asked him, taking a step back.

He shrugged his shoulders and gestured to the portal with the ocean of souls.

"You'll wind up back here." he explained. "I shall take you back to the fog, and you will cease to exist. But this time, you'll know you went out trying to make a difference before you fade away. My realm needs a hero, Asher Merrick, and I believe that hero is you. I know that that hero is you."

Alarm bells went off in my head. This guy was insanely powerful, but he was also downright insane. First, I died and came back to life. Then he told me he's a god. Now I'm expected to save an entire dimension?

"Listen," I started, "I appreciate the second chance at living. Genuinely. Death wasn't my cup of tea."

His enthusiastic smile dimmed a little as I spoke.

"But you've got the wrong guy. I'm not a hero. I'm not some dimension-saving legend or whatever."

A twinkle in his eye formed. The excitement on his face transformed into a confident grin. He shrugged at me and chuckled.

"I never mentioned you saving the realm or anything about you becoming a legend."

"Well, I know that. I just meant those as, like, examples of what I could be or—"

"Exactly!" He said, pounding his fist into his palm. "You can become a

15

legend. And you can become a hero. And you might save Echo Veil." His face became less joyful and turned flat and neutral.

"However," he said in a cold, distant voice that sent a shiver down to my core. "That doesn't mean you will, Asher. You may fail. You may die. This world is very real. And it is very dangerous."

The darkness surrounding us dissolved and transformed into a massive landscape as he spoke. Replacing the dark blue void were rolling hills filled with bright blue trees that stretched towards the morning sky. The platform beneath my feet was replaced with the soft fluff of a wispy cloud.

As the area came into focus, I saw a creature off in the distance, flying from the horizon. It was larger than any creature I had ever seen flying. Its massive wings beat against the air as it soared. The red morning sun gave the creature an ethereal glow.

The skyward beast let out a mighty roar to the heavens. As it bellowed, sparks and flames sprouted from its maw, evaporating a cloud that it flew through. The sounds I had not noticed before of birds chirping, the wind blowing, and the general life below all hushed to deathly quiet.

"Dragon," I whispered to myself as the beast disappeared into the horizon.

Gathos gazed towards the horizon with me, saying nothing as his face soaked in the sun's warmth on the brisk autumnal morning. The wind in the clouds slipped and streamed along at a breakneck pace, but he and I were unaffected. We stood on this cloud, solid as the mountains that rose straight from the ground.

"Swords and sorcery," I whispered quietly. "Might and magic. Terrors and triumphs, all of it?"

"Yes." Gathos said just as quietly.

"Tragedy too?"

"Guaranteed."

I looked back at him. He knew my next question.

"There will be others like her, Asher," he said, confirming my suspicions. "Fiends disguised as friends. You will be betrayed. Your heart will be broken."

The excitement and wonder slipped away to icy discontent.

"So, what do you say? One more chance at life? A chance at true adventure? A quest to save the lost from a fate like yours own?"

16

As the remnants of the dragon's roar echoed in my chest, I felt something inside of me. Something that I had only felt for brief spurts or periods before. The embers of life started to burn inside of me again. I looked out into this horizon of a new world.

"You've got a deal," I said finally, turning and staring at him. "When do we get started?"

Gathos smiled at me in victory.

"Right now."

Gathos waved his hands, and a large mirror appeared in front of me. I saw my own reflection staring back at me. I looked like death. For good reason, of course. I was in nothing but the pants I had been sleeping in before I died.

I looked at myself in the mirror and thought for a minute. This felt like the first part of a game where you build your character.

My body was pale and gray with no color to it. My muscles had become emaciated—not that they had ever been much to boast about. My reddish-brown hair had turned pale and sickly. Even my eyes had lost what little color they held.

Looking closely, I could see deep scarring on my chest. It must be from the two bullets that went straight into my heart. I touched them and felt their rough bumps against my hand.

"I'm not sure if I'll look different, but I'd like to keep these," I said to Gathos, who nodded.

"Let's get you ready for the world of Echo Veil," he said with a clap of his hands. "I have a question for you. Would you prefer to slice your enemies into bits, or blow them up with some magical concoction?"

As he said those words, my appearance shimmered. At first, a sword appeared in one hand while a shield was in the other. I wore heavy banded armor while my face was obscured by a helmet made of steel. Next, I was in a black and silver robe with a large book. I could feel a strange sensation radiate through my body. It was similar to the feeling of electricity, but it had more of a... flowy feel, like a breeze that ran through my body.

"You'll have the basics down, depending on what you pick." He explained. "No deeper understanding of the mechanics, but a good starting point."

When I concentrated, I could make either version of myself up. I was

17

several inches taller, and my muscles grew tremendously.

My physical appearance didn't change when I concentrated on the more magical version. However, my aura was different. In fact, I felt empowered. It was strange, feeling pure power radiating outward.

I pondered on the possibilities. Both options offered advantages. If I lost my spell book, would I be able to cast any spells? And if I were to fight something like that dragon off in the distance, what good would a sword really be? Did I even want to use a sword? What if I preferred a bow and arrow? Why did I even have to choose between either? Wait a minute... did I?

"I'd like both," I said finally. "No point in limiting myself before I even get started."

"I knew I picked the right one," he said as he studied me intently. "You won't be as adept, but your possibilities will be greater."

My appearance changed as I concentrated once again on my new self. The combination of leather and strategic metal banding around my joints felt protective but not too heavy. On my side was a straight broadsword decorated with a golden inlay and a red and purple wrapping on the handle. Meanwhile, a shield was strapped to my back.

The shield was silver and red on each side, with a curved black line in the middle. At its center was a crescent moon and three stars. On inspection, the same symbol appeared on the pommel of my sword.

"Hope you don't mind having my symbol on your shield," Gathos quipped.

Considering he was bringing me back from the dead, I wasn't going to complain. I rustled through the backpack I had been given. There were several notebooks and pieces of charcoal for writing. Digging deeper into the backpack's main compartment, I found a bedroll, a mess kit, a tinderbox, a bar of soap, torches, food rations, and a waterskin. On the side was a sack with about a hundred gold coins the size of half-dollars stamped with a fleur-de-lis.

"Just enough to get you started," Gathos explained. "Now, let's also add some life to you," he said, pointing at me.

I watched as my face regained its color—perhaps a little more than was there beforehand. My hair changed in color as well. My formerly ruddy ginger locks turned golden. Not blonde, mind you. It was as if my hair had been dipped into molten gold and polished to a perfect shine. My eyes had been changed from a cool metallic gray to bright and silvery. All my features were the same, if a bit sharper.

It was weird. Not only had life been restored to me, but it also looked like I had more vigor than I'd ever had before.

"Huh, I guess that's how my grandmother thought I looked," I quipped to myself.

"It's how Annie saw you as well," Gathos said wryly.

I chose to ignore his comment. Regardless, I had to admit that I looked great. It was interesting to see somebody in the mirror so different yet so familiar. A sad smile crept along my face as I looked at my leather armor and a dark purple cloak. The person in this mirror wasn't just in the mirror. It's who I was. The old me truly was gone.

"At least I'm taller."

"Ha! Yes, well, I think that's about everything. Are you ready, Asher?"

I tore my eyes away from looking in the mirror and looked at him. It was funny. He had the same expression my mom had when I first went to school as a kid. It was the same look that Annie gave me when we both graduated. I turned and looked away, off to the horizon.

I took in the vast sweeping the forest and the tall mountains off in the distance. I looked down at the grass below and imagined taking those first steps. Excitement and worry mixed about in my stomach. What would be the first thing that tried to kill me? What would be my most outstanding achievement? Would I even achieve anything? I didn't know.

"I don't know if I'm ready," I admitted. "But it's time for me to go."

"Alright then," he said quietly with a nod.

The thin cloud around us grew dark and heavy. Thunder began to rumble all around us. Gathos reached out and touched me on the chest. I felt electricity begin to zip and flutter all around me as he did. Tiny arcs of cobalt blue appeared. The thick smell of ozone infiltrated my nostrils.

"You will be given a gift before you go down there, Asher," Gathos whispered to me. "You will be able to see what your potential truly is. You will test how far you can truly push your limits."

The arcing lightning grew in its brightness. It flashed as it illuminated his face in the blackness of the cloud surrounding us.

"Unlock your potential, Asher Merrick. Become great."

The lightning raced towards him at his words, condensing in a giant ball of electricity in his free hand. With one final flash, he brought the hand to my chest. Thunder clattered around us at a deafening roar. My vision blurred as I felt the cold sting of electricity.

My whole body was on fire! Every nerve was overwhelmed at the sensation sweeping across me. My vision began to blur as my brain started to shut down. Gathos disappeared in front of me, or perhaps I was going blind. I put my hands in front of me to block the lightning, but light also radiated from my hands. My whole body had become a giant blob of lightning and energy.

I heard Gathos' voice one last time before I faded from consciousness.

"Don't limit yourself, Asher. I took the liberties of removing those for you."

Chapter 3

Xaliasday Morning, 21st of Wirdin, Year 678, 4th Age

When I woke up, I felt something soft beneath me. It tickled the few bits of exposed skin on my body. My eyes slowly blinked open, and I was greeted with a view of the canopy from below. As I brushed my hands against the ground, I felt soft blades of grass that had just been kissed with the morning dew.

As I acclimated to my surroundings, I took a deep breath and inhaled the scents around me. The air was wet and earthy, but floral and pleasant. It was as if somebody had grated cinnamon and nutmeg over a garden of fresh spring flowers.

I heard the calls of birds and other creatures calling through their mates through the trees. Looking above, I could see that the leaves of these trees were blueish-green, rather than the harsh emerald that I was used to.

I took a deep breath and pulled out my sword. As I did, it shone like a beacon under the shade of the forest. The blade was silver and polished to a near mirror finish.

The pommel felt natural in my hands. I twisted the blade around and made a few rudimentary cuts, slices, and thrusts. The sword felt... like an extension of my body. As if I'd spent my whole life with it.

"Well," I said, sheathing the blade with a flourish. "At least he gave me the basics to start with."

Unsure of where to begin this new journey, I decided to look for a river or stream. I could follow it downstream and hit a town or hamlet if I was lucky. I listened carefully for any sounds of running water but could find no evidence. Checking for any footprints also proved futile. The thick carpeting of the squishy grass absorbed all footsteps like memory foam.

Eventually deciding to just go east, or my closest approximation of east based on the sun's position, I took my journey's "official" start. As I walked along the forest floor, I noticed that few animals stayed anywhere near me. They kept their distance. Hushed their songs. Ran away. I guess they were more afraid of humans in this world than we were of them.

Despite being in a forest so obviously full of life, it was as if none were around me. Silence followed wherever I went. For hours, I walked in apparent isolation while still nature of the area gave me a much-needed chance to simply think.

I still wasn't sure that any of this was real. Perhaps I was still in the throes of death's cruel transition to the afterlife. Perhaps those thousand years of nothing I experienced was a funny little glitch in my brain. But this was more real than any dream I'd ever had. More visceral than any vision or out-of-body experience before it.

When I pinched my skin, I felt pain. When I pressed the cold steel of my sword against my fingertips, I bled. I could smell the soggy smell of life and death when I breathed in. Wait. Life and death?

Snap!

I heard a twig snap behind me. My heart rate shot up, and I grabbed for my sword. As I did, I heard an awful growl.

I turned to discover the source of the quiet that had followed me through the forest.

A gigantic wolf stood snarling at me. The monster had to be at least six feet tall at the shoulders—larger than a Kodiak bear.

Its mangy black fur was matted, and bony spikes protruded from its spine and joints. Its bright red eyes stared hungrily at me through tiny slits. Bits of flesh and blood from its latest victim still hung messily from its rows of jagged broken canines.

It growled at me again, low and guttural, and began to slowly circle inward. As the wolf bore down on me, my grip on my sword tightened.

My immediate urge was to run. But I knew that I could never realistically hope to outrun this beast.

"Oh, fuck you," I said aloud, as I tried to bolster my courage. Was I really going to die again before I'd gotten my chance to explore this strange new world?

"Haaah!"

I let out a scream and charged at the beast.

If I had to die, I would go out fighting. I wouldn't cower and plead, like I had before.

I swung my sword as hard as I could directly at the wolf. It matched my

22

charge with one of its own, ducking beneath my strike. I brought my shield up at the last second and managed to catch its attempt at a bite.

Its jaws enveloped almost the entire shield. It bit down, but the shield did not budge.

Despite my block, the sheer size and strength of the wolf bowled me over. My arm burned from the impact while straining to keep my hold on the shield. The wolf kept its teeth firmly locked as it pinned me to the ground.

"Shit!" I grunted.

I tried to swing at it with my sword but I lost my grip, and the weapon clattered away, out of reach. My vision blurred from the impact of my head smacking into the ground.

When I got into town, investing in a helmet would be one of my first priorities.

The wolf's putrid breath blew into my face, taunting me as I lay trapped beneath it.

Suddenly it released its grip on the shield and snapped again, trying to go for my head. I swatted it away with the shield, barely avoiding having my face bitten off.

The wolf growled in frustration and anger, it's maw a frothy black and red. I felt its claws dig into my armor, further cinching me in place. Its spikes mainly were on its back, save for one on its left front shoulder. This one curled in a nasty forward twist like a knight's lance.

The sadistic animal leaned down, its spike inching toward my skull. I managed to pry my right arm free, trying to hold the animal back. I could swear I heard the wolf laugh as it snarled, slowly pressing its spike further.

I pushed back desperately on the spike. My muscles strained as I tried to slow its progress Something welled up inside my chest as I struggled. The wolf simply pressed its way down further as I felt its spike begin to dig into my throat. With the way the spike curved, it could rip my head off.

Suddenly, a strange sensation burned inside my chest. My muscles screamed out in unison as I held what could be my very last breath inside of me. My face turned right red and then purple as I strained.

The spike finally began to pierce into my neck. Blood trickled onto my shoulder as I desperately gripped at it.

The strange burning sensation became even more potent. The fire burned my insides, every vein, every fiber. It burned hotter and hotter. Brighter

23

and brighter. And right as it was about to explode felt that fire begin to coalesce.

The sensation started to tighten around my muscles, and the spike began to move backward.

Realization dawned on both of us.

Before the wolf could do anything, I tightened my grip around the bone. Tiny pieces and chunks flew in every direction. I ripped and twisted before the wolf could try to slip away.

The wolf let out a pained yell as I snapped the protruding spike off its body. It slammed into the ground on its backside, howling in agony.

Sensing my opportunity, I jumped to my feet and grabbed my sword.

The wolf let out a whimper, lowering its torso before me in a kind of bow, as if to beg for mercy. Its breathing was ragged, as it tried to avoid eye contact. It was trying to tell me that I had won.

We both knew that was bullshit.

With my sword in hand, I went for the beast as it leapt at me. This time, I ducked underneath its attack, and with one single thrust upward, my sword pierced its chest.

The force of my stab lifted the entire beast up into the air. With a surprised bark, the wolf shuddered for a second. Finishing the thrust, I turned my hips and arced my sword downward. As I did, the wolf slammed into the ground.

The beast died after a few last twitches.

As suddenly as my newfound strength arrived, it escaped me. My whole body collapsed onto the ground. Every muscle inside of me screamed for relief from the pain and overexertion. I lay on my back, sucking in precious air.

I felt that I could pass out at any moment and sleep a thousand nights.

"Yeah," I labored. "I really shouldn't be falling asleep in the forest next to a giant carcass."

After a few more prolonged moments of rest, I shakily stood up. The wolf's eyes had gone milky white, and the blood had stopped pooling around it. It looked like the spikes were for defensive measures—protecting joints and parts of the body the mouth couldn't easily reach.

The spike I had torn off the beast was heavy in my hand.

"Glad I didn't get stabbed by that," I remarked. "I wonder if it's valuable?"

As soon as I said that, a voice could be heard right behind my head.

"You could probably get a few coppers."

"Gah!" I shouted out, swiveling around and brandishing my sword.

When I turned around, I came face to face with a tiny green pixie floated just around my eye level.

"Eep!" she squealed, covering her head with her tiny little hands.

She was maybe a foot and a half tall with shimmering silver wings like a butterfly. She had a tiny crown made of flower petals on her head.

"Sorry!" I said sheepishly, putting my sword back.

"I'll say!" she retorted. "I was only trying to help." She looked past me and down at the wolf that I had killed. "Thanks for taking care of that spire wolf, by the way. It has been terrorizing this part of the forest for a while. We asked a group of adventurers to help, but…."

"Adventurers?" My ears perked up. "Do you remember seeing them, little pixie?"

She gave me a long look with an arched eyebrow. I definitely said something wrong. My awkward sensor was going off the charts.

"You are clearly not an intelligent person," she said with a sigh. "That's to be expected from humans, but still. Pixies don't like being called a little. And for your information, I'm probably four times as old as you."

She had placed her tiny hands on her hips as she fluttered into my personal space around my nose.

"Sorry," I said again.

"Is that all you say? Besides dumb comments about pixies, that is. Or is that your name?"

This pixie was not very nice. But then again, I had just insulted her without realizing it.

"No, that's not my name. I am... Asher."

"Never heard of a human named Asher," she said, eyeing me.

"I'm not from around here."

"That much is obvious. Nobody comes into this part of the forest unless they have a death wish, thanks to these wolves. And if you weren't with the adventurers we hired, then you're either not from here or dumb. Or both."

"Probably both," I sighed. The pixie giggled at my self-deprecating humor.

25

"Well, you're lucky you're cute, Asher. You might want to link up with the adventurers I mentioned. They could use a hand last I heard. And like I said, you should get a couple of coppers for each of the bones from the spire wolf if you feel like carrying them."

"Thanks," I said. "I never heard your name by the way."

The pixie smiled at me. "You can call me Trella. The adventurers are that way."

Trella pointed me into the forest, and I thanked her again. Using a knife from my backpack, I quickly cut out a few more of the wolf's spikes. I told Trella she could have the rest if she wanted them, before I headed off in the direction she had indicated.

I couldn't help but marvel that a pixie had told me she thought I was cute. The thought made me laugh to myself.

As I ran towards a bright spot in the forest, I heard voices, the clang of steel, and the familiar growl of spire wolves.

"Gi!" I heard a woman's voice shout. "Get behind me and start healing!"

I dropped into a crouch and slowly crept towards the source of the commotion. Hiding in the bushes, I saw two people, one holding a sword and shield, the other pointing a staff, fighting three spire wolves encircling them. The wolves snapped their jaws and growled at the people. They appeared to be moving in for the kill.

The woman with the sword was in armor similar to mine. However, her sword was bright green, and she had red hair closer to blood-red than orange. She swung her sword back and forth, trying to keep the one in front of her at bay.

Behind her was an enormously tall woman with grey skin and black and silver robes with stars on them, a purple circlet atop her crimped black hair, and a massive set of circular glasses on her nose. She pointed her staff at the red-haired woman, muttering rapidly.

"Zliuo Azkhaba Weemla, Zliuo Azkhaba Weemla, Zliuo Azkhaba Weemla."

As the large woman chanted, they were washed over with a faint golden glow. Cuts and bruises on the women started to fade. Right as I noticed that, the woman in red looked over and caught sight of where I stood in the bushes.

"Who the fu—"

26

Before she could continue, one of the wolves attacked from behind. It leapt out at the extremely tall woman and bit down on her shoulder. Up on its hindlegs, the wolf was taller than she was.

She cried out as the beast bit down on her shoulder.

The bite seemed not to fully penetrate through the thin layer of golden light. It was as if the light had absorbed most of the damage. Shrugging off the bite, she continued her defense.

"Giezha," the redhead exclaimed. As she turned to defend her companion, her wolf sensed the opportunity.

Without thinking, I leapt into action. In the blink of an eye, I had my sword drawn, and was charging straight at the wolf, not even bothering with my shield. Hearing my footsteps, the wolf quickly spun around to stare at its would-be attacker.

"Hey!" I screamed at the wolf, trying to maintain its attention. "I'm your entertainment now!"

Just like the previous wolf, this one jumped directly at me. Now I was the one who had the opportunity. I sped up and collapsed onto my knees. Momentum carried me forward across the ground, I thrust my sword straight up.

The sword collided with the beast right in the underside of its throat. It would have been a guaranteed killing blow if it were not for its jaw's bony protrusion. Instead, the sword sliced into the side of the wolf's neck.

"Graaaarr!" The wolf howled in pain as it landed. Blood dripped from its open wound. Its eyes stared at me in hatred as it began to circle me again.

Not daring to take my eyes off my adversary, I called back to check on the others.

"How are you holding up on your end?"

"Just fine, thanks!" came the voice of the red-haired woman. I couldn't tell if her tone was sarcastic or preoccupied. "Gi! Hit him hard! "

The sound of wood cracking over a skull echoed through the forest. Fighting the urge to look behind me, I kept my eyes on the wolf. Whatever the source of that sound was, it did plenty to distract the wolf. It stopped growling and turned its head to the right, looking past me.

Sword pointed forward, I charged straight ahead at the wolf. Before it could react, I swung directly downward on its neck. Its thick fur and hide absorbed most of the swing. However, as I tried to continue my swing, I

27

felt the sensation in my heart return. My entire body was on fire from the inside out for a brief moment. I felt my muscles swell and exude power. Gripping my blade as the wolf tried to fight at me desperately, I planted my feet and shoved my sword down.

Shink!

My sword went straight through the wolf. For half a second, it looked like the wolf blinked in surprise . Then, its head separated from its neck, hitting the ground with a thud. Blood spurted over my shoulder and onto the ground. Looking back around, I saw that the other two wolves were also dead. One of them had a sword directly in its chest, while the other looked like it had been beaten to a pulp.

"Well." My shoulders heaved up and down as I tried to catch my breath. "Not really sure you needed my help now."

Retrieving her sword from the wolf, the red warrior woman approached me.

She walked straight up to me, invaded my personal space, and looked me up and down. Her eyes were a violent shade of green. Her skin was pale as the moon, save for freckles across her nose and cheeks, which were high and defined. She was reminiscent of pictures of a warrior princess from a 1970s fantasy novel cover. Oh, and her ears came to a point. That was neat. After studying me for a moment, she met my eyes.

"Thanks, stranger!"

Wiping the sweat off her brow, she laughed heartily and patted me on the shoulder twice. She looked past me and whistled.

"First time I've ever seen someone take a wolf's head clean off. I'm impressed."

"Uh, thanks," I said, grinning back at her. "Pretty impressive work yourself."

She rolled her eyes and smiled, waving my compliment away.

"Please, these things are supposed to be child's play. Even three on two, we shouldn't have struggled this bad."

Behind her, the tall and gray woman was lamenting over her broken staff.

"Mara," the woman said glumly in a deep voice. "I broke my magic staff again."

Mara's smile and laughter instantly died. She made a face like she'd just eaten an extremely ripe lemon and gritted her teeth.

"I take it they're expensive," I said.

Mara simply nodded her head as the pain of the impending expense glazed over her face. She shook her head and sighed.

"Oh well, that's how it goes in this line of work." She extended a hand for me to shake. "I'm Mara, as you've probably gathered. Mara Brightwood."

"Asher Merrick," I said, clasping her hand. "Need some help?"

The process of removing the spines from the wolves was long and arduous. Mara and the tall Goliath woman, named Giezha Nightstrike, taught me the proper procedure of removing them.

"I don't know how you managed to break off one," Giezha said, her voice as small as her stature was large. "But without the end caps that connect to the subdermal tissue, they're basically worthless."

"Sorry," I said awkwardly.

"Well, as you helped save our skins with the spire wolves, you're entitled to part of the loot," Mara said as she finished the last wolf. "Between spires, meat, pelts, and this silver coin I found in one of their paws, I'd say we did all right."

"How much?" I asked, wondering about the cost of things.

"With the silver coin...." Mara said, calculating everything while waving her finger around.

"About three gold and six silver total between sale of goods and the contract." Giezha said, her shoulders slumped over. "One gold and two silver for each of us." Giezha sighed heavily. "A new staff will cost me almost four gold pieces."

Mara winced again while I felt the bag of gold pieces in my backpack weigh all the heavier.

"You know, I wasn't contracted for the job," I said while placing the wolf spires into a pile. "You two can take the money yourselves on one condition."

Mara's eyes lit up and she grabbed me in a bear hug.

"Thank you, thank you, thank you, Asher!" she said, jumping up and down, lifting me in the air with with ease. She then burst out into a rapid-fire story about their situation. Mara stopped to take a breath. Before she continued, she realized what she was doing and let me have a turn to talk, coughing awkwardly.

"If it's alright with you," I said, rubbing my ribs, "I'd like to join you in your journey beyond here. I'm not from around here and could use a guide."

Mara and Giezha both raised their eyebrows at me. They nodded and shook their heads as their expressions changed, looking at each other. Whether they were aware of my presence in front of them was debatable. After prolonged and silent deliberation, they shrugged their shoulders and looked at me.

"Deal. On two conditions," Mara said, putting her index and middle fingers in the air.

"Sounds fair."

"First, you tell us how you managed to rip off that spire wolf's spike like that," Giezha said, towering over me. From this angle, I could appreciate her impressive assets and the well-defined, rippling muscles all over her body.

"Okay..." I said, unsure of how to answer. "And the second?"

"You get to find that out later," Mara said with a mischievous smile.

Alarm bells went off in my head. "Well, that doesn't sound fair."

"Don't worry," Mara said with a wink. "It's nothing bad. Now hurry up and take some of those spikes! We've got to hurry up towards Naled before we make camp.

"Naled?" I asked, still unsure about joining them.

"City north of here," Giezha said, picking up all but two of the spikes. "Guild is waiting for us there."

Despite my worry about their second condition, I felt the need to join Mara and Giezha. Rather, I wanted to join them. Before I could ask, they were already marching out of the clearing and into the forest.

"Wait up!" I shouted while scrambling to pick up the other spikes.

It may not have been the smartest play, but it felt right in my gut.

Chapter 4

Xaliasday, 21st of Wirdin, Year 678, th Age

We found a dirt path that cut through the trees and other foliage walking through the forest. I walked in the back while Giezha took the front, with Mara in the middle.

After a few hours, Mara turned to me.

"So, you really have no idea how you managed to rip off the spike?" Mara asked me.

"Not a clue," I said, shaking my head. "That thing got me pinned down, and the only thing I could think of was 'I am not dying again this soon'."

"Dying again?" Mara asked curiously.

"Well, not dead, dead," I exclaimed, trying to cover my tracks. "I've had a few close calls, though. You know how it is."

"Ahhhh, yes. That makes sense," Mara said, clearly pretending to understand. "Still, ripping a spire wolf's spike like that is some seriously impressive stuff. I don't even think Mick could do something like that."

"Mick?"

"Half-human-half-goliath from the guild," Giezha muttered. Her voice sounded surprisingly angry. "He prides himself on being the toughest and strongest of both races."

Mara came up and nudged me in the shoulder as we walked.

"She really hates him," she whispered, not remotely quietly.

"He's a walking stereotype that gets reflected on goliaths like me. Not to mention he's a complete idiot who follows along with whatever that chauvinistic pig tells him," Giezha hissed as she turned around. Giezha's eyes flashed dangerously as she snarled back at us. Before we could apologize, her attention snapped back forward, and her expression

31

softened.

"We're here, by the way." Giezha said quietly.

Up ahead was a small campsite next to the road. There was an ash circle where many campfires had had been burnt. Much of the grass in the area was also worn out from heavy traffic. Giezha and Mara quickly set up a pair of tents and unloaded their equipment.

I decided to get the fire ready and fetching water from the pond next to camp while they unpacked. I had no intention of letting either out of my sight. For all I knew, these girls could be assassins or something. Best to stay on guard. Once the fire started, we decided to sacrifice some of the wolf meat for a decent meal of stew and root vegetables. The prospect of surviving off hardtack and rations was already unappealing to me.

Once the camp was set up, we all got out of our armor and into more comfortable clothes.

My undershirt was bright blue and purple with a short V-cut down the front. Giezha stayed in her mage outfit but took her circlet off, replacing it with an extremely wide-brimmed hat that came to a curled point at the top. Mara took off her leather armor and gambeson, leaving a heavy cotton shirt that was wide and billowy. My eyes lingered just long enough for her to catch me.

Mara's gregarious nature led to dozens of stories throughout dinner. Most of Mara's stories were about quests they had done for the Red Breaker Guild. Giezha tossed the occasional stick or log into the fire.

"So, the old lady said her cat was missing," Mara said while gnawing on one of the remaining rib bones. "But Giezha just stands outside for a minute, and next thing you know—"

"—Mr. Widdles was on my shoulder, taking a nap." Giezha smiled softly as she sat on the ground, hugging her knees. "I liked that quest."

Mara threw a heavily chewed bone into the fire and snorted.

"Hard to call it a quest. We were animal control."

"Still got paid though, right?" I asked.

Mara rolled her eyes. "Yeah, all three gold that the three of us got to split after giving half to the guild."

"Three of you?"

"We work best as a threesome, with our friend Uli." Mara explained. "She's why we took the wolf hunting job."

32

"We were hoping to find her on the mission," Giezha said, hugging her knees more tightly into her large chest.

"Yeah," Mara sighed. "Haven't heard from her in weeks. Just heard a rumor that she was working in the southern region near the Attlebron Mountain range."

"How far away is that from here?"

"About a hundred miles southwest as the crow flies," Mara said suspiciously. "You really aren't from here, are you?"

"Got dropped out of the sky here this morning," I said, using the ridiculousness of my situation as cover.

To my surprise, they both just shrugged as if it were nothing.

"Anyways, after we get done with this job, we want to try and go south to look for her," Mara declared. "We're at our strongest when we are all together."

As nightfall came, the sky turned completely pitch black. Clouds covered any potential stars above. After casting a few spells on the tents and campsite, Giezha quietly retreated to her tent, which was twice the size of Mara's. The loud sound of her snores could be heard less than a minute later.

"Not going to set up your tent?" Mara asked from behind me while I stared out into the sky, wishing I could see this world's constellations.

"Forgot to pack one," I joked, feeling the warmth of the fire on the back of my neck. "I'll just sleep on my bedroll and wait for the stars to come out."

"You sure you want to?" Mara whispered into my ear.

I flinched forward, managing not to jump out of my skin.

"Yes, Mara," I said, turning around. "You don't have to worry about—"

Once I'd turned, I finally got a really good look at Mara. Her silky white skin glowed like a warm candle as the fire crackled behind her. I nearly fell off my seat as she stood there, baring her skin for all the world to see.

"I think I might have a better idea of what you can do tonight," She smirked as she slowly walked toward me.

As she walked closer, I could see the finer details of her muscles wrapping around her like taut ropes along her arms and legs. My hungry eyes traced down her abdomen to a hard set of abs, which were perfectly symmetrical and dotted with freckles. Then I looked up at her breasts, which were finally freed from her armor. They were much bigger than I'd expected.

"I… umm…" I said, struggling to find the right words. "Damn."

Clearly enjoying the look on my face, she bit her lip and took another step. "You wanted to know what that other condition was, right?" Mara teased. "Let's see what you've got, Mr. Merrick."

As she reached down to my belt, I stood up and backed away, falling over a log behind me. Before I could move, Mara climbed on top of me. Her body radiated warmth, that was comforting and inviting. Her eyes reminded me of the wolf's earlier when they had fixed on their prey. As turned on as I was, I couldn't quite shake a horrible feeling in the pit of my stomach.

"Now, hold on," I started, trying to keep the rabid woman at bay. "How do I know I can trust that Giezha won't smash my skull in while you distract me or blow me up."

A voice came from Giezha's tent. "Because if you don't hurry up and fuck her, I'm going to have to deal with her complaining about not getting laid. And if I have to deal with that even one more day, I will bash your brain in."

"She doesn't mean that," Mara whispered into my ear. "She's just jealous."

"Yes, I do, and no, I'm not."

"Point is…if I was going to pull out a knife to cut your throat, it'd be stashed where your right hand is now," Mara said, pressing her body against mine.

Without realizing it, I had placed my right hand on the small of her back. My left hand was resting on her thigh, and there definitely wasn't a knife there. Just some very tight and well-defined muscles. The hormones were quickly telling me that that was good enough.

Mara knelt her face down and kissed my lips. Before I knew it, our tongues were intertwined while Mara let out a few soft moans. Wanting to go somewhere with even a modicum of privacy, I lifted myself up, carrying Mara as we continued to kiss. Once we entered the tent and I released her, she pulled me onto the ground while helping me take off my armor and clothes.

After I tore off my trousers and shirt, we both sat and stared at each

34

other's naked bodies. Mara looked stunning, even in the dark. The light from the fire bled into the tent's fabric, casting a faint glow. Her chest heaved as she tried to gain her breath while we just looked at each other. It was as if we were hypnotized by each other's bodies. Her hand had drifted toward her pussy, and mine to my erection. As I grasped it, it felt a little odd. Looking down, I saw a pleasant, but unexpected surprise.

"Admiring yourself there, Asher?" Mara giggled.

She wasn't exactly wrong. I had never had any problems with my "equipment" beforehand. Quite the opposite. In fact, I was rather confident. But looking down, I saw I had gained a few inches. No point in complaining, though, right?

"Never had this happen before," I said, looking up at her, feeling a deep-seated hunger in me. "It never got this big before. Must be the company."

As we locked eyes again, we both looked at each other for a moment. And then another moment. And another. Tense energy built up between us. Neither dared to make the first move, but we desperately wanted to. Simultaneously, we wrapped our arms around each other again. We both fished for what we wanted in our hands.

As I traced my fingers along the outside of her pussy, I noticed that she was already incredibly wet. She grabbed me and began to pull and tug along my cock. Both of us moaned at the others' efforts. I opened her up with my index finger and ring finger while my middle finger pressed and circled around her clit. She gasped and sucked in air as she pressed her face into my shoulder. Hearing and feeling how violently she responded turned me on even more.

Every breath I took, I inhaled more of Mara's intoxicating aroma. It was like the forest's flowers coalesced into her and turned my brain into an animal's.

"You're so fucking sexy," I whispered into her ear. Not Shakespeare, but what could I say? Shakespeare doesn't exist here. "I want all of you right now." As I spoke, she began to moan more and more.

"Oh Gods, Asher," she said, unable to hold onto my cock anymore. She placed both hands on my shoulders while I fingered her.

"I want to make you feel like you're about to burst. I want to touch you." My finger went inside her while my free hand grabbed her firm ass and squeezed. "I want to taste you. I want to fuck you."

35

"Please;" She gasped. "Please do that, Asher."

Her body writhed as she pressed against me, moving along with my fingers in rhythm. Obliging her needs, I slowly pushed her down onto the bedroll and placed my head between her legs. For a moment, I simply looked at her. Her pussy was beautiful; a small flower with petals, white and pink, glistening with morning dew.

I traced my tongue around her thighs, careful to just barely graze her labia. She moaned and protested, wiggling her hips.

"Don't tease me," she pleaded, "give me what I need. Please."

Not wanting to waste too much time either, I pressed my face between her thighs. I licked, nuzzled, kissed, and gently sucked at her flesh, making her wait for a bit before I finally turned my attention to her clit.

Her hips twisted and flexed as she squirmed with pleasure. I used one arm to pin them down, holding her locked in place so that I could continue to enjoy her body.

At first, I was slow and deliberate, making sure that she felt every movement of my tongue. She moaned and squealed as her body turned to putty in my hands. I grabbed her knees and spread her thighs wider.

I began to lick more sloppily, becoming a bit rougher and more passionate with my kisses.

Mara showed a special appreciation for the new approach. Her body writhed and wiggled while her thighs tried to tighten around my head.

I thrust two fingers back inside her, pressing against a slightly textured spot that I felt on her inner walls.

"Yes! Asher, right there. Right there, yes!"

Her muscles started to tense. Sensing she was getting close, I circled her clit with a little more force.

"Asher! Oh, Goddess, I'm gonna—"

Mara screamed out as her whole body seized, her pussy pulsing around my fingers. She let out a few more moans and her legs shook as I gently extracted myself.

Wiping my mouth with my shirt, I watched as Mara's chest heaved up and down while her eyes rolled around in her head. Breathing deeply, she looked at me with pleading eyes.

"Please."

And with those magic words, I took my rock-hard cock in hand and

36

backed away so that I could kneel before her. Slowly, I pressed the head into her sopping wet opening. It slid in with ease at first. She let out another gasp and moaned as her eyes squeezed.

"You're a monster, Asher," she whispered with a laugh. "Oh Gods, yes, deeper."

At first, she struggled to stretch out, but slowly I was able to follow her orders and go deeper and deeper. Laying down on top of her, I wrapped one arm around her while the other took hold of her bottom. Squeezing and massaging her ass, I finally managed to get every last bit inside her soaking wet pussy.

"Fuck-ing hell." I groaned in pleasure. She felt like a vice made of wet silk around me. Slowly, I began to thrust in and out of her.

"Asher," Mara moaned, "It's so fucking good. It's so big." Her nails dug into my shoulder. I could feel them tear and scratch at my back, but I was too preoccupied to feel pain. For now, it only felt good.

I started to thrust into her harder and faster. She refused to let go and her pussy clamped down on me tighter and tighter. I moaned out, unable to contain the feeling. Mara whimpered as the sound of our bodies filled the air.

"Mara, I don't know how much longer I can go," I said with my teeth clenched. "I'm close."

"Me too!" she moaned.

I felt the warm splatter of her juices squirt onto my dick as my whole body tensed up. I laid down on her and kissed her deeply as I kept my hand loosely around her neck. She desperately returned the favor, sliding her tongue back between my lips. We felt each other's short breaths as her legs tightened around me. Our bodies tightened up, threatening to come undone.

"Oh Gods, oh Gods, oh Gods!" She groaned. "Fuck!"

I felt the warmth of her release as her pussy clamped down even harder on my cock.

"Gah!" I groaned. I pulled out of her milliseconds before I exploded. Cum spurted out as I exhaled in pleasure, plastering her belly and breasts. Some went as far as her face, splattering on her cheek.

Mara breathed in and out for a few moments, her breath ragged and strained. Her body glistened with sweat and seed. She strained to look up at me, her eyes barely a sliver.

"W-Why'd you pull out?" she asked breathlessly.

I took a moment to catch my breath.

"Too risky," I said, looking at the defeated warrior before me.

"You boys are so clueless about girls," Mara joked, her breath slowly returning to normal. "A single spell keeps the little monsters at bay for months at a time."

I raised an eyebrow at the thought of magical birth control. It made sense, honestly.

"No way of knowing you've got that," I retorted while wetting a piece of cloth with a bucket of water.

Mara looked at me and smiled. "You're sweet."

I pressed the rag against her skin, wiping up the absolute mess I'd made of her. I might not have had much knowledge of magical birth control, but that wasn't the case when it came to aftercare. Laying down, I gently pulled her towards me. I wrapped one arm around her waist and the other behind her back. For a moment, she said nothing, nestling herself into me while pulling a blanket up from under the bedroll.

"Guess you're not going to look for the stars?" she asked with the smallest laugh.

"No. I like the view here a lot better."

I held her and realized I wasn't really done yet. Her body pressed against me, the smell of her pheromones, and my renewed life had me raring to go.

"Oh!" Mara exclaimed, rubbing her butt up against me. "Looks like somebody is still awake."

As my cock throbbed against her, I gently started to massage her breasts from behind.

"Seems like you are too. Maybe we should..."

I rubbed against her clit, and her soft moans combined with pressing against me were all the confirmation I needed. I had been given another chance at life and was told to live up to my potential. This was as good a place to start as any.

38

Chapter 5

I woke up feeling a bolt of electricity through my chest. I bolted upward out of the bedroll. Jumping to my feet, I looked around in every direction. My nostrils flared as my eyeballs bulged out of my skull. Looking down, I saw Mara. She had a short sword pointed at me. I was back in the tent, and the shocking sensation percolated around my chest.

"Sorry about that, I don't know what happened," I murmured as Mara slowly put her sword down. "Felt like a shock to my cehst."

Mara reached out her hand, and gently touched my chest. Two bullet-sized scars marked where Anastasia shot me.

"Did a person do this to you?" she asked as her thumb traced down to the scars on my chest.

At her touch, the electricity circled around the scars. It did not physically hurt, but it gave me a horrid sense of unease. I flinched at her touch, and she retracted her hand.

"I'm sorry! I shouldn't have—"

"It's fine," I said, cutting her off, my voice unsteady. "Yes, someone did that to me. Someone... close."

After an awkward moment, Mara excused herself to prepare for the day. I quickly got dressed and followed her. Outside, Giezha stared at me with her broken staff pointed in my direction. It glowed a nasty shade of yellow as sparks flew out of the broken section.

Giezha was covered in sweat, in nothing but a loose tunic, and a black headband. After a tense moment, she nodded to me and lowered her staff. I was more afraid of what would happen if her spells backfired than what she would actually do to me. Then again, I wasn't a fan of her throwing the staff down and deciding to rip me in half with her bare hands.

"I need to finish my morning workout before we leave," Giezha told Mara, turning away from me. "I can skip the pushups if we're in a rush."

Mara turned and looked at me uncomfortably. "We still need to pack up, so you can do it while we finish."

Giezha, having already dismantled her tent and cleaned the firepit,

39

immediately dropped to the ground and started doing one-armed pushups. All that was left to disassemble was Mara's tent and we could hit the road.

After Giezha completed a hundred pushups with each hand, we got back on the trail and headed north to Naled. Despite fighting those spire wolves twice yesterday and the evening's activities, my feet were the sorest. Hours of walking with no end in sight was a tough row to hoe.

As we walked, the two had another one of their silent conversations, communicating through expressive glances. Occasionally they would look back at me, which was very annoying. I did my best to respect their privacy, however. I was still some stranger they had known for less than a day.

After a few hours of walking, the grasses and more flamboyant flowers began to disappear from my sight. Replacing them were dead leaves and dirt along the forest floor.

The midday sun burned brightly in the sky as sunlight pierced through the canopy all around us, drying whatever water we had left.

The worst part about wearing leather armor so far? It gets really hot when you've got so many layers on. After another few hours of walking, we took a break near a stream and refilled our waterskins.

Giezha muttered another spell as she pointed her staff at the waterskin in her hand. With a sizzling sound, the waterskin's rope began to smoke. A fire burst forth from the rope, causing her to drop it on the ground.

"Ow!" she exclaimed.

Before the fire could spread to the rest of the water skin, Mara and I quickly dumped our water, extinguishing the flame. Giezha blew on her hand and sucked on the part that had been contact with the flame.

"Sorry," she muttered, barely audible. "Just wanted to boil the water for safety."

"That's okay, Gi," Mara said, patting her shoulder.

"Oh geez," I said in genuine surprise. "I never woulda thought of that. This water could be swarming with parasites. Good thinking, Giezha."

She looked at me with a funny expression cocking her head to the side.

"Why wouldn't you think to do that?" she said disbelievingly.

Rubbing the back of my head in embarrassment. "I'm uhh... Kind of new at all of this. I never really had to worry about parasites in my water where I lived before."

"Where was that?"

"Ever heard of a place called Louisville?" I asked sarcastically.

Both of them looked at me with raised eyebrows.

"Never mind," I said evasively. "Thank you again, Giezha. I appreciate you looking out for a newbie like me."

Giezha gave me a small smile, and we collected the water for boiling. Despite the brightness of the sun, the temperature was mild for the rest of the day. After making camp, we boiled the water, salted the wolf meat a second time, and had another round of wolf and potato stew. The hearty meal filled our bellies with its savory (if a bit bland) flavor.

After eating, we went to the stream to freshen up. I pulled out a bar of soap and a wooden toothbrush from my pack. After cleaning myself up, I realized there was no toothpaste.

"Ah nuts," I muttered.

Doing my best not to take a peek, I shouted to Mara. "Hey, you got any toothpaste I could borrow?"

"Tooth what?" she called back. "Oh, you mean tooth gel?"

"Uhh... yeah?" I said, confused.

"Just grab a couple of those blue leaves from the Aeflon bushes by the water and get the jelly from the middle."

Looking down, I saw tiny bushes with long purple vines sprouting blue clovers the size of maple leaves.

Tentatively picking a few leaves, I looked them over. They had a smell reminiscent of mint and clover, and when squeezed, a translucent blue gel popped out. Placing some on my brush, I cleaned my teeth and dried off with a spare shirt.

"Ahhh, nothing like a nice fresh bath! And I grabbed some of those Aeflon bulbs and vines for later," Mara said, her hair still wet. "What are you going to do once you get to Naled?" she asked me while wringing her hair out by the fire.

"Dunno," I tried to ignore the my aching feet as I sat down. "Might see if I can find some work. Not sure how long a hundred gold will last me, but it won't be forever."

"You could try to join the Red Breaker guild," Mara suggested.

Giezha looked over at us with a stern expression.

"What?" Mara demanded.

41

Giezha continued to stare at her, completely ignoring me. I shifted uncomfortably in my seat and decided to get back to my dinner. It wasn't a bad idea. If I could get in with a guild, I'd have a good chance at finding work.

"Maybe," I said softly to myself.

That night, I decided to sleep under the stars. The clouds from last night had passed and what was left was a beautiful brightly lit galaxy in the sky.

Bright blue and pink swaths of far-off star systems painted backdrops for the sky's bright white and yellow stars. As the cool breeze of the night tickled my face, I looked at the planets far off in the distance. There was a bright green planet with rings in the sky about the size of my pinky nail.

Closer in was a large bright white moon, at least twice the size of the Moon from Earth. To the left of it was a much smaller moon that was cyan in color.

I let out a small sigh and soaked in the beauty until I was interrupted. I felt a hard poke on the back of my head. Turning my head, I saw Giezha staring down, staff pointed directly between my eyes.

"Sit up," she commanded.

I complied and put my hands up as I moved into a cross-legged seat. Her face was almost entirely emotionless, but I could sense her anger.

"Where are you from?" she demanded, sparks flying out of her staff. "How did you kill that wolf? And what are your intentions with Mara?"

This very tall, powerful woman was ready to split my skull in half at a moment's notice. Or smash it into a paste. Probably something between the two. Either way, I took a deep breath and looked at her. Try as I might, I couldn't think of any good lies about her first two questions. I had no idea where I was or what was going on.

"Giezha," I started, my voice doing its best to remain calm. "I am going to answer your questions honestly. However, I doubt what I am about to say will satisfy you."

"I don't believe you."

"If you already don't believe anything I'm saying, what's the point of telling you anything?"

Sparks began to fly from her staff, singeing the ground. One of the sparks jumped up and bit me in the nose.

"Shit!"

Rubbing my nose, I kept my eyes fixed squarely on her. Slowly, she reached into her robe and pulled out a scroll.

As she did, a rustling noise came from Mara's tent. Poking her head out, she looked at us in confusion.

"What's going on?!" She exclaimed.

"This scroll will let me cast the Truth Circle spell." Giezha said, ignoring Mara. "If you try to lie, I'll know. And I'll kill you for making me waste a two hundred gold scroll on you. And for putting Mara in danger."

As Mara quickly stumbled out of her tent, I couldn't help but feel relieved. This was a best-case scenario.

"Giezha, is this really the best time?" Mara pleaded, grimacing my way.

She shot Mara an impatient look. "I understand you're interested in him, Mara. But you are too trusting. People don't just fall out of the sky into the middle of nowhere! He's not telling us everything." She turned back to me and narrowed her eyes. "But he's going to. Or I'm going to blast him into the ground."

"Better now than later I suppose," I said with a small grin. "I agree to your terms."

Mara looked at me curiously as Giezha unfurled the spell scroll and began to speak an incantation. As she spoke, a white circle surrounded both of us and began to draw an intricate series of lines, circles, and shapes. A script I was unfamiliar with encircled the entire thing as she finished speaking.

"If you tell the truth, it stays white. Lies make it turn black. Try to hide something, it turns red." Giezha explained curtly. "Now answer my questions."

I sat down in the middle of the circle and collected my thoughts. I needed to make sure to tell her the truth. But would my truth be even believable? What would happen if she still thought I was lying? My sword was behind me— I could probably outrun her and Mara. Probably.

"Alright. Let's take it from the top," I said, clapping my hands on my knees. "I'm from a place called Ohio from the planet Earth. I was brought here by a deity named Gathos."

Giezha and Mara both blinked twice at my last statement; it clearly wasn't what either expected. The Truth Circle stayed bright white, indicating that I was telling the truth. I decided to keep going before

Giezha could ask questions.

"I have no idea how I managed to rip off that wolf's spike. I was about to die, and all of a sudden, my strength grew a hundredfold. It was like magic. It probably was magic. I have no idea how magic works in this world because magic isn't a thing where I'm from."

Again, the circle stayed white from my words. And again, Giezha didn't say anything. She simply absorbed what I told her. Mara looked at me with a wide-eyed expression as I went on.

Now for the fun question.

"I don't wish Mara any harm. Quite the opposite," I said, smiling at Mara. "She seems like a lovely woman, and I am extremely attracted to her. I can't speak of anything any deeper than that, since we met yesterday. However, I can't lie, she is quite enchanting."

The circle stayed pure white, while Mara's cheeks burned bright pink. I sat there with her for a few tense minutes, Giezha's staff pointing at my chest. Her breathing was strained, eyes ice-cold, and body unmoving.

Finally, she pointed her staff away from me and said, "If you promise to not hurt Mara, I will make sure neither of us tell anybody what you just told us."

"I take it that what I told you is a bad thing?" I asked with a wince.

"It's not a good thing, that's for sure. As for this Gathos, I have no idea what deity it is of which you speak. But the pantheon is long, and the number of gods is like the number of leaves on the trees." Before I could ask her any questions, she retired to her tent.

Mara was clearly just as perturbed by how I arrived in Echo Veil. However, before I could ask her anything, she quickly retired for the evening.

Not exactly the warm reception I'd been hoping for, but you can't win them all.

Once that was over, I laid back down in my bedroll and looked at the night sky. I sat and watched shooting stars flare in and out. I saw tiny blips of light come and go, imaging myself out there. Lost in space. Well, I was lost now. Lost in an alien world with no chance of returning home.

The following day was a quick affair. We packed up our things and hit the road as soon as possible. The only time we stopped was so Mara could pick wildflowers. I helped her pick the roses, daisies, and a wild star-shaped

44

flower and placed them into her bag.

"I take it she's not a gardener?" I joked with Giezha to no response.

After walking so much, my feet were still sore, but less so than the day before. Giezha more or less ignored me for the trip while Mara explained in great detail the difficulty she had in a dream with a monster known as a Qua'loth.

"Hey, why didn't we keep walking last night?" I asked as the forest disappeared behind us, replaced with wide-open fields. Off in the distance, you could see a walled city.

"Because the guards would have killed us," Mara explained simply. "Nobody is allowed into the city at night, lest they be ready for a dozen arrows in the chest. It's a security measure against theft and spies."

"Huh. Fair enough."

"Doesn't help at all," Giezha interjected. "Just another excuse for them to collect taxes."

"Oh shit, taxes!" Mara exclaimed. "We forgot to pay our exit tax and we're gonna get hit with a late fee. Plus our entry tax as non-citizens! And the import taxes!"

Giezha added up the rolling list in her head, and her already grey skin paled.

"That'll come to about ten gold. This trip is going to cost more than it would've ever made us."

"Can't the guild pay it?" I asked cluelessly.

Mara and Giezha scoffed at my proposal.

"Gotta pay when you get there," Mara said, her pace slowing to a crawl. "And we don't have it."

A light bulb went off in my head. "Yea, we do," I said, pulling out the bag of coins. "This should be able to easily cover the cost. We can get in and tell the guild they need to reimburse you guys."

"That's really sweet, Asher, but we can't accept that. It's inappropriate. Besides, the guild would tell us to take a hike," Mara said, her eyes looking off at the city walls. Her voice was filled with dread.

"She's right," Giezha added.

Unperturbed, I pressed on. "Well, then let's make it a business agreement. I will help you guys get into the city, and you help me get started with your guild."

45

Mara eyes lit up and she. "That's a great idea!"

Giezha gave me a skeptical look, but I simply responded with a thumbs up and a smile. These two had been good to me. They had every right to be suspicious of me, but they gave me a chance to explain what was going on, and they promised to keep my status as an Otherwolder secret. It felt good to help them. They also felt a little... lost.

"Gathos," I chuckled to myself. "I think I know why I landed in the forest."

Any sailor coming into the city would look for the massive lighthouse, the Endeavor, to guide them.

47

Chapter 6

Evlanday, 23rd of Wirdin, Year 678, 4th Age

"I've told you for the tenth time, he's our guest in the city as a liaison for the Red Breaker Guild!" Mara shouted to the guard impatiently.

The guard was a hulking combination of dragon and human, towering over all except Giezha with black and green scales. He tilted his halberd downward slightly towards Mara, who was in his face.

"And I shall repeat for the tenth time that no paperwork has been submitted, and neither of you are registered as captains or members of decision-making authority." The other two guards, a half-elf and minotaur, took a step forward, surrounding Mara.

Hearing the unmistakable sparks of Giezha's broken staff, I decided to interject.

"Gentlemen, gentlemen, gentlemen." I said as I leaped between Mara and the minotaur. "You are correct. The proper procedures need to be followed." I flashed a big smile and danced with my intonation. "I mean... Without a way proper enforcement of laws and regulations, how are we any different than animals? Livestock, that is."

The three of them trained their eyes on me. I could feel a noose starting to wrap around my neck and needed to get to the point fast.

"I apologize for not following the guidelines for entry to the city. It's a lot of paperwork, but it's necessary. Tell me, how much would it be to requisition the forms necessary for entry?" I punctuated this question by making my coin pouch jingle at my hip. "I'm assuming I'll need to file this in triplicate, yes?"

I looked at each of them as I spoke, hoping that the subtext was obvious, but palatable. For a tense moment, nobody moved or spoke. My eyes darted to Mara and Giezha, who were also ready to fight or take flight. After a moment, the dragonborn spoke up, pulling out some papers.

"Documentation is five gold pieces, which will need to be done in triplicate. So, fifteen total. We will make sure to have the forms expedited in their filing."

48

Mara looked like she was about to speak up, but before she could, I placed five coins in the hands of each guard, scribbled on the blank piece of paper with an ink quill, and rushed into the city. The large gate slammed down to the ground behind us. I checked the dating on the paper: 23rd of Wirdin, Year 678, 4th Age. My eyes blinked several times, realizing I'd need to learn the calendar system.

If you looked at the city of Naled on the map, you'd see it at the center of the southern portion of Lake Shabba. The lake was an important center for transport, connecting two of the largest rivers in the western part of the Narag Kingdom. Naled was flush with buildings, shops, and purveyors of food, curios, and anything else an adventurer may need. Any sailor coming into the city would look for the massive lighthouse, the Endeavor, to guide them.

With two roads, you could get pretty much everywhere. Mountain Road took you north to The Docks, through Castle's District, and out on the main road at the gate. The West-to-East road, called Setter's Crossing, would get you from Iron Court to Settler's Valley. Our destination was near the heart of town.

"What'd you do that for? That was a total shakedown!" Mara protested further, stomping her foot on the ground as we walked past two goblins bartering over a bucket of toad's eyes and cockatrice feathers in an alley.

"I consider it an investment," I replied. "Sometimes, it's better to just go with it and worry about revenge later."

"They'll try to shake us down again." Giezha sighed forlornly.

"Not if we get some clout in the guild," I retorted hopefully.

Mara and Giezha both sighed at my ceaseless optimism. As we walked towards the guild, we passed a large plaza filled with people walking from stall to stall. This looks like it was the more legitimate place for bartering and quick sales in the city. Mara waved to another human in armor similar to hers, juggling a series of flaming daggers. Noticing us, the woman stopped juggling and waved back at us. The daggers all froze in mid-air, lazily rotating in place as she waved.

"We both come from Kiragaz," Mara said with a funny smile. "She left a few years before I did. Her parents used to run the mill."

For a moment, the smile plastered on her face faded. She stared off into the far distance.

When we turned the corner, nothing looked very different. Ramshackle buildings stacked atop each other like boxes in every direction. Giezha and Mara walked up to a wooden building, which had evidently been painted many different shades of red over the years. Above the solid stone door was a carving of a sloop cresting over a wave.

Mara knocked on the door in a rhythmic pattern from left to right. At first, nothing happened. Then, rather suddenly, the door burst open.

A grumpy-looking man covered in scars with a red bandanna on his head stood in the doorway. He scowled at the three of us with several teeth missing. He pointed a thick, gnarled finger at Giezha and Mara.

"Ah, the Rookies..." he said, spitting off to the side. Eyeing them up and down, he shifted his attention to me in the middle. His eyes glinted as his mouth formed a slight scowl. "And who, in the holy name of Adar, are you?"

My tongue was caught in the back of my throat for a moment. The guy's gnarled hand was covered in scars, and his hairy arms were the size of tree trunks. He wasn't particularly tall, but he cut an imposing figure. Doing my best not to cower, I answered him.

"I'm the newest rookie. Asher Merrick. I helped them with a job they were contracted on through you."

"Did you, now?" he asked in a sarcastic tone. "Killed a few wolves for some elf-bugs and backwater farmers? Congratulations! Now get the fuck out."

As he was about to slam the door shut, Giezha put her hand out and stopped it. He looked like he was about to stab her in the throat, but she stared a hole right through his head. She put down her staff and grabbed the broken spike from her backpack with her free hand.

"He did this to one of them with his bare hands, Valdir." Giezha told the man sternly. "He just got on the road recently and is already capable of doing this."

He snatched the spike out of her hands and inspected it all over. When the ripped section was in front of his face, he paused and brought it closer to his eyes. His eyes scanned the spike over and over again for a solid minute. After a moment of deliberation, he looked at us all.

"Looks like the real deal," he said with defeat in his voice. "If he wants to join you lot, it's no skin off my nose."

50

He turned around and walked back into the building. Mara, Giezha, and I followed, despite the lack of invitation. There was ample space with tables, chairs, and a fireplace crackling underneath a pot of stew.

The room was full of people of all different magical races talking, arguing, and fighting. Notably, every one of them had a red bandanna on their head.

Valdir walked us to a table with a female dark elf sitting alone, reading a book in a script I was unfamiliar with. Using context clues, it was probably Elvish or Elvish-derived. The woman had silver hair that ran down past her shoulder and steel-gray eyes colder than a blizzard in the mountains. Her skin was as dark as the starless midnight sky I had seen the other night. Valdir coughed, and the woman turned her thin, pointed face towards us. Her expression held a mixture of annoyance and boredom.

"Yes, yes, what is it, Valdir? Did those two manage not to screw up this time?" As soon as she finished speaking, her eyes set on me. "Evidently, that is not the case." She snapped the book shut and stood up. She turned to Mara and started barking at her.

"Brightwood!"

Mara stiffened up and saluted her. "Yes, Captain Dawnthorn!"

The dark elf walked around Mara, her shoulders swaying back and forth like a cobra. "What was the assignment given to you?"

"Eliminate the spire wolf problem contracted by the pixie named Trella Sigold—"

"I DON'T REMEMBER ASKING THE NAME OF THE CONTRACTOR!" the woman screamed into Mara's ear.

I felt Giezha's fist tremble as her left foot began to bounce up and down. Valdir simply looked on in amusement.

"Now tell me the contract again!"

"Kill the spire wolves in the southern forest as contracted and not a single one more."

The captain spun around Mara again before putting her face right next to the side of Mara's.

"Exactly. And where in the contract did it say to pick up hitchhikers?"

Valdir was about to interject before the captain pointed a long finger at him. As I looked around, most of the people in here stopped what they were doing and watched. They all clearly took a lot of joy in watching

Mara be humiliated by the captain.

"Well?"

"It wasn't in the contract." Mara said, her voice and posture as resolute as could be.

"Exactly! So, where the fuck do you rookie pieces of shit get the gall to—"

"I asked to join them and offered to pay," I interrupted her. She put her full attention on me. Her eyes looked like they were about the bulge out of her skull as she bared her teeth.

"Come again?" she said through gritted teeth.

As intense as this woman was, I didn't feel intimidated. Only annoyed. I hated people like her—the kind that will dress you down in front of as many people as possible.

"I got attacked by one of the spire wolves. After killing it, I ran into them and offered them a contract to escort me to this city to join you."

She narrowed her eyes. "What kind of contract?"

Mara tried to speak, but I cut her off, doing my best to take all possible guilt.

"Verbal contract paying out twenty-five gold minus administrative fees upon reaching my destination. Which would be now, I suppose."

A twisted grin spread across her face. Her smile was almost unnaturally wide as the sides of her lips curled inwards much too far.

"And where is the payment?" she asked, jabbing a hand into my chest.

"Here."

She took the sack I offered her and counted out ten coins. She looked down and scowled at me. "Where's the other fifteen?"

I turned my head to the side and kept my face neutral. "They were used up for the administrative fees we needed to get into the city. I had to sign an entry form in triplicate with the guards. If you want the remainder of the payment, you'll need to seek reimbursement from them."

She made a move as if to grab me by the throat but pulled her hand back at the last second. I have no idea how I managed to not flinch as her hand shot up like a bullet towards me.

She turned around and walked over towards a dragonborn who looked similar to the guard at the entrance. The captain whispered something into his ears, making his eyes turn to slits. The dragonborn got up and

52

rushed out the door without a word, muttering the words "good for nothing sibling."

Returning her attention to me, the captain looked me up and down. She made no gestures, and her expression remained absolutely still.

"I heard something about a spike?" she asked nonchalantly.

Valdir presented the spike to her, which she analyzed. After a moment, she looked at me and tossed the spike onto her table.

"Alright, you've completed the contract. You got into the Red Breaker Guild. Now you need to get IN to the guild. We'll add you on a trial basis for a few jobs around the city and see if you're worth the trouble. Be ready to suck hind teat. You're also on your own for lodging and food until otherwise stated."

Mara and I both let out a sigh of relief. The three of us were all quickly ushered out of the guildhall. Mara pulled Giezha and me into a group hug as the door slammed in front of our faces.

"We did it!" Mara squealed. "That was the best mission report yet! I really think Captain Dawnthorn is starting to like me."

Giezha looked like she was about to say something but decided to let it go.

"So where to now?" I asked.

Mara and Giezha took me to a nearby tavern a few blocks from the guildhall. It was a dusty building built from stone and vertical logs on the outside with a broken sign that read 'Silver Cup Inn.' Inside the tavern's heavy oak door was a dusty room with a short bar, and a few tables and chairs were strewn about. Only a few patrons sat in the dimly lit watering hole.

"Girls!" A voice came from behind the bar, which appeared to be more ancient than the rusted door.

Polishing a dusty glass was an older-looking satyr with a long beard. He had a pair of yellow goat's eyes that sank into his wrinkled skin on his round face. The parts of him not covered in fur were bright pink like someone's cheeks after a few too many drinks. His fur was tightly coiled and jet black, save for a peppering of silver. Behind him at the bar were a pair of massive caskets and a pot of stew bubbling over a fire in a stone fireplace.

"Hello, Salvatore."

53

"Hi, Sally!" Mara said, reaching over to scratch his beard. The old goat blushed bright red, and you could hear his tail flail about behind him.

"You girls get those wolves taken care of?" he asked with the warmth of a grandfather asking his favorite grandchild about their favorite birthday present.

"You know we can't go into details Mr. Salvatore," Giezha said slowly.

"Oh, pish posh, Giezha! It's only me and a few regulars. And good lord, girl! Your staff!"

He put the glass down and stroked his beard as he looked at the staff she presented.

"Did you forget to add the components in the correct order for a potion again?"

"No," Giezha said, her gray cheeks starting to match his in color.

"Say the incantation backwards?"

"No."

"Lose your temper?"

"..."

Salvatore just smiled and started wiping his pince-nez with the same rag he had been "cleaning" the glass with. He just shook his head and poured out some drinks for the girls with a chuckle.

As if noticing me for the first time, he looked at me and cocked his head.

"Mara, did you pick up another boyfriend?" His voice lost all merriment and intonation.

"Sal!" Mara shouted, dribbling half the foamy beer onto herself. "You do not need to talk about me like that, and that is NOT what is going on."

Sal gave a mischievous laugh and winked at me. Mara buried herself in her beer while Giezha tapped her forehead, looking off into the distance. I could swear that she smirked for a half-second. Pouring me a ninety percent foam beer, he looked at me.

"So, what brings you here, stranger?"

"Sal..." Mara started. He cut her off by handing her a second glass of beer and gestured for me to answer.

I shrugged. "I helped them take care of the wolves and asked if I could join their Guild."

Sal looked at the girls, then turned back, raising his eyebrow. "Oh? What'd that old crone Ylsysea Dawnthorn say?"

54

"Not much after I flashed that greedy bitch some gold."

Salvatore let out a bleating laugh at my remark as I took a sip from my still foamy beer and kept eye contact with him. His opinion of the captain was just the same as mine.

"Well, anybody who can shut that woman up is good in my books. Oh girls, you don't mind if I ask another question, do you?"

Mara finished her second beer in one go and let out a long sigh.

"No, Sal, Uli is still gone. We had hoped there'd have been some word about her, but no luck."

"We spent a few days out looking for her before looking for the wolves," Giezha added. Despite the fact that she had barely sipped at her drink, Sal replaced it with a fresh glass.

"That little missy gets into more trouble in a week than I did in a lifetime with the Breakers," Sal said while having a drink of his own.

"You were—" I started,

Sal nodded and chuckled before alluding to some previous experiences.

"I'm sure she'll turn up eventually." Sal reassured us. "In the meantime, if you're looking for work, I heard that a lot of goats have gone missing in the area."

"Goats?" Giezha asked incredulously.

"Yes, goats! A couple hundred gold coins worth at this point!"

"We'll look into it, Sal. Of course, you'll need to put a contract up for bid if you want the captain to approve us working on it. And even then..."

"Oh, don't you girls worry about something like that," Salvatore added quickly. "Just some gossip I heard. Nothing more."

The girls and I finished our drinks, and they took me to a room off to the side of the tavern's second floor. As the door was opening, Sal whistled for me. I turned back and saw him pointing a knife at me. He gave me the "Don't get my girls into trouble" look that every father figure has perfected.

I gave him a reassuring thumbs up and turned around. Like the rest of the building, the room was extraordinarily shabby and dusty. It was simultaneously empty and cramped, no more than ten feet wide by ten feet long.

In one corner was a collection of broken and rusty swords with tattered scraps of leather armor. On the other was a bucket filled with half-broken

55

staffs painted with the same markings as Giezha's current one. The walls were plastered with papers written with descriptions of jobs and various training notes. The floor was completely covered in books, scrolls, and various bits of adventuring gear.

"Welcome to our humble abode," Mara said, tossing her backpack into the corner by the swords.

"Where do y'all even sleep?" I asked, trying not to step on anything.

Mara dragged her feet as she walked over to the other corner, clearing a path as she walked. "On the floor, in our bedrolls."

"We sold our beds last month to pay rent," Mara said while struggling to take off her armor. After yanking it off, she looked into her reflection in the dirt-caked window, brushing her hair.

"Sal doesn't know that yet, but once we get paid, we'll be able to get our beds back. Or at least one of them. I'll go buy it back in the morning while you two get supplies."

I looked at the two of them like they were insane. Who sells their bed to make rent? As I thought that, a wave of guilt hit me. Who was I to judge how they made a living?

"I need to get a new staff before we take another job," Giezha said, putting her tent tarp across the ceiling as a makeshift divider.

"I know, Gi. You and Asher can do that while I'm out. You should show him the basics of magic and stuff while you're at it."

The divider separated me from the two of them. I could hear articles of clothing fall to the ground before redressing with what they'd left on the floor beforehand.

"How much does renting a room cost here?" I asked curiously. As intimate as I had already become with Mara, I didn't feel comfortable sharing a room this cramped with them. I liked my privacy. And I'm sure they could use some as well.

"One silver a day, or about three gold per month," Mara said.

Mara walked back to my side in a pale green dress, and her hair no longer braided. It fell down in waves past her shoulders. Giezha walked out in almost the exact same robe as before, except it was now trimmed with blue instead of silver, and she had put her large witch hat back on.

"So, somebody who has roughly sixty gold to his name could get a place rented for the year and have plenty to spare."

56

Giezha snorted. "If you don't mind risking going without food or supplies for your next job."

"Speaking from experience, don't recommend you try," Mara said, placing a hand over her stomach. "You can make good money in a guild. But being the rookie in a guild is rough without money saved up. The pay is only one gold per week, assuming you get any jobs assigned to you."

"Right now, we've got maybe four gold and a couple of dozen copper between the two of us," Giezha said, pulling her makeshift curtain down.

I furrowed my brows, trying to do the math on that one. I had just paid them a month's worth of expenses and then some from the sound of it. Plus, there was the money they should be guaranteed from the job.

"But what about the money you made from this job? Shouldn't you be getting like six gold plus the regular wage?"

Both of them shook their heads. Giezha turned around and started picking things up off the floor while Mara leaned against a wall while she spoke. She looked off towards the grimy window as if she could see through it in the dimly lit room.

"That should be the case, but right now we're pretty heavy in the red. We all had to take loans out from the guild in order to pay our application fees. In addition to that, we need to pay them for any equipment we can't supply ourselves. Add room and board plus just the cost of being alive and…"

"That's highway robbery," I said incredulously. "They're scamming you guys!"

"Thank you for the obvious commentary," Giezha grumbled.

"Don't mind her," Mara said, waving her hand. "We knew that going into it, Me, Uli, and Gi wanted to make a name for ourselves. Y'know? Get some references before applying for some of the bigger guilds, maybe even move onto a bigger city. We've just had a couple of bad breaks. But we'll pay our debts off soon!"

Even Mara's chipper attitude could not mask the doubt in her voice.

"How much debt are you in?" I asked, already afraid of the answer.

"Since the incident? Six hundred gold," Giezha grumbled. "And that was before Ulilee ran off."

Mara's face grew bright red, and she started to argue. "She did not—"

"Whatever." Giezha brushed past us and walked out of the room, slamming the door behind her.

57

I turned and looked at Mara uncomfortably. "Sore subject?"

Mara just shook her head and looked down sadly. "Doesn't even begin to describe it. Giezha's not been herself lately."

An uncomfortable thought popped into my head. "I hope my being here hasn't made things worse. Especially since I am an Other—"

"Don't be silly Asher," Mara said, cutting me off. "I wouldn't use that word much around town, but Giezha's slow to warm up to everyone."

"And it doesn't bother you?" I asked, referring to my status as an Otherworlder.

Mara smiled and shook her head. "Not unless you give me a reason." Mara looked out a window, where Giezha could be seen stomping off down the road. "She's been having a rough go of it since Uli said she had a solo job to take care of a while ago. Haven't heard from her since. Giezha's paranoid that she got a better offer somewhere else and didn't want to tell us."

This mysterious Uli girl made more and more questions pop into my head every time she was mentioned.

"Was she the leader of you guys?" I asked while helping to clean up the rest of the mess in the room.

"Yeah," Mara said with a grimace. "She was the one that brought us together. We were making pretty good progress towards our goal until recently."

"Recently referring to 'The Incident' I presume?"

Mara clenched her jaw and looked away from me. Rather than speak, she just gave a quick nod. An awkward, pregnant pause ensued. Now wasn't the time to keep prying. I had better ideas.

"Any clue as to when Giezha will be back?" I asked as I finished stacking up a pile of books.

"She usually takes a couple of hours to cool off. She'll probably go and find some stray cats to pet or magic tricks to impress the local kids with."

"Never took her for the kind that enjoys being around kids."

"She acts like an ice-bear, but she's a big softie when you get to know her." Mara had just finished stacking the last of her notes.

"Well, if you don't have any plans..."

Mara turned and looked at me with an eyebrow cocked and a mischievous grin. She sauntered over to me.

58

"Who says I don't have plans?" she asked with a wink.

"Well," I started, reciprocating her flirtatious demeanor. "I haven't had a chance to really look around the city. I would love the opportunity to learn the ins and outs."

"And here I thought you were going to ask me to get out of my clothes," she half-joked. "Sounds like fun! But you have to buy me dinner, and some food for Gi. She won't be mad about missing the tour, but she is dangerous when she's hangry."

"Noted. I also need to talk to Sal about renting a room. You said it's seven silver per week?"

"Nine silver for you," she said, walking out of the room. "He charges us less because he likes us."

Mara left the room and shut the door behind her, leaving me alone in the ladies' room with my thoughts. How come Sal didn't like me? He'd only known me for about ten minutes.

Walking through the city of Naled with Mara was a chaotic experience. Buildings crammed together as tightly as possible, sometimes only inches apart. Most of the buildings were only a few stories tall and varied widely in their width. Homes and shops made of wood, stone, and daub crammed in, fighting for every bit of real estate.

The Silver Cup Inn was nestled into the western portion of Settler's Valley bordering Main Gate and Iron Court only a stone's throw away.

Being so close to Iron Court, the area was rough-and-tumble with businesses and guilds of both legal and dubious origin nestled in the shadow of the Naled Fortress. Sitting in the very center of Naled, Fortress was an imposing keep with thick stone walls surrounding it. Every ten feet, we saw guards with spears surrounding the perimeter.

"The big wig councilmen all stay there. Fat pigs living in their castle; playing King-of-the-Day." Mara made a gesture of a peace symbol with her thumb between the index and middle finger. One of the guards saw this and began to chase after us.

"I wonder what that kind of gesture means," I joked as we hid in a narrow alleyway.

Up next was a walk up to The Docks. Filled to the brim with fishermen and travelers was a chaotic mess even as evening approached. Fishmongers threatened the competition with giant tuna and salmon in hand. At the

59

same time, they rubbed elbows with ship captains, offering rides as far as the ocean.

A halfling with ghostly white hair hailed us as we walked. Mara tried to ignore him, but my excitement and curiosity dragged her over.

"Interested in a romantic boat ride, young man?" He asked while smoothing his tightly parted hair. "Special pricing, for one hour only: two silvers instead of the usual seven!"

Paying that much for a boat ride just off the shore made my stomach turn. Mara rolled her eyes and tried to pull me away. I felt somebody brush past me as we thanked the halfling and headed towards Iron Court. With an instinctual grab towards my side, I felt the absence of my coin sack.

"Son of a—" I turned around and the halfling was nowhere to be seen. "Bitch."

Mara looked at me and instantly knew what had happened. With a single glance, she bolted off away from me.

"Get back here!" Mara shouted.

Running to catch up with her, I pushed my way past a gaggle of sailors. I ignored their cursing as I tried to follow her bright red hair. Mara made her way to the edge of The Docks near the water. When I reached her, I saw her panting as she shook a fist at a ship.

The ship was setting out to sail and already making distance. At the very front of the ship, I could see a white-haired halfling flaunting his catch—a pouch with all the gold I had. A second halfing joined in his mocking of us.

"Evlana and Gods Above..." Mara lamented.

"Oh, they are not getting away from me," I said, pulling out a dagger I had kept stashed at my side.

"And what are you going to do now? Throw it at them? Give them another gift?"

The halflings on the ship seemed to have the same thought as Mara. They hooped and hollered, goading for me to throw the dagger at them. No doubt to be sold the second they landed. Gritting my teeth, a wicked idea crossed my mind.

As the ship got a few more yards out, I backed up a dozen paces. As I did so, I focused all of my energy on jumping. I thought about how I needed to jump twenty feet across and almost ten feet high. My legs began to burn, and my muscles contracted and tightened like before with the wolf. The

60

ship continued to drift out as I burst into a full-on sprint.

"What are you doing?" Mara asked as I ran past her.

"Something stupid!"

I felt energy swirl inside my calves and feet, and I kicked off the ground with all my might. I left the ground with the force of a cannonball being shot into the air. I soared up into the air over the water and towards the boat. The wind stung against my face as I zeroed in on my targets. The halfling with my gold dropped it in unison with their jaw.

Bracing for impact, I tucked my knees in, ready to roll forward. With a knife in my right hand, I guarded my face and neck with my arms as I landed. I hit the wooden deck of the ship with a deafening impact. I rolled forward several times before jumping at the halflings.

The female halfling sprinted away from me, while the thief was stiff as a board in shock and horror. I pointed my dagger inches from his neck. He flinched but couldn't move due to his paralyzed fear. Several other members of the ship all stared at me in stunned silence.

The sound of my blood pumping pounded in my ears as the rush of adrenaline coursed through my veins. As I opened my mouth, I struggled to catch my breath. "I... believe... you have something... of mine."

Out of the corner of my eye, I could see the female halfling trying to get below deck. Keeping the knife trained on the one in front of me, I pointed at her with my free hand.

"Where... do you think... you're going?" I panted.

She froze in place while a couple of the sailors walked towards me slowly. Lumbering up the stairs near the halfing and pushing past her, a half-orc with a chipped tusk approached me. From the look of his fancy hat, he was probably the captain.

"What's going on? Why are you on my ship?" he demanded. His words were slow and heavy.

Having finally caught my breath, I could speak clearly. "Those two halflings stole my gold pouch and tried to make a getaway."

He looked at the halfling I held at knifepoint and the one he had pushed past. He scowled at them and growled. They both looked like they were moments from pissing themselves.

"And how'd you get here?" he said suspiciously.

"He jumped!" one of the sailors exclaimed. "From The Docks! Ran up and flew here like a bird or something!"

The captain looked back at me and scanned me up and down.

"Magic user?" he asked.

I wasn't exactly sure if it was magic that I was in control of, but I wouldn't let him know that.

"You could say that."

"Hmph. Well, I never saw a magic user threaten someone with a knife. Take your gold and get off my ship."

"Sure thing."

Grabbing my coins beside the petrified halfling, I turned around and took another running start. My legs burned as I prepared to soar like a triumphant eagle. As I kicked off the ground, I felt my body catch a breeze and fly into the air. However, I had failed to notice how much further I was from shore now.

Splash!

I hit the cold water with so much force my body sank at least ten feet into the water. The force of hitting the water was excruciating. A rush of bubbles blasted across my face, disorienting me. For a moment, my grip on the gold pouch slipped, and several coins drifted into the depths of the still waters. My dagger had also fallen out of my hands. Well, shit.

Floating back up to the top, I saw that I was still a ways from shore. I looked back at the ship and saw two tiny figures get thrown off the edge. Before I could laugh at the misfortune of the tiny thieves, I heard Mara shouting my name.

"Asher! Asher!"

She was frantically rowing to me in a small boat. Her face was screwed up with panic and confusion as she heaved the boat towards me. I swam up to it and clumsily made my way aboard.

"Thanks," I said, trying to catch my breath again.

"Asher, that was amazing! You must have jumped at least twenty feet. How'd you do that?"

"That is an excellent question, Mara. I would love to find out the answer with you."

Mara gave me a look and just started laughing.

"You are full of surprises, Asher Merrick. You are full of surprises."

I sat down on the boat while Mara paddled. A different kind of burning was coursing up and down my legs. The regular sort of pain that happens when you overexert yourself. As we got back to shore, I needed help stepping out of the boat. Walking back to the tavern, Mara offered to carry me.

"I'll have to respectfully decline, Madam Brightwood." I joked as my legs screamed and cursed at me for forcing them back into service.

The walk back to the tavern was slow but enjoyable. We stopped and grabbed some street food from a vendor that had seen my incredible leap onto the ship.

Mara and I laughed and joked the whole way back, stopping only once more so Mara could buy a large amount of bean pods. As we walked, I felt a faint tingling in my legs and a thought crossed my mind.

Maybe that's what Gathos meant by unleashing my potential.

Chapter 7

Gethsday Evening, 24th of Wirdin, Year 678, 4th Age

I spent the entire next day sleeping in my new apartment. I had taken a room in the same tavern as the girls. Salvatore absolutely refused to put my room next to theirs, but I didn't mind. My room was a basic wooden box with a bed, desk, chair, and a shabby chest.

Despite how exhausted I was, I slept terribly. Over and over, I'd randomly wake up, feeling an electric shock in my chest. I'd hear a 'bang!' and jump out of bed.

The first few times, I'd wake up in a cold sweat. Around the third, I gave up and decided to get going for the day. The only problem was, the evening had come and gone. It was well into the night when I got back to my room. Leaving my gear locked away, I stretched as I descended the second-floor balcony.

"Welcome back to the land of the living!" I heard Salvatore chide me while cleaning the tables. "The girls went to check on you, thinking something had happened, but I sent them away. Sometimes a young man just needs some rest."

Something in his intonation made me not believe him, but I ignored it. Sal seemed like a nice enough guy. I walked up to the bar and ordered a meat and cheese plate for breakfast/dinner. While Sal prepared my meal, I asked him about the girls.

"Where are they right now? Over at the guild?"

"Hard to say really," Sal replied while I tossed a couple coppers to him. "If I were a betting man, although I'm not, I'd say Mara is training with her guildmasters, and Giezha is at the Arcana Library near the Naled Fortress. Poor girl spends all her money accessing the Arcana Library."

"How much is it to enter?" I asked while munching some spiced pork.

"Oh, about two silvers I'd guess," Sal said while shaking his head. "Gi misses rent the most out of those girls because of that place."

"Can't she get a library card or something?"

Sal gave me a funny look, clearly indicating a library card wasn't a thing here. Changing the subject, I got back to Gi and the Library.

"So, what is it she's trying to find there?"

"She's looking for what every other magic user is looking for. Spells,

64

incantations, potions, whatever she can find to make herself a more powerful wizard. Or sorcerer. Or whatever it is she is."

"There are different types?"

Sal gave me another funny look, and I waved my hand in his direction.

"Let's just say magic ain't much of a thing where I'm from."

"It must be an unusual place... Well, anyway, magic users get their magic from only a few places. From the gods, from their ancestry, from a curse, or from a special circumstance. No matter what though, they must study magic in order to improve themselves. Their source is just the spark, it's up to them to light the flame and provide the fuel."

His words reminded me that Gathos had given me magical abilities. The last few days had been such a blur that I hadn't even stopped to think that I was probably able to use magic. Out of morbid curiosity, I held a piece of cheese in my hands and pointed my finger at it. For a moment, I imagined a tiny little flame shooting out of that finger, melting the cheese.

Nothing.

"You interrogating the cheese for more info, boy?"

I shook my head and chuckled. "No, just testing something out. Thank you for the information, Sal, I really appreciate it."

Sal grunted in response, and I left him a few copper pieces as a tip. I hadn't gotten around to finding out if tipping was a thing in Echo Veil, but I figured I might as well. Hopping out of my seat, I left the tavern and headed for the Naled Fortress.

"Sal, where is the—"

"It's a bright white marble building with turrets on all four corners." Sal said, cutting me off. "Look for a bunch of dopes in wizard hats and robes."

With a thumbs-up, I turned around and dashed out of the inn.

Thanks to its proximity to the Naled Fortress, the journey towards the library wasn't difficult. This massive castle and its walls ripped into the skyline higher than any other building. All I needed to do was walk in that general direction, and I'd get there eventually. Just as Sal had predicted, there were wizards everywhere walking in and out of the library.

The entrance was a massive wrought iron and wooden door nearly two stories tall. It appeared that the wizards entering and leaving the library were walking straight through the wall.

As I prepared to walk through it as well, a voice stopped me.

65

"Halt," came a bored, nasally voice. I looked to my and saw a female gnome with dirty blond hair, not bothering to look up from the large book in her lap. "What color is the door?"

"Uhhh, come again?"

The gnome woman rolled her eyes and looked at me.

"In order to gain entrance to the library, you must first show that you are capable of the arcane. What color is the door?"

"I thought that in order to enter we needed two silvers."

The woman just looked at me with an impatient expression. As she tapped her fingers, I could see the faintest twinkling of lights at her fingertips. Looking back at the door, it looked like the door's wood was brown. No, wait, it was black. Maybe it was orange? Oh wait, she was changing the color of the door.

I looked at her, raising my eyebrows. She shrugged her shoulders and didn't say a word. Apparently, magic could be done without an incantation as well.

Looking at the door, I strained my eyes, trying to figure out what the original color of the door must be. Perhaps there was a riddle to it. Perhaps there was a way to figure out what color of the door was beforehand. As I tried to ascertain it, a mouse scurried out from a hole in the wall, straight through the door.

"I'm an idiot," I said to myself under my breath. I turned and looked at the gnome. "There is no door."

The gnome rolled her eyes and stuck a hand out. Digging into my pocket, I grabbed a couple loose silver coins and stuffed them into her hands. I walked towards the door and phased right through it. The inside of the library was enormous. Shelves of books that lined every wall, going as far up as the eye could see. Sunlight lazily drifted downward from windows at the very top of the ceiling.

Wizards and mages of all shapes, sizes, and colors surrounded me, discussing their research, engrossed in their tomes, or searching the stacks. I looked for a nearly-eight-foot-tall, grey-skinned woman but couldn't find her in the central area. She was not in any of the other rooms I tried either.

"Looking for something in particular?" A green dragonborn mage asked me.

Looking around to see if I could find Giezha again, I sighed. "Someone

66

actually. Really tall, gray skin, doesn't talk much."

The dragonborn nodded his head.

"Oh yes, the goliath. You will find her in the room just across from this in the main foyer. She will most likely be studying alone. Strange. Usually, it's her smaller friend that comes to get her."

"Mara?" I asked

"No, that's not it... I believe her name was Ooo-lalee?"

"Ulilee?"

"That's the one," he said, snapping his clawed fingers. "I take it she understood she's no longer welcome here?"

I looked to my left and right. "Uhhh, no. She's... out at the moment."

"Ah, just as well." The dragonborn left, satisfied that the ever-mysterious Ulilee wouldn't be disgracing the hallowed library with her presence.

Following the dragonborn's directions, I found myself in a peculiar room. It was much smaller than the others but no less fascinating. The room was filled with narrow halls of books and floating chairs, candles and scrolls. I saw people floating in the chairs while they studied as I looked around. None of them, however, were Giezha.

"Askanda's Tome of Scaled Foes," I heard a young boy in a set of blue robes command behind me. When I turned around, I saw him sitting in a chair that floated up to a specific row of books. Sticking his hand out, he picked out a book that had a title to match his words—Askanda's Tome of Scaled Foes.

Sitting in another of the chairs, I cleared my throat.

"Umm... Giezha Nightstrike?" I whispered.

The rickety wooden chair shuddered to life before floating upwards. It continued to float higher and higher and higher... until I looked up and saw a figure floating near the ceiling.

"Giezha!" I hissed.

She was entranced in a large purple and black book with a very harsh-looking script on the front. It emanated a faint hum and glow of purple energy as her eyes rapidly scanned its pages. Her concentration was broken when she heard me. She darted her eyes towards me and cocked her head to one side. I held onto the chair's arms with a vice grip as I floated up. The fall down didn't look fun.

"If you're looking for Mara, she's at the guildhall."

"I've actually been looking for you," I said, struggling to not look down. "I was hoping you could tutor me in this magic stuff."

Giezha pulled her head back in surprise, and her eyes widened.

"Why have me tutor you?" she asked like I'd proposed we go dancing.

"Because," I murmured while pulling my feet up and under my bottom. "You are the only person I can ask, and the most knowledgeable person I know with regards to magic."

For a moment, she said nothing.

"You need a tutor? What makes you think you have any magical abilities? From what I could tell, you are proficient with the sword you carry."

"Call it divine intervention from another world."

Her hand snapped forward, covering my mouth. Her eyes were narrowed, and she put her other hand's finger to her lips.

"I told you not to talk about that around anyone but me. It would be very bad if somebody else heard."

Doing my best to not tip over, I nodded and pushed her large hand away from me.

"Yeah, I know. So, will you teach me?"

"I don't think it'd be a wise use of either of our time." Giezha floated her chair over to where she had been previously studying. An idea popped into my head as she started to read again.

"I'll buy you a new staff and get your old one fixed."

Giezha's head shot back up, and she looked at me.

"I agree to the terms."

Giezha tapped my chair and announced a command for both chairs.

"Floor."

We descended like a rock, gaining momentum faster and faster. All of our momenta disappeared before we were about to splat onto the floor, and gently landed. I expected my head to smash into my knees, but instead, I hopped down on my feet.

Walking past me, Giezha made a beeline out the room. I followed her into a room with no foot traffic. It was even smaller than the last few.

This room was a single story tall, with one large bookshelf on the back wall. The rest of the room was filled with younger wizards reading from books aloud to their teachers. Puffs of smoke and dancing lights filled the

68

room while the sounds of overlapping tutelage filled my ears. Carving a path straight through the din, Giezha quickly walked straight to the bookshelf, picked up a book, and turned around, nearly bowling me over.

"Where are we going?" I asked to no response.

Instead, she walked back into the main room before ascending a large white marble staircase. I followed her as we walked up and up and up the stairs. My legs burned as they trudged higher and higher. I struggled to keep up as she ascended two to three stairs at a time with a single step while I had to run behind her.

Just as suddenly as she started, she stopped. Turning to her right, she opened a dusty wooden door. Inside was an empty classroom with a few desks, a large board, and a square with chest-high walls encircling a badly burnt and scarred section of floor. Giezha pointed to an empty desk with two chairs.

"Sit here, please," she said quietly.

She placed the book in front of me as we sat down, opening it a few pages in. The pages were filled with text and illustrations of a small dwarf in a wizard's hat. Illustrations showed him doing magic and other diagrams.

"You know next to nothing about magic, do you?" Giezha said as she scanned the pages.

"Yeah," I said, reading the descriptor on the foundations of magic. "Where I'm from, magic is just a fancy card trick and sleight of hand."

Giezha's eyes halted and darted over to me. The last time she looked at me like that was when she was ready to brain me. Shifting uncomfortably in my seat, I could no longer concentrate on my reading.

"No magic whatsoever?"

"None."

Giezha looked up and breathed deeply while pinching her nose.

"Your ignorance of the most basic of concepts in magic will make training you difficult."

I winced at her bluntness, but she pressed on. "It will be difficult, but not impossible. If you are diligent in your studies, you may learn the mystic ways and arcane arts."

I nodded my head and got back to reading. Before I could get another paragraph in, she pulled the book away from me.

69

"This book, however," she said, snapping the book shut, "is completely useless. This is basic instruction with reading levels for a child. It would be an insult to try to teach you this way. I suggest a more practical approach."

"That sounds great!" I said as my eyes shined like stars. I was going to learn magic! Real magic!

Giezha didn't share the same level of enthusiasm as me. She stood up and pulled out a small piece of paper from her robe. The paper unfolded itself in the palm of her hand. I stood up and got a closer to look at it. It looked no different from any other scrap at first glance, but you could barely make out a different shade of white. There were intricate patterns and shapes similar to the one from the Truth Circle she had created the other day.

"Most ignorant of magic think of it as an art. Something created from nothing but the imagination of its caster." As Giezha spoke, a small green light rose from the paper in her hand. It glittered like an emerald floating in her palm. "They are not wrong, but they are not entirely right. Magic is a science. You will always need a catalyst of some sort to create something."

"I suppose it's like energy," I said, watching the emerald light float. "It can't be created or destroyed. Only changed."

"If that helps you remember it, sure." Giezha pulled out a small vial from her robe. It was filled with grey powder. Uncorking it released the smell of burnt wood. "For a less experienced wizard, the catalyst will often need to be in larger quantities. To make fire, one would need a catalyst for the fire."

She dumped a small amount of the ashes onto the paper. With a moment's concentration and a slight twitch in her finger muscles, the green light began to change colors. It started to emit heat as it changed from green to orange and yellow. The emerald in her hand shifted into a small flame that burned continuously over the ashes.

"However, as your understanding of magic and your control over your abilities increases, you will no longer need such a large catalyst. Memorizing runes and their formulas can unlock the same effects."

She shook the flame out and dropped the paper to the ground. Cupping both hands, Giezha closed her eyes and began to mutter an incantation. As she did, a fire sparked from nothing in her hands. The flame made no sound, but I felt its heat radiate towards me.

"A simple incantation and the creation of a chain reaction will be enough to bring forth the effects you desire. These effects can take many forms."

As she said this, the fire began to dissipate and turn into another set of lights in her hand. Its brightly colored lights danced in her palm.

"The changes that you create can be an illusion, like a dance of light, or maybe the sound of chirping birds."

As she said that, I could hear the sweet sounds of songbirds fill the room.

"You can create things, destroy them, change them. As you become more and more adept, what you do with your magic truly does become limited only by your imagination and the mana in your system, and the vessel in which you cast your magic. With a proper staff, I'm normally more... competent."

My mind raced at the possibilities. "So, I could make a nice and juicy steak appear in my hands if I wanted to."

Giezha suppressed a laugh that came out through her nose. "If you knew how to conjure the cow, slaughter it, cook it, and include all of the other components... Yes, you could."

"Can I affect other people directly?"

"Depending on what you're trying to do, yes. Some folk, like the fey, enjoy playing tricks on the mind. They may modify memories or create false emotions. There was once a pixie in Naled that became the grand vizier to the emperor through his trickery of the King's feeble mind."

"Can you physically change other people?" I asked excitedly, my mind racing with possibilities. "Like if somebody were really annoying, could I turn them into a goldfish to shut them up? What about things? Could I turn lead into gold? There were a lot of stories about wizards doing that where I'm from."

"I thought you said magic didn't exist where you are from," she said skeptically.

"It's true, magic wasn't real where I'm from. But we still imagined it. Myths and legends and stuff."

Giezha thought about what I said for a moment. "Hmm. Well, yes, it is possible to change the physical nature of a person or a thing. However, all magic can leave traces of itself on whatever you have cast your spells on. Playing tricks and other misdeeds can lead to severe consequences. It's often that wizards, sorcerers, and the like will receive a stricter form of punishment for the same crime as a non-magical person. And Asher..."

She gave me a warning look.

71

"What? I'm listening, I swear."

"I know, that's why I am about to say this. Do not under any circumstances ever practice necromancy. It is considered the foulest and most heinous form of magic that exists in this world. Some consider it to be the greatest sin possibly committed. Only a few twisted individuals partake in this forsaken path of magic."

"Got it, no raising a giant zombie horde to take on my enemies."

For the next hour, she continued to explain the inner machinations of magic. The need for incantations, using magical conduits to increase the potency and precision of magic, storing magic in spell scrolls and other objects, and creating the chain reaction that leads to magical effects.

As she spoke, I did my best to commit everything to memory. I borrowed a notebook of hers and a writing quill. My hand cramped as I hurriedly wrote down notes while she spoke at a breakneck speed. This was the first time I had seen her speak with such enthusiasm. But the more she talked about magic, the more briskly she spoke. I could see her expression soften and her eyes light up in excitement.

I even saw her crack the occasional smile as she answered my questions. As she continued to teach me, the sun began to set even further and the moon started to rise. I asked her a question, trying to clarify some points of the lesson she had given me.

"So, let's say I was trying to go and create a fire without the proper runes or catalyst—"

"You'd likely create no less than a puff of smoke. Or in rare cases, you may create an inferno that could burn down an entire forest. It's all dependent on where your magical gifts have come from. For most people, it's about unlocking more and more of the power that you have inside of you. Some have more power in them to begin with. Some are given such immense powers that the secret is locking enough of it away for it to be usable."

As we walked back to the entrance, my mind drifted towards my patron. He had gifted me with power that I had no idea was possible. I shuddered to think about what could happen if I weren't careful. Gathos did not seem like the type of fellow to exercise great restraint.

Giezha pulled out a set of runes, having me focus on their design and order. She also brought me over to an unlit candle she'd placed on the

72

windowsill.

"Dip your finger in some ash and try to focus your mana on these runes," She instructed. "This is a basic flame spell you will use to light the candle. Now point your finger at the wick and read the runes."

Reading the spell was hard when I didn't know what the runes were saying or how they worked on the most basic level. However, I was able to recognize their patterns and imagine them in my head. Focusing my mana on the vision of the runes, I tried to feel the warmth of fire at my fingertip.

"There you go," Giezha quietly encouraged me. "Really try to focus on getting their order and form correct."

The vision of the runes became clearer in my head, and I began to pour mana into my hand. It felt like warm wax running down my body and coalescing into my fingertip. It grew larger and larger. Hotter and hotter. I could even hear the flicker of the flame!

"Asher!" Giezha shouted.

My eyes snapped open, and I saw a ball of fire the size of a soccer ball engulfing the candle. In a panic, I snapped concentration and the fire sphere shot off into the midnight sky. I watched in horror as it thankfully fizzled into nothing up in the sky.

I turned to Giezha, worried she would be mad. I was pleasantly surprised when I saw Giezha giving me a look of approval.

"Your control is shit, but you've certainly got the mana for it. Not bad, Merrick."

I was about to say something when the sound of bells could be heard from the turrets of the library's walls. Giezha turned and looked towards where the bells had been emanating from. The cold expression she often wore returned firmly to its place. She turned to me and gestured for me to follow.

"We'll need to pick this up another time. The library is closing for the likes of us." Giezha picked up the book she had brought. "Return."

As she said that, the book floated into the air and out the door, we had entered from. I followed her down the steps towards the foyer.

"Let's hurry up, Asher," Giezha said, picking up the pace. "We'll be meeting Mara at the guild."

As I caught up, she looked at me and nodded her head.

"Good job today."

Chapter 8

Gethsday Afternoon, 24th of Wirdin, Year 678, 4th Age

"We'll need to make a quick stop before going to the guild," Giezha said, entering the Silver Cup Inn.

Before I could ask her any questions, she walked out with two staffs in her hand. The shorter staff was the one I had seen her carrying the previous days. Both sported cracks and breaks along the top ends of them. The taller staff curled at the top, the same shade of gray as her skin with black markings across it.

"You said you were going to pay for lessons, and I intend to receive payment immediately."

Next to the guildhall was a small collection of buildings with signs hanging out the front advertising different magical services and curios. Giezha walked us into a shop named Tomes and Tiaras. The inside was warm and inviting, with the faint smell of incense, which created a light haze in the room. I walked along the chest-high shelves looking at rows of magical items, ingredients, and potions.

"See anything you like?" a voice came from the other room behind the sales counter. A youthful-looking elf walked into the room. He had a slender face and cheekbones next to ears that protruded up and outward. After looking at Giezha and me, a look of disappointment briefly flashed across his face.

"Evening, Perrin," Giezha said, placing the two magical staffs on his counter. "I can't afford to buy anything today. I'd just like these fixed."

The elf picked up and inspected them. Perrin held them with both hands looking down the wood at different angles. As he did, a look of disapproval flashed across his face. Giezha shifted her feet as he made his inspection, drumming her fingers on her hips. She managed to look everywhere but at the elf, who inspected her precious magical items.

74

My eyes settled on a small green potion in a spherical bottle as he worked. The liquid inside swirled rapidly on its own, and its inscription identified it as a stamina potion. Most of the potions were selling for at least seventy-five gold. This one, however, was going for forty.

"You need to watch that temper of yours, young lady," Perrin said as he finally set them back down. "It doesn't make sense to keep buying staffs if you are going to turn them into clubs. Do you want to be a sorceress? Act like one. We don't need a goliath ruining the good name of magic users."

Before I could say anything, Giezha slammed her fists on the counter, splintering the wood. Perrin's eyes were as big as dinner plates, and he took a half step back. Perrin started to reach for something under the counter, but Giezha got into his face. Her eyes were slits as she glared at him.

"I did not come to this establishment to be spoken down to as if I were a child. I did not come here to have my race belittled. And I did not come here to be treated as a lesser mage. I came here to purchase your services. I suggest that you remember this. How much will it be to have this one repaired?"

Perrin stood there frozen solid in fear as she shoved the grey and black magic staff out. He stammered, trying to find his voice.

"F-f-f-four gold"

Giezha turned and looked me up and down before returning her attention to Perrin.

"I want to trade this staff for a spellcasting focus for him. Something he can use while fighting with a sword or shield. What do you have?"

Before Perrin could protest, Giezha shook him with a bored look on her face. He nearly wet himself as he summoned a collection of rings, bracelets, and other objects. Giezha nodded for me to look, and I inspected the different items.

They looked like little trinkets and dollar-store rings using battered metal instead of cheap plastic. After quickly picking through the pile, I settled on a copper ring wrapped around a solid purple stone. You could see little twinkles—like starlight in the night sky—inside the ring on closer inspection.

"That'll be five g-gold, plus the cost of the counter, so a few extra coppers."

75

Giezha leaned over further, and her hands crunched the wood below. After it groaned and creaked to her satisfaction, she leaned back and nodded her head. I came up to the counter and paid him in exact change. After receiving payments, he took a deep breath and held one staff in his hands.

Placing the broken section in his palms, Perrin squeezed his eyes shut. A bright white light emanated from his hands, and when Perrin let go, the staff was repaired. He quickly fixed the second before waving his hand over the counter, which snapped back into place.

"I'd appreciate it if you'd stop breaking my counter," Perrin said shakily.

Giezha flashed a wicked smile. I thought she looked terrifying, and Perrin clearly agreed.

"Then stop making racist remarks about my people. It's a simple solution."

I decided to leave the potion of stamina behind as we walked out, and I made sure to leave it on a different countertop than the one I had picked it upon. Take that Perrin, the racist, magic shop-owning elf. Giezha kept the grey and black staff and looked at the ring I put on my middle finger.

"Consider that an investment in your magical career," Giezha said with a nod of approval. "I hate that stupid man."

"Then why do you still shop there?"

"He's the only one I found that is willing to serve me," Giezha said with a shrug. "Magic users tend to have a poor opinion of goliath folk, and they've never seen one that does magic instead of swinging a giant hammer or sword. They consider what I do to be unnatural and perverse."

"That's awful."

"It is. But my kinfolk agree with them. My decision to pursue the magical arts was one of the reasons I... Well, never mind. It's not important. What is important is that I pursue my destiny on my terms. And I won't let anybody get in the way of that."

"Admirable," I said with a shrug.

Neither of us spoke as we walked into the guildhall. The Red Breaker guild was just as rowdy and noisy as before. Most guild members drank, laughed at the tables, discussed upcoming jobs, and shot the breeze. Scanning the room, I could see Mara in the back, and it looked as though she was speaking with the captain.

"Mara doesn't look happy," I observed.

"That's a bad sign." Giezha leaned down and whispered.

"The captain looks very happy though."

"That's an even worse sign."

Mara stood up from the table and stormed over to us. Her face was bright pink, and her eyes stung with tears. Her fists trembled as she walked while other guild members hooted and hollered at us.

"Rooks done fucked up now."

"Dead crew walkin'!"

Ignoring all of that, she grabbed us and took us to a corner table, drawing an extra chair. Giezha and I sat down, looking at each other, unsure of what to do or say. Had we just been fired? Had a bounty been placed on us or something?

"Mara," I asked, afraid of what the answer might be. "What's going on?"

Mara tried to speak, but her voice wouldn't come out. She put a finger up and tried to clear her throat. When she opened her mouth again, a hiccup came out as tears continued to stream. Half of the guild members avoided watching, while the other half looked like they were watching their favorite show unfold.

"Mar," Giezha said, holding Mara's shoulder. "Is it about Uli? Have we heard anything?"

She shook her head and made another attempt at gathering herself. With a sniff, she looked up at us.

"It's not about Uli, though she is expected to return in a few days. We got a job request." Mara finally managed to mumble. "One that we were personally requested for."

"Well, that's a good thing, right?" I asked. "The more jobs we do, the better."

"It's the job that's the problem," Mara said, tossing a lavender-colored envelope that had been previously opened on the table. "Read this."

The writing was of beautiful penmanship and lackluster authorship.

Dear Pemalina,

I have a small confession. Forgive this pouring of my heart.

I cherish The High Street Market Festival, where we first met. The moment I clapped my eyes on you, I knew you were an amazing girl.

Recently, I have begun to regard you as much more than just a beautiful shrine girl.

My feelings intensified when I saw you smiling in the moonlight that festival evening.

You have eyes as deep purple a color as aubergine and the most dazzling smile I've ever seen. When I look at you, I just want to kiss you all over.

You're so special in your kind ways. The way you handle your petty father shows tremendous empathy and temperance.

I know I'm just a fair fool to you, but I think we could be happy together, soaring through life like two beautiful doves.

Please, say you'll be mine Pemalina, and accept this Ivory Rose as a token of my affection.

All my love,

Sir Randal Arasalor

Giezha and I both lifted our heads from reading and exchanged looks. Mara had her head buried in her hands. A pair of fat and greasy guild members were behind us, laughing and pointing in our direction.

"The man who wrote this letter is a knight who serves the Fortress. He's apparently fallen for one of the shrine maidens of the Temple of Ihena, the Goddess of Dreams. He wants us to find him an Ivory Rose to be added to his letter. He contracted the job for two hundred and fifty gold. Ugh! We could not have received a worse possible mission."

"What's so bad about collecting the stupid rose? Is it a rare type of flower?"

Giezha's face lit up with understanding, and she hung her head low, trying to hide her face under her witch's hat.

"They're roses that have been dipped in a special potion that turns them into a white crystal," Mara explained. "They're very fragile and ridiculously expensive. The kind of expensive we can't afford. He plans to send this letter to her next week."

Looking back at the captain, who winked at me, a sinking feeling came into my stomach. Other members of The Guild joined in on the jeering at us. Whatever this was, it was starting to stink.

"The Guild isn't going to reimburse us for the cost of the rose, are they?"

Both Mara and Giezha shook their heads slowly. They both got up and

78

walked out of the guildhall. I followed suit, not wanting to sit and be the sole participant in these bastards' cruel game.

Try as we might, there was no conceivable way to pool our resources together and get that kind of gold together for the rose.

All the guild members offered to "loan" us the money, of course, but that would simply further entrench everyone in more debt.

Later, we took a job outside the city, finding some missing sheep in the woods for a local farmer. While rustling up the last one, I offered to pay for the rose myself.

Although I technically had the money for it, I'd be throwing away a ton of money just to play these bastards' game. I was shot down immediately.

"All that would do is put us into debt with you," Giezha explained.

"We appreciate it, Asher, but we can't do that," Mara sighed, accepting the ten silver pieces for the job as we went to our next menial task. "We'll figure something out."

The next afternoon, I asked a pretty obvious question. "Why don't we ask Sal?"

They both shot me deathly glares at the thought of asking him for such a large sum.

"We already owe him basically everything," Mara said glumly. "Asking for that kind of cash would be downright insulting."

Day after day, we worked around the city doing whatever jobs we could find that were too small for the guilds to gobble up. But try as we might, no matter how many odd jobs we picked up, we just couldn't scrounge up enough coin for the rose. The night, before delivery was due, we walked back to the Silver Cup Inn and sat at the bar, defeated.

Without hesitation, Sal pulled out glasses and poured us our drinks. He set his elbows on the bar and looked at us. Neither touched their drink but instead just sat and looked at them. Unable to diffuse the awkwardness, I started drinking my ale.

"Oh, girls," Sal said, frowning at them. "What have those idiots got you up to now? You've been dejected all week."

Rather than force them to speak, I gave Sal the rundown. He put down the other glass as gently as possible. The look on his face reminded me of when I told my mom that my teacher had been "forgetting" to grade my homework after I broke up with her niece in middle school.

79

"When I was a member of that guild," he said while pouring drinks for another few patrons at the end of the bar. "Being a Breaker meant you were willing to go above and beyond the call of duty. It meant that you could break through the things that sent others back to shore. Nowadays, it's just an excuse used to bully rookies."

After sitting at the bar another half-hour while Sal and I tried to stimulate conversation, the two left their drinks untouched and went to their room. The sound of the door locking could be heard faintly above the small crowd at the bar.

Sal sighed and started to pick up the two drinks. I quickly grabbed them and laid down a piece of copper for each. I hadn't had a good drink in what felt like a hundred years, and I needed one badly. And even if these beers weren't particularly good, they'd do.

Sal didn't stick around to chat and got back to serving the other patrons. I turned around and looked at the people coming to the inn. Unsure what to do about the rose, I ordered another beer and resigned myself to people watching.

A few hours and a half dozen beers later, I was having trouble watching the fight between a gnome and his halfling wife while his dwarfish girlfriend tried to escape the bar. Sal decided not to intervene and took bets with the others sitting at the bar.

"Busy figuring out the job, Asher?" Salvatore asked me while the unfaithful husband chased after his crying wife and girlfriend.

"Just trying to get my sea legs," I said while doing my best not to take his bait. "I ain't been here but a few days, and it's already a crisis. Ain't going to accomplish nothing tonight, so I might as well enjoy myself."

Sal clasped onto my shoulder and looked me in the eyes. "Yes, well, I think you've had enough. Go on up to bed and make sure you're sober enough to help the girls in the morning."

I pulled my shoulder away from his tight grip and slipped off the chair, grumbling.

"Dusty old codger," I mumbled, loud enough for him to hear.

As I attempted to make it to the staircase, I felt a pair of hands grab me by each shoulder. Turning around, I saw the two fat slobs from the guild. The two of them had tied their headbands askew to their foreheads, and their eyes were bloodshot. I hadn't seen them in the inn, but they were deep

80

into the night as it was.

"What'd you just say to the fine purveyor of the Tin Cup Inn?" The fatter one, a pot-bellied half-orc with brown tufts of hair on his face, sneered. "He may be an old codger, aye, but it's rude to point it out. Ain't that right, Sal, you old codger?"

The smell coming off him put the word putrid to shame. He smelled like a sweat-stained shirt that baked in the sun for weeks. The other Breaker, an extremely tall and wide man with an eyepatch and suspenders over his white shirt, laughed as bits of saliva rolled down his face.

"You two haven't been allowed in this establishment for five years," Sal said stiffly. "Get out."

The half-orc tossed me chest first into the bar counter. I barely managed to catch myself, though I still slumped against the bar.

"Remind me what it was that got us kicked out of a founding Red Breaker's bar, again?"

"Harassing my customers and starting a bar fight," Sal said with a glance towards me.

"Awwww, Cmon, Sally!" The other one jeered. "It's not harassment if they're just a rookie. Ain't that right? Rookie?"

Memories of my last bar fight flashed before my eyes. I didn't want to have a repeat of how that wound up. I just turned around and stared at them.

"I ain't looking for trouble, alright?" I said, trying to diffuse the situation.

"Oh," the half-orc said, pushing his face into mine. "Not looking for trouble, eh?"

I stayed silent and kept my hands up. He wasn't as tall or as strong as Giezha. The other just laughed at the half-orc's words. I decided to just walk away. It would be better to deal with the two idiots tomorrow in the guildhall. Right now, it would just be asking for trouble.

Slipping through the tables, I got out of dodge and walked out of the bar. Hopefully, the crisp night air would do me some good. As I was opening the bar's door, the half-orc spoke again.

"Shame about the rose. You could really do for one of these little things."

I looked across the bar and saw a white crystalline rose held daintily in his massive green hand. My stomach churned as I watched him wave the rose back and forth. Whether it was my anger or the beers, I felt sick to my stomach. Clenching my teeth, I considered my options. If he was just trying to play me, he was doing an excellent job. On the other hand, it wasn't a good idea to let the opportunity slip by.

"That's it," he said, goading me. "Why don't we take this business outside?"

Following orders, the two of them cornered me in an alleyway not far from the Inn. It was taking all the patience in the world not to pick a fight, but even drunk Asher knew this wasn't a fight I'd likely win.

The half-orc twiddled the rose between his fingers as he spoke. "Now let's get down to brass tacks. You need the rose, and you all are too broke to buy so much as the glass case it comes in."

I bit the inside of my cheek to stop myself from making a sarcastic remark. The half-orc continued his speech.

"So, let's have ourselves a little wager, eh?"

I cocked my head to the side and made a sound like I was interested in learning more.

"Been hearing some interesting things about you, Rook. Spire wolves and jumpin' thirty feet to chase some thieves. Impressive stuff, Rook! Impressive stuff!" He clapped my shoulder excessively hard.

"'Issall bullshit." Spitty dismissed.

"Maybe," I admitted.

"Ha! I knew it."

"Shut up, Mick!" the half-orc snapped. Regaining his composure, the half-orc placed an arm on the bar top. "If you can last ten seconds with me in a fight, I'll consider giving you the rose."

I looked at him and then Mick who was grumbling and looking at both of us. I felt he didn't find this as entertaining as the half-orc did.

"Right," I said, sure of an angle somewhere. "And if I lose?"

Mhurren laughed heartily and squared up like a boxer, leaving the rose on a loose crate. I felt the muscles in my arm begin to burn. They burned hotter and hotter like the insides were ready to melt.

"Well, when I snap you like a twig, you'll be leaving those miscreants and become our personal pack mule."

"Our bitch." Mick added eloquently.

I looked at them both, anger boiling to the top. The second I agreed, they'd both jump me and beat me down. I wanted nothing more than to say fuck it and try to bash their brains it, but I knew this was a bad idea.

"Fuck off." I said, brushing past them, still feeling the fire burn in my arms.

"Hey!" Mhurren shouted, grabbing my arm as I walked away.

In one motion, I grabbed him by the wrist and smashed it onto the wall. SNAP!

The sickening wet crunch of bones breaking filled my ears. Mhurren let out a howl of pain and went down to the ground in a heap, grasping at his arm. I looked at Mick, remembering that he was the half-goliath Giezha hated.

He didn't say anything, but instead tried to grab me as I made a run for it. Right as I was about to get clobbered, Salvatore appeared out of nowhere and blasted him with some spell that sent him flying through the air. The spell missed me by inches as Mick spiraled into the air before crumpling to the ground next to Mhurren.

"Damn fools," Sal muttered angrily, holding the door open for me. "Always trying to start fights and cause trouble."

As I looked around, most of the bar had huddled by the windows to watch everything go down. They all quickly returned to their drinks, games, and stories once the excitement had ended.

"Thanks," I said, quietly.

"Don't mention it," Sal assured me. "When I had heard rumors about you from other people, I wasn't quite sure what to make of it. Until now, I hadn't made up my mind about you."

"What's the verdict?" I asked, looking up with a grin on my face.

Sal just laughed and handed me the rose from Mhurren and Mick.

"I'd say you lasted longer than ten seconds, eh?"

Sal placed the rose on the bar. Light trickled in and out of the crystal rose. Tiny rainbows dotted across the rose, mixing with its pearlescent coloring. Indeed, it was a beautiful little thing. I marveled at its beauty, trying to figure out how Sal heard all that.

"How?"

Sal poured himself a drink and grinned. "This dusty old codger's got a few tricks up his sleeve."

Incantations flowed from her mouth as she shot out blasts of magic towards me. One missed my stomach by inches while an icy blue bolt sliced into my shoulder, leaving a superficial cut that burned cold.

Chapter 9

Orosday Afternoon, 4th of Ulenen, Year 678, 4th Age

I spent most of the next day sleeping, not waking up until late into the afternoon. When I woke up, there was a heavy presence on my right side. My entire right arm and hand were paralyzed. Lifting my body up, it fell to the side like a tube filled with wet sand.

"Well now..." I said in concern.

Concentrating, I tried to focus on moving my fingertips. Only my index finger managed to budge. My forearm, bicep, and triceps muscles all refused to activate. My shoulder was useless too.

84

"What in the—" Initially, I worried that the orc may have crushed my hand or something, and I had not realized it. Upon closer inspection, I didn't appear to have any injuries. There were no visible markings, bruising, or scars.

"Oh, dear."

A knock came at my door.

"Asher?" came the voice of Mara. "You finally up?"

Stumbling towards the door, I saw Mara and Giezha looking at me anxiously.

"What happened last night?" Mara asked, noticing my limp arm. "Sal told us you got in a fight?"

I did my best to explain how everything went down between me and the two Breakers. Mara and Giezha didn't look surprised that Mhurren and Mick got themselves involved. However, hearing about the rose made them very happy.

"REALLY?" Mara gasped.

I nodded my head and gestured to the rose on my desk. Giezha inspected it, her eyes shining much like the crystalline rose.

"What happened to your arm?" Mara asked, realizing just how bad it was.

"No idea," I admitted.

Giezha came over and inspected my arm, stroking her chin.

"That's peculiar." She finally said, "We should have a professional look at it. You stay here and rest, Asher, we'll go get the reward money and find someone."

Happy to lie down, I obliged to her idea. I was frighteningly exhausted. About an hour later, they came back with a guest. A brown-haired dwarf in silver robes. He had a metal symbol in his hand of the sun and moon with an eyeball in the middle.

The dwarf stuck a hand forward for me to shake.

"Rangrim Holderhek," he said gruffly. "Blessings of Naukitha upon you." I attempted to lift my right hand and shake his, but it only swayed lazily.

"Asher Merrick," I responded, waving with my left hand. Thanks for looking at my arm. It's um... not working."

The dwarf nodded his head and sat me down at the chair in my room. Pulling his long hair and beard into respective ponytails, he poked and

85

prodded my arm, lifting it and speaking a few incantations to himself while grasping his holy symbol. No lights or visual effects alerted me to what he was doing, but when he finished up, he nodded his head.

"Well, either you're the hardest-working young man I've ever met, or you have a very peculiar affliction."

"Sir?" Giezha asked.

"His arm has been worked beyond exhaustion for a normal body. It's as if his arm has been digging stones and gems out of the Bastard Mountains for the last thirty years."

My stomach churned and backflipped at the news. Had I already worked my arm to the point of permanent paralysis? If so, I was in for a rough time. I was so inadequate with my left hand, I couldn't tell you anything I'd ever used it for.

"So, what you're saying is, I'm cursed? I have never done any digging outside of sandcastles at the beach."

"It may well be a curse," he admitted, lifting my arm and letting it fall to my side. "It could also be related to some other ability of yours. We magic users pull from within when using magic. Perhaps you pulled something too hard. Overexerting yourself."

"Impossible," Giezha said resolutely. "He just started learning how to use magic."

The cleric shrugged his shoulders, continuing to inspect me.

"Maybe it has something to do with the jumping?" Mara suggested. "And the thing with the spire wolf."

Giezha gave her a stern look, but Mara ignored her.

"Jumping?" The dwarf said, his eyes perking up. "You wouldn't happen to be that fellow that leaped across the harbor?"

I just laughed and scratched the back of my head with my usable hand.

"You got me there."

"Well, that may be a clue," Rangrim said as his hands began to glow light red while wrapped around my arm.

As the light shone brighter, the muscles in my arm began to crawl back to life. First came the familiar pins and needles sensation, followed by a warm, relaxed feeling. When Rangrim took his hands away, I was able to flex my right arm and move it around. My fingers were back in perfect working order as well.

86

Rangrim clapped his hands and gave a bow. "Seems to me that when you do that thing with your jumping Mr. Merrick, you pull everything you've got into whatever you're doing. However, after so much exertion, it's like attempting to draw blood from a stone. Your body can no longer support itself and well...." He gestured to my formerly paralyzed arm. "What put you in this state?"

"I uh, got in a fight."

The dwarf shook his head as he began to take his leave.

"Try to avoid doing that in the future. You may take someone's head off next time."

Mara tried to stop him and give him payment for his service, but he waved her off. Before leaving the end, he stopped and shook hands with Salvatore.

With my arm back in working order, I met Mara and Giezha in their room to see what was on the agenda. Giezha was patching a hole in her witch's hat and robes while Mara was painting on a massive piece of parchment.

"Sal's gonna love what I make him," she said proudly.

My curiosity piqued, I noticed that Mara was surrounded by bowls of colored water. Floating inside the bowls were the flowers from her backpack.

I watched Mara stroking a brush against the parchment, layering dark greens over a sketch she'd drawn.

"Whoa," I said, impressed. "You make your own paint?"

Mara giggled and shook her head. "Sorta. They're watercolor pigments. I'm doing a painting of Lake Shabba."

When I thought of watercolors, I imagined the finger painting I did as a child. But Mara's painting was out of this world. It was super rich in detail, with a large ship off in the distance and stars littering the purple and blue night sky. I couldn't help but watch in awe as she turned a few simple brush strokes into a planet and its rings.

"That's amazing."

Mara blushed slightly as she concentrated, smiling while she painted.

"Oh, this is nothing," she said coyly. "My little brother, Nol, is the real artist. He could paint the leaves of a tree from the top of a mountain with a single glance."

While I was sure her brother Nol was a great artist in his own right, I was too busy admiring Mara's skills. Giezha finished patching her hat and joined me in watching Mara finish up the details on her painting.

"We should get some lunch after this," Mara suggested, placing the painting in sunlight to dry. "After that, I can give this to Sal."

My stomach growled in unison with Giezha's. Heading out into the city, Mara and Giezha made a beeline for a place called the Golden Sky Tavern. Having already collected the reward for delivery of the rose, they were ready to spend it.

We sat down for a meal at a local cafe outside. Mara pulled out a handful of copper coins from a leather pouch inside her gear and handed it to a woman working tables, asking for a heavy food platter.

"Don't worry about Mhurren and Mick, Asher," Mara said, her eyes beaming. "Even the captain hates them."

"Why are they still members of the guild?"

"They pay their yearly dues and make the guild money," Giezha explained. "That's all Captain Dawnthorn cares about. She doesn't care how much of a violent, cruel, idiotic, or chauvinistic pig you are. If you make money, you're in."

The woman returned with a large platter of meats, cheeses, and other delicious charcuterie. Giezha picked and nibbled on it while Mara ate voraciously.

"Sal left them because of stuff like that?" I asked, taking a slice of salami.

"Not exactly," Mara said in with a cheese wheel section in her hand. "Captain and Sal had a huge falling out a long time ago. He took his cut and made the Inn. She decided to turn it from a proper feeder guild into a personal bank."

"Feeder guild?"

The maiden brought us our drinks and left after staring at me. The large mug of ale frothed in front of me, enticing me to forget about five o'clock and have a breakfast beer. I may have just woken up, but this stuff was light compared to Sal's swill, so... down the hatch!

"Basically, it's a guild that somebody joins to cut their teeth and hopefully get scouted. Most guilds don't go more than a few cities out, and Naled is an important port city for the Empire. If people are traveling north, south, east, or west, they'll probably make a stop here. And with such a large and diverse population coming and going all the time—"

"—there's plenty of opportunity for work for people like us," Giezha finished. "They neglect to mention how terrible the pay is while recruiting you."

"It sounded like you're not getting paid at all."

Mara made a painful expression. "We are, technically."

"Technically?"

Giezha nodded her head. "They pay us, but we are in debt to the guild for joining. Most guilds have an application fee and yearly dues. They can run several hundred gold pieces. It's common for a guild to offer free entry to a rookie on the condition they pay off the fees plus interest on their first contract. They can still get paid while they're on that contract, but it's always looming over your head."

"You could be working a ten thousand gold job and only get fifty if you're on a bad rookie contract. It'd pay that contract off course, but you'd have no right to claim the reward."

The words student loans rang in my head.

"Is that why you guys are in such bad debt?"

They both exchanged glances.

"That's one reason," Giezha said while eating a tiny bit of yellow cheese. "In addition, there was an incident a few months ago during an escort mission. Things went wrong..."

Mara hung her head in shame. "And we were held liable to pay it off. The guild got it squared away with the contractor, but we, in turn, owed the guild the money back."

I nodded my head, putting all the pieces together. "But once your debt is gone, you'll be free to contract with them again at a better rate, or go somewhere else where you can get higher-paying jobs, benefits, and all that."

"Basically," Mara said, finishing off the last of the meat. "The only problem now is that we've run out of jobs the guild is willing to give us. Unless we want to bid for a contract ourselves. But that would be suicide in more ways than one. We just look for odd jobs around the city when we're between contracts."

"So how much did we get for the rose job?" I asked, curious about the

89

final pay.

"We got a hundred gold, with sixty going to our debt. That leaves each of us with ten, plus ten for Uli when she gets back."

Mara emphasized the word 'when' and looked at Giezha as she said it. Deciding not to challenge her words, Giezha threw her hands up in mock surrender, finishing off the last bit of cheese. I looked down at the empty wooden board in disappointment. I had barely eaten anything.

"Well, we should get going, guys," Mara said, standing up and patting her belly. "Gods, what a tasty meal. We should come here after we get done with training."

Before they left, Mara and Giezha both hugged the maiden and chatted briefly. As we walked down the street, I lamented over the tasty food that was eaten right under my nose. Before I got up, I felt a tap on my shoulder. It was the woman who had been serving us. She held out a thick sandwich for me. Accepting the food, I had to do a double take. For the first time, I noticed how beautiful she was.

Let me rephrase that. She was fucking gorgeous.

"Sorry about them! Mara and Giezha didn't leave you anything to eat, so I thought it'd be a nice snack for the road." Her cheeks burned bright red. I accepted the sandwich and thanked her. I couldn't help but stare at her, quickly getting lost in her deep blue eyes.

Her face was round with full cheeks that stretched into a smile warm enough to melt steel. I couldn't help but notice how curvaceous she was, given that she was wearing a green and blue bodice that lifted her chest rather strategically. But the thing that struck me the most was how her face shined like pearlescent rays of the moon on burnished bronze, framed by curls of silver and copper hair.

"See you around, adventurer," she said with a giggle.

"Yes," I said as I felt my throat go dry. "I'll look forward to it."

Making sure not to trip on my way out, I caught up with the girls munching on my sandwich. I looked back to steal one last glance and met her gaze. I guess she had the same idea. With a mutual laugh of embarrassment, I took my leave.

"Ooohhh!" Mara exclaimed. "That looks good! Where'd you get it?"

"Kiersa gave it to him as we were leaving," Giezha said, the slightest grin tracing her face. "You've got competition, Mara."

90

"As if," Mara huffed, her face turning a light shade of pink. "Besides, he's free to do whatever he wants. Friends can enjoy themselves and each other, right Asher?"

I hadn't really thought about it, but Mara and I had already slept together. If she was down for a mutually beneficial friendship, I wouldn't say no.

"Sure thing," I said, looking back in Kiersa's. "Just don't get jealous."

Giezha let out a small chuckle while Mara playfully stuck her tongue out at me.

"Oh, don't worry," Mara said, a devious look forming on her face. "I don't get jealous. Giezha told me all about your 'private' lessons with her yesterday while I was out. I'll be sure to get plenty of training with you."

I looked at Giezha incredulously, but she just looked away and shrugged. We wound up walking to a large open area inside the city. There were few buildings around, and the open-air arena was recessed about ten feet into the ground. You could see people fully decked in armor fighting one another. Not just with weapons at hand but also casting magical spells at one another.

A fireball whizzed past the head of a half-elf and exploded next to a different group fighting. The fireball burned brightly but did not actually damage the others thanks to an invisible wall. The heat and light from the fireball were nothing more than an annoyance and a distraction.

"Welcome to the Warren!" Mara jumped up and down in excitement, a glint of hunger and malevolence in her eyes. "A guild-neutral location to spar and hone your skills. Kind of like the library for the nerds, but focused on combat."

She nudged Giezha's side while saying that. Giezha had switched from her hat to her circlet, and her eyes were focused on the combating mages.

"Those nerds would've torched the other two fighting next to them if not for the barriers," Giezha muttered

"She's right, you know!" an exuberant voice behind me called out.

Walking up behind us was a dragonborn in heavy armor. He had two swords on his back and a large rectangular shield in his left hand. With his helmet on, you could almost mistake him for a human knight. Well, except that he was seven and a half feet tall and had an armored tail.

The two swords on his back were very different. One was a classic hand-and-a-half longsword with a silver hilt. The other was jet black with

91

a thick blade, heavily curved and gnarled at the handle. Spikes and curly protrusions came out the sides of the blade as well.

"What-ho, young Breakers!" he called out, grinning with sharp teeth across his red and green scales. "How lucky we are to get such bright young stars here in the mid-afternoon of a fine autumnal day."

The knight gave Mara and Giezha a deep bow before noticing me. Stiffening up, he extended a hand with a warm smile.

"Ah, and this must be the new sloop out to sea, yes?" My hand disappeared in his as he shook it. "I have heard many, many good things about you, sir...?"

"Merrick," I said, hoping he wouldn't break my hand with his tight grasp. "Asher Merrick."

"Wonderful to meet you, young Asher. Yes, this your first time in the Warren, I take it?"

"He's having a lot of firsts, Vurshung," Mara said, devilishly. "We were just about to start his training with a sparring match."

"Jolly good!" Vurshung said, clapping his hands. "Why don't I join you lot? It could give him the chance to face the both of you without having the chance of utter defeat."

Giezha and Mara gave each other looks of amusement and nodded. They gestured for me to follow them down into the Warren without a word. Small walkways split the arenas apart, providing walking space for moving between the mini-arenas. Battles and lessons continued all around us. The sounds of swords clattering, arrows whizzing through the air, and spells cascading into explosions of sound and color were muffled by the force fields separating the different combatants.

Vurshung chattered away in an endless stream of stories and diatribes about his adventuring days as we walked to our area.

"Yes, and after that, I had to fight off against this horde of bandits believing themselves to be the descendants of the Goddess of the Hunt, Evlena! Of course, it was actually the result of their water source being spiked by the Anburtak mushrooms in the area. It gave them psychedelic dreams and psychotic episodes, mind you. As well as an awful case of dia—"

"We're here!" Mara pointed to an empty spot with several broken sections of stone flooring and singes.

92

"Ah yes! Section Dorva Seven-Seven," Vurshung said while stretching his large arms out. "Now, will this be a traditional two-on-two battle, or will it be more of an objective-based match?"

Giezha sat on the ground next to Mara, giving her staff its last once-over. Mara rolled her neck around, popping a few tight spots.

"I figured we could give him the crash course," she said lightly. "Go ahead and get your weapons out, Asher. And remember: Don't cheat your way out of this."

As my stomach tightened into knots, I pulled out my sword and shield, attaching the shield to my left arm. With my sword at the ready, I got into a defensive posture. The sounds of combat whirling around me did nothing to ease my anxiety. Mara just stood there about twenty feet from me while Giezha stood up and leaned on her magical staff.

I looked over to my left with Vurshung having adorned his helmet. He looked over to me and gestured back to them.

"When you're ready," he said with a hearty laugh.

"Alright," I said, slowly looking back. "Let's start the crash—"

Pang! Pang!

Two bursts of dazzling pink energy whizzed by my head. If I had been a second slower to duck, god knows what would have happened to me. Er, gods knows. Before I had a second to comprehend what was going on, Mara was in my face with her sword thrusting upwards.

"Lesson one!" She shouted with her upward thrust. "Never take your eyes off the enemy!"

My left arm jerked forward and managed to block her strike with my shield. Before I could step attack back, she flowed into her second attack, slashing horizontally at my legs. I leaped backward, trying to create some distance. Mara's eyes were cold as steel, and her face was twisted and vicious like a tiger's when it pounces on its prey.

Swinging my arm back, I avoided her. I spun my body in the direction of my attack, preventing her from closing any distance on me. Facing her, I sprung forward with a thrust. Mara's vicious look didn't change as I forced her on the defensive. She blocked my strike with her sword.

"Not bad. Now, for lesson two."

I felt a burning sensation across the right side of my body as a bright light raced towards me. As I looked, a gigantic fireball was headed straight

93

for me. Leaping out of the way, I saw Vurshung jump into the fireball, with his shield out in front of him.

"Be aware of the battleground, Asher!" I heard him shout as the fire slammed against the shield. The impact of the fireball pushed him back as he dug his feet into the ground. The fire streamed around all sides of him before he sliced at it with his black curved blade. The flames evaporated at its touch.

Looking back at the source, Giezha had her staff pointed straight at where I had been. She was nearly on the other side of our marked-off section of the Warren, and she had created nearly a hundred feet of distance between us.

"Are you crazy?" I shouted.

"Yes," Giezha deadpanned.

"Get the mage, Asher!" Vurshung said, pointing towards her. "I'll battle the sword maiden. Rule three, always take out the magical targets!"

With a nod, I burst forward, kicking away from Mara. Sprinting off, I made a beeline towards Giezha. Incantations flowed from her mouth as she shot out blasts of magic towards me. One missed my stomach by inches while an icy blue bolt sliced into my shoulder, leaving a superficial cut that burned cold. My muscles, however, burned hot as an idea flashed across my mind.

"No!" I whispered under my breath to myself. "I need to watch that."

Abandoning the idea, I suppressed the fiery sensation in my muscles. I couldn't resort to using my trump card every single fight. Or else I'd have nothing left to fight with. Blocking the last set of icicles with my shield, I closed the distance on Giezha. With my left arm stung in pain, I flung my shield out at her face. Instinctively, Giezha lifted her hands in front of her face, giving me an opening. Launching my whole body at her, attempting to tackle her.

She may have been much too big and strong to tackle to the ground, but I didn't need to. Swatting the shield down, Giezha looked down and couldn't react as I dove into her. My shoulder slammed into her side as I wrapped my arms around her waist. Her whole body felt like it was made of concrete, and the impact of my head against her hips nearly knocked me out.

Still, the impact shoved her back into the forcefield. Her head snapped

94

backward, and the literal shockwave of the impact created a ripple effect against the translucent field.

"Guh!" she groaned.

Tightening my grip on her waist, I pushed my body underneath for leverage and whipped it around into the ground. Body slamming her down, I pulled out my sword and held it at her throat.

"Yield!" I shouted, my vision blurry and my muscles heavy.

She held her neck back and blinked several times. A look of astonishment on her face as my blade was mere inches from her throat. For a half-moment, her bottom lip quivered, but she quickly replaced it with a sneer.

"You're outnumbered," she said with her hat askew.

"And you've got a sword at your throat," I retorted with a grin.

"Rule four, Merrick."

SMACK!

My jaw crunched as a massive boot slashed into my face. The metallic taste of blood mixed with flesh in my mouth. The impact of whatever had just kicked me caused me to bite part of my lip off. The dizziness of my vision was replaced with patches of black spots and a ringing sensation in my ears. Blood continued to pool out of my mouth as I felt a tooth fall out.

"What the—?"

SMACK!

A second kick hit my stomach, knocking whatever air I had left out. A second and third stomp crunched my chest after that. Rolling onto my back, I saw a gnarled sword pointed at my face. Vurshung stood over me with both swords drawn and placed in a cross between my neck.

"Never trust anyone, young Asher," Vurshung said, his voice carrying a sinister edge. I looked and saw his eyes had gone fully reptilian, like an anaconda ready to kill its prey. "Goodbye."

As he swung upward for the coup de gras, Mara jumped in and yanked him off me. My head swirled as I struggled to see clearly.

"Ms. Brightwood! What is it?" Vurshung asked.

Looking at the state of me, Mara's whole body shook before she grabbed her sword and bashed Vurshung in the face with the hilt of her sword. He stumbled back at the impact, his eyes returning to normal.

"What the fuck is wrong with you!" Mara screamed, pulling me up. "We said help him train, not try and kill him!"

95

My vision refused to improve as my whole body began to get woozy. Vurshung's flurry of blows felt like I'd been hit by a truck. Mara pointed her sword at Vurshung as her body began to coil for another strike.

"I was doing exactly what I was supposed to do! Why in my day..." Before he could finish his sentence, an explosive fireball lifted him off his feet, sending him crashing into the force field. Sitting me up, Giezha began administering a healing spell she had demonstrated the day before.

The blistering pain in my face and stomach dulled as the warm golden light and twinkling stars emanated from her spell. My aching muscles relaxed, and I felt the bruises dissipate into nothingness. Looking down, I saw the tooth that had been knocked out of me.

"Any chanth you can reattath thith?" I asked with a heavy lisp.

Vurshung groaned in a crumpled heap on the ground. His helmet had been knocked off his head by the force field. Giezha motioned for me to wait a moment, and she turned and picked him up. Holding him by his chest plate, Giezha balled her right fist up and punched him square in the nose several times.

Her face made no emotion as she punched him several more times before the last blow knocked him back to the ground. Cracking her knuckles, she turned back to me.

"Open wide," she instructed, to which I complied. "Put the tooth back, and I might be able to repair it."

As I clumsily placed the tooth back, Mara looked nervously from me to Giezha and back again. Giezha began to mutter the same healing incantation as before. Instead of a large swath of golden light enveloping my whole body, a small stream of concentrated light slithered out of the staff towards my teeth.

Before the magical light touched me, I realized my tooth was backward and flipped it into the correct orientation. I felt the strange sensation of nerves reattaching themselves and my tooth digging back into position. With one final push, my tooth reattached itself and clicked into place.

"Asher, we're so sorry," Mara said, jumping up and down. "This was not the plan! We just wanted to teach you fighting and some stuff to remember until—"

"Until a foolish old man tried to relive his glory days at the expense of a young adventurer." Vurshung said as he shakily got back up before dusting

96

himself off. Mara whipped around and pointed her sword at Vurshung's neck.

"That was out of line, Vurshung! The Red Breakers will be filing a complaint with Ivory Forge's Guildmaster."

Throwing his hands into the air, Vurshung began to speak. "I know, I know! That wasn't the plan. Apologies for getting carried away."

"That was not getting 'carried away', Vurshung," Giezha said, muttering the preparations for what sounded to be another volley of icicles.

"That was a dirty trick, and you know it."

"Exactly," Vurshung said simply. "What else would it be?"

All three of us looked at him with confused expressions. He rolled his eyes and shrugged.

"Well, how else do you expect him to prepare for the life of adventure? It's bound to happen eventually, so he might as well be prepared! I don't know a single person who has ever managed to avoid getting betrayed at least once in their career."

"Hasn't happened to us," Mara said, her sword begging to go for the throat.

"Well, if it hasn't happened yet, it's bound to eventually," Vurshung said stubbornly. "To think it won't is just foolhardy."

He looked past the two of them and straight at me.

"I am truly sorry for injuring you, lad. I went overboard, and I recognize that."

Nobody said a thing as he kept his hands in the air. We both looked at each other unblinking. A few other groups stopped sparring and watched everything unfold.

Mara and Giezha were ready to rip this guy apart. Sensing that danger, I grasped Mara and Giezha's shoulders.

"It's alright, guys," I said, thankful that the lisp was gone.

"Well, not to us!" Mara protested. "He could have seriously hurt you! We're lucky Giezha's as fantastic at healing spells as she is!"

"That we are," I agreed. "But I still think it's okay."

I walked past the both of them and looked Vurshung up and down. They had really done a number on him, leaving several bruises and cuts along his face. There was also a distinct charred smell to him. Despite his battered state, he did his best to keep his regal demeanor.

"Well," I said, extending a hand. "Bygones be bygones, right?"

Relief spread across his face as he weakly took my hand.

"Thank you, young Asher. I am in your debt. Your heart is as big as the warrior spirit inside you."

I gave him a nod. He pulled me in a little closer and whispered.

"You'll put in a good word for me when they file that complaint, right? I don't need another demerit on my record this close to my retirement."

I couldn't do anything else but laugh at the old fool's blatant begging.

"No problem," I said, patting him on the shoulder. "Just remember something for me..."

Vurshung nodded vigorously. "What would that be— Whoa!"

Grabbing him by the neck and kicking his feet out from under him, I slammed Vurshung to the ground, putting a knife from my side at his throat. I made sure the knife just barely tickled his skin. His eyes were wild as he was powerless to get up.

"Make sure you remember Rule Four."

Chapter 10

Gethsday Morning, 17th of Dhivmirn, Year 678, 4th Age

The weeks drifted by like the summer's breeze. I was surprised how quickly I acclimated to life unplugged and unencumbered by the "modern world." There was always something to do, and without a computer to attach to for days on end, I was forced to find my own activities.

In the mornings, I'd be dragged out of bed to work out with Giezha. We ran through the forests outside the city at dawn and practiced intense calisthenics. According to Giezha, if I was going to tag along, I'd need to prove I was serious and not weigh them down. Despite her intellectual and magical aspirations, Giezha made sure that her body stayed in top form. And I mean top form.

The intensity and ferocity Giezha demanded pushed my newfound strength to the limit. My body would glisten with sweat by the end of each workout regime, and I'd thankfully wolf down every morsel Sal could sell to me. Giezha, however, barely broke a sweat and returned to her studies immediately after getting home. One evening, I caught her doing more advanced and high-intensity exercises while studying from her scrolls and tomes.

There were few jobs we could bid on at the guild, so Giezha and Mara were doing odd jobs around the tavern and with a few local shopkeepers. I tried to pitch in where I could, which usually meant lugging crates and hunting down rats the size of Labradors in the sewers. Giezha would take the lion's share of lugging cargo while Mara sliced through rats with terrifying efficiency.

Besides the physical training, Mara and Giezha also started training me in combat and magic. Mara's teaching style was almost entirely based on combat scenarios and staying calm under pressure. Giezha refused to teach anything outside of the absolute basics, saying my ungodly mana pool

99

made control an absolute necessity. Refusing any gold in return, they spent alternating nights training me at the Warren or the Library.

"Misremembering a single rune will be the difference between amplifying the sound of a Kharian Kodabird, and blowing up the tree it's in," Giezha would constantly remind me. She'd usually switch up the specific bird, but the sentiment remained. "In your case though, it'd blow up every tree in twenty feet."

When not working out, working jobs, or working in time to hang out with Mara, I helped tend the bar with Sal to earn some spending money. Usually, that meant a dozen coppers at the end of the night. Sal allowed me to pay their rent portions for a few months to help them get ahead. He had taken much more kindly to me ever since the scrap with Mhurren and Mick.

Between the constant work, training, and adjusting to the new reality I lived in, I was exhausted every night before bed. And that wasn't even considering the nights Mara would sneak in. We'd just sit and talk most nights while playing cards, dice, backgammon, and painting using whatever pigments we could scrounge up and make.

Of course, we also made plenty of time for more intimate activities.

Without much actual fighting going on, I kept my usage of my ability to a minimum. It wiped me out completely whenever I used it. And of course, I still wasn't sleeping well.

"Gah!" I shouted, bolting out of bed.

"Asher?" Mara reached for my arm, gently pulling me back. "Your heart's racing again."

"Sorry," I croaked as the sunrise lazily drifted through the grimy window in my room. "It happened again."

That damned shock kept waking me up right around my scar.

"Don't be sorry." She gently pulled me back to the bed. As I regained my composure, she traced one of her fingers across my chest. Mara pressed her chest into my side as she worked her way to my right arm, where a fresh burn was fading away. "Giezha's work?"

She had an unsatisfied tone in her voice. I just shook my head at her question and rolled towards her. Mara had the uncanny ability to twist her beautiful face into that of an apex predator. Whenever she fixated on something, a chill ran up my spine.

100

"Not hers," I sighed. "Mine. I wanted to start doing more advanced stuff with magic besides reading and got uh… carried away."

Mara got out of bed and made a point to walk as slowly as possible towards my chest. I'd filled it with some potions and ingredients from that magic shop Giezha, and I had been to.

"You need to be careful with magic, Asher." As she turned towards me, she gave me a seductive look.

Mara walked back and started to massage the revitalizing cream into me, making the scars dissipate. Despite how hard she worked with her sword and the strict regimentation of her training, Mara's hands felt like soft silk against my skin. As she pressed the cream into me, my muscles relaxed, and I let out a sigh of relief. The new training was hard on my body.

"You know," Mara said, sliding one hand towards my crotch. "I feel like an encore for the other night may help."

I sat on the edge of the bed, watching Mara stroke my increasingly erect cock, while her free hand traveled down towards her lap. I felt the blood rush down to greet her hand.

"Mmmmm…" Mara closed her eyes and bit the bottom of her lip. "I've been wanting to do this since I woke up, Asher."

"You'll need to wait a bit longer." Giezha's voice came from outside the door. "I got done with my run around the city. Get dressed and meet me at the guildhall."

Mara scowled at the door. Her eyes moved back and forth in calculation and contemplation as to what to do next. Mara gave me a few playful pumps before Giezha rapped on the door even louder.

"Today, Mara! You too, Asher."

Mara called out to Giezha in annoyance. "Can't it wait? Why not do a thousand sit-ups while you study first?"

"I already did, Mara."

Rolling her eyes, Mara stopped and got up to get dressed. As we entered the main entrance of the Silver Cup Inn, Sal gave us both a look, and both of us waved him off in a non-committal fashion and walked out to meet with Giezha.

When we made it into the guildhall, the captain waited for us. There were fewer members in the hall than usual. The two idiots from the bar hadn't shown their faces since the incident, and were nowhere to be seen

101

here either.

The captain had a disgusted look on her face as she curled a finger towards us, beckoning for us to join her at her table. None of us said anything, but Mara swallowed nervously as we walked over.

"Sit," she commanded.

All three of us followed her orders. Captain Dawnthorn's eyes darted back and forth between the three of us as she rested on her folded hands. The captain's black eyes bored into my skull like a drill. It was like she was already prying the information out of me.

"Mhurren and Mick didn't show up yesterday," she said casually. "They were always late, of course, except for when there was money on the line. And this job certainly has a lot of money on the line."

I wanted to squirm and slither out of my chair out like a snake. Instead, I curled my toes inside my shoes while squeezing my thumbs to keep myself put. Giezha sat and looked at her, unmoving, unblinking. Mara was somewhere between Giezha and me.

"Permission to speak, Captain Dawnthorn," Mara said, her voice stiff as her posture.

"Permission not granted, Brightwood," Danwthorn snapped. "Shut up and listen to me."

Mara blinked several times but remained silent.

"Those two are good for nothing slobs that fuck up everything in sight. Despite that, they get the job done, and they make this guild money. You hear me? They. Make. Money."

She punctuated her last words with her finger jabbed into each of our chests. I started chewing on my cheek to keep quiet as my blood began to boil. Over a dozen witnesses could prove that Mhurren and Mick started that muck up. Besides, it was just me they messed with. Why get Giezha and Mara involved?

"Incidentally, that's not something that you do. You're all so far in debt I'm not convinced you'll ever pay it off. But beyond that, it's almost impossible to get jobs that you can even bid for."

"Boss, I swear we can—"

Brightwood reached across the table and smacked Mara across the face. The impact of the blow left a bright red welt on her cheek.

Giezha and I immediately stood up, ready to rip Dawnthorn in half.

Before we could reach across the table, Mara grabbed Giezha's arm. While rubbing her cheek, Mara gave her a calm look. Despite Giezha's rage, she nodded her head and sat down.

"As I was saying," the captain said, ignoring everything. "You lot don't make me or this guild any money. But those two do make me money. And now they've gone missing."

"They had nothing to do with the other night," I blurted out, ready to block her smack. However, no such strike came. Instead, she cocked her head to the side. "They didn't?"

"No," I said, trying to untie the knots in my stomach. "I take full responsibility for what happened at the bar."

The captain just rolled her eyes at me. "I'm not worried about a broken arm, Arthur. They came bumbling into the hall right after all that happened. Mhurren got his arm fixed up, and Mick's head got patched up. It's what happened afterward that has me angry."

"Like what," Giezha asked, her voice sharp enough to cut steel. "They disappear or something?".

"Yes. They've disappeared. And there is no sign of Mhurren or Mick leaving the city. Nor have they appeared in their usual hangouts. I checked the barracks, gambling dens, jails, whore houses, everywhere. It's like they disappeared into the air."

"So?" I asked.

The captain was on the last shred of whatever tiny bits of patience she had. She looked at me as if she were about to skip slapping me and go straight for a knife to the throat.

"So, you're going to investigate what happened to them. Talk around town and see what you can find from other people."

"Why us?" Mara asked quietly, doing her best to maintain eye contact with the captain.

"Because people like you for some reason. I don't give a shit about how some bumpkins feel about me or my guild. All I care about is running a tight ship that makes money and gets the job done. However, that seems to have rubbed people the wrong way in this town. I need the only people they're willing to talk to to do the talking. Understand?"

"What's in it for us?" Giezha asked, bowling over the captain's momentum.

103

The captain gave her a sarcastic smile. "The eternal admiration of your dear captain. And maybe a pat on the back while I'm at it."

"Money talks, Captain."

Giezha's eyes burned bright with hatred.

The captain didn't say or do anything for a moment. She just sat there and stared at us. Especially at Giezha. After a few uncomfortable moments of contemplation, she spoke.

"I'll be willing to forgive half of the debt you owe if you can get them back here."

Mara let out a low whistle.

"That's a lot of coin," Mara whispered.

"Money does talk, Gorina. Money certainly does talk." With that, she motioned for us to leave the table.

None of us said anything as we walked out of the guildhall. Several pairs of eyes followed us from around the room as we did. They all had strange expressions on their faces.

"Hey, Murdock." the captain called towards us, clearly addressing me. "Did you really break his arm?"

I turned back and looked her in the eyes.

"Like a twig."

Without another word, we left. By the time we had made it back to the Silver Cup Inn, a courier was waiting for us with Sal. He handed us a letter with the officially stamped Red Breaker wax seal. It was from the captain.

Inside the letter was an official contract for the job. We needed to find them alive. And if we did, the Red Breaker guild would forgive the debts owed by Giezha, Mara, myself, and their friend Ulilee. The job was also considered "need-to-know" and kept under wraps.

We'd also be expected to find other work, which the Guild would try and provide. It also had a list of their usual locations. I didn't like how it included me in the "having debts" part of the contract.

Needing to mull everything over, we decided to go out for lunch and discuss how we should tackle this job. We wound up back at the cafe with Kiersa, the cute maiden who had given me a sandwich before.

She brought us a slab of delicacies before we finished sitting down. As she laid it down, I couldn't help but notice that her shirt had a much deeper cut compared to before. It was definitely more revealing.

"Anything else I can get you?" she asked as I snapped my eyes to hers. The look on her face let me know I was completely busted.

"I think we're good for now," Mara said happily, munching on the salted venison. "Thanks."

As she left, Kiersa gave me a small wave before serving a different table. As I watched her working around the other patrons, I couldn't help but notice that even with the long skirt of hers, she had a very plump ass. Doing my best not to stare too long, I turned my attention to the others.

Neither Mara nor Giezha had noticed, as they were too focused on their food. Or they pretended not to.

"We're being set up for failure," Giezha said, nibbling a slice of bread.

Mara savored a piece of cheese while she thought. Swallowing the cheese, she looked at me and Giezha before sighing.

"That's no different than any other job we get from the captain."

"Why would she even bother giving us this job, though?" I asked as I filled myself. "Clearly, those two are important enough to keep around, so why bother with this whole charade if she thinks we can't do it?"

Both Giezha and Mara digested my words with unsure looks on their faces.

"Look, answer me one question: do the Red Breakers really have that bad of a reputation around here?"

"Aye, they fuckin' do!" an angry man from the other side of the table shouted as he spilled some of his ale.

"Skinflints and turncoats, the lot of ye!" his friend confirmed.

Walking past them, Kiersa tripped over him, and a bowl of honey'd ice shavings poured onto the first man's head. He screamed a collection of obscenities at her as she hurriedly tried to clean up the mess.

"You stupid bitch!" He screamed.

The man looked like he was about to start a fight, but before he could do anything, a muscular elf man with skin as dark as the midnight sky appeared behind Kiersa. He had a chef's hat atop his long silver hair and an oversized kitchen knife in his grip.

"Why are you screaming at my daughter?" he asked. "You made her spill the desserts I worked so hard on for my patrons."

"I didn't!" the man shouted, potatoes and slimy carrots dripping from his head. "That half-elf brat spilled it on me!"

The chef gripped the obscenely large knife tightly and growled. The angry man shrunk into his chair and said nothing. His friend sat there with an equally terrified look on his face. Without a word, the chef pointed them out the door, and they quickly complied. As she began to clean the mess, Kiersa's face was full of embarrassment. A few other people looked at us, murmuring.

"I suppose that answers my question about the Red Breakers. But you both seem well-liked as the captain said."

Mara blushed and scratched the back of her head. "Whenever somebody around town needs help, we're usually the first ones to offer assistance. Sometimes it's looking for special ingredients or looking for a missing pet. One time we helped this place out when they were low on staff. Anybody in a guild will usually charge out the nose, but it's just basic stuff that we don't mind doing."

"Most people in this city are struggling to make ends meet," Giezha said. "We know what that's like and don't want to make it worse."

"So that means you can get information," I said triumphantly. "I'm not saying that the captain thinks you can actually do it, but if there was anybody in the guild that could find them, it's you."

They both looked at me, their faces carrying looks of surprise.

"When you put it that way, it sounds possible," Mara said.

"Not likely, but possible," Giezha added. "I also don't trust the guild actually finding work for us."

"First time we ever got that in writing, though," Mara pointed out.

"She seems to be a big fan of contracts and their binding nature," I added. "C'mon, guys, this is a huge opportunity for you. Let's go for it!"

They both shrugged and grabbed their flagon of ale. We all made cheers to our new quest and enjoyed our meal.

Kiersa paid particular attention to our table as the three of us chatted about plans and ideas for finding clues to their whereabouts. Often, I found my beer would be refilled before I was even halfway finished. Once or twice, I felt her brush past me, smelling sweetly of roses. Mara tapped my hand after a while.

"You notice how often Kiersa is coming around, Asher?" Mara asked, leaning towards me to whisper.

I searched for Kiersa in the crowd of people and tables. When I found

106

her, I saw her eyes were on me. I couldn't help but grin to myself.

Deciding not to let my head grow any bigger than it already had, I changed the subject. After some idle chitchat and one more platter, we placed a silver on the table and left for the evening. But before I left, I waited for Kiersa to come back around. She noticed me waiting and smiled.

"Can I help you?" She asked quietly.

"Yeah," I said, trying not to blush. "I was wondering if you were busy tonight. I'd like to take you out, if that's alright."

Kiersa did a quick look towards her father who was focused on his cooking. Looking back at me she nodded excitedly.

"Meet me at the back entrance after nightfall." She whispered.

I nodded my head, and Kiersa smiled. She quickly returned to work, with some pep in her step. I turned and walked out to catch up with Giezha and Mara.

We decided to get an early start the next day and went to the top places on Mhurren and Mick's list. Neither the armorer nor the apothecary listed had seen either of them recently. Every bar, back alley gambling ring, and place of ill-conscious we visited hadn't seen them either. Their names weren't in the files of the Blue Lantern Inn for Precocious Gentlemen either.

I made a mental note to come back and check again by myself.

The last place on the list for the day was a magic shop. Located just south of the dock was a large building that twisted up a canopy of misaligned floors and broken wood. On the fourth floor was a room with a battered sign reading "Towser's Tomes and Talismans."

The shop was extremely cramped and dusty, every nook and cranny stuffed with potions and items along overfilled shelves. The air was thick and heavy with the smell of tobacco and mold. A faint bubbling sound could be heard in another room.

"Fascinating," Giezha said quietly as she contemplated a small, humanoid skull that was no larger than a baseball.

"That's a word for it," Mara said, plugging her nose. "Smells like my Uncle Sherwood's house."

"Oi! Who's'ere?"

A squat hobgoblin limped out of a back room. His skin was orange and leathery, wearing a pair of grey overalls and a greyer cotton shirt. Looking each of us up and down, he scowled.

"Who dares intrude on Towser's Tomes and Talismans?" he asked, leaning on the stone counter and revealing a severe hunch in his back.

"We were hoping to buy something," I said, pointing at the assorted collection of unmarked potions. "We've heard good things from a guild member."

Towser looked me up and down, shuffling over to me. Grumbling to himself, he picked up several potions, inspecting them visually and giving each a good sniff. Looking back at me, he picked out a few potions and sniffed again.

"Over here," he said gruffly as he walked back to the counter.

"Blue one gives you resistance to the cold. Red one gets the reaper's hands off ye. Orange gets you some wind back in your sails." He looked me up and down as I inspected the potions myself. "You're still wet behind the ears, ain't you? Can smell the inexperience on you same way a dog'll sniff out rabbits."

I was taken aback by how appropriate his selections were. Each one of these potions would have been handy the past few days.

"Which one of your girlies was it that shot you with them icicles? The elf?" he asked. I shook my head and he pointed a gnarled finger at Giezha. "Never seen a Goalie take up the Mystic Arts. Figured y'all were as thick in the head as you were in your muscles."

Giezha clicked her tongue and turned her face away from the hobgoblin.

"Oh, I meant no offense to ya', lass. Just be unnatural to be seeing magic users like yourself."

A vein was visibly throbbing in her temple as Giezha did her best to not repeat what happened at the last magic shop. Trying to pull his attention back to me, I stepped in front of his gaze.

"You're right about me being green, Sir Towser. That's the whole reason I'm here!"

"Oh?"

"Yes, my guild members actually recommended this place to me."

Towser scratched his chin with his dirty fingernails.

"Which guild ye' in, boy? Black Sparrow? Vines of Catharak?" Towser's eyes narrowed as he looked at me and growled. "You aren't with that damned Vurshung and that Ivory Forge, eh? Cuz if you are, I'll gut ye' like a fish before I let you close me shop down."

Punctuating his threat, Towser conjured a spectral knife in his hand. He took the twinkling red and pink blade and slammed it into the heavily scarred countertop, slicing through the stone as if it were tissue. He then pointed the knife in my face.

If this guy was going to try and intimidate me, two could play at this game.

"To hell with that old fool!" I shouted suddenly, making the others to jump back in surprise. "I'm not with any of those pathetic excuses for guilds, and I'm in this line of work for one thing. Money. And if there's one place I'm going to get that, it's with the Red Breaker Guild."

"Where's your bandanna?" he said unconvinced.

A bold sensation started to grasp me from the inside as he wafted the knife around. It was clear this old codger wasn't going to give up any information willingly.

"I haven't earned it yet, you old bastard. Like you said, I'm wet behind the ears. I was told to come here to make sure I had the right stuff for my missions."

Towser didn't move, while his scowl deepened. I could sense he was about to do something drastic soon, and I did my best not to let my muscles burn too hot.

"So, you're one of Mhurren and Mick's whelps, eh? Well fuck off. They know not to ask too many questions, unlike you."

God this dude was pissing me off. "I am nobody's whelp, Towser. And yes, I'm looking for them."

"Don't know nothin'," he muttered.

An idea popped into my head as I took a few steps back. Towser still had an evil glint in his eye, but he seemed satisfied I'd backed off.

"Mara," I said, picking up a potion off the shelf. "Why do you think Ivory Forge would want to close this place down?"

With a single look, Mara got the idea and played along. "Maybe he's dealing in illegal goods," she said, tapping her chin several times.

"Or he's not got a license to do business in the city with guilds," Giezha added, inspecting a large potion filled with black and white liquid.

"Maybe the councilmen want him gone," I nodded to Towser who was

109

getting angrier by the minute. "Maybe it'd be worth more to get rid of this place than it would be to Mhurren and Mick."

"A'right! I'll tell you what I know, dammit!" He shouted.

"Thank you." I smiled as I put the potion down.

Towser looked at all of us and growled.

"Those two ain't been seen since they had summin' go down at the Silver Cup. Weren't even supposed to be there, really. Came here the night before bragging about some covert mission they had in the morning. Something about maps, ancient weapons, prophecies, an' all that. Didn't think a word of it was true. Both of them were known for lying their asses off."

I looked back at the others, both of them wearing the same expression of bewilderment and concern as I had. Mhurren and Mick had appeared too dumb to tie their own shoelaces. Could they have been on a covert mission?

"I'm telling you the truth, damn it," Towser said. "Said they needed me to brew them up some special potions the next day before they left."

"Why would they come here?" Giezha asked. "Why come to this hole in the wall when there's a half dozen other magic shops in the city."

"Because I don't ask questions." Towser grinned. "I can also get some items you might need but can't find elsewhere."

"Explains why Ivory wants you shut down," Mara said with a smirk.

"Now you listen here!" Towser shouted, stamping his foot down. "I answered your questions! Now leave me be! I don't know what happened after. They never showed up the next day."

"What'd they ask you to brew?" I asked.

"Can't say. Just gave me a list of ingredients and instructions—which they said to burn once I finished the job."

"Well, where's the potion now?" Mara demanded, her sword still pointed towards Towser.

"Gone," he said simply. "Some good for nothing got in here and stole it along with some other potions."

Damn. That potion would have been our best lead, and it could have given us a clue as to what Mhurren and Mick were trying to do before they disappeared. We didn't even have the note to compare. Giezha began to mutter incantations, and a white circle with runes appeared on the floor.

"Don't you be trying that truth circle nonsense, you goalie oaf!" Towser shouted.

"Call her a goalie one more time, Towser..." I warned him.

She finished the spell, and a circle appeared squared solely on Towser. He started cursing in what I could only assume was a goblin language while picking up his knife and brandishing it. Mara and I gripped our swords, begging him to make the first move. Towser looked and realized his odds and swore.

"I said I don't know nothin' else already," he grumbled. "I finished the potion as instructed and got drunk like it said as well. Paid me in gold and a really nice bottle of dragon water. Twenty gold pieces a bottle!"

The circle changed color, indicating he was hiding something. All of us looked at him expectantly.

"Fine, it was ten gold a bottle. Got blackout drunk from it and woke up in my office."

The circle did nothing and stayed pure white. Evidently, Towser was telling the truth. Satisfied with what we found, we turned to leave.

"Oi! Ain't you gonna buy summin'?" he shouted at us.

Mara and Giezha kept walking, but I turned back and jogged to the counter. Pointing at the potions he had laid out previously, I asked how much he wanted for them.

"Hundred gold for the lot," he said proudly.

I quickly pocketed all three potions before he could do anything.

"How about free, and I don't tell Ivory Forge anything." I grinned.

At first, Towser looked like he was ready to gut me like a fish. But then his expression changed to a grin matching my own.

He laughed as he spoke. "I like you. You learn quick. Sounds like a deal."

I turned and quickly caught up with the others. Inspecting the potions, Giezha confirmed that they were what he said they were. My chances of being poisoned by them were apparently "minimal" at worst. The sun began to set over the horizon of The Docks, reminding me of something important. I burst out into a Sprint and waved at the two of them.

"Gotta go, guys!"

"Where are you going?" Mara shouted out as I ran.

"I've got a date!"

Chapter 11

Gethsday Night, 17th of Dhivmirn, Year 678, 4th Age

By the time I made it to the back entrance of the Inn, night had already fallen. The back alley was grimy, with boxes scattered about and rats scurrying behind them.

"Psst! Over here," a familiar voice called out to me.

When I looked down the alleyway, I saw Kiersa waiting for me on the street opposite the entrance. She quickly motioned for me to follow her. I jogged towards her, jolting slightly as a hissing cat streaked past me.

Without saying another word, Kiersa took my hand and ran off, pulling me after her. I noticed she had changed into a red and white tunic with a white shawl around her neck dotted with silver stars and golden crescents.

"What's the rush?" I asked, trying to keep up. "I wasn't that late, was I?"

Kiersa continued her brisk run, dodging between the carts and stalls. Her eyes sparkled as she glanced briefly back at me. She appeared nervous but excited. Her hand gripped mine tightly. After a few more minutes running, she seemed satisfied in her escape from whatever it was.

"Sorry about that, adventurer. I got a little excited."

She panted slightly as she sat down on the ground next to a vendor selling spiced slices of rabbit meat. I bent down and offered my hand after she caught her breath. She smiled as she took my hand, and I gently helped her up.

"Don't worry about it. You get used to the idea of running when somebody else starts to. And my name is Asher. Asher Marek. I believe I already know you as Kiersa, yes?"

"Kiersa Denrel, daughter of the great chef, Aire Denrel."

I ordered a couple skewers of rabbit meat and handed one to her.

"Hope you're not tired of salted meats and bread, Miss Denrel," I joked.

She laughed as she took the skewer, and we walked while eating.

"I wasn't sure if my father would approve of me being out with you. You seem like the classic adventurer, out to steal a fair maiden's heart." She looked up to the sky and held her hands together in mock adoration. "He's very protective of me, as you saw earlier today."

"Oh, you mean the part where he was about to slice that dude up and serve him on a platter?"

Kiersa laughed and finished her skewer.

"So, where are we headed?" I asked as she looped her arm through mine.

Kiersa grinned devilishly and didn't say anything.

As we walked, we passed The Docks and along the waterway to a section that turned into a beach. The buildings across from the water were large open-ended structures with people dancing and playing music, along with the sounds of meat sizzling on grills. A few people dancing around a fire on the beach waved to Kiersa, and she waved back as we went past them.

"Friends of yours?"

"From church," she said airily, "We often see each other around here as well. I love to walk along this beach."

As Kiersa spoke, her voice became airier. "The water is often too cold to swim in, but the sand is soft, and I can see the reflection of the moons in the water. It's peaceful. I like peaceful."

Her words stirred something in my chest. I looked out into the rippling water, thinking about my own bygone days.

"There was a beach I liked to visit as a child too. It didn't matter if the water was freezing. We still had to swim in it. Grandpa's orders."

I thought of the summers and winters I spent visiting my grandparents in Virginia Beach. My granddad always insisted on swimming in our coats on Christmas Eve as a "tradition". I think he just wanted an excuse to buy us all coats every year.

As she guided me on this walk down the beach, we talked about ourselves, our mutual love of reading, our friends. Her father had run his restaurant for fifty years when he received a knock on the door one night.

A former lover of his, a human, showed up soaking wet with a baby in her arms, and he knew from the second he saw her she was his daughter. Since then, Kiersa spent her days helping her father in the kitchen and serving tables while tending to her sick mother.

"My father isn't actually a dark elf. He's just confused for one. He's a moon elf. In the moonlight, he looks more blue than black. Mother is a human from the desert region of Galen. She was a trader who came by ship one day and spent a year here. Mother never meant to be a burden. She did not realize she was sick until a year after she had brought me to Naled. Father insists our arrival was a blessing from Ihena. Her sickness is simply a payment for the miracle."

"You mean, Ihena the Dream Goddess?" I asked.

She gave me an odd look. "Unless there's another goddess with her name. Blessed be she, the shepherd of our dreams."

As Kiersa said these words, she placed a hand on her chest and pulled out a necklace with three crescents surrounding each side of an equilateral triangle. It was silver with gold inlay twisting around it. It glowed slightly when she spoke a prayer in a language I did not understand.

"Blessed be she, indeed," I said, impressed.

Kiersa gripped my hand tightly and brought it to her chest. "You're a follower?" Kiersa asked, her tone completely surprised.

"Uh, no. Not a follower, just someone who deeply respects the goddess," I said, a little uncomfortable. It was hard to say, 'No, I'm actually on a mission from a different god.'

Kiersa gave me a small smile and nodded her head. "I suppose fate isn't that on the nose, is it?"

I gave a slight shrug, thinking about what fate had done for me lately. "You'd be surprised."

The buildings began to disappear as we walked further up the beach. Replacing them were walls made of conch and torches that lit the way. The sounds of people off in the distance grew softer. Kiersa and I talked about Giezha and Mara for a while. She told stories about working with them that left me in stitches.

"No, it's true!" Kiersa insisted. "Giezha absolutely insisted on wearing this ridiculous maid outfit. A friend of my father's actually bought it for him as a prank, but it fit Giezha better."

I stopped walking to hold my sides as I wheezed in laughter. The idea of Giezha in what amounted to a French maid's uniform was more fantastical than anything I'd yet encountered in this alien world.

114

"Oh lord, that is hilarious," I said, wiping away a tear. "I wish you had a picture of that. Giezha would probably kill me if I ever saw it, though."

"No! She loved it, actually. Mara, on the other hand, nearly got into a fight every hour for the three days they worked there. Still managed to get plenty of tips."

"Yeah," I laughed. "I suppose I don't have to wonder why."

The second those words came out of my lips, I regretted it.

Kiersa gave me a look and cocked her head. Sweat immediately began to come out of my pores as I tried to dig myself out of this impossibly deep hole I had stepped into.

"Uh, well. Y-you know," I stammered. "Mara is quite attractive, is all I meant. In an aesthetic sense." Kiersa held her hands on her hips as I floundered.

"Very smooth of you, Asher," she said sarcastically. "Wonderful recovery."

"Sorry, I really shouldn't be talking about—" Kiersa placed a finger on my lips to hush me.

"I could smell her on you this morning," she informed me. "She has a very distinctive perfume."

"Oh dear," I said with a gulp. "How much trouble am I in?"

Kiersa giggled and walked ahead of me. After a few paces, she turned back.

"None at all. It means you know what you're doing."

"Crisis averted," I whispered to myself as Kiersa continued to walk. As she walked ahead of me, I couldn't help but take the time to appreciate her curves.

Beyond the horizon, something rose into the sky. If not for a single red light atop it the structure, it would have been completely invisible in the night sky. Completely covered in vines and trees, it was a white and silver obelisk. The light barely poked through the trees.

"A lighthouse," I said to myself.

We walked up to its base, seeing it stretch up to touch the sky and send its beacon to the stars. Kiersa traced her hands along the stone exterior, brushing away the foliage and flowers.

Her eyes looked out into the water, which was flat as a mirror. In this reflection, you could see the millions upon millions of stars and galaxies up from the sky. From this angle, the lighthouse appeared to be just another star lost in the sky.

"Not many people know about this lighthouse anymore," Kiersa said. "When Naled was first formed, they built this lighthouse and named it Everlasting, so sailors had an everlasting light through the thick fog Lake Shabba creates. Most came from the Unbarad River, so it made more sense for the lighthouse to face the river."

"Why'd they change it?" I asked, looking back towards the city. The other lighthouse was clearly visible in the water, even from here.

Kiersa looked out to the city skyline where the Endeavor shined bright out to the lake. "Trade from the north increased and a second lighthouse was needed in the center of the city." She smiled and pointed towards the two moons. "Mother told me it could also pay homage to Avis and Xalia. This smaller lighthouse is to signify Avis, while the Endeavor represents Xalia out at sea."

"It isn't very bright," I said, noting the weak flame. "You barely even notice it."

Kiersa looked up to the lighthouse's pitiful flame sadly. She said nothing as she watched the dying ember flicker. As I stepped closer to her, I noticed that it wasn't just sadness in her eyes. It was longing. She looked like someone dying of thirst in the desert, their throat scratching for relief as they look at the massive chasm between them and an oasis.

"You're right. Mother used to tell me stories all the time about how it was brighter than any star, save for the sun, and how it was the single light that gave all hope to those who sought a better life in Naled."

"That's beautiful."

She looked at me, a few tears threatening along the edge of her eyes. "I guess the Everlasting isn't so Everlasting anymore. The firestone lighting will go out soon. It's only a matter of time. The city councilmen won't do anything for it, and nobody has stepped up to do it themselves."

"Why not?" I asked, thinking about the plethora of mages in the city.

"The Everlasting is a symbol and nothing more to most. Why go through the effort of restoring a relic from the past when the Endeavor is there?"

She sat down next to the lighthouse and stared off into the distance. The faint sounds of exuberance in the city were barely audible.

I sat beside her, and she leaned her head on my shoulder.

"Galen is really far north of here, isn't it?"

"Mhm."

"Did your mother come here by ship? Both times?"

She let out a small sigh and nodded her head.

"How long has your mother been sick?"

"For as long as I can remember." Kiersa said. "Mother prayed every day for my health as we sailed through the rivers and seas. It took us almost a year to arrive here, and she was skin and bones when we made it to Naled. But she said that when she first felt the warm glow of the Everlasting's light, she knew that everything would be okay."

"She sounds like my grandmother."

My mind went to my grandmother's stories about seeing the Statue of Liberty when she came to America during World War II. It meant so much to her. When she first saw it standing triumphantly at the shores, she knew she never had to go back to Germany. It gave her hope for a new life. Hope for herself and her family. Hope that things would get better.

"I hope this was an alright place for a date," Kiersa said, leaning against me. "Giezha and Mara said you were very sweet and earnest. More than just a handsome face and cute buttocks. I wanted to take you somewhere that meant a lot to me. I didn't think it'd make me like this."

I laughed at her first impression of me. I guess I did have a nice posterior. It was nothing like hers, though. I watched the lake as its gentle waves lapped against the rocky shore. The more I sat there, the more her words put a lump in my throat. It was a lot for a first date, but it was beautiful and real. It was vulnerable and authentic. It was who she really was.

"Hey, Kiersa," I said, nudging her shoulder. "I've got an idea."

"What?" she asked, wiping her eyes.

Grabbing her hand, I stood up and walked around the lighthouse. A section of dirt had grown on the front side of it. Looking up at the flickering light of the lighthouse, a fire started to brew inside of me. Not a raging inferno like before, but a small one. One that I tried to contain as best as I could. It warmed my insides, like sitting next to a campfire.

"How tall is this thing?" I asked her.

"About forty five feet," she said, looking confused. "Why?"

"Hold on tight." I picked her up in a bridal carry position.

"Oh!" Her eyes lit up as she blushed deep red.

117

"Let's go up top," I said excitedly. "I'll take us there. I can make this jump!"

"What?!"

Concentrating on the fire inside me like before, I felt my legs begin to shake in anticipation. My skin tingled with sweat as my breathing sped up. Bending my knees, I felt a rush of energy flowing through my body, begging for release. I held onto Kiersa tightly and unleashed the fire.

"Aaahhh!" Kiersa screamed as we flew into the air.

The wind stung my eyes as we flew up while I looked out and around. In a quick three-sixty, I could see the city's edges off in the distance. Ships sailing in and out to sea and the lush vegetation of the forest outside the city walls. The top of the lighthouse came into view, and I angled our descent towards the platform around it. Kiersa held onto me so tight I felt she may pop me open. She screamed prayers out to the Dream Goddess as we went up.

"Oh, Ihena, Shepherd of the Valley, guide me so that I may sleep a peaceful sleep and wake a rested woman. In your holy name, I pray."

As we slowly crested up, our feet pointed straight at the lighthouse's platform. A moment later, my feet were touching the stone floor. Kiersa had wrapped her legs around one of mine, making for a wobbly landing. She let out a squeal of terror and opened her eyes.

As she did, her jaw dropped as she looked out towards the city. Holding one hand at her chest, the other covered her mouth as she looked out, soaking in the view. She leaned up against a mossy wooden rail, the gentle glow of the lighthouse casting her shadow down onto the water.

"Asher, I..." she said, unable to articulate. "I never thought I'd..."

She turned and looked at me with the biggest smile on her face.

"Thank you."

A wonderfully dangerous idea grabbed the momentum in my mind as I looked at the firestone struggling to stay lit. It was a red and orange rock about the size of a basketball, floating in the center of the area with a mirror wrapping around it slowly. The rock was wrapped in flames licking the air gently.

"Ever see one wildfire connect with another?" I asked Kiersa.

She looked at me with concern as my eyes bubbled with excitement. As I looked at the flame, I did my best to remember Giezha's teachings. I picked up a small deposit of soot from under the stone and placed it in the palm of my hands before rolling up my right sleeve. I thought about the different runes and texts she wrote down for me to memorize. Closing my eyes, I imagined them swirling together in my hand.

"Ignis arolos, balryndaka!" I said, doing my best to enunciate every syllable.

As I spoke the words of the incantation, I felt a burning sensation in my palm. Tiny yellow letters and runes floated around my hand as I repeated the incantation. A small, smokeless flame was beginning to form in the soot. Remembering what Giezha said about mana, I imagined pulling my spirit out from within me and pouring it into the flame. I had plenty of mana, so I kept feeding it.

As I did, a strange prickling sensation radiated through me. I felt the gravity of the prickling waves concentrate on my palm. The flame grew larger and larger. From a tiny ember the size of a pea, it grew larger until it was the size of a cantaloupe. As hot as it was, it didn't burn me! It floated just above my hand. I knew I could make it bigger, so I tried to condense the mana I was flooding the fire with.

"Asher, you're a mage?" Kiersa asked in astonishment.

"Kinda." I said, turning my hand towards the firestone. "Let's see if this works. Ezoatra!"

Speaking the incantation that translated roughly to "throw," I heaved back and threw the fire like a baseball.

Fwooooosh!

The fire zipped out of my hand, straight towards the firestone. When it did, the flame exploded around the stone. The dancing flames connected with the firestone's and as it did, the stone began to grow in size. The stone swelled up as fire poured in and out of it. The firestone started emitting its own flames as it absorbed the ones around it.

The stone grew brighter and the fire warmer. The cool sea breeze was now overtaken by the warm glow of the lighthouse. Suddenly, the flames froze in mid-air.

Boom!

The fire sucked itself into the stone, glowing so bright I had to shield my eyes. The stone was impossibly bright, like if a tiny star floated in front of me. Blinded, I felt a hand grab me and pull me away from the firestone. Next thing I knew, I was running down a spiral staircase.

"Asher, what did you do?!" Kiersa shouted hysterically.

"I tried to restart the lighthouse," I said while blinking away the spots in my vision.

"I could see that. But how did you know how to do that? I thought you were a fighter or soldier type like Mara."

"I am!" I said, jumping over a missing staircase. "I'm also a magic user like Giezha. She's been teaching me."

Kiersa stopped and looked at me like I was insane.

"You've been in this town for a week, and you're already throwing balls of fire!"

"That's good, then?"

Kiersa sighed and threw her hands in the air before opening the lighthouse's base door. "It should be impossible. Never mind, though. Hopefully, the firestone is alright."

When we walked out of the lighthouse, we turned around to look up at its light. Kiersa immediately gasped her hands shot up to her mouth.

The formerly timid embers of the Everlasting were now triumphant, giant rays of orange and yellow light shining out into the sea. A ship coming up from the east let out a bellow of its horn toward the Everlasting as it sailed past.

Its light wasn't nearly as luminous as the main one back at The Docks, but it still shined bright. It shined true. It shined proudly.

I felt a great swell of pride in my chest as I looked up at it. I thought I'd done something really cool, until I heard Kiersa sniffling.

Kiersa was wiping her eyes with the back of her palms as she looked at the lighthouse. I gently placed a hand on her shoulder.

"I hope I didn't scare or offend you, Kiersa. I just wanted to..."

"No," Kiersa said, waving a hand at me. She looked up and smiled at me while a single tear rolled down her face. "Don't apologize, please don't. It's amazing. It's like a dream come true!"

She looked back at the lighthouse, unable to believe what was happening. "The stories my mother told me come to life. The way she felt when she finally came home to Father. I could feel what it meant now."

She got up and hugged me tightly, sniffling and giggling.

"Asher Merrick, that was the most wonderful thing someone ever did for me."

She held my face and kissed me.

"It was the most thoughtful thing too."

She kissed me again. This time a little bit deeper.

"The most romantic. The most—"

I stopped her with my lips this time. Holding her tightly in my arms. She kissed me again. And again. And again. She pulled me in closer, pressing her tongue into my mouth. She tasted sweet, and her moans sounded sweeter.

"Asher, I... I'd like to go somewhere else with you," she said breathlessly as I kissed her neck.

"I'd like that," I said, wrapping my hands around as much of her as possible.

We wound up at a hostel known as The Three Olives Inn. The tiny stone-walled building was a ten-minute walk from the lighthouse that we turned into a two-minute sprint. The Innkeeper was an overweight female halfling named Aria. With the lateness of the evening, she charged us half price on a room.

"Didn't think I'd get any customers this evening," she rambled while looking for the key. "An slog, this week's been! Haven't had any customers for a while now."

"Fascinating," I said, feeling Kiersa stealthily rubbing my leg with her hand hidden by her cloak. "Think you'll be getting more customers now that the Everlasting is back up?"

"It is?" Aria asked in bewilderment, handing me the key. She walked out the door to confirm what I said. "By Phieyr! The second moon rises! You two should come and see this!"

By the time she turned around, we were well on our way to our room.

Kiersa slammed the door shut, locking it behind her. Before I finished turning around, she was already halfway through stripping off her clothes. She stared back at me boldly as she removed the final layers.

She walked towards me slowly, giving my eyes an opportunity to rove over her naked flesh. I couldn't help staring at the luscious curves of her breasts as she approached.

As soon as she was within reach, I grabbed her and tried to put every

121

ounce of the lust I felt for her into a kiss. She scratched and clawed at my clothes, returning the favor.

"You're like a wildcat," I said to her, gently biting the curve of her neck.

"I'm just getting started," she teased, finally getting my shirt and pants off.

I picked her up and tossed her onto the bed, before climbing over her.

"I'm surprised you are able to pick up this much woman," she said.

"You're light as a feather," I replied. I squeezed her breasts together and buried my face between them, kissing and licking everything I could. "Soft as one too."

Kiersa's playful demeanor melted away, revealing a ravenously hungry individual hell-bent on getting what she wanted. She rolled me over and pushed me down into the bed.

Wrapping her lips around the tip of my cock, Kiersa straddled my shoulders with her legs, giving me a clear view of her soft, wet, inner lips.

Maybe her playfulness wasn't totally gone. She teased me a little, only lightly licking the tip of my cock as her hips swayed back and forth. My abs and legs contracted as I tried to keep my composure while she had her fun.

Clouds blanketed out the glow of the moon through the window. Her form almost disappeared in the darkness as her silver and orange curls danced like the galaxies in the sky.

When she began to take more of me into her mouth, I couldn't stand it anymore. Grabbing her hips, I pulled her down and placed the tip of my tongue squarely on her clit.

Her grip on me tightened, making me thankful she didn't have long nails. Kiersa let out a gasp and then a moan as she rocked her hips back and forth while pulling and tugging on my shaft. I felt her tremble and struggle to keep up as I began to lick faster and faster, massaging her ass with one hand and spanking her with the other.

"Oh fuck, that feels good," she gasped. "Keep going."

Obliging her, I continued to lick and suckle on her as she began to wrap her lips around my cock and suck more forcefully. She struggled at first, trying to catch her breath, but then she got into a rhythm. We both rocked back and forth making the bed squeak.

Things escalated quicker. She was practically dripping on my tongue, and whatever she was doing to my cock was beginning to make my vision go hazy.

"Fuck," I grunted.

I slid two fingers into her wet slit.

She moaned, no longer able to keep sucking. Grabbing me with both hands, she pumped me harder and I continued to rub her from the inside. I felt her squeeze on my fingers, getting closer to the edge.

"Oh, Ihena, please. Yes!"

Sensing my opportunity, I quickly maneuvered myself and got her under me. The swiftness of my movement caught her off guard and she looked up at me with wide eyes, her hair spread around her on the pillow. I looked down at her, taking a moment to appreciate my spectacular view as both of us struggled to catch our breath.

She bit her lip before snaking a hand down between us to finger herself as she stared at me.

"Show me what you've got, Asher. I'm ready."

I'd never had a more enticing invitation.

Grabbing my member, I placed the head at the entrance of her pussy. She was so wonderfully silky smooth that it was incredibly tempting to thrust into her immediately. Afraid I could potentially hurt her, I tried to go in as slowly as possible, rubbing her clit as I did so. Her eyes closed as she began to moan in pleasure.

My heart felt like it would explode from how fast it was beating. My whole body shuddered as I pushed almost completely inside, with only an inch or two left. Kiersa was so tight that I was worried I wouldn't fit, but she was so wet that I kept going deeper. Rocking my hips back and forth, I watched her writhe around on the bed beneath me.

"I could never tire of seeing you like this," I said, catching my breath.

She looked at me with that wicked playfulness and wrapped her legs around me. Her powerful thighs locked in place as she pulled me the rest of the way into her, causing us both to shout in pleasure. Her pussy spasmed and it took every fiber of my self-control to not explode.

After a moment, she looked at me again, smirking.

"Now fuck me like you mean it."

Following her orders, I began to move. The bed squeaked and groaned as I thrust into her, squeezing her breasts and leaning down to kiss her.

123

"Yes, yes, yes!" she screamed as I continued to thrust into her with as much force as possible. "Don't you dare stop."

She pulled me in, kissing me deeply and holding my head in place as I kept going. Her moans reverberated in my head as I kept going.

"Kiersa," I grunted. "I'm going to cum. Holy fuck. You feel so good." My body spasmed, and my cock throbbed inside her as what felt like an explosion bubbled inside me.

"Just do it! Finish inside me, Asher! I want it!" she moaned, staring me in the eyes. "I'm coming! Oh, Ihena! I'm coming!"

Her whole body seized, and with one powerful thrust, I felt her pussy tighten like a vice around me. With a last few desperate thrusts, I went as deep as possible before a wave of pleasure burst forward. My brain blanked out as I filled her one last time.

She whimpered with pleasure, wrapping her legs as tightly as possible around me. I grabbed onto her, shuddering and gasping.

Kiersa kissed me again as the pleasure continued to spiral. She held me tight and kissed me deeper than ever before. The whole world disappeared as we held each other. Only the occasional beams of moonlight filling the room intruded on us.

I laid on top of her, resting my head on her chest, feeling her rapid heartbeat. She played with my hair for a minute or two and turned my head up to kiss her again.

"That was..." I started.

"Amazing," she whispered, finishing my thoughts.

"Yeah." I kissed her and smiled. "That was some adventure."

Chapter 12

Orosday Morning, 18th of Dhivmirn, Year 678, 4th Age

When morning came, Kiersa was fast asleep in my arms. Morning light danced off her silver and orange curls as she snoozed. Her arm was draped over my chest, which, which made me realize something. The previous night's sleep was the first peaceful night's rest I'd had since coming to this world.

"Thank you for last night," I whispered gently.

"You too," she whispered back, blinking awake.

After a few moments, she got up and stretched her arms up, yawning. Her breasts swayed and pressed against me as she stretched her arms while the sun created a halo effect around her. She was like a beautiful, voluptuous angel. No doubt this effect was intentional.

She smiled and kissed me on the lips.

"I didn't think anything could top what you did at the lighthouse," she said, tracing her finger along my arm. "But you are certainly full of surprises."

"You are as well," I said, pulling her back down onto the bed.

Kiersa giggled as her hands drifted to the same destination as mine. Both of us were ready for round two before being unceremoniously interrupted by a knock at the door.

"Excuse me!" came the voice of the Innkeeper Aria. "Hate to interrupt you two, but there are two ladies outside asking to speak with Mr. Merrick about an urgent matter."

I groaned and laid my head on the bed. I hated getting interrupted like this.

"Tell them I'll meet them later!" I protested while Kiersa began to wrap

125

lips around my cock. "We can meet for lunch."

Suddenly, Kiersa stopped and bolted up with her eyes as wide as saucer plates.

"Oh no. Lunch!" Kiersa shouted, looking out the window at the rising sun. "I'm gonna be late and miss setting up before lunch! Father is not going to be happy about this! Asher! I—"

She gave me an uncomfortable look and sighed.

"I'm sorry, but I need to go."

I couldn't help but laugh as I waved her concern off.

"No, go! How could I ever expect more after a night like that?"

She smiled got dressed.

"We can take a raincheck," I said, handing Kiersa her top.

"Raincheck?" she asked while fitting it over herself.

"Like, we can't do this now, so we'll try to make time for it later," I explained while putting my clothes back on.

Kiersa looked out to the sun with her eyes filling in mild panic. Looking back at me, she gave a nervous smile.

"Assuming Father doesn't pitch me off the roof for being late." She laughed nervously.

Both of us finished getting dressed and quickly left the hostel. As we did, Aria gave me a wink and I bought a basket of fruits and bread for a mobile breakfast.

The city was already bustling, and to my horror, Giezha and Mara were waiting for me, gesturing for me to hurry up. As luck would have it, a man with an empty buggy and a horse was trotting along the street just ahead.

I quickly hailed him down, and he stopped. The main appeared to be a dwarf, with blond braided hair and a beard down at his feet.

"Whatcha need, stranger?" he grunted. "'Fraid I'm out of grains."

"I actually need transport across the city to the Golden Sky Tavern. As fast as possible, preferably."

The dwarf looked annoyed and started to snap the horse's reins.

"I ain't no deliverer and don't do no transport of anything but my grains."

As the horse began to trot, I jogged to keep pace.

"How about four silver and a meal?"

The horse stopped on a dime, and the dwarf looked at me, bristling his mustache.

"Got yourself a deal, sonnie."

I handed him a couple of silver coins and brought up the food basket. Handing the horse an apple, I uncovered a small glass vial. Grabbing it before he could see it, I gave the dwarf the basket of bread and fruits.

"Courtesy of the Three Olives Inn. You should check them out sometime."

"Oh aye," The dwarf said, sticking a few berries in his mouth. "Have your lassie jump aboard. We're burning daylight!"

Kiersa ran up and jumped beside the dwarf. As they departed, she thanked me again and kissed me goodbye.

"Raincheck it is," she said with a smile.

Feeling rather satisfied with myself, I turned and walked back to Mara and Giezha.

Mara was doing a double-take between me and the direction Kiersa left in. Giezha simply raised an eyebrow and said nothing. As I looked at Mara, I got an uncomfortable sensation in my stomach. I just realized that she and Kiersa not only knew each other but were friends, based on Kiersa's stories. While I was free to see whomever I chose, would being with Kiersa, specifically, stir up trouble?

Mara looked at me with a strange look, pointing out towards the direction the cart went.

"Was that Kiersa?" she demanded.

Oh boy, more eels began to thrash around in my stomach. "Uh...yeah," I said slowly as Giezha shook her head.

"And was she your date?"

"Yep."

Mara didn't say anything and just looked back and forth a few times. A dangerous half-smile crossed her lips. She took a few steps towards me with a balled fist, and I got a notion to hightail it. As I braced for impact, I closed my eyes.

"Nice one!" Mara exclaimed, giving me a light punch on the shoulder. "I knew she was checking you out! You owe me three coppers, Giezha."

Giezha turned to me, pretending not to hear her.

"You didn't show up for morning workouts."

"Yeah." I laughed more than a little nervously.

"Where'd she take you?" Mara asked curiously.

Before I could say anything, Giezha answered for me.

"Knowing Kiersa, they went to the lighthouse," Giezha said, pointing towards the Everlasting. You could barely see it around the haphazardly stacked buildings in this part of the city. A faint orange glow beamed against the morning sunlight.

"Is it safe to assume that you had something to do with that?" Giezha asked without a shred of doubt.

Mara stuck her head toward the Everlasting and back at me. Her jaw dropped to the floor, and she started jumping up and down while speaking gibberish.

"You!" she shouted between nonsense words. "You-you were the one who lit the Everlasting?"

"Yep," I said simply.

"How'd you get up there?!"

"He jumped, probably."

"Right..." Mara said, nodding her head. "I forgot about the super jump thingy...Wait a minute!" This time, Mara punched me with some oomph behind it. "You dummy! Cleric Holderhek specifically said not to overuse it!"

"I didn't!" I protested. "Well, I used it yes. But I didn't overuse it! I jumped up once, and it was a much easier jump than the other time. And after that, we ran down the stairs of the lighthouse. I didn't do anything else with it, I swear."

Despite the quality sleep, I still felt dead tired. My legs ached like crazy. Mara pouted as she eyed me up and down while I feigned vigor. Giezha, meanwhile, kept looking at the lighthouse.

"Perhaps this ability is like a muscle. The more strenuously and consistently you exercise it, the more powerful it will become." She turned back to look at me. "I'd like to know how you got the firestone back up, but that's for later."

"Right," I said, an important question dawning. "How'd you find me?"

Giezha started listing reasons on her finger "You had a date with Kiersa. She was probably gonna take you to the lighthouse since it's important to her. Only you would have the ridiculous idea to relight a decades' retired lighthouse. We saw it was lit which meant..."

Mara finished the explanation for Giezha.

"Which meant she was gonna find somewhere close for you two to go and f—"

"Alright, I get the idea." I said, trying to quiet them as an elderly couple walked by.

Giezha smirked as my discomfort grew.

"Anyways… we just needed to pick you up, as there are more pressing matters to attend."

"Oh Gods, you're right, Giezha!" Mara said. She turned to me and grabbed both my shoulders. "Uli's back! She's back, she's back, she's back!"

That perked my ears up quite fast. The mysterious Ulilee, known everywhere I went, had finally returned. Despite hearing so much about her, I realized that there were several important things that I didn't know. Like what she looked like or what her place on the team was.

"Where is she now?" I asked, looking around to the dozens of people coming and going around us. "Did she not join you guys?"

Mara began to walk towards home as she explained. "She's at the guild right now. Apparently, whatever she had been doing was enough to warrant an immediate meeting with the captain. They've been talking for hours."

"Mara, it's only been forty-two minutes."

"Details."

On our way back to the guild, we passed by the Warren. I saw Vurshung sparring against several newbies to the Ivory Forge guild as we walked. He had almost no trouble taking them all on at the same time. In fact, he looked downright bored as he dispatched them with his cruelly shaped longsword. Catching my eye, he gave me an exuberant wave which I awkwardly returned. My jaw still clicked thanks to him.

"You think Uli's gonna like Asher?" Giezha asked Mara.

"She's either going to love him or try to kill him. Or both."

"Both?" I asked.

"Both." Giezha and Mara said simultaneously.

Unbothered by the potentiality of one of their teammates trying to kill the other, Giezha and Mara talked amongst themselves up ahead. Meanwhile, I tried to imagine what Ulilee looked like.

From the sound of it, she was capable of leaving destruction wherever she went. Being banned from the library near The Fortress, meant she was also likely a magic user. Perhaps she was a pyromaniac and had burned all of the books in the library at one point. Maybe she was sent on this mystery mission to get rid of her for a little while.

The foot traffic picked up immensely when we made our way towards the Guild District. Since it was the first day of the working week, contract jobs work would pour into all the different guilds. Ivory Forge would be receiving many officially sponsored and diplomatic quests. Captain's Harpy mostly worked in waterborne caravans. A half dozen or so others, including the Red Breakers, filled the gaps for the rest of the jobs.

The crowd wound up separating me from Giezha and Mara as we walked. Luckily, Giezha was so tall I could keep a decent eye on them. Several people bumped into me as we tried to cross our way to the guildhall.

As I tried to push my way through, an alarm went off in my head. My right pocket felt a little lighter. I felt to confirm, I realized that my gold had been taken from me. I couldn't see anybody through the sea of people. Panic started to set in as I tried to look for someone suspicious.

"Guys," I said, my voice growing louder as my chest thumped faster and faster. "I think someone just robbed me."

Mara looked and, for a moment, was concerned before she started beaming. "That's great to hear!"

I turned and looked at her. "Why is that a good thing?"

Mara's eyes grew wide, throwing her arms into the air. "Uli!"

Turning around, I didn't see anybody at first. After a moment's confusion, I heard a whistle directly underneath me. Looking down, I saw a slender woman with chartreuse green skin and cat's eyes colored like molten brass. Looking me up and down, she spoke in an easygoing manner.

"This the new guy I've heard so much about?" She tossed a familiar sack of coins up and down in her right hand as she spoke.

"Hey!" I thought I'd hidden it in a safer place this time. Something told me she was more competent than the twins from a while ago.

Trying to grab the sack of coins, I threw my hand out to grab it while it was in the air. When my hand wrapped around where it should have been, my hand went right through it, and the bag became translucent. Laughing, the green-skinned woman made the illusory coins disappear into nothing.

130

She somehow got behind me while I looked at the bag fly in the air. I jumped back in surprise.

"Oldest trick in the book," The green woman smirked. She lightly whipped her head back, resetting her hair which was cut short, save for a long ponytail and a few braids. Her hair was so dark a shade of green it almost looked black. As she grinned, a short pair of fangs popped out, and she reached behind her head, pulling out my bag.

Her pupils were narrowed like a cat, and the aura she generated made me know she was just getting started. I could feel Mara's snickers behind me as the people around ignored us and continued their business.

"That's another illusion, isn't it?" I deadpanned.

"Yep!" The woman said while dispelling the second illusion. "You catch on pretty quick."

"Thanks," I said, miffed I still didn't have my money back. "I take it you don't have it anymore?"

Giezha's hand appeared in my periphery, jingling a bag of coins. The woman, whom I could safely assume was Ulilee, laughed like a child playing their favorite game.

Giezha beckoned me to take the bag by jingling it again. "C'mon," she urged. "It's real, alright?"

I stuck out my hand for her to drop the coin bag into. Feeling its weight as it landed, I quickly stuck it inside the inner lining of my shirt. Ulilee gave me a look as if I'd challenged her as she eyed me up and down.

Doing the same, I could see she wore a shirt similar to the one I wore under my armor, save for its purple color and that it left her stomach exposed. It was something akin to a medieval crop top with golden coins wrapping around the shoulder to match one of her necklaces.

Continuing my... inspection, I noticed a series of blue-green and white tattoos along her arms, legs, and even one on her face. They were all horizontal bars and runes, except for a single purple triangle on her waist, partially hidden under a long blue skirt with golden ringlets and coins. Her lips were plump and glossy with black lipstick.

"Liking what you see, Asher?" Ulilee asked breezily.

My eyes snapped back Ulilee's, and she had her arms crossed in front of her while she smirked. Mara was ready to keel over laughing, and even Giezha snickered. Doing my best to keep my eyes on hers, I tried to project the same confident energy.

"Probably about as much as you are." I said, doing a decent job of sounding casual.

"Oh?"

Without making a single sound, Ulilee vanished for a moment before appearing right in front of me. Her head barely came up to my chest, which she gently pressed her hand against. The stern expression in her eyes suddenly became as soft as a lamb.

"Then that must mean you think I look amazing," she whispered, putting a chill into my spine.

My mouth turned dry as I tried to compose myself. Something about this Ulilee kept me off balance.

"Well, I think we both know the answer to that." I said plainly, before changing the subject. "I take you're back from your… trip?"

Ulilee smirked and turned towards Giezha and Mara.

"Yes, the trip was certainly… interesting. Let's go to our usual spot and talk."

Ulilee hugged Giezha and Mara and began to walk opposite the crowd. Unsure of what to do, I awkwardly stood there, trying to figure out if that was an invitation for me to join. The certainly didn't seem lost with Ulilee around.

"Yo! Merrick!" Ulilee shouted, jumping atop Giezha's shoulders. "Hustle up!"

I jogged to catch up, staying a few paces behind them. As we walked, everybody gave Giezha and Ulilee a wide berth. Many people, especially those appearing to be from guilds, waved at Ulilee and exchanged pleasantries. Ulilee's demeanor could only be described as "cool." She had a gravitas to her that pulled you in.

"So, where was it they sent you, Uli?" Mara asked, her eyes shining like stars.

"Classified," Ulilee said in a tone of mock seriousness. "Captain wanted me to stay out in the field another few weeks, and I told her she could kiss my ass."

"Really?" Giezha asked with concern.

"Ha! No, I'm just pulling your wand, Gi." Ulilee laughed and pulled a bag of nuts from nowhere and started eating from it. She would alternate between handing one to Giezha and herself as she ate.

"So, Asher," Ulilee said, turning and looking me up and down again. I felt very naked as she did so. "Heard you're building quite the reputation around town. Snapping arms, storming ships, and breaking hearts. Right Mara?"

Ulilee gave Mara the thumbs up while I did my best not to blush. Although I had only really been with Mara and recently Kiersa, I couldn't deny that I had caught several wandering eyes over the past few weeks.

"Uh-huh," Ulilee said, turning back the other way. "Guess that answers that."

I looked at the back of her head, dumbfounded and tongue-tied. I would have to watch out for her. She was more dangerous with her words than she was in combat. At least, I assumed so. I hadn't seen her fight yet. Then again, if she was anything like Mara or Giezha, she could more than hold her own.

As we walked, we took a direction into the city that was new to me. It took us deep into a seedy neighborhood west of the Fortress. The crowd thinned out. Ulilee hopped off Giezha, and in a flash, her outfit changed to a gray cloak with a hood.

I looked around and noticed several eyes following our progress. A few sketchy individuals stopped whatever business they were conducting and watched as we walked through the slums. The buildings were all broken down and stunk of animal dung and garbage. Most of the shops didn't have names. Instead, pictograph symbols in long strings were hung up on wooden boards.

"They're coded messages," Ulilee said, reading my mind. "Means something different depending on who's the one that's reading it."

"How's that work?" I asked, trying to decipher what a fish, triangle, finger, crossed swords, and a unicorn head had to do with the row underneath it.

"Depends on your imagination."

"So, which one are we going to?" Mara asked, her face back in hunting mode and her hand on her weapon.

Uli pulled Mara down to her level and whispered something in her ear. Mara nodded and stayed silent. I was about to say something when Giezha put a hand on my chest. She shook her head and put a finger against her mouth. Apparently, whatever we were doing was on a need-to-know basis. And I didn't need to know. Yet.

As we zigzagged our way through the maze of slums, I noticed a pair of individuals begin to follow us. I brushed against Giezha and tried to covertly gesture what I saw. She muttered something under her breath, and I noticed one of her lenses in her glasses turn into a mirror. A second later, the glasses were back to normal.

Giezha started whistling a tune, and I immediately noticed Ulilee's long ears twitch.

"How many?" she asked quietly.

Giezha whistled some coded message, and Ulilee's ear's twitched again. As we walked, she turned a corner ahead of us. When we turned, she quickly gestured for us to slide up against the wall. I wound up behind her while Mara was behind me and Giezha took the rear. After a pregnant pause, Ulilee looked back where we had been. She gestured to follow her, and the two individuals were gone.

"Got to love being tailed," Mara sighed.

Ulilee stretched her arms behind her head. "Meh, keeps things interesting. Espionage and all that junk. C'mon, we're almost there."

Ulilee led us to a small cart that had an extremely short and squat goblin with nearly closed eyes and a pipe as long as he was tall in his mouth. The slits of his red eyes flicked over to us, and he took a long puff. As he exhaled, he began to speak a language that I recognized as Goblin.

Ulilee waved her hand while he spoke. "Let's skip the pleasantries, Rogorm. I've got a lot to do today, and we need to make it quick."

Rogorm made a sour face that wrinkled his skin to near-impossible levels. Fixing himself another batch of whatever he was smoking, he tapped the extremely long pipe on his cart while looking us all over. He looked back at Ulilee and started speaking to her again in Goblin at length. With an annoyed look, Ulilee replied to him in Goblin in a curt manner.

"Let's stick to Common so my compatriots can listen in, Rogorm. I won't ask again."

Rogorm scratched a long fingernail against the chipped blue paint of his cart.

"You neglect your heritage, Ulilee Iron Will."

A sour expression crossed Ulilee's face, and a white dagger appeared in

134

her hand. She kept the knife out of view under the cart. Giezha and Mara looked unworried. The old goblin was either unaware or unimpressed.

"I do not neglect any of my heritage. The name is Ulilee Siannodel, daughter of the human Carmine Siannodel and the Goblin Una Noxead, and I'm proud of it."

"Oh, aye. Ye' be only halfkin, it's true." The goblin puffed out a few smoke rings before settling his eyes on me. He ignored Ulilee and spoke to me. "What's your business here, boy?"

Everybody's eyes snapped toward me. I looked around and checked to see if anybody was watching us. The area wasn't abandoned, but the few people that were milling about seemed more interested in their own business. Ulilee gave me a deathly severe look, while Giezha and Mara gave me the side-eye.

"I know you." he asked, picking his teeth. "Gave Towser some trouble. Don't take kindly to that."

"Towser's an ass, Rogorm. Just leave him be."

"Towser and I had a... conversation. And I'm their friend and partner," I said, gesturing to the girls. "Their business is my business. And mine is theirs."

The goblin considered my words for a few moments and blew out more smoke rings in the shape of perfect squares. He punctuated the smoke trick with an arrow that pierced through each. He grinned, exposing a set of razor-sharp teeth.

"Friends?" he asked thoughtfully. "Bold claim."

Before anybody could interrupt me, I swooped in next to Ulilee and got in his face. I placed my elbows on the cracked wood of his cart, which splintered under my weight. If this little bastard wanted to play games with me, he could go right ahead. My face was only a few inches from his. He slowly blinked while he frowned at me.

"I consider anybody to be my friend, Rogorm," I said with a beaming smile and one hand on my sword. "We could be friends too. So long as you show them the respect they deserve."

"Respect?" Rogorm muttered.

"Yes," I said, pressing more weight on the cart. "Respect as in, you address Ms. Siannodel as such. And that you stick to a language we can all understand if possible. It's rude to talk about someone in front of them.

135

And we both know that's what you were doing."

Ulilee gave me a smirk while Rogorm held an expression reminiscent of Towser's. After a moment, he knelt down and grabbed something in his cart. He pulled out a box wrapped in black fabric, handing it to Ulilee. She gave a curtsy and handed a few coppers to him.

As we walked away from Rogorm, Ulilee tapped me on the elbow.

"Held your own pretty well in there, Asher," she complimented. "Didn't peg you as so confrontational."

"Bad habit of mine," I said, eyeing the box she carried. "It's gotten me into trouble more times than I'd like to admit."

"I hear ya. It could get you killed."

My eyes flashed back to that night. The fight. Her. The shots. "You have no idea," I muttered, ignoring the tingle on my scars.

"What? Speak up. My ears aren't that big."

"Uhh, I said I have no idea what's in the box."

"Oh, this?" She undid the linens on the box, revealing the delicious smell of greasy, fried foods and a collection of rich, dark brown chicken cuts, battered and fried. "Yeah, you can't find a better place for authentic Cezian Goblin-style chicken cuts."

Ulilee started handing out tiny pieces of crispy, steaming fried chicken bits. The flavor was black pepper and cinnamon, with a hint of garlic. It was also super spicy. I enjoyed sweating out the burn of the chicken while Mara was quick to buy a block of cheese to cool off. Giezha avoided them altogether.

Popping a chicken bite into her mouth, Ulilee looked to the tall sorceress. "Don't worry, Gi, I got you covered." She pulled out a box with candied nuts and fruits from nowhere, handing it to Giezha.

After finishing the snack, Ulilee brought us to their "usual spot" which amounted to a secluded alley. She jumped behind a large garbage sack and gestured for us to hide. Sticking behind a couple large boxes, I looked back where we had come from.

After a moment, we saw the two that had been tailing us again. One of them, a half-elf with long black hair and a scar across their nose, stopped and stared in our direction. The other, a goliath with red tattoos, leaned down and muttered in the half-elf's ears while looking the direction we all came from.

Giezha had somehow become invisible while Mara stuck behind me. I was wedged so deeply behind the boxes with Mara that you'd have to be right above them to see me.

After a moment, the half-elf turned and kept walking in the direction we were initially headed. We all waited a few more minutes before coming out of hiding. Ulilee jumped out of her hiding spot and had us cut through the alleyway.

"Uli, what's going on?" Mara asked as we walked towards the Warren.

"I've been followed for the past few weeks," Uli said, her head on a swivel, darting in every direction. "Those two have been following me since I left the city in the first place. I thought I lost them a few days ago."

"Which guild are they from?" Giezha asked, also scanning for them.

"No idea. But what I do know is that they're hard to lose and even harder to find." She turned and gave us all a deadly-serious look. "I'm worried this job we were given is a trap."

Chapter 13

Tavilday Night, 20th of Seeyrn, Year 678, 4th Age

A few nights after her arrival, Ulilee gave the rundown on our assigned job in their shared room. It was an escort mission to the city of Zizar, about four days east by land and sea. We had the option of either taking the road or hitching a ride on a trading vessel for the first leg of the journey. Otherwise, it'd be a week each way.

Once she finished explaining the job, Ulilee asked me a pointed question. "You ever been on the road that long, Merrick?"

Crap. I hadn't forgotten my conversation with Giezha and how being from another world wasn't a good thing. I turned to look at Giezha behind Ulilee, who shrugged her shoulders noncommittally.

"I've been... around, y'know?" I said unconvincingly. "Typically, I try to go from place to place as quick as possible. I'm sure I'll be able to manage the journey."

There was an unmistakable glint in Ulilee's eye as she digested my blatant lie. Rather than pursue it further, she didn't say anything and got back to planning. She was going to call in a favor from a merchant sailor who could get us halfway there. The noble in question was a merchant who specialized in trading magical gemstones in Zizar.

"He's in a hurry to get back since his contract to buy the firestone from the Everlasting as a cultural item went up in smoke." Ulilee turned and smirked at me. "Know anything about that, Asher?"

Mara snickered behind Ulilee's back as I squirmed in the seat I'd brought from the bar. The lighthouse coming back on had caused quite a stir. Several ships had mistakenly tried to make port before quickly adjusting course. Luckily, no ships had accidentally beached yet.

It was still a mystery to everybody else how it had happened. The entire lighthouse was off-limits according to a council decree, which Kiersa forgot to mention to me. Now the area was becoming a popular destination again.

"I can neither confirm nor deny anything."

"Good idea," Ulilee said while rolling her eyes. "Well, let's try to get some shut-eye. We'll need to leave in the morning if we want to get paid."

"How much is the job?" Mara asked as I got up to leave.

"Hundred gold each," Ulilee said while getting out a bedroll. "There's a little upside to the contract, but that bitch, Dawnthorn, staked a claim to it, so we're just getting base fees."

"I'm assuming that means we pretend there was no upside?" I asked while about to slip out the door.

All three of them laughed sarcastically. "Good luck getting that to pass inspection," Giezha said while setting up a game of cards.

"Captain's ruthless with paperwork," Mara said, getting ready to deal in. "She can smell a lie better than anyone. Except for Uli."

Uli jumped into a game of cards, anteing in a few coppers. I was about to offer to join in as well, but a look from Ulilee made me reconsider. I quietly slipped out of the room and went to my room for the evening.

As the season began to slip towards autumn, nights came earlier. The dusk of the evening swayed into nightfall as I sat by my table, writing in my journal and occasionally looking out at the moons and the city. It took some getting used to the whole two moons thing. But the view that the sky provided unpolluted by light was astonishing.

Looking out below at the city streets, I could see a couple friends still trying to get the last few sales for the night. Business was slow, and most entertainers had packed up for the evening or tried to make their coin at the taverns. All that was left were the stragglers and drunks.

I noticed a few regulars in the area from the weeks I'd spent people-watching at night. There was a pot-bellied ogre who bought a whole chicken from the tavern and enjoyed it on his way home. Another was a group of young hooligans who could never hold their liquor and would leave sickly markers of their merriment on the street. Finally, there was a local bum I had run into a few times in the Market Square. He was an old half-elf named George with bright red hair that stuck out in every direction.

"Speak of the devil," I mumbled to myself as the man of the hour had arrived.

George was even more intoxicated than usual. At least, that's how it appeared, based on how he was walking. Shambling was a better way to describe it. His movements were stiff and mechanical as he wandered around in circles. At least twice, he bumped into people as if they weren't even there.

As he began to walk past a building in front of me, I saw him walk face-first into a wall. Feeling bad for the poor guy, I decided to go down and help him.

"Yo, George!" I called out.

When I got there, he was still lying down on the ground. The whole street had finally emptied for the night. My nose was assaulted by a seriously foul odor when I got close. He'd hadn't smelled pleasant when I ran into him in the market, but this was downright putrid.

"Hey, Georgie," I said, kneeling down. "Remember me? I bought you that wheel of cheese a couple days ago at the market? You okay?"

"Murreghhh," he moaned throatily.

I tapped his shoulders a few times before trying to roll him onto his back. As I did, he began to push off the ground, with his arms shaking like a leaf.

"I'm gonna help you up, alright?"

Rolling him over, I jumped back at the first look at his face. It looked like part of his face had been sliced off and the skin peeled back. I recoiled in shock, falling onto my backside.

"George?" I asked, trying to scramble back to my feet.

I slowly approached him with my hands out in front of me. George was still lying on the ground staring straight up into the sky. The putrid smell emanated as he moaned quietly. It was hard to see details with the tiny bit of light out, but he was really messed up. The left side of his face had its skin removed, and his eyes had a dull gray look to them. His nose had been shaved to the bone while his skin had become gray and rotted.

"What the—?"

Before saying anything else, he reached out to grab me at my ankle. It felt like a vise had been planted on my foot as he did. I tried to shake him off, but he would not let go. I fell back onto the ground as he tried to pull my foot up to his mouth. He let out another moan, and I could see his teeth begin to bite down onto my boot.

Panicking, I kicked him in the face, which did nothing to stop him. I kicked him again, and it was as if I had brushed him with a feather. His teeth struggled to break through the thick leather of my boot, but it felt like

140

he was tearing my leg off in the process. As my heart raced and I struggled to think of what to do, I felt a burning sensation in my stomach. With no other ideas, I welled up all the power I could and kicked Zombie-George in the arm.

When I made contact, I ripped through his arm at the elbow like it was wet paper. His arm snapped off his body and he was sent him flying. Propelled into the air, George's body flew into an alleyway. The alley was completely pitch black as he disappeared into it. My chest heaved as I waited like an idiot. I expected him to crawl out of the alley for several moments. However, he never did.

"George?" I asked timidly.

I got up and walked into the alley to investigate. It was impossible to see anything in the dark, but there was no trace of him! The alley was narrow, and he should have hit something in here. A box, the walls... something! But there was no sign of him! His moaning had stopped, and nothing looked out of place. The rats in the alley scurried about as if nothing had happened.

"George?" I whispered again.

As I stood there for a few minutes. I realized that I hadn't taken the hand off my ankle. Looking down, the hand was gone. I stood there in the dark silence for another few moments. This... just wasn't right.

When I walked into the bar, I sat down and ordered a drink. My heart was still racing as I tried to make sense of this impossible situation. George had just tried to eat me! And when I kicked him away from me, the guy disappeared into thin air. Just disappeared.

Sensing my troubles, Sal poured me a double. Turning back to straighten the painting Mara had done, Sal asked me a question.

"What's the matter, son? Sad the girls didn't want to invite you to poker night?"

I didn't answer and just drank from my beer. I was afraid to say anything and seem crazy. I shook my head and tried to take a drink without spilling onto the bar. Nearly choking, I put the beer down ran my hand through my hair. I felt skittish and jittery with my leg bouncing on the stool.

"Everything alright, Asher? Look like ya seen a ghost."

Before I could answer, a figure sat down next to me at the bar. A ghost, in fact. Or at least, a zombie. I looked to my left and saw George sitting right next to me, happy as a clam. His skin was back on, and his nose was reattached. His vocal cords seemed to be working as well as he hummed a little ditty to himself. It sounded oddly familiar, but I couldn't place it.

"How's it going, Salvatore? Let me get a couple drinks and some food. The dice have been good to me."

I stared at George, my mouth on the bar and my eyes wide as the horizon. George saw how I was staring and did a double-take. He gave me an awkward smile and tried to make some small talk.

"How's... it going, Asher?" He asked, trying to keep his smile. "Rough uh... night?"

I shook my head and tried to regain my composure. I slapped a few coppers on the bar without finishing my drink and headed up to bed.

"Giezha must've given me a bad potion during class," I murmured.

When I opened the door, I saw Ulilee sitting at my desk. She was reading from my journal, apparently. I should have been agitated at the invasion of my privacy, but I was too distracted.

"Giezha's been teaching me the basics of potion brewing in the mornings after workouts," Ulilee read aloud as I brushed past her. "Mara has helped with my shield fighting. I hate shields, but better not get complacent. Haven't had a job in a week now, and I'm getting antsy." Ulilee stopped and turned around to look at me before continuing. "They keep bringing up this Ulilee, but I'm a little suspicious. What's she been gone for so long for? Why all the secrets?"

Ignoring her, I rifled through my chest and pulled out a Potion of Calming Giezha had used for instruction a few weeks ago. Downing the faintly lemony concoction, I felt a tingling sensation envelop me. The pins and needles in my extremities faded as the adrenaline quickly evaporated out of my bloodstream.

My mind buzzed with everything still, but it was slow enough to not get overwhelmed. With my body catching up to my mind, I looked at Ulilee.

"Why all the secrets, indeed?" Ulilee said, tapping her chin, looking up to the sky. Her voice was peppy, but there was a dangerous undertone.

Finally able to relax, I looked at her and crossed my arms.

"Look," I said, trying to locate where I'd put my sword and shield. "I don't know you. And you don't know me. Neither of us trusts each other. Let's get that out of the way."

"Oh, I trust you, Asher," Ulilee said airily, hopping to her feet and walking towards me. "I trust that I'll know when you're lying at least. You're a terrible liar. You've got a tick in your eye when you do. You also look away when you're about to lie." She took a few more steps towards me, and I stepped back, bumping into my bed. "And when you say the lie? Well, the rubbish that comes out of your mouth is just hilariously, obviously, untrue as well."

I kept scanning the room for my sword and shield to no avail. Sensing what I was up to, Ulilee revealed them by her side. Tossing them into the trunk, she sauntered towards me.

"I have the feeling you're a great liar," I said, crawling backward on the bed. "I don't take it that you'll teach me how to do that thing where you pull something out of thin air."

"What? Sleight of hand?" she asked coyly.

"I doubt it's that easy."

"Nothing special," Ulilee said, successfully cornering me. "Just wanted to send a little message."

She placed a hand on my chest, and I slowly put my hands up. "And that is?"

"I don't know who you are. I don't know where you're from. And I don't know why you're here. There's a lot of rumors about you, Asher…"

She leaned in closer to me, which gave me the cue to slip away. I wasn't convinced I could take her in a fight and running out of my own room was out of the question. I needed to keep my defense up while I weathered the storm.

"I'll keep that in mind," I said, sitting on the trunk. "Anything else?"

Ulilee pulled a curved, white dagger from nowhere and tossed it into the air a few times.

"Just a warning that I'll skin you alive if you hurt Mara or Gi," she said with a sickly sweet smile as she spoke. Her irises widened from their usual vertical slits.

"Fair enough," I said, getting in a defensive posture. "And the first time any of you try to screw me over will also be the last."

Ulilee stopped and cocked her head to the side, her irises growing and turning fully circular as she studied me. I stood there with my sword at the ready and my muscles burning for a fight. I'd be sleeping long into the next day, but I'd rather sleep longer than sleep forever.

With a flick of the wrist, the knife disappeared behind her arm. Ulilee's tense posture loosened up. Her eyes slowly returned to normal as her trademark smirk reformed onto her face.

"Good to know, Asher. Good to know."

Ulilee slowly walked back to the door and made her leave. She turned and gave me a cheeky look with one foot out the door.

"I hope the rumors from Mara and Kiersa are true."

Putting my fists down, I shrugged.

"Don't tell the others about this, by the way."

I nodded my head, and she left. I stood for a moment, weighing my options. I didn't feel good about being on my own, but I was getting tired of being threatened as well.

However, she had every right to be suspicious of me. At the end of the day, I was just some dude who invited himself to her team. I needed to prove myself if I wanted to earn her trust. Maybe I could start now, I thought to myself. I ran to my door and called for her.

"Oi, Ulilee!" I shouted, opening my door. When I opened my door, she was right there. She still held that seductive gaze.

"Need something?" she asked flirtatiously.

Ignoring her advances, I pointed to George, who was still at the bar chatting it up with Salvatore.

"You see that guy at the bar? George. Hobo who usually hangs out around here?"

"What about him?"

I placed a hand on her shoulder and looked her in the eyes. "You know the thing about trust? What I'm about to say might be crazy, but I need you to believe me."

She didn't say anything and just waited.

"When I came into my room, I was distracted by something that I saw a little bit ago. I was here people watching from my window and saw George stumbling around in the street."

"And? That's no different than how he always is."

I tried to keep calm as the potion I took fought against how I was really feeling. "I went down to check on him to see that he was okay, and when I did, his nose was cut off, and his skin was peeling back. He smelled like

144

death and acted like it too. He was a zombie!"

Ulilee looked at me, her mouth opened slightly. She looked to the left and then the right, saying nothing. Clearly, she was unconvinced.

"And then he turned back to normal?" She pointed towards George, who was clearly not a zombie.

"I know," I admitted. "It sounds crazy, but look!"

I reached down and pulled one of my pant legs up. When I did, you could see bruising and indentation around my ankle that matched the outlines of finger bones. I also discovered something attached to my pant leg. A tiny bone fragment near the ankle and another embedded in my boots.

I picked them out and handed them to Ulilee. She looked at me, then back to the bones, and then at George before returning to the bones.

She looked back at me, handing over the bone chips.

"That's why I was so frazzled when I came in and chugged that potion. I feel like I'm going crazy, but I know what I saw. And felt."

She looked at me again and nodded her head. She spoke gently and rubbed the side of my arm.

"I believe you, Asher. You should get some sleep while that potion is still working. We can talk about this later."

I nodded my head and turned back to my room.

"Thanks again, Asher."

"No problem Ulilee."

"Hey!" she called back.

I turned and looked at her with the door nearly closed behind me.

"It's Uli. Just Uli." She gave a toothy smile. "At least, that's what my friends call me."

Before I could say anything, Uli winked and turned back down the stairs.

"That girl is just as strange as the others," I muttered.

Unable to think of anything other than what happened with "George," I decided to call it a night and go to sleep.

I woke up feeling a heavy sensation on top of my chest. My first worry was that I somehow immobilized my chest by using my ability last night. When I opened my eyes, I saw my knapsack filled with equipment on my lap.

"C'mon, we're late!" I heard a voice call out. "Hurry it up!"

145

I struggled to sit up as I became aware of Uli clapping beside me, trying to wake me up. I waved her off and told her to wait outside while I dressed. Lumbering out of bed, I strapped on my gear and armor, which I'd lazily discarded by the bed.

Sal had a plate of sausage and coffee ready for me. Downing a cup of joe and picking up the sausages, I thanked him and made my way outside.

The three of them waited impatiently for me while I munched on cold sausage. Mara was bouncing up and down as was par for the course when she was excited. Giezha, meanwhile, was buried deep in her book. Uli was tapping her foot on the ground with her arms crossed.

"Sleep well?" she asked sarcastically as she turned to walk towards The Docks.

"Not really," I said, stifling a yawn. The sun was barely cresting over the horizon, and my muscles ached while my legs felt like bags of wet cement.

"Well, too bad. We're on the clock."

We made our way towards The Docks, passing by the Golden Sky Tavern. Kiersa was sweeping the front of the building and saw us. We all waved to her, and she quickly ducked into the tavern before emerging with a collection of sandwiches.

"For the road! Better than living off hardtack for the whole journey." She handed us each a large sandwich packed with meats, cheeses, and some veggies. When she gave me mine, she kissed me on the cheek and whispered in my ear.

"I haven't forgotten the raincheck."

I just nodded and grinned like an idiot as she giggled and got back to work.

The others gave me a teasing look but didn't say anything except for warning me not to let her father see. Once we made it to The Dock, Uli instructed us to wait for her as she met her contact.

"The noble will know to look for you guys. Gi is unmistakable."

Giezha looked annoyed but said nothing while Uli ran off. The three of us just stood in the middle of a market section of The Docks, awkwardly waiting for the noble to show up. Mara clutched her rucksack and smiled from ear to ear, bouncing up and down.

"Isn't this exciting!?" she squealed. "Back on the road and escorting a merchant all the way to Zizar! Oh, I hope there's a bandit camp or a giant

146

spider nest we have to torch. Oooh! Or maybe an evil coven of witches." Mara happily chattered away, listing all the various dangers she hoped to encounter.

"You hoping for the same?" I whispered to Giezha.

She pulled her face out of her book and looked at me. Her face was just as blank and unreadable as always. She looked at Mara, who was still listing off interesting deadly encounters, and back to me.

"I'm looking forward to seeing Zizar's magic shops. I heard there's an orc-owned apothecary."

"That would be correct!" boomed a deep voice behind us.

Turning around, we saw an extremely tall and rotund man approaching us. Clad in bright red and silver robes was a large human male with slicked-back hair in a ponytail that ran to his waist. His face was round and shiny, especially where a scar traced down his throat and his right ear. It looked like a scar from a burn long since healed.

"Isaac Geney, magi-gemologist and amateur lutist at your service."

Isaac bowed as far as his large belly would allow, and a lute, slung behind his back, became visible. At his side a small moleskin sack, presumably filled with gems, jingled around as he swayed back and forth. Isaac looked at us with heavily sunken hazel eye

"The Red Breakers said one of their most promising young teams will be escorting me to my home of Zizar at the foot of the Childock's. Am I safe to assume that is you?"

"Yes!" Mara said excitedly, nearly shouting. "That's us, Mr. Geney!"

Isaac smiled warmly and shook Mara's hand, kissing her knuckles. So close to us now, I could smell the thick aroma of patchuli.

Unphased, Mara beamed and bounced on her heels, ready to get going.

Uli came back with the captain of the vessel we'd be riding, a caravel called the MSS Argojet. The captain was a tall, white-haired Drow named Sillaesa Moonwalker. Her stern expression and military-style uniform conveyed an aura that demanded respect.

The ship itself was about forty feet long and housed a crew of twenty or so rough and tough sailors. As we made our way onto the ship, we all kept in a tight formation around Isaac. I took rearguard, watching the prying eyes around us. More than one person looked suspiciously long at Isaac's sack of gems.

147

"Be on the lookout for anybody getting too close," Uli reminded us as we set ourselves up in a small bunk area. "According to the captain, rough seas mean we are going to be at sea for three days instead of two. That means an extra day for things to go wrong."

Once we made our way back to the top, we did our best to blend in. Uli took Isaac to talk things over with the captain. At the same time, Mara disappeared into the kitchen under the guise of helping the chef. Giezha and I helped with the rigging and getting the sails in order. Neither of us had any sailing experience and may have been a hindrance more than help.

Once the ship was ready to sail, the captain had the sailors lift the anchor and let out a blow of the horns to signify we were leaving port. Apparently, it was a sign of respect to gain favor from the gods of the seas and sailing.

The swaying and lurching of the sea told me I'd need my sea legs fast. It's hard and heavy lurches swirled my gut, and I was nauseous with in moments. I leaned over the ship's side, trying not to lose the lunch I had eaten only an hour before.

"You alright, Asher?" Giezha asked, keeping a solid distance.

"Yeah," I grunted, trying to focus on one of the ships leaving The Docks simultaneously to us. "Just need to..."

Something cuaght my eye as I looked at the small ship about twenty yards from us. The sails had just been let loose as it was getting ready to hit the open sea. The ship was half our size and crewed by even fewer people. Two of them looked familiar. Very familiar.

"Giezha, you wouldn't happen to have a spyglass, would you?"

She handed me a brass spyglass that was beaten up on all sides. "Yeah, one of the crewmen let me borrow it."

Pulling out the spyglass to its full length, I inspected the ship we were passing. Training my eye on two individuals, I confirmed my suspicions. The pair were the half-elf and the goliath that tailed us in the Iron Court. I relayed this information to Giezha.

"Hope they aren't looking for us," Giezha said, her voice hinting at a touch of nervousness.

"Well," I said as they both stared directly at me. "I wouldn't get your hopes up."

Chapter 14

Avisday Night, 22nd of Dhivmirn, Year 678, 4th Age

Despite our paranoia with the crew aboard the ship, the days on the water were peaceful, uneventful, and downright dull. Despite reporting that I had seen the two following us to Uli and Captain Moonwalker, nothing came of it. The ship wound up leaving in the opposite direction from the port, and none of us saw it once we were in open water.

Trying not to crowd Isaac too much, we watched him in shifts, with two of us staying close, one patrolling the ship and another taking a break. I had mornings off and night shifts on personal duty. Mara's free time was afternoons, which she split between practicing her swordsmanship and painting dozens of beautiful watercolors. Giezha and Ulilee split evening shifts so Giezha could practice her potions after dinner and squeeze in some lifting, using the anchor and metal chains as weights.

Isaac was easily the most entertaining part of the journey aboard the ship. When he wasn't recounting his journeys around the continent searching for gemstones, he would spend hours playing his flute and singing ballads of heroes past. The day before we were set to land, he offered to teach me a few chords.

"You know, the ladies do enjoy a man who can bring the music in their hearts to life," he cajoled me as the two of us walked aboard the topside while the others were away for a moment. "Although, I doubt you have trouble with the ladies. Eh, Mr. Merrick?"

Scratching the back of my head, I gave an embarrassed laugh. "I didn't know that it was that obvious. Mara and I have tried to be discreet."

Isaac laughed as he diddled away on his lute. "Oh, don't be so modest! I've seen the way those girls look at you. You aren't picking fruit from too many trees, are you?"

149

I shook my head and laughed. "Ulilee doesn't trust me as far as she can throw me. And Giezha... well, let's say she's hard to read."

Laughing, Isaac reached into his bag of gems. He pulled out a tiny pearl-sized ruby and pressed it into my hands.

"Well, whatever you choose to do, when you get the notion to do something for that special someone, use this."

Isaac gave me a wink and got back to his music. My shift was about to end, and I looked for Ulilee. Surprisingly, I found her sitting on the ship's side with a pole in her hands.

"He give you any trouble, Asher?" Ulilee said, watching her bobber trail off further and further.

I looked at Isaac, who gave me a cherubic smile and whistled along with his music. I couldn't deny that I caught Ulilee staring at me a few times, and she seemed to enjoy relentlessly flirting with me. Then again, she seemed to enjoy flirting with everybody. That, combined with the fact that she had threatened to kill me a few nights ago, gave me the distinct impression she wasn't interested.

"Oh, not really." I said, watching her tranquil expression as she stared out into the calm waters. "Catch anything good?"

"Nah, ship's moving too fast through the water for anything to come to the surface. I just like to take my mind off things for a minute."

The longer Ulillee stared out, the more I realized I was interested in her. Ulilee was stunningly gorgeous with a great body. She had a slim and athletic build accentuated by her revealing clothing.

She also moved with grace and precision that made everything she did look easy. Besides her obvious physical beauty, she also had a charm that gave her a magnetic quality. In a word, Ulilee was just cool.

It was hard to describe, but she just made you want to be around her. She made quick friends with everybody around her, and the crew had already welcomed her into their ranks.

"Is it my shift?" she asked, snapping me back to reality.

"Huh? Oh, yeah. It's your shift. I'm gonna go grab some food then."

Ulilee didn't say anything and nodded, reeling in her line. It took almost a full minute for it to reel in, and once Ulilee did, she nodded to me and gestured to leave. As I headed below deck, Isaac gave me some more words of encouragement that I sorely needed. Or maybe I didn't. Who knows?

I went down to grab some food and meet up with Mara and Giezha. It was cards night, which meant it was time to win back the money I'd lost playing Mara in backgammon previously. However, we'd only be able to play a few hands before returning to our duties.

After several quick rounds, we started talking about rumors on the deck. The biggest was that Captain Moonwalker offered Ulilee a job on the ship. Apparently, she turned it down on the spot.

"She get a lot of job offers like that?" I asked as I continued losing hand after hand.

"Oh yeah," Mara said, throwing down a full house. "Never gives them a wink of a thought, though. She likes this kind of work and doesn't want to get tied down by anything."

"Plus, she'd miss us," Giezha added, throwing down a ten-high straight in frustration.

"You seem to spend a lot of time staring at her," Mara mentioned casually, dealing in the next round.

"About as much time as he spends staring at you and me," Giezha said in her usual deadpan.

I felt as if there was something in my throat preventing me from being able to speak as I looked at another particularly terrible hand. No potential flushes, no pairs, and my highest card were a nine of diamonds. Mara and Giezha were more interested in my response than in the game. Neither picked up their cards and looked at me expectantly.

"Well, to be fair..." I trailed off, trying to come up with something good. "To be fair, you ladies are all gorgeous." I gestured to both of them and continued. "It's true I might've been checking out Ulilee a few times, but it's hard not to when she flirts so heavily."

They looked unimpressed, refusing to start the round as I tried to dig myself out of this hole.

"And yes, Giezha is well... She's not only tall and strong but also extremely intelligent and, yes, quite pretty."

"That why you tackled her during training?" Mara chided while nudging Giezha, who looked at me with a blank expression. Feeling like I was making no progress, I pushed on.

"As for Mara, I mean, do I even need to say it?"

151

"Yes," they both said simultaneously.

I sighed in defeat and hung my head.

"Fair enough." I looked at Mara, who accidentally showed the straight flush in her hand as she smiled in anticipation. "Mara is what we call a bombshell where I'm from. Just ridiculously hot.A rocking body, super sweet personality, I'm pretty sure any guy's mother would beg you to be their daughter. Satisfied?"

Neither of them said anything, but I noticed they held their cards to their faces trying to hide their blushing. I'm sure my face was crimson red in embarrassment as well, but I ignored it and immediately folded my hand. As they started the next round, neither said anything as we played in silence. After a few rounds, Mara spoke up again.

"You know, Uli's totally got the hots for you, right?" Mara said, still pink in the cheeks. "You should totally take her out when we get to Zizar. She could really use a night out."

I blew a raspberry out while I raised it to five coppers. "She likes to flirt, but I doubt that," I said dismissively.

Both Giezha and Mara exchanged looks while calling my bet. The next card gave me a three of a kind.

"She does if she wants to make someone jealous," Giezha said, which Mara nodded to. "When she was dating a member of the Black Sapphire Guild, she wouldn't even look at another man, let alone flirt."

"But," Mara said, going all in. "She suspected he was cheating on her. After that, she started flirting with everybody."

Giezha and I both called her obvious bluff while Mara continued the story.

"Turned out he really was cheating. Had been the entire time. We think she kept flirting with everyone to cope."

"Yeah... that bastard Mithx really broke her heart. That was what... a year ago? She hasn't seen anybody since then."

Mara plopped down a pair of twos.

"That sucks," I said while dropping a threesome of queens. "I know what it's like to get betrayed by someone you thought you loved."

Realizing what I said, I looked at Giezha and motioned for her to hurry up and show her cards.

"Yes, well... The point is, we think you and her would be good for each other. She needs to let loose a little bit and enjoy herself." Giezha plopped down a straight flush and pulled the pot in a while, nodding towards Mara. "And this one is hoping you two will let her watch while you two have sex."

"Huh?"

Before I could really process what Giezha said, Mara exploded into a cacophony of swearing and denialism.

"What the fuck did you say!?" She screamed, jumping to her feet. "That is an absolute fucking lie, Giezha! I'm not some-some p-p-pervert who gets off watching other people fuck!"

"Hold on," Giezha tried to interject.

"No, don't you tell me to fucking hold on!" Mara seethed.

Giezha sat there gobsmacked as Mara unleashed a verbal lashing. Her eyes widened in horror as Mara's face got redder and redder.

Mara shook violently as she tried and failed to come up with the words to defend herself besides her maze of swearing and anger. I sat there dumbfounded, looking back and forth at the two of them. It was quite the accusation of sorts, but then again...

"To be fair," I said slowly, as Mara snapped her attention to me. "You do seem to be very excited about the prospect of me dating other women. Like with Kiersa. And you were trying to set me up with Ulilee just now."

"Asher," Mara looked as if she were about to cry as she trembled in rage and embarrassment. "Why would you say that?"

"There's no shame in it, though!" I said quickly while giving Giezha a furtive look. "People like what they like! Seriously, if that's what you enjoy, anybody who has a problem with it can go fuck themselves." I punctuated this by giving another angry look to Giezha.

Giezha shrank inwardly, and just as Mara was about to explode again, the door opened behind us. Ulilee was laughing with Isaac before turning and looking at the situation. I sat there with my hands in front of me, afraid of what Mara may do while the others were frozen in place.

"What's going on," Ulilee asked, her smile vanishing from her face. "Did poker night get too crazy or something?"

Mara burst into tears and ran out of the room, down the halls. Giezha stayed put, shock and shame planted firmly on her face. Ulilee turned her attention to me while I tried to form the words to explain the situation.

Sensing the tension in the room, Isaac quietly excused himself to the room we shared next door.

"Merrick?" Ulilee said, her voice rising dangerously.

I fumbled over myself, trying to come up with something to say. "I..."

"It's my fault," Giezha said quietly. "I talked about Mara and her... likes and dislikes... and she got... you know." Giezha avoided looking at Ulilee while she mumbled her explanation.

Ulilee pinched her eyes while shaking her head.

"Gods dammit." She muttered. "I'll go—"

"Wait!" I shouted, getting up from the ground. "I should go talk to her." Ulilee gave me a look, daring me to leave. "I'm serious. I made the situation worse with what I said too. I need to go and apologize to her."

"Asher, if you hurt her..."

"I know," I pleaded, holding Ulilee's arm. "But, please. I need to go talk to her. She deserves an apology."

Ulilee didn't say anything as she thought for a while. After a few moments, she silently motioned for me to go.

"We'll watch over Isaac, you go." Uli said to which Giezha nodded.

I thanked Uli and dashed out of the room trying to find where she had run off. After searching the lower decks, a sailor stopped me while he was walking from the topside.

"Hey Goldie," he said in a surly voice. "If you're looking for Red, she's topside bawling her eyes out."

I thanked him and made my way up to the top. There was hardly anybody on the top of the ship by this point. The sea was calm, and the winds had died down. Most of the crew topside were talking amongst themselves.

"Then she ran up the crow's nest!" a dragonborn sailor exclaimed. "Crazy bitch just crying like she got the clouds for eyeballs."

Several of them laughed at his story. I walked up to them, ready to knock his head off, but calmed myself. Having seen my approach, they all quickly shut up. The dragonborn who had been complaining looked at me and snarled.

"Here to come 'n get your girlfriend, eh?" He sneered.

"Where is she?" I asked shortly.

"Shove it up your ass, Goldie," he said while flipping the bird. "Breaker's like you don't get to be talkin' like that."

Grabbing him by the shirt, I lifted him, my muscles beginning to heat up. He struggled and kicked me in the chest, trying to get me to let go. His pathetic kicks bounced off me as the fire rose in my insides. The others didn't move a muscle, stunned I had lifted the dragonborn in the air when he had a good foot on me and eighty pounds to boot.

"Where?" I demanded.

"Crow's nest," he grunted.

"Thanks."

I dropped him on the ground and turned, looking upwards. A faint bit of red could be seen atop one of the crow's nests on the central mast. I looked up from below, where the soft sound of crying could be heard from above.

Grabbing the ladder, I clambered up to the top of the crow's nest. It was about fifty feet into the air, and the breeze of the sea was beginning to pick up. When I got to the top, I saw Mara crying, curled up in a ball. She ignored me, looking down at her feet as she sniffled.

"Hope you don't mind if I climb in," I said, struggling to get over the hump. "I'd rather not climb down sixty feet without getting the chance to talk to you."

Mara stayed perfectly still and continued to ignore me. I climbed in and sat down beside her. I wanted to wrap my arm around her, but she nudged me away when I got close. For a few minutes, I just sat there while she cried. After a while, Mara looked away from me and gave a heavy sigh.

"What are you doing here, Asher?"

My throat was dry as I struggled to come up with the words again. I was never good in these situations, but I'd put myself here. So, I needed to see it through to the end.

"I-I came here to apologize," I said, struggling to get the words out. "You were clearly upset, and all I did was make it worse. I didn't mean to make you embarrassed or anything."

"A little late for that," she said quietly, looking at the wall of the crow's nest.

"Yeah... True..."

Rather than say something else, I waited, hoping she would speak up. I just wanted to give her a chance to talk and not feel judged. After a few more minutes of awkward silence, she finally started to speak. Every word

155

looked like it was hurting her to say.

"They both know," she said, struggling at each consonant. "Gi and Uli both know about how I like to..." she trailed off before collecting herself again. "I got really drunk one night when we were talking about stuff we like, and I talked about how I fantasized about... watching."

I didn't say anything and just let her keep talking.

"They didn't mean to, but they started laughing. They thought it was weird, and I ran out of the room crying. Just like tonight. They've always assured me since then that it was fine, that it wasn't weird... and all that."

"And?" I asked quietly, scooting closer.

A tear stung Mara's eye as she leaned into me.

"And I've never been able to talk about it since then. I've never tried to... I've always felt embarrassed, and I've always felt like I'm a freak. But then again, that's how I've always been made to feel."

I squeezed her arm reassuringly. I felt like there was more to the word she was saying. I didn't press further. She wiped her eyes and did her best to keep talking.

"It's just really frustrating because everybody has things they like. Everybody has fetishes and kinks and stuff. But I'm the weird one because I want to see my partners enjoying themselves. I'm a freak because I want to watch someone I'm attracted to be with somebody else. Somebody else I'm..." Mara bit her lip for a moment before finishing her sentence. "...with somebody else who I'm also attracted to."

She probably practiced this speech a hundred times to herself with the way she carefully articulated each word. But the way the last sentence was spoken, that was something she had never practiced before. Something she probably didn't admit to herself.

"Other women, you mean," I said quietly.

"Yes," she said, wiping her face. "Am I a fool for feeling this way?"

"No!" I said, trying my best not to shout. "We all have desires inside of us. Ways of being, I guess. It's hard to put into words, but you know what I mean, right? You are who you are, and it's nobody's business. It's for you, and your... and your partner."

Mara said nothing for a few moments before speaking again.

"I've been repressed almost my whole life in more ways than one. My family is very close-minded and bigoted. They follow the perverted words of a thief gallivanting as a woman of the cloth, perverting the words of Evlana. I'd be kicked out of the family just for speaking of such of desires."

Hearing her words, I felt my blood begin to boil and the fire return inside of my muscles. I felt a strong desire to find her hometown and smack her family upside the head. She took another moment to catch her breath. "That is the reason I left. I wanted to be free, to be the real me. Strong, adventurous, authentic."

I had switched from holding her shoulder to stroking her hair without realizing it. She kept her head pressed against my chest as more tears silently fell.

"Your family should all rot in hell for what they've done to you," I said, frustration boiling over in my words. "You are your own person, Mara. You aren't just strong, Mara, you're a total badass. Anytime we spar with people at the Warren, you mop the floor with them. The moment I met you, you were fighting off a horde of giant wolves with spikes sticking out of their sides!"

She sniffled and placed a hand on my chest, which I squeezed tightly.

"You've been traveling the world with your friends, adventuring wherever you go. You've lived more in the months I've known you than I ever lived in my entire life before meeting you. You're just getting started but you've already done so much. It's truly amazing. You're amazing."

She gave a small laugh that sounded half like a sob as she clutched me tightly. I gently cupped her face, turning it towards me. I looked into her deep emerald eyes, getting lost in them all over again.

Never had I wanted to kiss her as badly as I did now. I wanted to make the pain in her heart go away. I ached for the gentle feeling of her lips pressed against mine but managed to hold back.

"Mara, you are a beautiful, hard-working, kind woman who lights up the room everywhere you go. Anybody who wants you to be anything less than your truest self is robbing the world of its beauty."

Her eyes widened as she sniffled. "Asher," she whispered.

"You have nothing to be embarrassed about. You have nothing to be ashamed of. The only shame that should be felt is that the people who have made you feel that way about yourself. I'm so sorry if I'm one of them, I promise I will never do that again."

I had not realized it, but I'd begun to tear up when I heard her speak so tenderly and vulnerably. The tiniest trace of a smile appeared as her quivering lips curled. Unable to stop myself, I leaned in and kissed her. She gave out another tiny laugh while I pulled her into my embrace. I wiped away her tears as she wiped away mine.

"I promise, Mara," I said breathlessly as I kissed her and kissed her again.

Mara held me tightly, the taste of salt stinging on her lips. "I believe you, Asher. I believe you."

A gentle breeze rolled into the crow's nest as we embraced each other. The two full moons shined brightly as the clouds disappeared into the ether. Our hands began to explore each other's bodies like the many times they had before.

"The breeze feels nice," Mara whispered into my ear. "We'll have to make sure not to get caught."

Mara and I made love under the gentle twinkling of the stars that night, never once letting go of another. The tight space of the crow's nest had her ride on top of me, something that she was more than happy to oblige to. Her soft breasts pressed into me as her vigorous and hungry movements threatened to break the wood beneath us.

More than once, I silenced her cries in pleasure with a deep kiss as we quenched our lust for each other in the salty breeze. Mara's face, still strewn with tears, changed to a joyful expression as we laughed and loved. As she bounced atop me, tightly wrapped around my swollen member, we climaxed as the ship's rocking provided an extra final thrust. She mumbled a promise about taking a potion she'd saved for the trip as I held her in my arms just a little while longer.

Later, as the midnight hour rolled in, we quietly snuck out of the crow's nest and into the sleeping quarters. The door to her room was locked, so rather than wake Ulilee and Giezha, she simply slept in my hammock in the room I shared with Isaac.

Locking the door behind me, I pulled out a protective scroll Giezha had given me to use at night. I could tell Isaac was pretending to sleep for my sake as he let out exaggerated snores that had never been present the previous few nights.

Once the room was safe, I got in the hammock with Mara. As I closed my eyes, I held her tightly, promising to myself to not let go.

Chapter 15

Evlanday, 23rd of Dhivmirn, Year 678, 4th Age

Somehow, Mara was more chipper than ever the next day. Neither Ulilee nor Giezha asked about what happened last night, but they both gave me the thumbs-up after seeing how happy Mara was when leaving our room. As we approached our drop-off point, Giezha awkwardly shuffled over to Mara.

"Mara, about last night," she mumbled, afraid to look her in the eyes. "I'm really, sorry. I shouldn't have said—"

Mara cut her off with a tight hug around her waist. Giezha returned the favor, along with a stifled sniffle. Ulilee gave me a back slap as congratulations and led us topside. Rumors were spreading around the ship about what I did to the dragonborn the previous night. Although some shot dirty looks my way, they kept a wide berth from us as we prepared to dock.

Ulilee thanked Captain Moonwalker as we departed and got on the rowboat back to dry land. Isaac insisted on paying for the boat with a pair of sapphires for the captain. The rest of the crew looked hungrily at the precious gems while the captain stowed them away in her breast pocket.

"Let's get a move on!" Ulilee commanded while Giezha and I began rowing the boat towards dry land. The section of the river was only a few hundred yards wide at this point, but the speed of the water flow made for a challenging job of angling the boat.

Luckily, Isaac was well-traveled and capable and helped us steer the boat toward dry land. After getting the team off the water and into the dirt, I pulled the boat onto the ground, and we chopped up the wood, deciding to keep it as firewood. While we stored the wood in a spare pack that Isaac had on him, Ulilee studied the map she'd brought.

"It'll take us about half the day to get back onto the main road that gets

159

to Zizar."

"Excellent!" Isaac boomed while clapping Ulilee on the shoulder. "I'll be home in three days! You Red Breakers sure know how to work a contract."

With our supplies ready, and our exuberant customer eager to get home, we started the long walk through the grasslands. Although the southern portion of Naled was thick and forested, the eastern side of the river was mainly rolling hills of grasslands. Unfortunately, we ran into a hard rain, which slowed us down.

Isaac passed the time by playing the lute and delved deeper into his music. In the four days we traveled, I never once heard the same song twice. That was almost as impressive as how long every song was. And how every song seems to be about a tragic hero who longed for his love back home.

"I will break that lute," Giezha grumbled while on rear duty with me a few hours and three songs into Isaac's concert. "I will break it over my own head for a moment's peace."

Ulilee stayed ahead of everyone, scouting ahead and pointing out the best route for us to take. Once or twice, she'd stop to a halt and order us to get down while she looked out to the hills. After a minute or two, she'd give the signal to keep going. None of us ever saw whatever made her paranoid.

"She always like this?" I asked Mara, who happily skipped to the tempo of Isaac's playing.

"Only on jobs that she's worried about."

"That a common occurrence?"

"No. It's not," Ulilee shouted over Isaac's high note.

Deciding not to ask any more stupid questions, I resigned myself to listening to Isaac's moderately skilled playing of the lute. Less than four hours later, we were graced with the presence of a beaten-down road that led east by northeast toward the city of Zizar. Far off in the distance, you could just make the outline of the city, with one large tower spiraling high into the clouds.

"May the Spire of Zizar inspire all near and far," Isaac said before breaking into a soliloquy on the founding of his hometown.

My feet ached much the same as they had in my first march toward Naled with Giezha and Mara. I began to noticeably lag behind everybody during the last few hours of walking. When the sun began to set, I could barely

160

keep them within eyeshot going up and down the area's many hills.

"Move it, slowpoke!" Ulilee shouted back to me.

Try as I might, I could not muster the strength to pick up the pace. My legs burned, and they screamed in protest as I tried to keep plodding ahead. Every step I took felt more laborious than the last, as each step became smaller and smaller. Eventually, Mara had to double back and come get me.

"You'd think someone with all those muscles would find this to be easy," she joked, staying behind with me.

As I huffed and puffed, I tried to sound nonchalant. "You'd think, but I've never been good with long distances."

Mara giggled and rolled her eyes. "Yeah, I've noticed." She got behind me as we walked and inspected my knapsack. "Did you bring anything that might help?"

Shit. I'd forgotten to pack the potions from my trunk. I was so excited the night before leaving I didn't think to inspect my inventory before leaving. My reward for my lack of planning was legs ready to collapse under my body at any moment. Mara pulled something out of my pack as I was about to crash into a soft patch of grass.

"Oh! This should be perfect!"

Mara handed me a small spherical bottle with sparkling orange liquid swirling inside. One of the potions that I had bought at the hobgoblin's shop the other day.

"Don't drink the whole thing, or you'll be up all night," she warned me as I opened it for a sniff. "Stamina potions are finicky, and it's hard to tell how strong it will be."

Its smell was a pungent combination of citrus and more citrus that shot into my brain and started firing neurons off left and right. The smell alone of this stuff was enough to get your heart racing. Mara gave me the double thumbs up and nodded her head, urging me to take a drink.

"Down the hatch," I said with a sigh.

Taking her advice, I only drank about a quarter of the bottle. The second the liquid touched my tongue, I battled the urge to gag on this impossibly sweet drink.

Forget any energy drink you've ever had. This stuff swirled around the bend from sweet and into impossibly sour. As I forced it down my gullet, I instantly felt all my muscles and arteries seize up simultaneously.

161

Putting the stopper back on the bottle, I took a deep breath of air and felt fresh oxygen fill my lungs. When I looked around, everything looked brighter and sharper all at once. My legs begin to vibrate, itching for some action. I snapped my head toward Mara, my eyes no doubt bulging out of their sockets. My heart began to race at the speed of light.

"Wow! That is some strong stuff!" I shouted, my voice booming out into the valley. "Let's go!"

Turning back toward where I saw Ulilee leading the others, my feet exploded underneath me as I sprinted forward. Dust and grass kicked up behind me as my feet slammed against the ground at an impossible pace. The sensation was similar to what I felt whenever I activated my ability, minus the literal burning feeling.

As I zoomed down the hill, my mind raced through a million fractured thoughts that had no relationship to each other.

"That is some strong stuff!" I shouted at the top of my lungs to nobody. As I crested down the hill and began to see the others, I spoke to myself as my thoughts refused to stay in my head. "You know I really should think of a different word for how I describe the thing I do when I get really strong all of a sudden I mean, I really need to just figure out what I'm actually going to call it because if I just want to keep calling it my 'ability' because it's going to be really weird whenever I think that to myself because if I'm honest all I'm really saying is a whole lot of nothing whenever I say that."

I caught up to the others in the blink of an eye and accidentally ran past them. My legs were on autopilot, and they had stepped on the gas. Any soreness in my legs was replaced with unbridled energy that needed to be expelled as quickly as possible.

Looking back, I started to lose them and spun in the air to run back towards them. A few minutes later, and they finally caught up with me. Or I caught up with them. Something like that. As I ran in tight circles around them as they walked forward, Giezha pulled out her staff and shouted an incantation. When she did, smokey purple tendrils crawled out of her staff and snatched me.

When they did, I felt all my muscles strain against an invisible force all around me. It was like I had gone from freely running to trying to run in a tub of molasses. I felt slow and heavy failing to gain traction on the ground.

"What in the nightmares of Ihena happened?" Ulilee asked incredulously as I tried with all my might to run full speed.

Having just caught up, Mara explained that I took the orange potion. Ulilee went bug-eyed and looked at me with astonishment and amusement. Giezha grumbled something about unsafe potion-making while keeping up her spell to slow me down. It didn't make me slow, so much as it made me slower. Unfortunately, it did nothing for my rapid heart rate and over-stimulated brain.

With evening approaching, we decided to stop for the night. I set up camp in record time. Once every menial task they could give me was done, I was like a puppy running around trying to grab his tail. The others watched me in amusement as I put Mara's energetic outbursts to shame.

"You gonna be all right, Asher?" Ulilee asked as I fidgeted constantly.

As I twitched and walked around aimlessly, the words flowed out of like a torrent of water, my broken dam.

"Oh yeah, of course never better I feel fantastic there's no way I could ever be feeling any better than I'm feeling right now I mean seriously this stuff is really got that get-up-and-go type of stuff for you, you know what I mean it's seriously just fantastic stuff I'm definitely gonna be all right I will gladly take the first watch, and you guys can go ahead and get yourself some nice sleep while I make sure that nobody sneaks up behind us and gives us the old stabby-stabby."

Never had I strung so many words with so few punctuation marks as I did that night. Mara, Giezha, and Ulilee took turns getting me to set off on another endless conversation. I kept Isaac up late into the night, asking him to play song after song while I exuberantly danced around the camp. When Isaac finally managed to slip into his tent, I was mercifully beginning to feel the tail end of the potion.

The sounds of cricket's buzzing provided an invisible white noise that had me looking in every direction. Once the moons came up high in the sky and the only light came from the fire in the camp center, I couldn't help but feel nervous. The adrenaline-fueled pumping of my heart was replaced by a nervous tick.

"Calm down, Asher," I whispered to myself, looking around at the swath of hills and grasses.

We had made our camp on the top of a hill, giving us a good vantage point of the area around us. However, it was like looking out into a sea of blackness in the dead of night as the grasses waved in front of me with the gentle breeze rolling over the hillside.

I tried to keep myself busy by reading one of the textbooks that Giezha had given me every couple of minutes. They assured me that I could do some light reading during my watch, so long as I didn't forget to keep myself aware of my surroundings. However, I could not keep any information on the different runes representing the Gods in my head as I kept looking up at the slightest sound.

After re-reading the same paragraph without any luck for fifteen minutes, I gave up and pulled out my journal. My entry for today was sparse compared to the extended writings I had been trying to do each previous day. Besides narration of events, I'd been keeping notes about my ability. The situations I was using it in, how long I was able to use it, the after-effects, and their severity, all documented in my journal.

The more I used it, the less serious my recovery time became. I still couldn't use it more than once without suffering debilitating exhaustion. However, it wasn't knocking me out the entire next day.

And I still couldn't find a good origin for it, though, nor could I find any references to an ability like this from the library. There were potions, scrolls, and spells that made you stronger, but none that fit the description of my ability.

Additionally, I had been coming up with names for it as well. I really did hate calling it my 'ability' and couldn't help but to try and find an effective and 'cool' name for it..

"Let's see, Burster, Afterburner, Turbo Charge, Explosion..." I mumbled to myself, pouring over a series of scratched-out ideas.

Most of them were generic or ripped off from shows, comics, and anime I had seen before. I thought about going with "booster," but that sounded lame in my head. The phrase "crank up" made me laugh because of how stupid it sounded, and I was sure Marvel would sue me even in this world if I went with "flame on." Hitting a wall, I got out my astronomy notebook and decided to relax and watch the stars.

I had begun to recognize a few distinct constellations in the sky. One was a collection of stars in the rough approximation of a sword. Three stars in a triangle made the point, followed by four stars under the tip made the blade. Finally, a curved collection of six stars made up an uneven crossguard and hilt. This constellation was known as Ziapho the Divider. A blade used in the Cosmic Tearing by Oros the God-King, apparently.

According to legend, his sword tore a hole in the realm that set the Second Age of All into motion. From that tear, beasts, monsters, and creatures descended on Echo Veil from far-off realms. Some of them included dragons, hydras, giants, and the onwuntaku, a giant shadow with pearlescent eyes that feasts on the souls of its victims. Literally.

Stories like that sounded like pure fantasy to me, but I was living in a fantasy world now.

As I studied Ziapho's position in the sky, I noticed an extremely bright red object next to the tip of the constellation. It was bright red and white, standing out against the black, purple, and blue sky. It was also enormous, with two rings around the central white dot. Whatever this thing was, it was large enough to be visually distinct in a sea of stars and galaxies in the midnight sky.

I gasped in realization. Thinking back to my astronomy class from college, I recognized it. Amongst the collection of stars and planets in the sky, I observed the slow explosive death of a star—a supernova.

"Supernova," I muttered to myself. "That's got a ring to it."

As I wrote the idea down, I saw a list of the names of gods I had encountered so far. The list was about a dozen or so, with a particular God of the Lost at the top. I made a note to begin researching the history of the world and the pantheons of the gods. My "patron," so to speak, Gathos, would be my first order of business in my research. Those thoughts and plans for future study were quickly put to the side when I heard a noise.

Cshshshshsh.

The rustling of grass in the wind was constant, but this was different. It was too sudden and localized to be the wind. I dropped my notebook and grabbed my sword at my side, sheath in it and ready for whatever came. After a few moments, the grass rustled again, moving towards me. My muscles tensed as a small rabbit suddenly appeared out of the grass and into the firelight.

It's sniffed and hopped around silently by the fire. It gave me a cursory look before returning to the grass. I washed it as the rabbit hopped into the grass and bolted off in the same direction I had first seen it emerge from. As I sat there, sword firmly in my grasp, I couldn't shake this funny feeling. That rabbit had done more than just look at me.

It observed me.

It made a beeline straight for the fire and stopped to look at me. Any rabbit I had ever known, wild or domesticated, was scared of people it didn't know.

Sensing danger, I slowly crept towards the tents. As I did, I heard heavy footsteps off in the distance. We had either been followed or found. And whoever it was had waited until we went to sleep or were distracted. I first slunk into Ulilee's tent as she instructed before I went on watch. I moved as quietly as possible as I gently shook Ulilee awake.

"Wake up," I hissed, hearing the footsteps inch closer. "We've got company."

Ulilee's eyes snapped open, grabbing her knife and a multicolored stone. Her expression was stone cold as she crouched low, listening outside. When she heard the footsteps, she pointed toward Isaac's tent situated between her tent and mine.

"Wake him up," she said, barely audible even from this distance. "Keep him quiet, and I'll get the others."

She disappeared out of the tent in a flash, and I quickly made my way to his tent. Ducking out of the fabric of Uli's tent, I dashed to Isaac. Coming from behind the woods, I pulled back the red fabric of his tent. When I looked inside, there was a woman crouched over him as he snored.

When the light from the fire outside flooded the tent, her head snapped up towards me with her eyes widening. She wore all black with a mask over her face and hood covering all but her black reptilian eyes. Her sword was rose up, ready to stab Isaac in the throat as I launched myself forward into her.

Catching her by surprise, I knocked her and myself out into the open.

"Uli, they flanked us!" I shouted, rolling onto the ground with the would-be assassin.

As I shouted, the sound of swords clattering against each other rang through the air. Jumping to my feet, I saw Mara fighting a large man with a sword nearly as long as she was. The goliath had made its way right into the middle of our camp somehow. My attention was brought back to the assassin in front of me when I heard her hiss at me.

166

I had not realized it before, but the assassin was not human. The woman's hood got knocked off, revealing sharp, reptilian features. Looking down, I saw that she did not possess a pair of legs, but instead, her bottom half was serpentine with a snake's tail.

"Get the gems!" came the burly voice of the goliath as he fought off Mara while Giezha could be heard casting an assortment of spells.

The snake-woman hissed at me and lunged with her sword. Her movements were janky and slow compared to my training with Mara. I was still forced onto the defense with her lunge as I blocked her strike with my shield.

"Bastard!" she screamed, overemphasizing the 's' consonant.

Pulling my shield back, I slashed at her with my sword. She jumped back and coiled before lunging again. I pulled my sword back and jumped forward, thrusting with my blade, over and over. Our swords connected and bounced off each other. I felt the sword slice into my hair as it grazed just past my ear. My sword made a superficial cut into her shoulder.

Advancing, I jumped forward and slammed my shoulder into her trying to knock her back. She grunted as I tackled her, and her sword flew out of her hands. As I was about to go in for a finishing blow, the sound of sizzling air alerted me to an attack from behind.

"Duck!" I heard Ulilee shout as she tackled me to the ground.

A bright red beam of light shot through the air where my head was less than a moment before. The beam of light hit a tree, bursting it into flames. I looked at Ulilee in shock and nodded my head.

"Thanks."

She was already preoccupied with the snake woman, jumping back to her feet. I scrambled to mine, joining her against the snake woman who recoiled, pulling out a second, heavily curved shortsword. I could just make out a few black drips off the sword as an acrid smell pierced my nose.

"Poison," I warned Ulilee as the assassin waved her sword in front of her.

A droplet came for my face, which I blocked with my shield, while Ulilee rolled out of the way. The poison hissed as it burned against the metal and wood of the shield. The assassin swayed back and forth like a cobra dancing to a snake charmer's song. There was no telling how many more there were, and we could get surrounded at any moment. Ulilee had disappeared into the dark.

167

As I prepared to attack, I saw Giezha unleash a blast of fire at the Goliath while Mara dashed towards Isaac's tent. Resisting the urge to pull out my trump card, I had an idea.

Taking another step back from the advancing snake woman, I began to mutter incantations as I remembered the fireball I made with Kiersa. Tiny red runes danced across my arms as I pulled the energy from inside me into my hand. With an orange flash, a flame lit up in my hand. I coalesced the flame into the size of a baseball, curling my fingers around it.

The assassin stopped her advance, hesitating at the sight of my flame.

"A swordsman and a mage?" she hissed in confusion. She sneered and began to sway back and forth again. "You still can't hit me."

"Oh yeah?" I chided, "Try me!"

I lunged straight at her with the ball of fire in my hand. She deftly maneuvered around my attack. With her eyes focused on the fire, I threw my right hand forward, slicing upward into the air. She would have had her right arm cleaved off if she were an average human. However, she curled her body around the blade at the last second. She then wrapped her tail around my leg and arm.

"Perfect." I grinned.

Right as she was about to stab me in the gut with the sword, I clinched the fireball in my hand and grabbed her tail as hard as I could. My hand burned as she screamed in pain from the flames. Before she could try to escape, a knife plunged straight through her chest from the back. The snake woman grunted as her eyes rolled to the back of her skull and she dropped to the ground. Ulilee appeared from behind, pulling her knife out.

Frantically, we looked around the camp. A goliath's body had been pierced twice in the chest. Next to him was a wizard gnome who'd been frozen solid. His eyes had utterly glossed over. With no sign of any other bandits, we rushed to Isaac's tent.

By the time we made it back, he was already being tended to. Isaac looked unharmed but shaken. His eyes jumped over towards Ulilee and me, flinching. When Isaac realized it was us, he gave us a nervous smile and nodded his head.

"You all did a fine job cleaning up those bandits!" he congratulated us as his voice cracked. "The fine warrior Mara c-cut that goliath down while Ms. Giezha froze th-the uh, Gnomish wizard in place."

168

We brought everyone back outside to do a post-mortem on the attack. Giezha used the last of her mana, healing a cut on Mara's shoulder, while Ulilee and I looked around the campsite. From the looks of things, Mara's was the only injury any of us had incurred. Ulilee and I knelt beside everyone as we tried to recount what had happened.

"It had to be the rabbit," I sighed, coming down from the adrenaline. "It was most likely a familiar or summoned from the gnome they used to scout the area and distract me."

"The goliath was most likely a diversion, while the snake woman was the real threat," Mara said, rubbing her shoulder.

It made me sick to my stomach to think we had come so close to losing Isaac. It pissed me off. "If I was a moment slower..." I said through gritted teeth.

"No," Ulilee said, her trademark confidence evaporating, replaced with nervousness and fidgeting. "No, this is my fault. I should have been on the first watch. I'm always the one who goes on watch first. There's no reason for them to have gotten this close. We should have been able to see them or found some trace of them. I was scouting ahead, and I still didn't catch them."

Ulilee paced back and forth, muttering to herself. Her eyes rapidly moved back and forth as she talked to herself before heading off to her tent. Giezha and Mara exchanged nervous glances while Ulilee did this.

Mara tried to get up, but her shoulder started to spout blood.

"Shit!" Giezha hissed. "Sit still and let me finish. I'm low on mana right now, so it's not going to be as fast."

As Giezha healed Mara, she looked at me and nodded. I nodded and walked over to Ulilee's tent. She was walking around randomly, muttering to herself. It took her almost a full minute to notice me.

"Ahem," I coughed.

Uli's eyes bolted towards me. "Hey..."

"Hey to you too," I responded. "You alright?"

Uli ignored my question and got back to pacing. Walking back and forth, she asked me a question. "W-Were there any signs of others?" Ulilee asked me, her tone warbly. "Besides the rabbit, I mean."

I shook my head, entering the tent fully.

"No, there was no sign of anybody. The rabbit staring at me was the only

169

thing that tipped me off. If I hadn't told you, I don't know what would have happened."

Before I could react, Ulilee turned and dashed out of the back of the tent.

She ran to a forested section of the area. "I'll go scout for any others that might be waiting for us!"

"Wait!" I shouted, following her.

She was nearly out of the tent as I tried to grab her shoulder to stop her, but she shrugged me off and kept running. I shouted for her to slow down, but she just ducked in and out of trees, muttering to herself.

"Can't let this happen, not again, not again," she muttered, oblivious to my presence.

"Hey!" I shouted, grabbing her with both hands.

Reflexively, she pulled her knife back out and slashed at me. When I saw the knife slice in front of my face, I felt the most dreadful deja vu. As its brilliant white pearlescence flashed against the moonlight, I felt a painful sting in my chest. Tripping over a tree root on the ground, I hit the dirt. When I looked down, I thought I saw two bullet holes in my chest.

"Fuck!" I screamed as blood began to pool in my chest. "Annie, what the fuck!?"

I ripped off my armor and clothes, looking for a wound. As I scratched and clawed in my own skin, I realized I had imagined the wound. The blood I had seen magically vanished. Ulilee's strike was several inches short of contact. Ulilee's eyes went from murderous to horror when she realized it was me. She dropped the knife in terror. Stammering, she tried to form the words for an apology.

"Asher, I-I-I I'm so sorry!" Her hand trembled as she stepped closer to me.

For a moment, I panicked and stumbled backward, trying to get away from her. Her face was not hers. It was Annie's. But when I blinked again, it was Ulilee.

"Please, tell me I missed, please!" she whispered, panic-stricken and checking me for wounds

"I'm okay, I'm okay," I said to myself, gently pushing her off and putting my clothes back on. "I'm good. I'm good. No wounds, for sure for sure yeah, yeah..."

Ulilee reached a hand out to me but pulled back, biting her lip. She shook her head and wiped her face, snapping her serious expression back into place.

"Ulilee, I-it's all right," I said again, trying to calm her down. "Mistakes happen. W-we should get moving, I think."

I got up and dusted myself off. She stood there dumbfounded as I left and immediately started packing my tent up. As I did, Ulilee walked over to Mara and Giezha.

"Everybody, pack up," she said, taking a deep breath. "We are going to go through the night and get into town before morning. We are about five hours out, and sunrise should be in about six."

At her words, Mara and Giezha leapt into action and started to tear down their tents. I continued packing, but Isaac grabbed me by the side. His panicked expression pleaded for me to intervene. He did not want to walk another five hours. Seeing this, Ulilee placed a hand on his shoulder.

"Mr. Geney, we are going to get you home and get you in a nice and cozy bed sooner than you can shake the fangs off a viper." Ulilee turned her attention to me, pausing at first.

"Asher, I need you to give everyone a small dose of that stamina potion and put some pep in our step."

I gave her a pensive nod and gave everybody a sip for the long march ahead. Isaac still had his reservations, but he decided it was best to get moving as quickly as possible after the ambush on our camp. Once we had everything torn down, we were ready to embark on our journey.

The first few hours were totally silent as our legs begrudgingly trod along, taking us up the path. Glancing off in every direction, we kept our weapons at the ready. The potion's jolt of energy, mixed with the terror of the sneak attack, had us all on edge. We had taken so little that it didn't make us giddy, but it was enough to keep us wired.

Isaac, ever the gentleman, did his best to not complain about the long march. Having your life threatened by roving bandits will make you happier to get moving, I suppose.

The entire time we walked, Ulilee and I both caught the other looking before quickly turning away. The awkwardness was thick enough to cut with a knife. As terrified as I was by everything, I knew that we needed to come to some resolution.

Eventually, Isaac had too much walking, and we needed to rest. While

171

Giezha watched over Isaac and Mara refilled her waterskin, I found Ulilee sitting by a tree.

"Yo," I said while nudging her. "Are we good?"

She didn't say anything and just watched the others, drumming her fingers on her lap. Finally, she shook her head and spoke. "Are we? I nearly took your life with my carelessness."

I sat down next to her gingerly. I was still spooked by the whole incident, but for totally different reasons. "You also saved my life back there, Ulilee," I pointed out. "If it weren't for you, that snake woman would have gutted me like a fish, and I'd be the one dead on the ground. At best, I'd be writhing in agony as I died a slow death. So, thank you."

"Thanks for that visual," Ulilee joked while giving me a funny face. "I see your point, though, and you're welcome."

I turned to go and give everybody the jitter-juice when Ulilee stopped me again.

"And Asher, I've already told you this."

I cocked my head and looked at her, confused.

"My friends call me Uli."

Friends. That sounded nice.

Even if they nearly cut your head off.

"Oh Gods, yes!" Mara agreed, jumping up and down at the idea. "I could use a nice hot soak and some fancy soaps on me."

Chapter 16

Xaliasday Morning, 28th of Dhivmirn, Year 678, 4th Age

After a paranoid sprint through the night, we made it to the city gates of Zizar. Isaac's rotund frame made it difficult for him to keep pace with us the entire time. Still, he was nonetheless delighted to have returned home. Roosters making their morning songs to the sunrise could be heard off in the distance.

We trudged through the shantytown of Copper Road with heavy eyelids and heavier footsteps. The arduous march and lack of sleep left Giezha extremely irritable. She scowled at every passerby who got too close. One of them, a person with a cat's tails and ears, made a move on Isaac's sack of gems. Before he knew what had happened, Uli was behind him, poking a dagger in his back.

173

"Ghk!"

"Would you believe me if I told you I was the best option for you?" Uli whispered in his trembling ears as she stifled a yawn. "Our mage would love nothing more than to cast a fireball down your throat and call it a day. Our sword maiden looks like she could turn you into a pincushion at any moment."

Giezha and Mara both made threatening gestures at the scared cat person. With a sadistic smile, Uli turned him to me. Struggling to keep my eyes open, I opened them wide as I stared him down. "And him? Oh, you don't want to know. Trust me. He's a sick, sadistic man."

The failed thief ran off with his tail quite literally between his legs. We all gave a round of applause for Uli's performance, laughing as much as our tired souls would allow. Truth be told, we were all so tired, hungry, and sleep-deprived that she was pretty accurate in her descriptions of the team. Even Isaac looked ready to bash the man's brains in.

After waving off the guardsman at the front gate, Isaac gave us a tour through the densely populated city. At least, he tried to until he fell asleep in the street, forcing us to heave him up and bring him to a nearby tavern.

The Hag's Mug Inn was a tiny old hole in the wall stuck between a blacksmith and a tailor's building. Inside was a circular room with walls, floors, and even furniture carved out of cobblestone. The main feature was a circle of stone that sank into the floor with built-in seating and a small fireplace. The place was empty besides the barkeeper, an orc with long black hair who barely looked up to acknowledge us.

"Any rooms vacant?" I asked while leaning a snoring Isaac in the corner next to the bar.

"Mmhmm," the orc grunted, polishing off a drink of his own. "Pay by the head, not by the room. Be seven silvers for the lot of ye."

The orc ignored the coins Uli put on the bar as he poured himself another drink. He gestured to a room up a flight of spiral stairs in the corner of the room next to a snoring dwarvish woman in a wizard's hat. As I dragged Isaac upstairs and flopped him onto the bed, his snores somehow managed to stay just as rhythmic as his loot playing. We all collapsed in exhaustion, ready to pass out at any moment.

"Who's taking the first watch?" Mara asked while stretching.

"Not me," Giezha grumbled, laying down and placing her hat over her

174

face. "Fuck that."

As Uli struggled to stay awake, she raised her hand. "I volunteer. I got this."

Mara waved her hand while flopping her head back and forth. "Noooo, you go to bed, Uli. You've had a long day."

"Nope. I'm in charge. I'll do it."

They argued back and forth as they unconvincingly tried to prove they were wide awake and ready for action. My sleepy brain managed to come up with a brilliant idea. While they argued, I got up and made my way out of the room.

Walking back to the day-drinking barkeep, I slumped into the chair in front of him. He didn't bother to look up as he worked on a breakfast stacked high with bacon and pancakes. The smell of coffee with cream liqueur wafted into my nostrils.

"Need su'mn?" he asked uninterestedly.

Looking at the collection of swords and trophies, I figured him for a retired adventurer. This bar was more than likely a place for him to hang out with friends rather than make money. Hence the drinking at the crack of dawn.

Before I started, I gave myself a quick pinch to keep awake. "Look, Mr. Barkeeper, I'll be honest with you."

He continued to enjoy the juicy bacon that still sizzled on his plate.

"I just finished walking for the better part of the last dozen or so hours. My only respite was a short break at midnight. And that was promptly ruined by ambush on my camp." He stopped and looked up at me, slowly chewing his bacon. "I have been up for more than a day, and I am exhausted like never before in my life."

I pulled out the ruby that Isaac had given me a few days ago. He looked at it curiously. This man probably had bottles of wine more expensive than this ruby, but it was all I had to entice him.

"This was given to me as a bonus for this quest. I want to pay you to ensure that nobody comes in that room while we sleep for the better part of today and possibly tomorrow. I'm going to lock the door, I'm going to fall asleep, and nobody is going to stay up to watch out for whatever is out there." I punctuated my story by pointing out the door.

The orc sighed as he stopped eating and looked at me. He studied me

175

long and intensely before picking up the ruby in my palm. He looked it over a few times with his blank expression and nodded his head.

"Yup," he said with a belch. "Been there before, young blood. I'll make sure nobody messes with you lot."

Getting up from his seat, he pulled a silver pole down from the wall and gestured for me to follow him. Walking to the front door of our room, he smacked one end of the pole on the ground, which ignited it in flames. Placing it on the barricade latches, a wall of flame appeared in front of the door, which quickly turned invisible. Despite its invisibility, flames could still be felt up close. Handing me an end cap from the latch, he demonstrated opening and closing the door.

"No cap, no entry," he said.

I nodded and opened the door, ready to collapse. A lovely side effect of the fire barricade the barkeeper provided was how perfectly warm the room became. My eyelids became heavier than mountains as the warm air beckoned me to join the others in their sleep. Astoundingly, four more beds had appeared in the room.

I quietly picked each of the girls up, laying them down in their own beds. None of the others so much as flinched. Even Giezha, who was heavier than the others combined, made no noise as I struggled to put her to bed. With everybody nice and cozy, I gratefully got into my bed. Once the blankets were over me, I laid my head to rest. I was asleep before my head hit the pillow.

* * *

I was woken up by the exuberant voice of Mara as she rattled the frame of my bed. Coming back to the land of consciousness, I saw all of them gearing up for the day. Looking under my blankets, I realized that I was still in my gear. My nostrils were treated to the stink of the past few days' worth of grime.

"C'mon, Asher!" Mara urged me, bounding with energy. "Isaac said he'd take us on a tour of the city before he takes out to dinner!"

A free meal was always welcome, in this world or the last. I could hear Isaac laughing at his own jokes on the other side of the door, no doubt regaling his adventures to the barkeep. Grabbing the gear that I had hastily

176

thrown on the floor last night, I was ready to go once I jumped out of bed.

"I don't suppose there's a bathhouse we could visit?" I asked, marching out of the room.

"Oh Gods, yes!" Mara agreed, jumping up and down at the idea. "I could use a nice hot soak and some fancy soaps on me."

"Yeah," Giezha grumbled, trying to brush her hair into submission. "We all smell awful."

Agreeing to take a siesta after getting the job done, we met Isaac out room by the bar, chatting up the silent orc.

"Yes, yes. It was quite the spectacle to see the Red Breakers trounce the villainous bandits with such skill, precision, and brutality." Isaac laughed while the orc ignored him. Isaac turned and noticed us. "Ah! The heroes of the story! Time to give you a tour of the town, yes?"

Once we were outside, I was greeted by the sun now cresting to the west as evening struck. We'd been asleep the entire day, it seemed. I lamented that my sleep schedule would be in tatters because of this. Mara joked that she'd help me get my schedule back on track with a giggle and a lascivious look.

Picking up right where he had left off the previous morning, Isaac gave us an intimate look at the city of Zizar.

"Yes, Zizar was once one of the mightiest cities in the continent!" Isaac boomed. "This was the former capital of the long-since-dead Dwarven Empire from the Third Age. Today Zizar remains a cosmopolitan rest stop between the capital city Clearmire to the southeast and Kharbian Plains to the northwest."

Isaac showed us each of the main boroughs of the city. He explained their significance, starting in West Town and going clockwise through Ghostsprawl, Three Courts, and Rookwood. I'd be lying if I said I paid any attention.

During his tour, Isaac pointed out his favorite places to visit. Places like stores, restaurants, venues of music, a café run by an old lady rumored to be an ancient dragon in disguise, and of course, his store.

"Why don't we go in for a spell and get payments taken care of?" Isaac asked, his eyes hungrily looking at the front of his store.

We all followed him into an ostentatiously decorated store. The bottom floor was used as his place of business, while he rented out several floors above to tenants. The bottom floor was decorated with ornate tapestries that depicted a slimmer version of Isaac and his adventures.

Apparently, he really had been all over the continent while looking for magic gemstones. One showed him climbing a mountain with a yeti at the top, another him dueling a troll on a bridge.

Several displays of different gems and inscriptions explained their magical properties. Most were magical conduits that could increase the effectiveness or strength of magical spells. A few of them could produce spells of their own, and some were elemental gems—stones imbued with the power of fire, water, earth, wind, and light.

"I had a Stone of Death once," Isaac mentioned not-to-humbly. "But a damn thief stole it when I had a buyer all lined up for it. Necrotic energy is quite nasty when applied offensively, and he was willing to pay top coinage!"

Isaac poured his collection of gems onto the table and quickly sorted them, placing them into their appropriate section. With a wave of his hand, several magical locks wrapped their spectral energy around the different displays.

"Now," Isaac said, pulling out several pouches jingling with gold. "I believe you are each owned one hundred gold, yes?"

"That's what the contract says," Uli said, her eyes hungrily staring at the money.

"Excellent. Feel free to grab a gemstone from this case. You could use it as the centerpiece for building an item of some sort."

"Right," Giezha quietly scoffed. "Like we could ever afford that."

Each of us picked out a small gemstone from a collection of loose stones. Giezha picked a rectangular emerald and attached it to her staff. It glowed bright green, making her eyes twinkle and nostrils flare with excitement. Mara went with a circle of amethyst.

"It was my mother's birthstone," she said, smiling at the purple and pink stone. "I'll have a necklace made of it."

Uli went with a pearl, which Isaac then insisted she take a second of.

"I wonder if I could turn these into Luck Pearl earrings?" she asked while pretending to have them on the tips of her earlobes.

Having already been given a gem by Isaac, I decided to grab a moonstone and give it to Kiersa when I got back. I had heard somewhere that a holiday for followers of Ihena and a few other deities was coming up soon.

"Awwww!" Uli and Mara teased me as I held the white and purple stone. It was incredibly soft to the touch but somehow firm at the same time.

"They're known for bringing good dreams and having healing properties," Giezha mentioned, her eyes still locked firmly on her staff.

"Follower of the Goddess of Dreams getting a moonstone? She's gonna love it." Mara said with a hint of jealousy.

Once we wrapped up the payment for the quest, Isaac insisted that he finish up the tour for us. Not wanting to be rude, we obliged.

"You'll notice how this street is many times wider than any of the others you've seen it so far," he pointed out as we walked along a road nearly the width of a football field. "This road is where every church must be located in accordance with the Broken Shrine Treaty. This was done to prevent more religious Civil Wars like the one during the Third Age. Every official place of worship in the city must be located here now."

Dozens of buildings representing the worship of different deities smashed against each other as hundreds streamed in and out of the buildings. One highlight was an exquisitely crafted marble church worshiping Xorcha, God of Storms, that touched the sky. It was flanked by tiny shrines to the gods of wheat and leatherworkers capable of holding a dozen people or less.

Ulilee and Mara asked for a break to pay respects to their gods. We first went to Mara's place of worship, a thin building adorned with silver inlaid silk on all of the walls. In the center of the building was a large fireplace where people deposited weapons into the flames. Mara pulled out a set of arrows and shot them into the fire from close range with her bow.

"May Evlana's wisdom guide me and let her strength flow through me," she whispered to herself in prayer. I placed a dagger in the flames as everybody left before catching back up. It felt right to participate in my friends' culture and respect their religion.

Mara was the last to leave as she spoke with one of the clerics near the fire. She ran back excitedly, handing me a small topaz ring.

"I saw you donated to the church, and the cleric wanted to thank you. It's a gift of the Goddess' protection."

I put the ring on my right-hand ring finger and was surprised it was such a perfect fit. As I wore it, I felt an odd sensation. It almost felt like I was being wrapped with a warm blanket.

After that, we found ourselves in the house of worship for the Goblin God of Fortune, Dusyr. This church was on the third floor of a large wooden building hosting gods primarily worshiped by goblins, orcs, dragonborn, and cat-folk. This church was less a solemn place of worship and more akin to a rambunctious family gathering. Goblins, hobgoblins, and halfkin drank and laughed as some tossed coins into a black stone urn, held by a statue of Dusyr.

"Even though goblins are considered greedy and treacherous, Dusyr always preached fairness and helping the most beaten-down tribe member," Uli explained.

Uli chatted up a few halfkin, standing away from the full-blooded goblins and hobgoblins. It was also apparent that Uli didn't look the same as the others. The goblins here had small, beaded eyes that were either black or red entirely. And the half-goblins looked closer to goblins than humans. Ulilee's cat's eyes made her stand out from everybody else. As did her fantastic body.

"Keep it in your pants, Asher," Mara hissed, elbowing me in the shoulder, pointing out some of the goblins in the room.

None of them looked happy as they picked over the fish and chicken livers. In fact, all of the goblins and hobgoblins eyed the half-goblins with contempt and distrust before noticing us. Once they saw the humans and Goliath in the room, they shifted their scornful looks towards us. With a shrug, I also decided to pay some respect to Dusyr.

I saw a couple of goblins place a few copper pieces into the urn, which made the top glow orange. Walking up to the statue, I realized it was lower than I was. They had made Dusyr taller than the average goblin, but he only stood about five feet or so at the eyes. I saw the urn was somehow smelting the copper to liquid.

When I checked my coin sack, I didn't have any coppers left, and I only had silver and gold coins.

"Welp," I muttered.

Trying not to make too much of a splash, I threw a few silvers in the urn. Roughly what I would have gotten for the dagger I placed in the fire.

When the silvers clattered in the urn, the glow it generated was bright

180

white. The air smelled of pine trees as all eyes turned towards me. The bright white glow of the urn began to fade as cinnamon replaced the pine smell. Everyone started jabbering in Goblin, while Uli ran over to my side, her eyes wide and jaw slackened.

"What'd you do?" She whispered as others got closer to us.

"Put a few silvers in the urn," I shrugged.

"Why?" she asked urgently.

"Respect, I guess. I don't know."

As we spoke, the urn had changed color to a dull gray. The sweet smell of cinnamon hung in the air as all eyes remained on us. The goblins spoke in hurried tones.

An ancient-looking goblin with a huge, crooked nose in light blue and pink robes approached Uli and me. Wearing a hat that appeared to cover his eyes, he looked at Uli and spoke to her in Goblin. Uli looked at him with consternation as she responded, also in Goblin.

Whatever she said gave the shaman pause for thought. He tapped his finger against his cheek as he thought for a moment before turning to me.

His eyes began glowing red as he looked at me, and I suddenly felt naked. It was as if he could see right through me as he looked at my chest. His eyes stopped glowing, and he nodded his head, speaking to Uli again.

After a few moments, he addressed the crowd in their native tongue. A few half goblins didn't understand, but those who did whispered something in their ears. They all looked at me in shock when they heard whatever was whispered. The goblin priest threw his hands up and shouted a harsh command. All of the goblins quickly looked away from me and returned to their business.

"Let's go," Uli whispered, grabbing me and the others as we left.

Once we were back onto the main street, I asked what that was all about. Mara, Giezha, and Isaac were all as confused as I was. I noticed a few goblins had followed us out into the street. They stayed several yards away from us, but no doubt watching. Uli was clearly trying to stay calm.

"Uli, what the heck was all that?" Mara asked in confusion.

Giezha kept an eye on the goblins. "Yeah..."

"Look," Uli said, pacing back and forth. "It's complicated. I can't get into everything, but, Asher, how many coins did you put in the urn?"

I tried to think about how many I put in.

181

"Two," I said confidently.

My words made Uli's face drop and her shoulders slump.

"You are such a dummy," she moaned, putting her hands to her face. "Two!"

"Yeah...?" I said, unsure and afraid of the consequences.

"Congrats!" a half-goblin snickered to Uli as they passed by.

We all looked at Uli, who was blushing bright red.

"Silver is sacred metal for goblins. Gold may be more valuable, but silver is sacred. Dusyr's Tome of Wits was written in silver ink, and his dagger was forged from a silver star."

"So, it's bad that I put silver in?"

A few more goblins walked by and gave us curious glances. Uli moved us away from the crowd, trying to avoid looking at me as her face grew pinker and pinker. Fidgeting with her hands, she continued.

"In goblin culture, you offer silver to a chieftain or a shaman if you want to yourself. Two if you want to protect someone. They will accept it even if it comes from someone who don't follow Dusyr." She looked at me, pursing her lips. "To give silver in the presence of a shaman is to offer your life to protect someone. At least, if they're a goblin."

"Oh," we all said simultaneously. After a second, the realization hit. "Oh..."

All eyes were on me as I realized the connotation. The look on Uli's face made it all the clearer.

This was some serious stuff.

"So, I just made a declaration to protect you in front of a bunch of goblins and a shaman."

"Yeah," Uli said, scowling at goblin onlookers. "Basically, letting everyone know you'd give your life to save me. Not exactly something people who are just buddies would do."

"So, what happens now?" Mara asked.

"What happens next is we celebrate!" Isaac shouted exuberantly, bringing us all in. "I haven't gotten to celebrate a Goblin Oath of Protection since my visit to the Republic of Galen! We must feast! We must sing! We must celebrate! Follow me!"

"Wait!" Uli shouted, wiggling free from the group hug. "Oaths have different meanings, depending on who gives them." Uli looked around

182

and brought us close together as she whispered. "To do that, Isaac, would be as good as announcing marriage between Asher and me. The shaman understood that Asher didn't understand all that. I explained that we were part of an adventuring party together. A team."

"What'd he say to that?" I asked.

"He wanted to observe your soul," Uli explained. "When he peered into you, he told me he… respected your heart and would accept the unusual oath. He warned me that not every goblin may see it that way. If we go out and celebrate too much, it will confirm their suspicions."

Giezha and Mara asked the same question simultaneously. "Which is...?"

By this point, Uli was beet red. "That it was a secret marriage proposal."

"Ah," I said, feeling like I just had a brick thrown onto my chest.

Uli and I looked at each other awkwardly as Giezha and Mara burst out laughing uncontrollably. Isaac was disappointed about the lack of celebration. Still, he quickly turned his attention to an elf woman with a large diamond necklace.

As the other two roared with laughter, I decided to break the awkward silence between Uli and me.

"You know what I need? A bath. A really good soak. Right, Mara? Didn't we say we wanted to hit up a bathhouse? I'd like to do that right now. Yep."

Looking back, Isaac had become too preoccupied with procuring the woman's diamond necklace.

"Please, madam, I assure you that you would receive top coin for such a precious gemstone. Perhaps we could have a chance to discuss things… alone? Maybe over dinner and a glass of brandy?"

Isaac abandoned us as the woman took his arm, and they walked off discussing business. Seeing the opportunity, I made a beeline for anywhere but where I was. Uli quickly caught up with me as we made our escape. Giezha and Mara were close behind, laughing to themselves.

Chapter 17

Xaliasday Night, 28th of Dhivmirn, Year 678, 4th Age

As we walked, Uli led the way. Taking us back towards the northern part of the city, we wound up near Snow Gate's entrance. Presumably named by the view of the massive snowcapped mountains that the gate pointed directly towards when opened.

After zigging and zagging through the maze of streets and alleyways, she walked to a staircase that led underground. Walking down the stairs took us to a black wooden door with an eyehole.

Uli knocked twice and a set of yellow eyes appeared at the slot. The gentle sound of a harp being played could be heard. My nose was also filled with an intoxicating mix of flowers and other aromas.

"Need something?" asked an accented, feminine voice.

"Rest and relaxation," Uli responded.

The eyes disappeared as the slat shut. The sound of doors unlocking and wood creaking could be heard before the door opened. A large half-orc woman dressed in pink and white robes held the door open for us. She gestured for us to enter, and we made our way inside.

As we walked down a short hallway, the beautiful music from the harp wrapped itself around me. The smells emanating from the end of the hall put me in a trance as I began to feel warm and comfortable. At the end of the hall was a small room made of dark brown wood with a single desk in the middle. A blonde half-orc-half-elf with bright pink eyes sat behind the desk, scribbling onto a ledger.

"Welcome to my place of business," the man said, looking over a pair of halfmoon glasses. "How may I be of service to you?"

"Baths," Giezha said desperately. "And food."

My stomach growled in the realization that I had not eaten in quite a while. Despite promising us a delicious meal, Isaac had forgotten all about us. He took the elf with the diamond out to dinner instead. Mara's stomach growled in unison with mine as she nodded vigorously.

"And will it be just the four of you?" he asked, inspecting each of us.

"The four of us, Sir Willowden," Uli said. "It was originally for five, under Isaac Geney, but he became... preoccupied."

The man looked Uli up and down before checking his ledger. Uli's expression was confident, calm, and impossible to read. Pointing his finger at an entry near the bottom of the page, he checked again and studied us. After a few moments of pondering, he pulled out a second ledger wrapped in blue leather.

"Geney, Geney, Geney... Ah! Here it is." He snapped his fingers to summon the woman, nodding his head. "Yes, this all seems to be in order. He has paid ahead for this, so you are free to go ahead. Please follow Mrs. Ashhearth. She will take you to the bathing area. You are free to choose whichever bath is open. Dinner will be served after you finish up. Will you be staying here for the night?"

This place was like an all-inclusive hotel.

"Yes!" Mara whispered excitedly.

"Was that part of the reservations?" Uli asked, trying to keep the excitement in her voice to a minimum.

"No," he said, looking back at the ledger. "If you would like, we can set you up in a suite for seventy gold. Otherwise, it'd be thirty gold per room."

"No!" Mara cried while Uli made a noise like she got punched in the gut.

"Um," Uli said, trying to remain casual. "I think that we'll pass on the overnight accommodation. We'll just go get cleaned up. Thank you, though."

The elf smiled and nodded.

"That is fine; please be sure to drop your weapons and effects off before entering."

A pair of human butlers took us to a storage area, where we placed our equipment into an empty green chest before giving us a key wrapped around a silver string.

"The only clothes permitted are our robes, sir," the man said, wrinkling his nose.

"Ah, right," I said, embarrassed as I'd nearly walked in still wearing my regular clothes.

The robes were made of the softest cotton I'd ever encountered. It felt like I was wearing a baby blue cloud as I walked back to the entrance. The girls were all wearing robes of different pastel colors flanked by Mrs. Ashhearth and the other butler.

The elf/orc at the desk gestured for us to follow Mrs. Ashhearth, who led us through the other door. Walking down a hallway, the sound of the harp grew louder as we passed other patrons who chatted to one another. The stones underneath our feet became warm as the humidity increased.

Most rooms appeared large enough for only one or two people, while a few others were large communal baths with a dozen people. Some had closed doors, while others simply had curtains. All types of people were relaxing in pools of steaming water, with glass bottles all around them in the rooms with open doors.

Ornate marble statues flanked each of the doors, depicting different animals. The ethereal sound of the harp emanated from every direction as we went down the hall. It may have been piped in from above or magically placed there.

"Feel free to choose whichever bath you please, but clean yourself in the cleansing pool first," Mrs. Ashhearth instructed in a soft voice before leaving.

I turned and made my way towards a single-person room flanked by tiger statues. I told the girls I would meet them for dinner. They waved as they made their way towards another room down the hall. My muscles ached for a chance to relax and have a moment alone.

Closing the curtain behind me, I opted to close the sliding wooden door for some privacy. I stretched and exhaled, ready for a nice warm bath. The room was divided into two pools. One was a large rectangular pool with steam that lifted into the air. To the large pool's right, a smaller pool of deep blue water was swirling counterclockwise. The sign read 'cleansing pool' in half a dozen different languages, of which I could only read one.

"Man," I muttered to myself as I undressed. "I need to learn some of these languages."

My muscles sighed in relief as I stepped into the bath and soaked in the water. Beside the pool was a small box with several bars in it.

I relaxed, feeling the gentle current. I picked out a bar of soap that smelled like mint and cedarwood as I began to clean myself. After thoroughly cleaning and exfoliating, I picked out a golden oil bottle and soaked it into my hair, giving myself a pleasant aroma of honey and cinnamon.

Once I had cleaned myself thoroughly and enjoyed the warm water. I decided to try out the steaming bath to my left.

The water was warm like a perfectly heated hot tub. I waded in further until I found a spot where the water went up to my neck when I sat down. This was one of the most luxurious moments of my life, past or otherwise. The hot water, luxurious smells, and gentle strings of the harp made me drift to sleep.

"Ah, that's the stuff," I said to myself.

I closed my eyes and relaxed. My mind went blank as I drifted away into that weird space where you're awake and asleep at the same time. For the first time in a while, I didn't have to do anything. I was able to just enjoy myself alone.

I sat there for about a half-hour in total silence, enjoying the hot water that bubbled underneath. As I was about to fall asleep, I heard the noise of wet footsteps. Shaken awake, I saw Uli wrapped in a towel, picking up one of the decanters.

"Uli!" I shouted in surprise, seeing the door was still closed. "What are you doing here?"

Uli smiled and poured the oil into the water. As the purple liquid hit the water, it frothed and bubbled, letting out an aroma of lavender. Taking her towel off once in the water, she sat at the basin, her body covered in the bubbles.

"Just taking care of business," she teased, letting out a rich sigh as she stretched her arms.

"What's that supposed to mean?" I asked, sensing danger.

"Don't worry, stud. Nothing like that tonight," she said with a wink. "No, unfortunately, I need to talk to you about some actual business."

Her expression changed to a deceptively calm smile. I could tell that she was holding something back as she stared at me. I felt the urge to inch away from her but figured I should stand my ground. Any weakness I showed would just be exploited.

"I take it that it's a private kind of business," I said, gesturing to the locked entrance. "The kind where you sneak in to have a private conversation."

"You could say that," she said coyly. She looked at me for a moment, her expression telling me nothing. "Who are you, really?"

Damn. I knew it would be something like this. Uli wanted answers, and I didn't have any. One of her ears flickered as her golden eyes pierced through me.

"Ah, fuck," I muttered to myself.

"I've been talking to some contacts about you, and it's like you dropped out of the sky. Nobody's heard about you. There were no rumors about you before you showed up in Naled. It's like you didn't exist until a few months ago."

I chewed my lip as I thought of what to say. I did not have Giezha around to cast a Circle of Truth on me to prove anything, and even if I could, I wasn't sure I wanted to. Uli wasn't the type I wanted to know too much about me. As I looked at Uli's expectant face, I realized she had a point. I had only been in this world for a month or so.

Uli frowned as she read my expression. I half expected her to make a knife appear out of thin air, but she stayed perfectly still. It was bad enough I had already told one person where I was from. I couldn't risk telling anyone else. Not right now.

"I'm... a drifter," I said, finally. "I'm not going to sit here and explain it, but I lost everything a while ago. My home, my friends, family..." I stopped myself and exhaled. It was still hard coming to grips with my new reality. "Everyone and everything I ever knew is gone."

She didn't react whatsoever to what I said. She just sat there and stared at me. I felt that this was similar to what she'd expected to hear.

"What did Giezha tell you?" I asked.

Uli kept her poker face. "Not enough." Uli shook her head and poured water on herself. "She didn't tell me anything you haven't already said. She said that you're not from here and that all of this is new. Every time I asked her, she told me to drop it. Mara was tight lipped as well."

Uli scowled at me. "And that's not good! How do I know you're not going to stab us in the back? How do I know you're not going to hurt them?"

I still stood up and pointed at her, frustration boiling over.

"I could've left in the middle of that ambush, you know! I didn't have

188

to tell you it was alright when you nearly cut me in half! You want to talk about trust, but what have you done to earn mine?"

That perked her ears up.

"Last I checked, you're the one who stole from me within thirty seconds of meeting me. Last I checked, I didn't hit you with some crazy-ass knife illusion, making me see fucking ghosts!"

Before realizing it, I was right in front of Uli, towering over her. Despite the awkward feeling, I stood my ground and kept eye contact—a difficult feat considering how good she looked covered in soap.

"You're right. I'm sorry, Asher," Uli said softly as she looked me in the eyes. "I really like you, honestly. But I have to stay on guard. I need to protect Gi and Mara. And you being here makes it…."

"I make it what?" I asked impatiently.

"Complicated. Alright?" Uli shouted as she stood up. "You're a fucking paradox! You've hardly known any of us long, and yet you're throwing yourself into the line of fire for us! Every chance you get, you go out of your way. It's suspicious! I don't know what to do with you!"

I did a double-take, trying to not watch the soap run down her body. "What the fuck does that even mean?"

This time it was Uli who stood up.

"It means you must want something in return. It means there's an ulterior motive. Because there always is."

"Not with me."

"I can't know that. I can't just look into your soul."

I arched my eyebrow at her. "Well, the shaman at the temple did."

Uli's cheeks burned bright, and her ears flopped down. She looked away, silently contemplating as we stood next to each other. I sat down cattycorner to her at the edge of the bath. There was strange energy in the space between Uli and me. Slowly building up.

After several minutes, her lips formed a small smile. "Well, I guess you really just might be that good, huh?"

I scratched the back of my head and blushed. "Wouldn't say that, but what you see is what you get, Uli."

Uli chuckled and nodded her head. "This goes against everything I learned. But I trust Gi and Mara's judgment."

"They're good people."

Ulilee smiled and looked away. "They are..." She shook her head again and looked at me with a slight grimace. "Look, I'm sorry about earlier. About all this. It's just hard to trust people, and I...I don't want them to get hurt. I don't want to get hurt."

"I get that," I admitted. "I know what it's like to get hurt by somebody. Somebody you thought you could trust."

Uli looked at the scarred remains of where I'd been shot.

"Is that why you shouted the name 'Annie' the other day? When I..." She couldn't finish her sentence as shame washed over her.

I thought back to when Uli's knife flashed against my face, and in a split second, I saw Annie instead of Uli. Unable to speak, I gave a noncommittal shrug. Uli decided not to dwell on the topic.

"I'll tell you the other reason I'm here. I already told the girls about most of it."

"Does it have something to do with Mhurren and Mick?" I asked.

"Yes," she said, massaging a shoulder. "It turns out that they were heading south for this job they were assigned, near the border with Zala— the same area I was scouting on my solo mission."

"Why? Think you were sent to scout out their job?" I presumed.

"Probably. Dawnthorn was real hush-hush about it. Only thing was, I didn't do much while I was south. Outside of some spirits and a few bandit camps, there's nothing out there. I spent the better part of three weeks milling around in the middle of nowhere. Except for one thing..." She looked out pensively. "On my last night in a mountainside farming village called Shadow's Pass, I thought I saw something. Something... weird. Undead, maybe."

"That's not good," I said, thinking about my run-in with George.

"No, it's not. Necromancy is rare in this region. You hear rumors about it, but there are few actual occurrences. It is almost unheard of."

"But in other places, it's not?" I asked uncertainly.

Uli nodded her head again, the gears in her head turning as she spoke. "Nulgat employed them during the Sun's War a hundred years ago. Since then, they've stayed there, far from Narag and the southern regions. But in Zala, necromancy is punishable by death."

I tried to keep up with where this was going. "What was the undead thing you saw?"

190

"I'm not even sure I saw it now. But I think it was a skeleton. One night in the forest, I saw it with a spear stuck in his rib cage as it shambled right past me. I was afraid it would attack me, so I stayed out of sight. When I went back to follow it, I couldn't find any trace of it. Dawnthorn told me I was seeing things when I reported it. I thought I was going crazy, but then you told me what you saw the other day."

"Yeah," I shuddered at the memory of his arm wrapped around my leg. "But then he showed up just fine less than a minute later."

Uli nodded her head, her brows furrowed in frustration.

"Something is going on. Something Dawnthorn and the others aren't telling anybody."

My mind hatched an idea. "You said those two guys we saw in Iron Court and The Docks were following you?"

"Yeah," Uli said, still processing everything. "I noticed them a couple days into my travel. Everywhere I went, they just showed up, clearly looking for somebody."

"It could have something to do with Mhurren and Mick going missing," I proposed. "Could have been them in disguise for this secret mission."

She shook her head. "I thought that too at first. But they're terrible at stealth missions. Whole guild knows it. It'd be hard for them to disguise themselves too. They were too dumb to do it on their own, and their affinity for magic is zip according to records."

I scratched my head, trying to keep all the new information straight. There were a lot of moving parts to this.

"So, we know you were sent there, we know Mhurren and Mick were sent there... and so were your stalkers..." I said, scratching my chin. "I feel like this stuff must be connected. We just don't know how, or in what way."

"Pretty much. I thought that you might be part of it, honestly." Uli laughed. "But I'm getting the sense that that's not the case."

I gave her a sarcastic bow. "Glad you could admit that." But I noticed something as I looked at her. "You know... we've been here a while. And now the bubbles are all gone."

She looked down through the crystal clear water. Her toned, trim body in all its glory, was a sight to behold. And so was the erection I got seeing her.

Totally undisturbed by this, Uli just smiled at me flirtatiously, wading closer. "That's fine. I don't mind the attention." She looked down at me, and her smile widened, biting her lip. "And I don't mind what I get to see either."

Uli placed one of her hands on my chest and gave me a sultry look. My face moved closer to hers, and I placed an arm on her waist. Touching the small of her back, I pulled her in.

"You're a dangerous man, Asher," she whispered into my ears. "Dangerous in all the right ways."

With my other hand, I grasped her butt and pulled her chest to mine. I felt her breasts rub against me and could feel her heartbeat betray her apparently relaxed demeanor. "Glad you approve."

She smelled like lavender and sex.

I kissed her, slowly and deliberately. The sensation of her fangs pressing against my lips was new and exciting. Uli let out a small moan as we kissed.

Uli sat on my lap, placing my erection precipitously between her buttocks. Grinding on me, Uli's movements became faster and more aggressive. We continued to make out as the hot water and oils swirled around us. My head was spinning as Uli leaned into me. But just as we headed to the point of no return, she stopped.

"What a lovely tease," she whispered, with her face flushed.

Uli got out of the water and grabbed a fresh towel, drying off. "See you at dinner." She licked her lips and winked before leaving.

After she left, I had to fight the temptation to take care of some business before getting out. I figured the person who had to clean these tubs wouldn't appreciate it. After drying off and getting back into my robe, I met the others in the hallway. One of the butlers took us to a private room.

Inside the room was a large dinner table ornately decorated with candlesticks and silver platters. The gentle crackle from the fireplace gave the room a cozy atmosphere. As we were sat down, the servers began to introduce several luxurious meals of exotic meats, cheeses, and fruits. The rib roast, was so flavorful that I had to stop eating to pause for a second and imprint it in my memory.

We discussed how we wanted to get back to Naled as we ate. Every so often, Uli and I caught each other staring before quickly turning away. Mara wanted to stay an extra day and explore the town, but Giezha pointed out that we needed to focus on the other assignment the guild had given us.

192

Mara relented with a pout.

"We can't go the way we came," Uli determined while ripping into a piece of lamb. "We've already run into trouble once on that road. And if we are still being followed, we might run into those two from before."

"Might be a good chance to get the drop on them," I countered, trying not to inhale the green beans and actually chew. "We could capture them and find out who sent them."

Giezha wiped her mouth while she placed the napkin on her lap. "Too dangerous. No way of telling how powerful these guys are. If they've been able to track Uli this whole way, they have to be bad news."

"Thank you for the vote of confidence, Giezha."

Giezha nodded to Uli while Mara chimed in. "I think that we should hitch a ride home to a river dock and take a ride on the next boat home. You know, undercover?"

That idea excited everybody at the table.

"That sounds fun," I admitted. "A little bit of espionage."

"Works for me," Giezha said, more interested in the assortment of pies brought in.

With the plan for returning home in tow, we celebrated our successful mission with the rest of the meal. Once we had eaten our fill and then some, we decided to leave and head to the tavern for one more night's rest.

As we made our way out the front door, we ran into Isaac and the woman he had run off with. They were apparently making a late-night visit to the bathhouse. Isaac quickly ushered us away as soon as he saw us.

"Yes, yes, good to see you again," he said quickly, with other things clearly on his mind. "Hope you enjoyed your time at the bathhouse. We should definitely get together again sometime. Have a nice night!"

The orc who ran the bar nodded to us as we returned to the tavern. The place was much rowdier than it had been when we first came in. Several of the people present were apparently famous adventurers. At least, according to Mara.

"Oh, Gods! The Platinum Avengers!" she whispered, pointing to a beautiful elf and orc in matching armor sets. "They just got back from the Abyssal Plains on a mission to save their friend. They had to fight a Dracolich while they were down there."

Uli let out a low whistle as we passed. The sheer presence they

193

commanded in the room was palpable. They could probably kill everybody in this tavern in a matter of moments. Interestingly, the orc in platinum armor had the same facial structure as the orc who ran the bar. My suspicions were confirmed when the Avenger introduced the barkeep to his compatriots as his brother.

As the party below us continued, we went straight to our beds fed, relaxed, and felt properly pampered. It was an easy and universal decision to make it an early night and go to sleep.

As I laid my head down to rest, I felt something hard in my pillow. Feeling for the hard object, I discovered the ruby with which I had attempted to pay the barkeeper. A note was attached to it.

"Don't ever give away the little things."

Chapter 18

Evlanday, 4th of Seeyrn, Year 678, 4th Age

Compared to our journey into Zizar, our return trip home was a cakewalk. After several days in the city, Mara managed to procure a place in a caravan headed to Naled on land, crossing the river via ferry. It meant an extra two days on the road, but it'd be easy to blend in with everybody.

The caravan was trading goods from all across the kingdom of Narag, picking up hitchhikers on the way. Our cover story was that we were travelers from the Northern region of Kahar near the capital city of Midania.

Isaac was kind enough to lend us silk robes from the region to sell the story. The caravan was a collection of wagons, horses, and people with a dream in one hand and a coin in the other. All told, there were three dozen men, women, and children going across the country.

The only one who spoke much with the others was Uli, who could imitate the northern accent. There was a close call when somebody from the region started asking questions about where we were from specifically. Luckily, a murderous look from Giezha stopped the dwarf in his tracks.

Crossing the river was only problematic in terms of bureaucracy. The caravan did not have proper documents for all forty of us. The guards in charge of the large stone bridge were sticklers for the rules, just like the guards at the gates of Naled. And also like the guards in Naled, a few coins pressed in their palms made the paperwork magically appear.

On the caravan, I spent much of the days studying the history of Echo Veil and its many deities, kingdoms, and customs. When not forcing myself to study history for hours on end, I did my best to learn what I could from Mara, Uli, and Giezha. On mornings before the caravan got started, I worked on my swordsmanship with Mara. She also started to teach me how to use a bow and arrow. I was a decent shot, but nowhere near the bullseye that Mara was.

"I actually grew up shooting a bow with my father," she explained one day, while pulling out an arrow, she shot into another arrow while

195

practicing on an elm tree.

Walking over, she adjusted my stance, making minute changes. My body felt tight and wound up as she moved my body into proper form.

"You're too stiff in your movements, Asher. Hold that thing any tighter, and you'll break the bow in half!"

While the caravan was moving, Giezha and I would sit on top of the back wagon while she continued to teach me the basics. So far, I was able to form physical manifestations of some of the basic elements like fire, water, lightning, and wind. Now, she was teaching me how to create auditory or visual effects. By manipulating the basic lightning formulation, I could change their color and make them appear as if they were fireflies flashing in the air.

"Well done, Asher," she said, complimenting my rudimentary illusion. "Now, back to water. Let's see a basic water blast."

I pointed my hand to the pond we were passing by and focused my mana. As I imagined the collection of runes used for the spell, I began muttering the incantation. My hand started to feel wet as if someone had stuck a hose to it. Then, a geyser of water shot out of my palm, about as strong as a garden hose on full blast.

"Nice!" I exclaimed, proud of my spigot of water.

"Not bad, Asher," Giezha complimented. "But your pronunciation was incorrect. The water stream should be the width of your entire hand, not a gold coin. Here, try this."

Giezha helped break down the phonetics of the runes with me, and I eventually turned my garden hose into a fire hose. As we started to wrap up class, Giezha asked me a question.

"Have you thought about what school of magic you wish to study in the future?"

"I wasn't aware I had to choose," I said, trying to make the lights turn blue and yellow. "Which school do you focus on?"

Giezha demonstrated the proper runes and their placement with her own spell as she answered. "Technically, abjuration. I need to keep Uli and Mara safe and well-healed in battle. However, I have a particular fondness for evocation spells. It's all about necessity versus want. As to your question about requirements, you don't technically have to choose."

"Huh," I said, finally turning the lights blue. "I'll figure out which type to

196

focus on once I get the hang of the basics."

Giezha grimaced at me and started to chastise me. "The Fifth Age will arrive by the time that happens at this rate. You refuse to use anything other than your sword when you fight. You must learn to use your magic outside of study. You will learn more in a minute of battle than you would a month of study."

"Giezha still won't tell me how she remembers the runes," I muttered to myself, sitting alone by a small pond, pouring over my notes. "Why?"

"Because she doesn't know." A voice came from behind me.

"Gah!" I shouted, falling on my back.

Looking up, I saw Uli hands on hips, and her ever-dangerous grin. She stuck out a hand and helped me up. Dusting myself off, I checked myself for my coin sack. She'd picked up a nasty habit of testing my perceptions any chance she got, and her way of testing me was seeing if she could steal from me. I stayed vigilant for her little game, and this time, I managed to prevent her theft.

I did my best to observe Uli, who had a habit of sneaking in and out of camp without anybody noticing. I'd been taking notes of her patterns of movement and methodology. She was impossibly light on her feet and had a knack for disappearing around corners. I still couldn't figure out how she made things appear and disappear out of her hand.

"Have your notes been helping you get more sneaky?" she asked, pulling out her fishing rod and casting.

"Have you been reading my journal?" I asked defensively.

The bobber plopped into the water as Uli stared out to the water. "Nope! Just guessed."

Damn. She got me again with that stuff. By this point, I was convinced she was more dangerous when talking than when sneaking.

"Well, to answer your question, yes. I've been taking notes about how you stay out of sight and ways to stay quiet."

"And you've been practicing?" she asked nonchalantly. "Get any better at it?"

I grinned malevolently. Uli didn't know what I'd been doing to practice, so I pulled out my coup de gras.

"Oh, I'd think so."

In my hand was Uli's backup dagger, which she kept on her hip opposite her larger white knife. Uli pupil's dilated and checked for the knife. Realizing I had stolen it from her, she gave me an impressed smirk.

"No bad, Merrick. Not bad."

"Thanks," I said, handing her the knife.

"Keep it," she said, sitting next to me. "Always good to keep a knife on you, and I heard you lost one in the harbor. Handy for shimming open doors, cleaning fish, picking a lock, marking exits, or keeping yourself armed when you're not supposed to. Just don't throw this one in a fire."

Uli reeled in a small trout and placed it in a basket. Casting her lure back out, she turned to me.

"Wanna join? I keep a couple spares on me."

Uli pulled out a spare fishing pole and I joined her, placing some bait on the line and tossing my line out. Neither of us spoke for a while as the sounds of night slowly joined us.

Uli had changed into a black kirtle with a blue sash wrapped around her waist. Seeing Uli fish showed me a completely different version of her. A calmer, more tranquil Uli.

Dragonflies buzzed along the top of the pond while fireflies slowly danced in the air, blinking bright blue and red.

Occasionally, my bobber would pull down, only to reveal an empty lure. Uli, on the other hand, caught fish quicker than I could replace my bait. I watched sullenly as a frog hopped out of the log we sat on and jumped into the water. Less than a minute later, the frog came back out with a small fish wedged in its large fangs. Frog with fangs. Go figure.

"How're you doing that?" I said, laughing at my comparative ineptitude.

Uli gave a smug grin and shrugged. "Just gotta know how to read the water. Father taught me how to fish before he taught me how to walk."

Uli gave me a few pointers, and by the time we finished, I'd caught a fish all by myself.

"Nice job," Uli said, placing my fish with the dozen she'd caught. "When did you get so capable?"

Something about the way she said that lit a fire in my belly. I looked at her and felt her nudge closer to me. We drew closer, feeling the same energy as in the bathhouse. Her mouth was open slightly, and I slowly traced my hand up her arm. Uli exhaled as I caressed her back and traced my thumb around her cheek.

"I don't know, Uli," I said in a low voice. "Did you get more beautiful since I last saw you? Because it seems to happen all the time."

She didn't say anything, but I slowly moved forward and touched my lips to hers. Uli dropped the fishing pole out of her hand and grasped my shoulder. After a moment, we pulled away.

"Why don't we pick up where we left off at the bathhouse?" I whispered in her ear.

Uli grinned her ears twitching. Her hand slowly traced down to my chest, before stopping. Hearts racing, Uli bit her lip.

"Not tonight, Asher." She said, before kissing my cheek. "Soon, though."

As Uli left, I couldn't help but watch her leave. I put my new knife at my hip and picked up the fishing poles and basket she left.

"Planning on banging her too?" Giezha asked, appearing behind me. "Mara might actually get jealous."

"Gah!" I shouted, faceplanting again. "Would you all stop sneaking up on me!"

"Ribbit."

When our caravan finally made it back to Naled the next day, Giezha was finishing up a lecture with me about mana and its use as a battery for magic. We thanked the halfling who brought us aboard and paid him three gold each for the service. Happy to get paid by hitchhikers, he didn't pay a lick of attention as we left quickly, shedding our costumes.

Although we desperately wanted to get home as soon as possible, we went to the guildhall first to report everything. Hoping for a quick report and rest at home, we were in for a surprise.

Opening the door, a cascade of explosions rocked us. We were mobbed by the sudden onset of flashing lights and shouting upon our arrival.

"Breaker!" the entire guild shouted, letting off fireworks and banging their fists on the tables. Valdir pushed his way through the crowd and raised all of our hands up in the air. When he did so, the whole crowd cheered again as the mob of people slapped us on our shoulders and shook our hands.

"What do we bleed?" Valdir shouted to the crowd.

"Red!" they shouted back to him.

"We break through waves?"

"We forge ahead!"

199

"If you weren't with us!?"

"Then I'd be dead!"

The crowd erupted into cheers again as the music began to play in the background. Valdir led us through the crowd while they started throwing red sashes on us. When Valdir finally led us to Captain Dawnthorn, we were like blood-stained mummies, wrapped head to toe in red cloth. The captain sat at her table, now adorned with a piece of red velvet fabric and four large steins frothing with ale.

"Alright, maggots!" Captain Dawnthorn shouted, bringing the crowd to a hush. "When these three came begging at our door to join, what'd I say?"

"Fuck off!" the crowd screamed.

"And did they?"

"Fuck no!"

"Did we kick their ass?" Dawnthorn asked while drinking from her own impressive mug.

"Kicked, we did!"

"Indeed, we did. We kicked their ass every step of the way. Even the little tag-along! But that was all a test to see if they could do it." Dawnthorn got up and handed a stein to each of us. "We tested them day in and day out. And after their mission to Zizar... I think they pass!"

The crowd erupted into deafening cheers. People stomped on the ground, slammed their fists into the tables, and made as much noise as possible. I felt the vibrations of the sound beating against my chest as the guild grew louder and louder.

"To our newest members! Welcome to the fuckin' guild!"

"Cheers!"

Banging her mugs against our steins, Dawnthorn and the crew drank to our new membership. We all managed to slug down the whole thing in a single pull. Surprisingly, Uli was the first to finish, and Giezha was the last. The crowd mobbed us all once we finished our drinks, and the celebration truly began.

The next several hours were a blur of stories, drinking, and gifts. Each of us was given a red and white headband, respectively. A red one from an older member of the guild to carry their title. And a white one for us to give our blood to the guild in the future. We were now allowed to wear our headbands anywhere on our bodies outside of the guild with this ceremony.

I looked over at Uli, Giezha, and Mara. All three of them were soaking in the moment in their own way. Mara was crying tears of joy while bouncing up and down, listening to stories from the former teammates of Sal. Giezha did her best to keep a straight face but had trouble wiping the grin off her face. Uli made gestures and played up to the crowd while occasionally stealing glances in my direction. I just smiled and gave a few high fives to members of the guild.

As the night wore on, Dawnthorn asked to speak with me privately. She swept me away to a corner of the room. At the same time, everybody else was preoccupied with an old Red Breaker drinking game involving four chairs and a magic hat. I decided not to drink too much so that one of us could keep our wits. Besides, the girls worked so hard to get to this point, and it was their celebration to have.

"So, Merrick," Dawnthorn said, leaning back on her chair like it was a throne. "You managed to go from rookie to full member in a little less than two months. Impressive."

"Thanks," I said, nodding my head to her. "But really, it was all them," I said, pointing to Uli, Giezha, and Mara, who were on the second chair stacked on top of the hat. "It feels like I've just been along for the ride."

"Don't be so modest," she said, tapping my glass of beer. "Those girls were like a kite caught in a hurricane before you got here. Lost, I'd say. Every time they had a job, something went wrong. Chance after chance I gave them, but they always managed to screw things up."

She looked at them with a sad expression on her face. She shook her head and gave me a wry smile.

"It was hard not to give up on them despite their obvious potential. But ever since you arrived, they've gotten their act together."

I just nodded my head and drank. The captain was incredibly intimidating, and I got a distinct impression as she spoke that she wanted to talk about something else. It was just a matter of when she got to it.

"Captain?" I asked, trying to create an opening.

"Hmm?"

"Why did you want to speak with me? And why did it need to be in private?"

Raising her eyebrows, Dawnthorn finished her drink and wiped her mouth.

"I see you have picked up Siannodel's impatience. It's one of the things I like about her. And you, I suppose. Get straight to the point! Time is money."

Dawnthorn laughed at her non-existent joke before continuing.

"I wanted to ask you if you had any updates on the... other mission you were assigned. I haven't heard any rumors, which means you haven't been talking. That's a good thing."

"Right," I said, trying to think of the best way to say we haven't done anything. "Mostly, we've been information gathering so far. Trying to find leads as to where they may have been headed. Following up on theories that might involve outside interference."

"Anything good?"

I exhaled and pursed my lips. "We know that they were headed south towards the border with Zala. We also know that you probably had Uli scouting for them beforehand."

Dawnthorn blinked once but said nothing.

"Other than that, I don't have much to tell you," I said while trying to avoid mentioning the two following Uli and us. "Well, there was one other thing."

Her ears perked up when I said that.

"What's the other thing?"

I took a moment to choose my words as carefully as possible.

"Captain... There isn't a chance their disappearance could have anything to do with the undead, right?"

The captain gave me a strange look when I said that.

"Undead?" she deadpanned.

"Yeah."

I quickly explained what I had experienced with George to her. When I asked if he had been seen lately, she said he'd been found dead. My stomach dropped as the captain shrugged at me.

"Dead?"

"Dead." the captain nodded. "Ripped apart from the neck down in some alleyway. Lot of rumors swirling around. It was close to the Silver Cup, actually. Near your... incident with Mhurren and Mick."

Fuck. Despite wanting to tell the captain what Uli saw, I didn't. Instead, I decided to mention seeing a skeleton on my way through the forest before

202

I came here. She didn't ask any questions about the second story, but I got the impression she knew I was holding back.

"That's... that's certainly interesting," Dawnthorn said, her eyes looking far off into the distance. "I won't lie. It might have something to do with that."

"Captain," I said, feeling something in my gut. "Why did you have Uli scout ahead for Mhurren and Mick? And why not send us there first? Perhaps they got there late or something."

Dawnthorn looked at me pensively, eyeing me up and down. "You're a sharp kid, Merrick. No stones left unturned. The reason I sent her to scout and didn't tell her why is simple: She wasn't a full member. Siannodel's got skills that far surpass her age, no doubt about it."

The faint sound of Uli and the others partying punctuated her statement.

"But she and others are kids. Rookies. Unknown variables. In other words, risky investments. If she knew too much or got caught by the wrong people with information in hand, it could cost a lot of people more than just money." Her tone was perfectly even and professional. "I have a guild to run, people to protect. Even if that means telling people less than what they want."

I didn't like the idea of her discounting Uli's moral fiber, but said nothing. I waited for her to answer the other question as well.

"As for why you're not down where I sent Uli, it's also simple. I have other people looking for them. Your job is to search nearby for Mhurren and Mick and along your other quests. I have a more... experienced team handling thing near the Zala border."

The captain didn't elaborate further and told me I should leave and get back to the party. I felt like she may have been hiding something, but I was hiding my own information as well. The rest of the night was filled with dancing, drink after drink, and a dozen different toasts to our new membership. We were given gifts by some of the members, as well as stories of their own hazing. I was given a coin with the Red Breaker logo on each side. Suitable for five uses at any brothel in the city.

"Better make sure Giezha doesn't see you take that!" a drunken Uli teased.

"Giezha?"

Uli was given a Potion of Invisibility which seemed redundant

203

considering how sneaky she was. Mara got a vial of oil that could sharpen a blade to such a fine point it could slice through a stone. And finally, Giezha was given a mighty scroll of defense that could protect an entire party.

Late in the night, we stumbled across the city and back to the Silver Cup. Well, I only stumbled because I had to keep the others from falling over so much. By the time I opened the tavern's door, I resorted to carrying Mara, piggyback style while pushing Giezha in a wooden wheelbarrow I'd borrowed. Uli was the soberest of the three and followed me while holding the back of my shirt.

"Good heavens!" Sal shouted while cleaning the empty bar. "I've been wondering when you would make it back! What happened?"

"Well, they—"

"We did it!" Mara shouted right next to my ear. "We went to Thighzar and did the thing! Then we got back here and—"

"And we officially made it into the guild!" Uli said while pumping her fists into the air. "Look at it, Sal! Look at it. Red headbands. On us, we're Breakers now!"

All four of us were wearing our red headbands. Giezha's was over her eyes as she snored in the wheelbarrow. Mara kept hers on her wrist while Uli's was unfurled and wrapped around her neck. I wore mine like usual on my forehead.

Realizing what had happened, Sal looked devastated for a moment. As quickly as it arrived, he shook his head and changed it to a strained smile.

"Sal, we did it! We did it!" Uli hugged Sal while jumping up and down in excitement.

With great difficulty, he broke away from her hug. Obviously, something was bothering him, but he did his best to look excited for the girls. He and I exchanged looks, and I could tell we should talk later.

"So, does that mean your debts are all paid up?" Sal asked hopefully.

Uli stopped doing her happy dance and thought for a moment. Her smile slipped away, replaced by a look of deep thought. Moving an invisible abacus back and forth, she did her best to run the calculations.

"Nope!" she finally said much too loudly. "Even if we got paid every copper we had left from this quest, we'd still be about five hundred gold short." Sal looked like he was about to have a heart attack until Uli started talking again. "But don't worry! We are also on a super-secret mission that's going to pay a bunch of it off."

Before Sal could ask any more questions, Uli slumped over the table she was sitting at and fell asleep. Mara was also gently snoring as I held her. Not wanting to press the issue, Sal just shook his head in exasperation and went to lock the front door.

I gently picked Uli up from her seat and carried/pushed the girls to their room.

"Why does this feel familiar?" I joked to myself, once again getting the girls to sleep.

"I don't know what Dawnthorn is up to, Asher," Sal said, furiously cleaning his glasses. "I don't know what it is, but I know it's no good. I've been—" He stopped short and looked at me. "It doesn't matter. I just know that bitch is up to something. That mission to Zizar would never get you in the guild in my day. She's working an angle, I can smell it!"

I scratched my head and nodded. "I think you might be right. When we were talking at the party, something definitely seemed off."

I then explained the entire story to Sal while including the bits that I did not tell the captain before. As worried as he was before, my story seemed much more upsetting to him. Unsettled, he poured himself a drink and one for me as well. Sal downed his entire drink and wiped his mouth and beard.

"That doesn't sound good." Sal poured himself another drink and downed it in one gulp as well. "I'm scared to say it, but this reminds me of something from a long time ago."

"Really?" I asked while taking a sip.

"Yes. If it's anything like then, we're in for a rough time." Sal tapped the bar several times while debating something in his head. "I'm going to call in some contacts and see what I can find out about this."

"Good idea. Maybe see what the captain is up to as well?" I added in suggestion.

"As sure as the sun shall rise to the glory of Oros."

We clinked our drinks in a final toast, and I headed off to bed soon afterwards.

"I'll be sure to have some Invigorating Potions and a hot breakfast ready for the girls tomorrow!" Sal called out to me as I walked up the stairs.

Taking off my headband and the rest of my clothes, I got ready to climb into the bed. I thought about things as I undressed. Whatever was going on, I was missing something. An essential piece to the puzzle.

"Something doesn't feel right," I muttered to myself.

"Sorry, Asher. I can scoot over."

I looked down and pulled up my blanket, revealing Uli lying asleep in my bed. And she was completely naked. When I pulled open the blanket, Uli blinked her eyes open. Once she saw me, she reached out, trying to grab onto me.

"C'mere and give me that good loving Mara keeps bragging about." Uli giggled.

I quickly pushed away from her hands and got out of the bed.

"Uli, what are you doing in my bed?"

Uli posed on the bed and gave a sultry look.

"Trying to get what you and I both want."

"No," I told her flatly.

She sat up straight and pouted.

"What do you mean no?"

"I mean, you're drunk. It-It wouldn't be right. I don't want you to wake up regretting something."

She crossed her arms over her chest.

"We both know I wouldn't."

"No, we don't," I retorted. "It's not right, and it's not happening."

She gave me a sad look, and her ears drooped. Even drunk, this woman could charm the pants off me. Not wanting to upset her, I thought of a compromise. Grabbing one of my spare shirts, I handed it to her.

"Here," I said, motioning for her to take it. "You can sleep here, but that's it."

Pursing her lips, she gave me an unsatisfied look but grabbed the shirt and laid back on the bed. Too tired to ask where her clothes were, I just got into bed and rested my head on my pillow. Uli scooted over and wrapped my arm around her. She mumbled to herself as she fell asleep while I slowly drifted away to the smell of honey and cinnamon in her hair.

"Did you steal that oil from the bathhouse?" I asked quietly.

Uli giggled and simply went, "Shh!"

206

Chapter 19

Xaliasday Evening, 7th of Seeyrn, Year 678, 4th Age

When I woke up the following day, Uli was already gone. I later found her downstairs nursing a plate of eggs and sausage with her hood up, blocking as much light as possible. Despite Sal's Invigorating Potions and plenty of hearty food, the girls took a while to fully recover. Nobody had much memory of that night, but luckily Uli knew full well that nothing happened between us.

I went to the guild to see if I could get any information. After chastising me for not displaying my Red Breaker band, Captain Dawnthorn made me swear not to tell anybody what was going on. I was only interested in learning about the quest.

When I questioned the other Breakers, I noticed how friendlier they were now that I was a full member.

"Mhurren?" asked a human mage named Brody. "Yeah, I seen him around a lot. Hard not to when he's always up in everybody's face. Your move, by the way."

The only way I could get him to talk was by agreeing to a game of chess. I had some experience with chess in my old life and recognized his opening. A basic opening at that.

Must've pegged me as a beginner. Playing along, I asked him some questions as we traded pieces.

"I got an up-close and personal view of that. What type of jobs did he typically take? Was it always with that Mick guy?"

Advancing my knights as he did the same, I waited for his response. He didn't seem very interested in my questions as much as he did the game. After moving his bishop, he looked up and answered.

"Mhm, they're thick as thieves. Mostly protection detail," he said as I

207

tried to pin one of his pieces. "They occasionally work the odd retrieval mission but prefer jobs that involve violence."

We continued to dance around each other with our pieces, forcing the other to sacrifice material and working our strategies. The more we played, the more I was able to ask questions. Too distracted by the game, he freely answered every question.

Mick and Mhurren rarely brought in repeat requests from quest-givers, but there were customers who specifically asked for them each time. They also had a penchant for making enemies everywhere they went.

"It's always a good day when they're not here," Brody said while putting me in checkmate. "Personally speaking, whatever job they're on right now, I pray they don't come back from it. And if they do, never work a job with them."

I thanked him for the game and left. As I got out of my seat, he said something to me.

"I could tell you were holding something back, by the way." I turned back and looked at him, my heart thumping. "You clearly knew how to play the game of chess, but rather than jump on my mistakes, you just let the game play out."

Realizing Brody was just talking about the game, I relaxed. "Yeah," I said, scratching my head. "I just wanted to get a feel for your skill level," I said, lying through my teeth. "Next time, I'll be sure to take you down nice and quick."

Brody rolled his eyes and welcomed the next challenger from the guild. The way the guild was so open and accommodating now was so peculiar. It felt like a fraternity from college.

I talked to a few other members of the guild, and they tended to echo Brody's sentiments. The general impression was that Mick and Mhurren had gone on a mission near the northern border to protect a traveling band of merchants.

In the few years they'd been here, neither was well-liked; they always worked together; and a trail of destruction followed wherever they went.

"That's the exact job we just completed," I told Dawnthorn, explaining my dislike of the cover story. "Doesn't that seem suspicious at all?"

Dawnthorn told me to keep my voice down despite being in her office.

"Quiet! And no, it won't be suspicious. Because it's not suspicious."

She pulled out a red leather-bound booklet and pointed to an entry line. "Assignment as a mobile sentry for merchants from Nulgat paid in advance to the order of seven hundred fifty gold, signed and notarized by Captain Ylsysea Dawnthorn."

She snapped the book shut and nodded her head curtly. She put the book back into a desk drawer and locked it before putting the key in one of her breast pockets.

"Nobody has the balls to insinuate that I would lie about what's in this ledger, Merrick. Have you found any new leads other than what you've told me already?"

"Still following up. Any word on the undead situation? I asked Sal about that, and he was pretty shaken up about it."

Dawnthorn made a rude gesture and blew a raspberry.

"That old goat starts shaking if the drinks aren't flowing." She looked out a window from her office and thought for a moment. Her expression was unreadable. "He's not wrong to be afraid if it's what he thinks it is, though."

"Why is that?" I asked, my knee bouncing rapidly.

"It's a really long story, Asher. But I'll give you the short version. A band of necromancers attacked the city about fifty years ago. They managed to bring an army of almost a thousand zombies and other undead right up to the heart of the city. Sal and I had just helped form the guild with some friends when it all went down. Only two of the necromancers escaped, and we managed to help save Naled. The emperor vowed to hunt them down."

"That's amazing," I said in awe.

She shook her head bitterly and pulled out a tobacco pipe. Lighting up the end, she took a few deep drags.

"No, what was amazing was how fucked over we got from it." She drummed her fingers on the table as she remembered a painful memory. "We lost some of our closest friends that day, and our guild was nearly destroyed before it even began. Despite being one of the main defenses for the city, we never saw so much as a single copper. All the other guilds got fat contracts because of friends on the Council, while I got to bury my friends in a pauper's grave."

I noticed a painting hanging on the wall behind her desk featured a dozen adventurers in the Red Breaker uniforms, all proudly displaying

209

their headbands. Sal was front and center with the captain's hand on his shoulder. She saw me look behind her and turned to the painting.

"I promised myself that anybody who put the same amount of work into this guild as I did would be rich. That they would never have to worry about money. That their descendants would never worry about money..."

She turned back to me and ran her hands through your hair a few times. "Look, I don't like being the bad guy. I don't like telling people they're not good enough to be in the guild. But this isn't a charity. It's a business."

I didn't say anything and just sat there. The captain seemed totally sincere with what she said. And I couldn't blame her. Getting screwed over and left to rot while everybody else got rich had to sting. Especially when you knew how much you and your loved ones sacrificed. I thanked the captain for her time and took my leave.

That night, I borrowed a book from Giezha's personal library that chronicled the history of guilds in the city. Sure enough, when it got to a two-paragraph entry on the Red Breakers, Sal was listed as a founder and even the first vice-captain of the guild. It also had a brief passage on their role in what was called the Undead Incursion. Compared to the other guilds from the time, the Red Breakers had a fraction of the coverage and words written about them. It was like they barely existed.

"I wonder what their reputation used to be like," I said, stretching as I got out of my seat to get dinner.

The others were still out of commission, and Sal left a note that morning that he'd be out on a personal errand, so the tavern was left closed for the night. That struck me as odd, and I realized he was the only person working at this tavern. After checking to make sure the girls didn't need anything, I left to grab some dinner and give the moonstone to Kiersa.

The Golden Sky Tavern was packed to the brim with customers. Many of the patrons wore white and purple robes with the three moon triangle formation of the symbol of Ihena that Kiersa wore as a necklace. Kiersa was taking orders from dozens of people by herself. Her father oversaw the roasting of a boar the size of a small elephant.

Noticing me, Kiersa gave me a quick wave while she desperately tried to fill orders by herself. Seeing that she could use some help, I decided to jump in.

Wrapping my Red Breaker cloth around my forehead, I ran up to Kiersa's father, Aire.

"Excuse me, sir," I said loudly, trying to be heard over the room's din.

Aire flicked his eyes to me for a half-second while he carved the meat of this gigantic boar. He used his massive knife to hack slices of the boar that was roasting over a giant open flame grill with one hand. With the other, he shook a collection of spices on the meat, which turned liquid when it hit the boar and quickly caramelized.

"What is it, Breaker?" he asked in his deep booming voice, still focused on the meat. "Can you not see that we are celebrating the Week of Tiur?"

The large front doors to the tavern were open, giving a brilliant view of the night sky. The smaller moon, Avis, was directly above the larger moon, Xalia. When I first arrived, it'd had been to the left of Xalia. Now, it was directly above. It dawned on me that Avis must have been orbiting its larger counterpart.

"Yes..." I said, hoping to catch an easy segue. "That's why I'm here. I'm here to help you celebrate! I even brought—"

The muscle-bound chef stopped what he was doing and stared at me. He wasn't taller than me, but he had a towering presence. He kept holding his gigantic knife, drumming his fingers against the handle. Luckily, Kiersa came to my rescue.

"Oh, thank the Shepherd!" she said breathlessly while grabbing my arm. "I hoped you would be able to make it sooner, but any help I can get waiting tables is appreciated."

I mouthed "thank you" to her as Aire looked at his daughter.

"Kiersa, why did you go through the trouble of hiring a Red Breaker, of all people?" he cast a disdainful look on me as he said the name of my guild. "No doubt he will try and take the entire offering to Ihena as payment. And the week of the equinox no less!"

"Oh!" I said, reaching into my shirt's inner pocket. "That reminds me. I wanted to give this to you both to celebrate the Week of Tiur."

I pulled out the moonstone and held it with my index finger and thumb. Under the moonlight, something interesting happened. Its soft white glow radiated white and blue. As I held it, I could almost feel the light from the moons in the sky warming my hands. A few people impatiently waiting for their meals whispered when they saw me pull out the stones.

Kiersa gasped and put her hands over her mouth while Aire's hand

211

slackened enough for the tip of the knife to clang onto the grill. Unsure of who to give the moonstone to, I held it there. Aire lifted his hand to receive the moonstone, and I placed it into his palm. Looking at it for a second, he breathed deeply before placing it into his apron pocket.

"Thank you, young Red Breaker," he said with a slight crack in his voice. "I would be honored to have you assist in our celebration."

He returned to his carving and seasoning duties and gestured for Kiersa and me to go. Kiersa still had a hand over her mouth as she looked at me. A little worried, I gave her a thumbs up, thumbs down gesture to gauge her. Looking back to make sure her father wasn't looking, she grabbed me by the shirt and kissed me before dragging me to the counter.

"You ever worked like this before?" she asked, throwing an apron at me.

I thought back to my time serving as a waiter at a bar in my sophomore year. I had spilled enough glasses of beer to make a viking cry. Deciding not to lead with that story, I simply nodded my head and waited for instructions.

"Just follow my lead, and make sure to say 'May our Shepherd guide you' when the customers leave."

The meals served were chopped dire boar, salted glowshroom, and pickled cabbages, traditionally eaten to celebrate the Week of Tiur. Kiersa and I ran ourselves silly seating people, taking orders, and cleaning tables. What'd I'd give for Giezha to have taught me the cleaning spell.

They had brought in so many extra chairs and tables we could barely squeeze between them to deliver food. And despite the front doors being opened, the roaring fire that cooked the massive boar turned the entire place into a veritable oven. Luckily, everybody was in a good mood, and for the most part, everybody tipped well.

As the last few patrons left a few hours later, I sat by the fire sweating as if I had run a marathon. Kiersa peeled off her apron and left to change her clothes. Aire looked completely unfazed and was finally digging into his own meal.

With Kiersa away, her father and I were in the room with only the midnight moons to accompany us. As I sat there, contemplating my lost weekend night, Aire walked over and sat next to me with a plate full to the brim.

"Eat, boy," he commanded.

212

I obliged, too tired and hungry to argue. I was taken aback by the flavors of the dishes. Anytime I had come here for a meal before, I always walked away full and satisfied. But this meal wasn't just food. It was more than that. It was a masterpiece.

With each bite I experienced a new flavor, a new texture. And as I ate, I sat next to its composer. Its sculptor. Its creator. This was a meal saved for special occasions.

"I take it that you enjoyed it." Aire smirked. "I'm honored that you think so highly of my cooking."

I looked down and realized that I had already eaten everything. My body was so entranced by the meal I'd forgotten to savor it. Before I had the time to regret my actions, Aire handed me another plate full of everything. He watched as I carefully dug into the meal, careful to savor every bite.

Mr. Denrel sat beside me, looking at the few bits and pieces of the boar left to be eaten. "I've seen you a few times around these parts lately. I take it you are new to the city."

Careful not to talk with my mouth full, I nodded my head.

"It's safe to assume you are the newest member of the team composed of my daughter's friends?"

His last question carried a dangerous intonation with it. Swallowing the last morsel, I placed my knife and fork down. Aire stared straight at me, a dangerous glint in his eyes. I felt that if we were speaking under different circumstances, I would be feeling a certain fire in my muscles. I looked Aire in the eyes as I spoke.

"Yes. You are correct in your assumptions."

He made a face that was like a combination of a smirk and a frown. He thought about something that made him laugh before he spoke to me.

"I've heard plenty of rumors about someone seeing my daughter a week ago. She didn't come home one night."

His words did not sit well with me. Kiersa was an adult, and no amount of doting from a father, or anyone, was enough to dictate what she could or could not do. I bit my tongue with that remark and tried to stay diplomatic with my words.

"That would be for you to discuss with your daughter, not with some stranger you just met."

"Ha!" he laughed with the sharpness of a wolf's bark. "How

noncommittal of you. You are correct. This is for me to discuss with my daughter. But there is a discussion to have with someone like you."

"Like me?" I noticed that he still had the knife in his hand. Or perhaps, he had just now grabbed it. Despite the knife's placement in his lap, I kept my eyes locked on his.

As Kiersa returned, having cleaned up, Aire spoke softly. "Yes. I've spent a long time in this city. And if I've learned anything, it's that humans can't be trusted around an elf."

Kiersa walked up to us, and just before she was in earshot, I decided to really piss this guy off.

"Humans? You mean like her mother?"

Before he could strangle me, Kiersa walked up and gave her father a hug. Kiersa said a short prayer thanking Ihena. Aire smiled at his daughter, and I did the same. She gave us a nervous glance as her father waved his hand and smiled. Neither of us wanted to worry her, so we kept up a facade of cordiality.

"You know," Aire said as Kiersa began to walk me outside. "I don't think I had the pleasure of learning your name, young man."

I turned around and looked him in the eyes. "It's Asher. Asher Merrick."

Kiersa squeezed my shoulder, and we both left the cafe. For at least two blocks, I could feel his piercing gaze in the back of my head. Kiersa kept turning back to make sure he didn't follow us.

"How many times did he threaten you?" she asked, her cheeks pink and brows furrowed.

I let out a humorless laugh. "Only about a dozen times in the two minutes you were gone."

Kiersa scowled back towards her father's direction and growled.

"He does that to all of your boyfriends?" I asked before correcting myself. "Friends with benefits, I mean."

My question made her blush a deeper shade of red. Turning down an alleyway, she squeezed my hand even tighter. Kiersa sat on a wooden box and put her hands to her face. She was deeply bothered by more than she was telling me. I sat down on an empty crate next to her and placed my hand on her back.

"He's a brutish, narrow-minded man," Kiersa said, looking back and forth in the abandoned alleyway. "But he has a reason for that."

214

I looked around the alleyway as well. At first, I thought Kiersa may have been afraid that somebody had followed us. But the alley was completely empty besides us. There wasn't even a rat that usually accompanied these types of locations.

"What do you mean?" I asked as she leaned into me.

She placed her head on my shoulders and breathed in and out slowly.

"My father has always been an outsider. Even among the elves, our kind is rare." She rubbed my leg with her hand as she thought for a moment. "Whether it was here or in the homelands, he has always felt the persecution and prejudice of being different."

I sat there for a moment as she closed her eyes.

"Have you?" I asked finally.

She didn't say anything. She did not confirm it. Nor did she deny it. Instead, she just held a sad smile. The more I thought about it, the more I realized that the only moon elves I had only ever seen were her and her father. I also realized that despite clearly needing help, nobody celebrating the evening had thought to help them.

I drummed my fingers angrily on the crate. I was a fool to not have realized the subtext before. Kiersa put her index finger on my lips and smiled as I was about to say something.

"I don't need you to make promises about changing the world, Asher Merrick. I just need you to promise you'll be there for me."

"Okay," I said, holding her hand. After a few moments, a peculiar thought came to mind. "Any particular reason you led me to an alleyway?"

Kiersa had a devilish grin and bit her bottom lip. Slowly, she ran a hand down to my leg and began to rub my crotch. At the same time, she placed one of my hands inside her shirt. Giggling, she pulled me in for a kiss.

I had almost forgotten how soft her lips were.

As we were about to tear into each other's clothes, a noise rang through the alleyway. The both of us stopped and jumped to our feet. It sounded like a cat screaming mixed with boxes breaking. There was also a sound like somebody groaning as if they were in pain. Or as if they had become a zombie...

"Get behind me!" I hissed, putting myself between her and the source of the noise. I reached for my non-existent sword. Realizing I had no weapon, I cursed myself for not gearing up before leaving the house.

215

The alleyway was so dark it was impossible to look down. Slowly, we began to back our way out. The piercing noise rang out again, and a black cat sprinted out and under our legs, yowling loudly.

"A cat couldn't have made all that noise," Kiersa whispered as we inched backward.

The groaning sound rang out again, sounding much closer this time. It also sounded... feral. My instincts told me this could be another zombie and a chance to find a clue. Everything else inside of me said I needed to protect her.

"Kiersa," I said, trying to remember a rune sequence from Giezha's class. "I need you to get out of here. I'll slow this thing down."

As I concentrated, a chill ran up my spine. Giezha had been teaching me ice-related spells and how they were good for damage but even better for slowing an enemy down or even stopping them.

"No!" She whispered as the noise got closer. It sounded inhuman. "I'm not leaving you!"

"GRAAAGGRH!"

A scream rang out through the alleyway, and in a flash, a creature leaped from the darkness at me. Throwing my hand out in front of me, a blast of ice erupted from my hand. The ice smashed against the blur of a creature, knocking it back. I saw part of the creature illuminated by a ray of moonlight for a split second.

It was humanoid, but the rest of this hulking, brutish creature had the face of a rat with beady gray eyes and broken teeth. The only reason I didn't think it was a mouse folk was they weren't seven feet tall and missing a chunk of the skin and flesh on their face.

"RUN!" I shouted.

The undead-rat-creature let out a bellowing roar as it shrugged off the attack. I tried to well up the energy for another blast and shot a set of three icicles. Kiersa turned and sprinted out of the alleyway while I tried to stand my ground. The creature absorbed the first two ice blasts without reacting and dodged the third. The creature ran with frightening speed and dexterity, deftly avoiding the boxes strewn in the alley.

Before I could react, it ducked down and tackled me to the ground. The creature screamed as it tore into me. Its claws scratched and scraped at me as I threw my hands up, trying to block the damage. Slices of my shirt flew

216

into the air as it dug into my skin, erupting a hail of red mist.

"Shit!" I howled in pain.

I struggled to get it off me, but it had me totally pinned down. As it scratched and slashed, it tried to hold me down on my shoulders. I punched and kicked and tried to elbow it, but nothing I did damaged it. Its jagged, broken teeth came down, ready to rip into my neck.

Right as it was about to deliver the killing blow, a blinding light erupted behind me. I could feel the literal force of this light slam into the both of us, and the harsh whiteness of the light illuminated the horrid creature. Its body was missing several patches of skin and flesh with bones sticking out of holes in tattered, shabby black clothes. The creature screamed in pain as it was thrown back.

The light hit me as well but did not do any damage. Instead, it felt invigorating. It felt like I was running at two hundred percent efficiency. I saw a silhouette that looked like Kiersa, pointing a shining light at us.

My body went into auto-pilot as I felt a righteous fire welling up inside my body. The rat-person was covering its eyes and trying to run away. Sensing my opportunity, I snapped off into a full spread as my whole body began to erupt from the inside out. I lined up my shot, focusing every last bit of energy into my legs.

"Hey, ugly!" I shouted, getting the zombie's attention. "FUCK YOU!"

I slammed my foot into the side of the zombie's head as I kicked it like a football. The force of the connection made a literal shockwave erupt from the point of contact. As I followed through, the head of the zombie ripped off like a piece of wet tissue. The head flew into the air, and once it hit the light, it vaporized into the air.

"Dammit!" I shouted, looking down at the dissolving lower half of the rat.

All I could see left was a piece of fabric lying on the ground. I turned back toward Kiersa as the lights slowly faded from her hand. She ran up and gave me a hug, wrapping her arms tightly around my neck and nearly bowling us both over.

"Are you okay?" Kiersa asked, burying her face in my shoulder.

"Yeah," I said breathlessly. "Better than I'd imagine, really."

I expected a stinging pain to be ringing out on my arms and shoulders, but they were totally unharmed when I looked. My whole body felt like it had just been healed.

Letting go of Kiersa, I saw that she held the moonstone I'd given her in my hand. Except, the stone was now half the size it once was.

I looked at her in awe. "Kiersa, did you use this?"

Rather than say anything, she grabbed me tightly and kissed me deeply. Unable to do anything but reciprocate, I held her tightly as I felt a tear streak against my cheek.

"I thought you would die, and I just moved without thinking."

"I didn't know you were a magic-user," I said, embarrassed to have not asked before.

"I'm not really," she said as we left the alleyway and got into the light of the empty streets. "I volunteer as a healer with the church occasionally. It's a natural talent I inherited from my family. This stone was able to amplify my Light of Ihena spell."

"That's awesome!" I exclaimed. "You saved my life, and you killed that zombie. Re-killed it, I mean."

Kiersa stopped and looked at me, terror in her eyes. She gripped my tattered shirt so hard it was liable to rip into pieces. Her lips quivered as it looked like she may cry again. I just held her tightly and stroked her head.

"Was it an undead, Asher?" she asked quietly. "Like the ones in the stories they tell of the Incursion?"

I looked around to make sure nobody was within earshot. A few people were in this street, but none were paying attention. It was odd that nobody had seen or heard what had happened just a few blocks away. But then again, noises like that were common in this area.

"Maybe, I don't know. I need to tell Dawnthorn about this."

"You need to tell the council!" she urged me, holding my hand tightly. "If this is anything like before, the city will need to use every bit of preparation it can. We can't wait for those Breakers to tell anyone!"

I didn't like the way she phrased that. "Kiersa, I'm a Red Breaker, remember?" I said, pointing to my sweat-filled headband. "So are Mara, Giezha, and Uli."

She looked like she was about to say something but bit her tongue.

"You still need to tell someone," she said resolutely. "You nearly died back there, Asher. I don't want to see you get hurt. And I don't want my city to be attacked!"

218

"I know!" I said quietly, trying to get her to lower her voice. "I need to report this to the guild immediately. I don't even know how to talk to the Council, but they do. They'll set something up, I swear."

As we got nearer, she had an annoyed look on her face. Clearly, whatever I was saying wasn't what she wanted to hear.

If I was going to be worth my salt as a member, I needed to tell the Breakers, but Kiersa was also correct. I chewed my lip as I thought.

"Okay," I said finally. "You win, Kiersa. You're right."

She put her hands on her hips and scowled. "I know I'm right, dummy. This is more important than some guild stuff. This could be the safety of your home! Of my home!"

I put my hands up in a non-threatening position as I talked. "Yes, and that's why I need your help."

She seemed surprised by that idea judging by her eyebrows disappearing into her hair. The captain would believe me, but others... not so much.

"Can you tell someone and warn the council?" I asked. "They might be able to detect some latent undead-ness to it or any magic that brought that thing back to life."

"Why can't you do that?" she asked, pursing her lips.

I sighed and shook my head. "The fact that I am a Red Breaker will make them less likely to believe me."

I put extra emphasis on my membership as I stared at Kiersa. Holding the fabric in her hands, she looked down and shifted her weight uncomfortably.

"Asher, I'm sorry. I shouldn't have said that stuff about the Breakers."

I waved my hand and front of me. "It's fine, Kiersa. I've just been dealing with that a lot since I got here."

"Sorry," she said quietly.

I pulled her in for a hug and kissed her head. I hated to admit it, but the Red Breaker's lousy reputation was more than earned. No point in holding a grudge over something like that. Especially when she just saved my life.

"Don't worry about it, Kiersa. Seriously." I bent down and kissed her on the lips. "But if you're feeling that bad, would you mind helping tell someone in the council?"

"Okay," she said after a minute. "I'll do what I can. Should I say it happened to you?"

I thought about it for a minute. "No, it could compromise more than one quest I'm on. There's a lot going on behind closed doors, and nobody can know what I'm working on. Just say that you encountered the zombie and used that moonstone to deal with it. Give them this fabric maybe there's some residual evidence on there."

We turned and began to walk back to her tavern as she pocketed the fabric. As we walked, she fussed and lamented over my tattered shirt. I laughed and joked that she shouldn't let her father think she was responsible for its condition. She laughed, admitting that he would probably suspect it.

"You know, you'd make a pretty good adventurer, Kiersa," I said conversationally. "You've got the magic, the guts, the charisma...."

Kiersa blew a raspberry. "Oh please, Father expects me to run the damned tavern for the next hundred years."

I just shrugged. "Not his decision, though, is it?"

By the time I walked Kiersa back to the Golden Sky Tavern, I was wobbly in the knees thanks to going "Nova" on the rat. When we arrived at the tavern, her father was waiting for us. She gave me a quick hug and kiss on the cheek as she slipped me a note.

Aire made a point to stare at me long after Kiersa ran into the tavern and up the stairs. Whatever kind of intimidation bullshit he was trying to pull had absolutely no effect after all that had happened. Especially since his daughter had just saved my life.

With a wave goodbye, I made my way home while reading the note Kiersa slipped in my hand.

"Missed you."

"Yeah," I said, laughing to myself, placing the note in my inner pocket. "Missed you too."

Chapter 20

Gethsday Morning, 10th of Seeyrn, Year 678, 4th Age

The next day, I gave my report to the captain with the girls present. She wasn't keen on having them in the room, but I insisted they hear everything. When I explained what happened, I made sure to leave out the part where Kiersa helped defeat the rodent. Instead, I told her that I blasted it with the moonstone until nothing was left.

The captain didn't look at me the entire time. Instead, she stared pensively at the painting of the original Red Breakers. After I finished the story, she turned back to us.

The others weren't happy with finding this stuff out at the same time as her, but when I'd gotten back the previous night, I'd collapsed at the front door. Sal had to drag me up to the bed and laid a vial of Daurag's Kip-Up Tonic by my bedside. Even with the tonic, my legs felt like lead weights.

I took a moment to sit down as Captain Dawnthorn gave out her orders. Dawnthorn walked by each of us, her hands behind her back and looking out to the window. The first person she spoke to was Uli, who kept her eyes straight and posture rigid.

"Siannodel," Dawnthorn said in a dangerously casual voice. "Mind telling me where the rest of the team was during Merrick's excursion?"

I was about to speak, but the captain put a finger in the air as I opened my mouth, silencing me. Uli never once broke her line of vision and stared directly forward.

"I and guild members, Brightwood and Nightstrike, were indisposed."

Mara cringed while Giezha looked at me, her eyes narrowed to slits.

"Personal decisions, Captain."

Dawnthorn stopped in front of Uli but refused to make eye contact. She just stared perpendicular to Uli and smiled.

221

"Because?"

Uli blinked once, and her jawline tightened.

"Because we were irresponsible and drank too much."

The four of us sat there waiting for the captain to explode. For her to rip into every single one of us about being idiots. To start smacking us in the face and asking if we really wanted to be here. If we were worth bringing into the guild and worth pinning this mission on.

But it didn't happen.

She just stood there, silently. As she stood there, the temperature in the room rose by a hundred degrees. I wanted to stand up and pace back and forth. But the sheer weight in the room left me unable to stand. The captain laughed to herself for a minute or two. Then she turned to Giezha.

"Didn't take you for a drinker," Dawnthorn said, patting Giezha on the back.

Stiffening up, she responded. "I'm not, Captain."

"But the other day?"

"Was the exception."

"Was the exception, yes." Tapping her lip, she then walked over to Mara.

"Anything to add, Brightwood?"

Mara was having trouble keeping a still face. Her bottom lip trembled, and she had to physically bite it to stop it from moving. Digging her fingernails into her palms, Mara took a deep breath.

"Only that Asher... should have had backup."

The captain stopped and slammed a hand on her desk. Mara and I flinched as her inkwell spilled onto the floor, dripping ink everywhere. I felt her long fingernails wrap around my shoulders and the heavy smell of tobacco and firewood filled my nostrils. Letting go, the captain sank into her heavily cushioned office chair. Looking into her eyes was like looking into a bottomless abyss, with only death waiting for you at the end.

Everything in my body was telling me it was either fight or flight. I was in no condition to be fighting. The captain pulled out a bottle of very expensive-looking whiskey and poured a glass for herself. After finishing the drink in a single pull, she smacked her lips and looked at all of us.

"I'm just fucking with you all." She grinned. "Asher was out on a date and got caught in a bad situation. Shit happens. As for you all being hungover, I mean, come on! It's a guild! You all got initiated!" Dawnthorn laughed and gestured for us to relax. "I guarantee nobody ever walked out of their initiation party sober. Well, except for this one." She made a lazy gesture to me and sipped her coffee.

"So, what are our orders now, Captain?" Uli asked, still standing at attention.

"Nothing," Dawnthorn told us, shaking her head. "The investigation is still ongoing. Find out what you can and keep reporting to me. Keep a low profile, keep working other quests, and we'll find out what we can."

We all finally relaxed and let out a collective sigh of relief. It seemed that we really weren't in trouble. Of course, we had no reason to be in trouble. We did exactly what was expected of us and told the truth. Mostly.

"Speaking of quests," the captain pulled out a piece of paper with a red wax seal of the Red Breaker logo. "You four are getting popular around town. This was another job that refused to go to bid and specifically asked for you."

Uli grabbed the notes and opened them up. She read through them silently as the captain explained.

"It's a local job. A church was supposed to have a shipment of silver bars brought in from the Childock Mountains. Shipment was reported to have come in sometime last week. After getting into the city, it went missing."

"And they hired the Red Breakers to find the silver?" I asked, confused, "Why not report to the police?"

"It was smuggled into the city," Giezha answered, to which the captain nodded her head.

"Why from there?" Mara asked. "That whole mountain range is no man's land."

"Special request from the Church of Sylo in Nara. They wanted to use metals in a ceremonial sword from the holy volcano that their god Sylo supposedly used as a forge so long ago. They don't care that the kingdoms of Narag and Nulgat lay claim to it. They just want to worship in peace."

Uli continued the line of thought. "And if the council finds out..."

"So does the Kingdom," the captain answered. "And then there will be potential for an international incident. No, the church understands the delicate nature of what they're asking. Going through us means unofficial channels. And unofficial channels mean even if it gets found out..."

I chimed in with my bit of wisdom. "It doesn't have the risk of leading to

223

war over regional disputes."

The captain gave me a slow clap and took a sip from her drink. "See? He's already catching up."

"Timeline?" Uli asked the captain.

"Flexible, due to the discretion needed. Now get out of here and go do your jobs. And remember, mum's the word."

All of us nodded and took our leave. With the fear of being turned into the captain's personal training dummies no longer hanging over our head, we all joked about how the others were so scared. Uli, of course, was not included in accusations of cowardice, but she was more than happy to chime in.

With about half the day left, we agreed to investigate the initial reports of the silver coming into the city. After that, we would need to talk to the church. There was no doubt somebody knew something they weren't admitting.

The guardsmen at the entrance mentioned in the job were the same ones I first met when I came to the city. They had no recollection of me, or if they did, they did an excellent job of feigning ignorance. Each of us took one of the guards and asked them questions. Uli naturally spoke to the squad captain, with each of us talking to another. After an uneventful conversation with one of the guards I'd previously bribed, I went back to the team, defeated.

"They're on edge," Giezha said as we walked away.

"No doubt," Mara agreed. "They didn't like having to deal with a whole team interrogating them. Something else is bothering them too."

"Maybe we're going about this the wrong way," Uli said, rubbing her chin. "Let's work on them individually for the rest of the week. See if we find anybody of interest coming in and out of the gate. We can talk to them in a more private capacity, perhaps grease a few palms."

"Think Captain'd give us a stipend for that?" I asked, thinking back to how much the guards' bribe was. "Probably have to be done on loan."

The others hung their heads in sorrow. That, of course, meant our bill kept going up. However, the payment for this job would be juicy, so we'd have to grin and bear it.

We spent the next few days working through the rest of the guards that patrolled that area at various times. Each of us interviewed different shifts on successive days. All told, there were the morning, afternoon, night, and overnight shifts. I got the short end of the stick and got stuck with the overnight shift.

The guards were just as dodgy about answers as the others, but I managed to use some charm with female guards to get some information. Unfortunately, it was nothing substantial and a bunch of hearsay.

Overnight shifts usually meant I slept well into the afternoon, resulting in having most of the day to do as I pleased. I spent all my free time studying at the library with Giezha's notes or training at the Warren. Well... all my free time when I wasn't having breakfast and dinner at the Golden Sky Tavern.

Kiersa was always happy to see my tired expression in the mornings and nursed me with an extra special soup du jour. Aire still didn't speak to me much, but my gift of a moonstone had certainly softened his opinion of me. Supper was usually whatever was leftover while we walked down the beaches and ended our evenings by the Everlasting.

Occasionally we'd sneak off to the Three Olives for a quick romp before my shift badgering the night guard began, but her father was growing suspicious. She implied that our friendship's "special" nature was still unknown to him, and she preferred to keep it that way.

Apparently, she had been walking funny at work lately.

After about a week of investigating, I still had nothing. There were a few vague descriptions, no hard leads, and a lot of "Fuck you, Breaker" shot at me. That was until I got to the last night of my patrol. I cornered a younger elven woman, who had been brought on last month, pretending to be a curious merchant. 'Younger' was relative, of course; she was probably two hundred and fifty.

You could only tell she was an elf because of her ears folding over and peeking out the side of her helmet. She was very excited to talk to me and, sensing an opportunity to get information, I turned on the charm.

After I batted my eyelashes a few times, she said that she was the one who signed their paperwork. She admitted that the person who'd brought the silver in had seemed strange.

"And did you get a good look at the cart it was brought in on?" I asked, taking notes with a charcoal stick.

"No, it just looked like a giant cart of silver. He was fully wrapped up

225

in black robes and wore an orange mask," she said with a dreamy look in her eye. "He didn't say anything, but he had a particular smell— like Kazherben Root. Based on that, I figured him as someone from maybe Midmanch. I think I saw their coat of arms on a sword or something too."

Once I finished asking her questions, I hurried back to the Silver Cup, doing my best to feign deafness to her question about when I got off my shift. I was brimming with energy about exciting information I had to tell the others. After breakfast at the Golden Sky. And a nap.

"Anything good?" Uli asked as we made a spread of our notes on the table at the Silver Cup that evening.

Sal was still gone on personal business, so we had the bar to ourselves. I had taken the liberty of putting some stew on before bed, and the collection of meat and potatoes was... passable.

"Got a whole lot of nothing," Mara said glumly. "Spent a lot of time hearing how they don't talk to Red Breakers. Then they danced around every question like it was the summer festival. Giezha?"

"Nah, the teams I interviewed were too busy asking what a goliath was doing with a magic staff to be useful. Even after they got tired of asking, none said they saw anything."

Uli nodded and checked her notes.

"Yep, I didn't get much outside of a couple possible sightings. Ash?"

I did a double-take when she said that. I knew she didn't mean anything, but when she said the name 'Ash,' I flashed back.

Hands up, 'don't do this', bang.

"You alright?" Uli asked me, eyebrows raised.

"Yeah," I flinched, snapping back to the real world. "Y-yeah uh, the guard I interviewed had a little bit of information. Just a general description of the guy and said that he might be from Midmanch."

Uli's eyes bugged out her head.

"Where?"

"Midmanch."

"That's where I went on my scouting mission!" she exclaimed. "Why pick someone from such a small town?"

"Could be a trader who also works in Zala?" Giezha suggested.

"Doubt Sylo's Church has a southern trader grabbing silver from the northern border. Way too risky," Uli said, shaking her head.

226

An idea flashed across Uli's face, and she rubbed her chin. "Only way to know who to look for is to ask the buyer. Why don't we pay a visit?"

After everybody finished their bowl, we geared up and headed for the Sylo church in the Castle District just south of the Fortress. To be inconspicuous, we wore our gear underneath white and purple robes. Mara and I couldn't hide our excitement to go undercover like this.

"This is going to be great!" Mara whispered as we walked up to the church.

The building lay just outside the Fortress's outer wall, giving it a natural camouflage against the cobblestone. It was a small, gray-stoned building shaped like the view of the Childock Mountain range if you were looking from Lake Shabba. The haunting sound of deep drums rhythmically echoed out of the front door.

A dwarf in gray robes and a grayer beard poked his head out the door as we approached the entrance. His eyes were invisible under the hood he wore, but his bulbous nose and facial hair poked out from underneath.

"Who seeks wisdom amongst the veins of silver and gold?" he asked in a low wheeze.

Oh great, puzzles. Wisdom. My absolute favorite. He stood by the door, watching us expectantly.

"A fool?" Giezha suggested.

"The poor?" added Uli.

Mara scratched her head. "Me?"

The man waited to hear from me as I thought to myself. I wanted to guess something profound and complimentary about his religion. Something that would really comb his beard hairs. Or... something.

"The blind," I said confidently. "The truly blind will not fret of treasures material in nature, but instead find wisdom, in the..." I had to think of something to tie it home. "Darkness. Of... life."

All three of my compatriots turned and raised an eyebrow at me. The dwarf holding the door stared longer at me than he did at the others combined. As my heart hammered in my chest like pickaxes against the Mountainside, the dwarf nodded.

"All acceptable answers," He wheezed. "Although the young man is... unorthodox."

"Or just wrong," Uli muttered, giving me a wink.

227

Inside was a service of sorts happening. In the center of the room was a dwarf with fiery red hair and a long beard best stretched past his ankles. He stood on a black obelisk while holding a hunk of some metallic ore. The congregation around him, almost entirely dwarves, listened as he spoke of their God Sylo.

"Sylo gave us these strings of silver and laid them here in the grounds beneath us." The dwarven man spoke with a booming voice that rhythmically bounced around the hall. All eyes were on him as the silver melted and floated in his hands. "The goddess Azira wove from the fabric of reality and helped create these metals before you. Silver, the metal of knowledge, was placed here so we may see into the past and know our future."

The silver metal slowly rose into the air and flattened itself into a thin oval. The silver metal began to shift as Shadows could be seen inside the metal. It looks like two people talking, but only in dark silhouettes. Suddenly, one of the figures attacked the other, and the silver exploded onto the walls. The liquid metal instantly solidified when it contacted the stone interior, glistening against dozens of other metal globules that peppered the walls.

The man standing at the top of the Obelisk noticed us and quickly wrapped up his speech. The Obelisk slowly sank into the ground as a chorus began to sing, and the other congregation members joined in. The priest had piercing blue eyes set in a severe-looking face. He wore a slight frown as he walked up to us.

"I've been waiting for you," he said, looking at each of us sternly.

"You have?" Mara asked.

"Yes," he said as he led us out of the main room. "The silver spoke to me during my preparations for today's sermon. It told me that I would be visited by four blind mice, lost in the maze."

Uli looked at me and gestured for me to speak up.

"Yes, well, I assure you we aren't looking for cheese, sir," I joked. "We are here for... other purposes."

"Other purposes?" The man asked, feigning ignorance as we walked down a deep staircase.

"Yes, you could say it has something to do with the procurement of your soothsaying metals."

228

The man's stern expression grew even more so at my comment. He stopped and placed his hands on the walls of the damp, rocky wall. As he did, a symbol like two trapezoids lit upon his hand. The rocky wall trembled, and the ground beneath us shook. As the silver and gold light in his hand faded, a large hole in the wall looked like it was being cut before dissolving. Inside the opening was a small study filled with books, a few chairs, and an oil lamp on a desk.

"Breakers," he said, almost growling, "Come."

Filing into the room, he waved his hand, and the hole in the wall sealed shut as the rocks coalesced back together. The faint sound of the choir could be barely heard from the inches of stone. The priest paced back and forth several times behind his desk. He pulled out a glass orb the size of a snow globe from his desk and tossed it into the air. Instead of crashing to the ground, the orb floated up and grew to twice the size of a beach ball before shining brightly.

"Sylo's greatest gift has been stolen from us," the dwarf announced gruffly. "After arranging for the delivery of silver, our courier decided not to deliver."

As he spoke, the image of a figure in green robes and a black hood could be seen running through a crowded street. The person running was carrying a small sack that jingled as he ran between the crowds of people. They were huffing and puffing as they looked back towards someone pursuing them.

"When the person set to deliver didn't show, we contacted our intermediary. We have not heard from them since then."

Uli leaned against the wall-to-wall bookshelf as she listened. "Any indication as to why?"

The dwarf pursed his lips behind his massive set of facial hair. "It is believed the courier had a change of heart. Possibly because of another buyer. Silver blessed from the Childock Mountains contains particularly fine components for spells, potions, and enchanted items. It's worth several times its weight."

The orb panned out to reveal the two people chasing the courier. It was two men. One was a huge goliath with zero expression, and the other a half-elf frantically searching for the courier. The goliath said something silently to the half-elf while pointing in the direction of where the courier

229

had been. A chill went up to my spine, as I'm sure it did for the others. We all silently looked at each other but said nothing. Once again, those two had shown up.

When the orb focused back to where the courier was, they had disappeared. The image slowly faded to nothing, and the orb fell to the ground silently. The dwarf picked up the orb and put it back on his desk. He took off his hood, scratched the back of his head, and let out an exasperated sigh.

"That was an eyewitness testimony we procured from somebody who had seen the courier," he explained. "This was two days ago, and the courier has not been seen since. There was no report of him at all. Until... recently."

"Did the two that chased him catch up?" Uli asked while looking at me and the others.

"That is unknown," the dwarf man said, reaching into an inner pocket. "As was what happened to the courier. Until this showed up."

The dwarf pulled out a piece of fabric from his cloak. It was torn and rough, stinking of death even from far away. He handed the cloth to me, and I inspected it closer while pinching my nose. The color of the fabric was black and gray. Tiny flecks of silver and gray splattered on top of the fibers, but the fabric was also gray. It looked like it was discolored slightly. Lighter in splotches, darker in others. Almost like someone had bleached the fabric. Like it was bleached by... by the sun...

"Son of a bitch," I whispered to myself. I looked up to the priest, whose eyes barely twitched as I stared at him. "Was this from the courier?"

"It was," he responded, nodding. "We were able to verify this based on the silver dust in the fabric. It was a perfect match for Childock Mountain Silver. The intermediary confirmed that the fabric came from the same type of cloak as the courier wore."

Giezha was the first to catch on to my train of thought. I could see it in her eyes and how she scowled at the fabric while pouring over the details. She gave me a look, silently asking if it was the same fabric I had found. I nodded to her, and Mara also seemed to understand, with her jaw going slack at the realization. The priest seemed to be putting two and two together as he saw our collective realization at something he was not privy to.

"I see there is an idea about what happened to the courier," he said with a sigh. "However, I have no interest in the dirty rotten scoundrel. I simply desire to have the silver that was promised to my congregation."

"Who was the eyewitness?" Uli asked while drumming her fingers on her leg.

"A goblin from Iron Court, Rogorbo, I believe. Before seeing the courier be chased, he was selling food from a cart that day. He then climbed on top of a building to watch."

"Rogorm," Uli corrected him with a scowl. "The witness was Rogorm the Unkind. A sleazy bastard who specializes in knowing what people don't want him to know."

The priest again nodded. "That sounds right, yes. He was certainly rude and unbecoming."

"Indeed," Uli said, standing straight and walking over to shake his hand. "Thank you for the information, your holiness. We will take our leave so that we may continue our investigation. If you have any other information you'd like to tell us, please don't hesitate."

The priest nodded and let us out of his office and the church. He could be heard retaking the stage and proselytizing about gold as we left.

As we walked down the streets, I looked at the fabric again. It had the exact same texture as the fabric that I had given to Kiersa the other night. Only this piece was shaped differently. There was no doubt that it was from the same cloak I had seen the rat person wearing.

"This is not good," I said out loud.

"Which part?" Uli asked in an annoyed tone as she pushed her way through the crowded Road. "The part where Mick and Mhurren showed up again? Or the part where it has something to do with whatever attacked you last night? Or maybe the part where we have to go and talk to that bastard, Rogorm?"

"All of the above," Giezha suggested.

"The part where I have a piece of this fabric too," I said.

Uli and stopped short. Her eyes bugged out of her skull as she bared her teeth and stuck a finger in my chest.

"You mind telling me when you were gonna mention that?" she said dangerously, causing others to look at us.

I put my hands up and tried to calm her down. "I-I was going to tell you

231

guys. Really!"

"But you didn't." Giezha's trademark glare was in full force.

Mara didn't say anything, but her face made it clear she was pissed. The three of them cornered me by an abandoned store, and I felt a noose starting to wrap around my neck.

"Look, I couldn't say it in front of the captain," I said, trying desperately to find the best words. "Kiersa didn't just run away when that happened." None of them reacted, so I continued speaking. "Kiersa was the one who saved me. She did something with the moonstone, and it shot out that crazy light. That thing pinned me down, and it was going to tear my throat out. Next thing I know, it's dissolving in the air after I kicked its head off."

"And the fabric?" Uli asked, doing her best impression of the captain from earlier.

"And the fabric was dissolving too. I only managed to save a single scrap. I have no idea what happened to the rest of it."

"Great, so where is the scrap?" Uli asked

I made an uncomfortable face and didn't answer. Realization spread across Mara's face. She facepalmed and just muttered to herself. Giezha and Uli looked at her, demanding an answer.

"Where?" Uli urged

"Kiersa has it." Mara and I said simultaneously.

Giezha dropped her staff, and Uli was gobsmacked. Mara continued to mutter to herself as I sat there squirming on the inside. I had thought I was being safe with this decision, that the council could find something I'd miss, but I now realized how bad of a mistake that was. I had messed up, and I had messed up badly. Uli began to tremble as her green skin turned bright pink. With her eyes turned to slits, she took a deep breath and spoke.

"Why... Would. You. Do. That?" she asked barely above a whisper. "We could've used it to tie the courier to the zombie. Giezha could've found traces of the magic used on the courier."

"This one was cleaned." Giezha said, pointing to the scrap.

No matter how hard I tried to pull the words out, they refused to cross my lips. "Because...because..."

"Because you don't trust us?" Mara asked, more hurt than angry.

"No!" I urged. "I do trust you guys. I just..."

"Don't trust the captain?" Uli asked, her voice rising dangerously.

"No! No! No!" I shouted, my cheeks bright red. "It's not about me, alright! Or you! It's because..."

Giezha finished my sentence for me. "It's because nobody would ever trust the words of a Red Breaker. Right?"

I sighed and hung my shoulders. "Right. Ever since I've gotten here, it seems like the guild is just mistrusted or downright hated. Guys, whatever is going on here is bigger than the guild. This could get really bad. Stuff like this is exactly how the Undead Incursion happened all those years ago."

Giezha nodded her head at this while Uli bit her thumbnail and gave me a look of deep disapproval.

"That was really dumb, Asher," she muttered before turning and walking.

"I mean, it kind of makes sense," Mara said timidly, turning to join Uli. "If this does wind up being like The Incursion, it could get really bad."

I stood there, afraid to follow them. As I watched them continue on, Giezha tapped me on the shoulders. The glint of danger in her eyes had left, replaced with her usual expression of neutrality mixed with boredom. She gestured with her head towards the others and just rolled her eyes.

"They'll be fine," she said quietly as she started walking towards them. "You could have handled it better, but don't worry too much."

Realizing that I was the last one left, I jogged to catch up.

Chapter 21

Xaliasday Evening, 14th of Seeyrn, Year 678, 4th Age

By the time we made our way into Iron Court, darkness had blanketed the city. We tried to keep a low profile and put our red bandannas underneath our white and purple robes. Although the guild worked with less-than-legal customers more than any guild, we were still unwelcome.

I felt a paranoid sensation that we were being followed more than once. But every time I turned and looked, everyone made a point of not looking at us. The others picked up on the same vibe, and we stayed in a tight formation.

As we walked, I got up near Giezha and whispered. "Would it be possible to make us look like different people?"

Giezha shook her head and said nothing. Uli walked beside me and spoke under her breath.

"That kind of illusion magic is out of her wheelhouse. Plus, she focuses on enchantments and evocation, remember?"

Giezha cast me an annoyed glance but said nothing else. I felt guilty about asking why she wasn't doing a specific type of magic.

We found Rogorm selling from his cart in the same spot as before. We approached him as he finished taking payment from a band of half-orcs. Noticing us, his eyes went wide. Looking back and forth rapidly, he picked a direction and sprinted away. We ran after him, forcing the crowd of people to make a hole.

"Dammit, Rogorm!" Uli shouted. "Giezha, try and slow him down."

Uli, Mara, and I chased after him, right on his tail, while Giezha pulled her staff out from under her cloak and shot a burst of icicles down the street. He managed to run into a building right as they were about to hit. As we got to the front door of the building, a muscle-bound human and a

234

dragonborn blocked our path with a pair of two-handed axes.

"Where do you think you're going?" the dragonborn growled. "Fighting in the streets is strictly forbidden."

"Let us through!" Uli shouted, her knife in hand. "That bastard Rogorm is getting away!"

"Mr. Rogorm is free to visit his home as he pleases," the human guard said, pointing the ax toward us. "Do not think you can get past us in one piece."

Judging by the armor they were wearing and muscles able to rival Giezha, they may have had a point. More people began to gather around us, and pointed in our direction, scowling as they talked. The look in Uli's eye made it clear she was ready to cut these guys' throats out and anybody else's who got in her way. I placed a hand on her shoulder and whispered into her ear.

"C'mon, Uli. Let's get out of here," I urged, sensing the guards could attack at any moment. "He can't stay in there forever."

Uli clenched her fists and kept looking at the guards. After a moment, she turned and walked away from them. Mara and Giezha kept their eyes on the guards as we went down the street. Several people kept looking at us as we walked, a few making threatening gestures. I looked at a few of them and lit a fireball in my hand, daring them to make a move.

"Bastard slipped through our fingers," Uli muttered angrily. "He's our main lead in this whole thing."

"We'll just need to catch him later," Mara suggested, patting Uli on the shoulders. "We could just wait him out, and then bam! Snatch and grab." Mara pounded a fist into her palm to visualize her idea.

"We should also investigate the rat attack," Giezha suggested. "Split into two teams and figure out what to do next."

"Fine," Uli sighed, kicking a rock on the ground. "I'll go investigate the cart with Mara. You take Asher to see if there's anything left from that rat thing."

"You sure?" Giezha asked, giving Mara a look. Mara had another unspoken conversation with Giezha before taking Uli towards the cart. Giezha turned and gave me the cloth piece. "Wasn't sure if you wanted this back. I inspected it on our way here, and it gave me an idea. Let's go to where the attack happened."

"Alright," I said, still wary of the surrounding area. "Will the other two be okay?"

Giezha gave me an evil grin and didn't say anything. Taking that as a positive sign, I led her to the alley. The streets were bustling with people when we got there, and the alleyway was no different. Boxes lined the ground as business folk hauled in cargo and brought out trash. Several times, a rat skittered across my foot as we inspected the area.

"There's no way we'll find anything," I complained. "This whole area has been contaminated with prints, other people, and junk."

I picked up a broken board on the ground and threw it behind me. Underneath was where I had been tackled to the ground by the rat-zombie. A few droplets of my blood still stained the ground. Around the blood droplets were scratch marks cleaved into the solid rock.

"Yo, Giezha, think this could help at all?" I asked, pointing to my discovery. "This is where the Undead Rat King decided I would make a good midnight snack."

Giezha leaned down to the blood and inspected it. She stood up and made a few motions as if she were pantomiming the attack based on how I'd described it. She also seemed to be taking some liberties.

"Hey, my face wasn't panicked when I got tackled," I protested as Giezha flailed on the ground. "And I went down fighting the whole time."

Giezha played dead for a moment before peeking with one eye. Once she was done with her performance, she jumped up and crouched low. She pointed her staff down and touched a bit of the blood splatter. The runes on her staff began to glow bright red, and as it did, the whole alley was cascaded in red light. It was like we were in a darkroom developing film. The red light revealed something on the walls. Darker red droplets and splatters contrasted against the red-lit walls.

"Blood splatter analysis," I muttered in amazement. "How'd you do that?"

Giezha did her best to not smile as she explained. "I used the locating spell, commonly used to keep an eye on objects or people, and applied it to your blood. After that, I combined it with the light spell, specifically red light. The magic locating mixed with the light and created a small area where we could easily reveal small and unseen objects."

"Giezha, you are seriously the most brilliant person I know." I said in wonder. "That's really clever."

Thanks to her spell, everything else looked washed out in the light, except for the blood splatter, which was bright and luminous. The rat really did a number on me, based on how much blood got on the walls, ground, and boxes nearby.

"That was when it got my arm," I said, pointing to the first splatter revealed. I turned behind and pointed to another. "Here was the second. After that, we got hit by the moonstone beam and... huh."

That stumped me. I was slashed a couple times by the rat, but only in two directions. You could clearly see the blood splatter on the walls from where I got hit. But when I turned and looked backward in the direction the rat initially came from, you could see more blood. A lot more blood.

"Giezha," I said, pointing to the splatter of previously invisible blood. "Follow me."

When we walked deeper into the alley, we saw these giant pools of blood and splatter patterns that looked like something out of a horror movie. On the opposite wall, it almost looked like the person was outlined with blood. Well, half of a person.

"What could have done this?" Giezha asked, clearly disturbed by the crude outlining of an abrupt cut in the middle.

I tried to inspect the area, but I could not find the other half of the blood splatter. At first, I thought it might have been a person being ripped in half. But why would their blood outline their entire body? How come there wasn't any splatter on the opposite side to coincide?

"Let me try this again," I told her, returning to where I was tackled initially. "Stay where you are."

I walked back to the original attack location and looked towards Giezha. Knowing where to look, and with the light on, I could see the blood splatter. Half of it. The half that was on the wall. But I still couldn't see where the other half went in this crowded alleyway. Wait. This crowded alleyway. Filled with boxes.

"Giezha!" I shouted excitedly. "Shine the light on those boxes we moved."

"Okay." when she shined the light directly on the boxes we had moved, they lit up with blood splatter. "Oh," she said, seeing the area lit up.

"It's a puzzle," I said confidently. "And I think I know the answer."

Working on a hunch, I remembered the shape of the rat person and tried to recreate their body shape with the boxes. Within a few minutes, I got my shape the way I wanted it and kept Giezha's revealing light on the boxes and the wall behind me. Running back to where Kiersa was when she saved me, everything fell into place.

"That blood splatter came from the rat," I said as I held a finger out like a pistol while pretending to be Kiersa. "Whatever that moonstone spell was, it disintegrated that thing. Left an imprint of the blood on the walls."

We collected a few samples of the blood and some dust found on the ground. Using Giezha's amazing spell, we managed to find more of the silver dust from the cloth on the ground. Most revealing was when we found traces of the silver dust layered over the top of the blood splatter.

"That settles it," Giezha said while wiping her brow. "The courier met a sticky end thanks to the rat."

"Yeah," I agreed. "And it was likely Rogorm made it happen, based on how he responded to our arrival." I looked at Giezha and noticed she was sweating despite the cool weather. Fall had finally started. "You alright, Giezha?"

"I'm fine," she said, fanning herself. "Just used a lot of mana on spells I'm not familiar with."

Giezha sat down on a box and pulled out a blue potion filled with tiny silver bubbles. After gulping it down heartily, Giezha wiped her forehead again and took a few deep breaths. She cast me an embarrassed glance, but I just patted her on the back.

"Gotta stay hydrated, Giezha," I joked. "Even I know that. Should we head to the tavern then and wait for them? Call it a night?"

Giezha walked past me and said nothing. Turning, she beckoned for me to follow her.

"No, we're all on stakeout duty tonight. Plus, we should inspect Rogorm's cart," she said, picking up her pace. "We drew straws, and you and Uli got the short straws."

I racked my brain, trying to think of when I drew straws. I did not draw straws. I did not. "When did this happen?" I asked incredulously.

"Before we left," she said, smirking. "We drew straws, and the only one left for you was the short one. So now you get to be on a stakeout with Uli on her birthday."

That stopped me dead in my tracks. "It's her birthday? Since when?"

"Since forever," Giezha said, not slowing at all. "She was born on the 15th of Seeyrn, 678 of the 4th Age."

"How old's that make her?" I asked curiously. I just realized I had never found out how old everyone was.

"She should be twenty-four. You remembered to get her a gift, right?" Giezha asked teasingly.

"Absolutely not, but you're going to help me shop for something!" I laughed.

"There is absolutely no way that I am helping you shop at the last minute," Giezha said stone-faced.

We found ourselves at a weapons shop in Iron Court, shopping for Uli's birthday. Giezha was stewing in the corner over being dragged into the store with me. I was trying to decide whether she would like a new knife or an accessory for her current one better. The shopkeeper, an elf with a scarred right ear, was someone I noticed watching our chase with the goblin Rogorm. Although he eyed us suspiciously, he did not stop us from shopping.

"Do you think she'd like a new blade or a sheath?" I asked Giezha while inspecting a red leather sheath.

"She'd prefer you not spend money on her," Giezha said with a grumble. "And I don't want to be here." I picked up the sheath and brought it over to Giezha. Barely glancing at it, she quickly looked away. "Yes, that will be fine. Let's get out of here."

"We've barely looked, though!" I protested.

"I don't care," she turned to leave. "I'm out of here."

Reflexively, I grabbed for her shoulder, but she brushed me away. "Wait! Giezha!"

Running in front of her at the door, I waved my hands to get her attention. When I looked at her, I noticed that she was scared, terrified even. She looked from left to right rapidly, and I could hear her fingers tapping against her staff. I let her pass and followed her out of the store.

"Giezha, what's wrong?" I asked quietly. "Is there something in the store?"

She didn't say anything and just looked away.

"Sorry," I mumbled. "I shouldn't have kept you in there since you were uncomfortable. You don't have to explain anything to me."

Realizing I was still holding the sheath, I turned to go into the store and return it. As I did, I felt a giant hand on my shoulder. Giezha grasped my shoulder with surprising gentleness. I stopped and turned around. Giezha's cheeks were bright pink, and she looked down at her feet.

"It's okay. It's just a bit embarrassing." She took a deep breath and kept going. "I didn't leave my kin just because of using magic." she struggled with the words she spoke. The pained expression on her face came from trying to articulate herself. "Weapons matter to most goliath clans. And I had an... incident when I was younger."

"Giezha, seriously." I squeezed her hand that was still resting on my shoulder. "You don't have to explain anything. If being in there makes you uncomfortable, that's all I need to know. We can talk about it some other time when it's easier for you."

Giezha thought for a minute and smiled. Although still bothered, her normal look came back.

"Thank you, Asher. I'll keep that in mind." she pointed at the sheath still in one of my hands. "Don't get her that. She's pretty attached to her current sheath. I suggest a different gift. She loves turquoise."

I looked at the sheath and then heard the elf from the store screaming at me.

"Ah, fuck."

By the time we made it back to meet up with Mara and Uli, I had settled on a pair of spherical turquoise charms she could put on her sheath or at the hilt of her dagger. They didn't have any at the weapon shop, but I found a vendor selling them on the street.

Rogorm's cart was gone when we made it back to the meet-up point. Mara and Uli were joking about something with another goblin when we found them. Giezha waved them down as Uli and Mara waved good-byes to the goblin. Uli seemed to be in a much better mood compared to when we had left her.

"Find anything interesting?" Uli asked, grinning from ear to ear.

"That blast from the moonstone disintegrated the thing that attacked me," I told them, excited to share our insight. "We found a literal outline of its body in an invisible blood splatter thanks to some nifty work by Giezha." Giezha tipped her giant witch's hat in response. "We also found silver dust

240

all over the area too. So, the courier had to have been attacked by the rat. Tell them the best part, Giezha."

Giezha didn't match my enthusiasm but was still happy to take the wheel.

"We will be able to prove if Rogorm was in contact with the silver thanks to my searching spell. I've also entertained the notion that the rat was the courier originally. They may have been cursed."

"Not a bad idea," Uli said. "Now we just need to wait for that bastard to appear again."

"Which means we get to stake out the area," I said, looking to Uli. "Sorry that we have to do it on your birthday."

Uli just shrugged. "Didn't have any other plans. We can use the time to go over notes. We should probably go get in position, shops will close soon, and we'll need to get food for our watch."

"Food does sound good," I admitted to my rumbling stomach. "Where would you like to go, Mara? Giezha...?" As I turned to the others, I saw that only Uli and I remained. Off in the distance, I saw the shadows of Mara and Giezha, both running off.

"Huh," Uli said in a tone of fake surprise. "Guess they were in a hurry."

"No kidding," I said with a vague sense of danger.

Chapter 22

Xaliasday Night, 14th of Seeyrn, Year 678, 4th Age

We wound up on the top level of a shady inn opposite the building Rogorm disappeared into. The two guards standing out front were still there, standing like a pair of muscly statues by the door. The room we had rented was only a single silver coin, which the dwarven woman at the front desk bit to test its authenticity.

To call the room small was the understatement of the century. The entire room was less than eighty square feet, with the bed taking up most of the space, despite being shorter than I was.

Uli sat on the raised straw mattress, peering out the window, spying on the opposite building. I walked into the room, carrying a baggie filled with beef and mushroom pies and a bowl of steamed rice. Uli's eyes widened at the smell of the meaty pies. She was practically lifted off the bed by the nostrils.

"Oh, I love hand pies!" she said as I flopped onto the bed, sending bits of hay into the air.

I took a grateful bite into one of the dozen pies I'd bought for us to split. The warm, juicy beef and mushrooms mixed with a spicy sauce lifted my tastebuds to heaven.

The both of us devoured our meals in silence, too focused on the delicious food to bother with conversation. I gestured for her to dig into the rice, and she scooped some into an empty pie shell.

I couldn't help but notice how Uli's ears fluttered as she savored the meal. Uli may not have had the ferocity of Mara when it came to eating, but she clearly shared the same appreciation. As did I. Once we plowed through the entire meal in no time flat, we let out a simultaneous sigh of satisfaction.

We took turns focusing on the window while telling jokes and swapping

242

stories of our adventures. Uli took special care not to ask about my past while giving precious few details of her own. From what I gathered, she was well-traveled by a young age. She came from the other side of the Kingdom and the Readisor Sea and had lived in a small city named Shabuled, roughly six hundred miles away.

"You must have spent at least a year on the road," I said in awe.

"Years, actually." Uli winked, playing a winning hand of cards. "Mother and Father made sure I had plenty growing up, but their time as tradesmen meant I had to be on the road with them."

I shuffled the deck of cards, hoping I'd catch her cheating this time. "So, they're here now?"

She shrugged, dealing out a perfect hand for herself, no doubt. "Nah, they retired back by The Woods a while ago. They knew I wanted to start my own life and helped me get set up before setting off back home." She looked out to check for movement outside with a wistful look. "We send each other letters often."

She changed the subject to pointers on stealth and diplomacy while I finally managed to King her Jack. Despite Uli's intimidating aura, she was incredibly easy to talk to and had a knack for getting me to open up.

After eating the scrumptious meal, and hours of conversation I felt my dry throat beg for a drink. Uli seemed to have the same idea as she pulled a bottle out of thin air, the same way she did with her knife.

"Hope you like cherry mead," she said, popping off the cork with one of her fangs.

Uli flicked the cork off her tooth and took a sip before handing it to me.

The mead was sweet and reminded me of maraschino cherry juice. It was thick and almost syrupy in its consistency. I certainly couldn't taste any alcohol.

"I'm not a womanizer, right?" I found myself asking out of the blue.

Uli's eyes snapped from the window, and she looked at me with a funny grin. Her ears fluttered—no doubt she was excited to tease me. She took a minute to collect her thoughts before speaking. She bit her lip as she spoke, and the mead must've put some color on her cheeks. I continued on, trying to provide context.

"Everyone knows I've had sex with Mara, with Kiersa. But neither really want to commit right now. I mean they do, and they don't. You know what

243

I mean? So, I kinda see myself as a free agent." I rubbed the back of my neck, feeling like a chauvinist as I spoke. "Is that bad? Like, should I not be doing that?"

Uli let out a burst of laughter, holding her sides. She let out a sigh and spoke.

"Nah, you're fine, Asher," she reassured me, "Have some fun! Mara's not the type to rush into relationships, and Kiersa… she's got other things to worry about."

I still felt unsure. "I just…"

Uli gave me a deadpan look. "Asher, in the name of Dusyr and my ancestors, you're fine. Live the adventurer's life."

"Which is?" I asked as she took a pull from the bottle.

"Ah!" She smacked her lips. "Fight hard, drink harder, and fuck hardest. Now get drinking."

She laughed and handed me the bottle. Checking the bottle, I saw that the mead was only three percent alcohol. Not exactly drinking hard, but that was for the best. Taking a sip, I took another look out the window and double-checked there was no movement. Still, nothing in the time we had been here.

"Think he's gonna make a move tonight?" I asked, setting the bottle down on the floor. It was about half empty.

"Doubt it," Uli said, writing in a journal she'd brought. "We spooked him something bad. He'd never leave that cart unattended unless it was something serious. Especially when it had this much coin still inside. Can't go out or around, and there aren't any underground passages either."

She casually pulled a bag of coins out of nowhere, jingling it lazily. Unable to contain my curiosity, I shut the curtain and looked at her.

"How do you do that?"

"Do what?"

"The thing where you pull stuff out of thin air?"

Uli shrugged and simply said, "Magic."

"C'mon," I said, pulling out my own journal and turning to my section on magic. "You can't just leave it like that. What type of magic? Is it a spell that I could learn? How does it work?"

Uli rolled her eyes and made the bag of coins disappear with a flourish of her wrist. "Well, aren't we curious?" She crawled over to me on the bed

244

and pulled her shirt up, revealing one of the tattoos on her stomach. "These tattoos aren't just for show." She pointed to the purple triangle on her waist, which started to glow. "A witch gave me this tattoo, and it allows me to store spells with my body. The only spells I know are sleight-of-hand, dance of light, and illusory sounds."

I'd heard of the last two spells she mentioned. Dance of light allowed you to create little lights that floated in the air. Illusory sounds are just sound you could mimic and throw out.

"What does sleight of hand do?" I asked, writing everything down in my journal.

"It lets me pull things out of my enchanted boxes or sacks," Uli said, magicking a pair of glasses out of thin air. "Giezha has helped me enchant a bunch of bags, boxes, and even a few pockets. All I have to do is imagine where I kept something and pull it out of its space."

With a flourish, an entire longbow and quiver appeared in her hands. I jumped back in surprise, which made her giggle. With a wave, she made it disappear again.

"Doesn't work if it's not where I'm thinking, though. Or too far."

"So, you just have a bunch of stuff hidden away to pull out of thin air whenever you need it?" I asked.

"Well, it's not that simple. If I'm too far away, the spell won't work either. And if I'm out of mana, I won't be able to use the summon either. The bigger the object, the more mana I use up."

"And the tattoo stores the spells?"

"Yep! There are no incantations, no runes to remember, just a simple mental image, and bam! It's useful because I don't look like I can do magic. And since there's no indication of me using magic, it helps me get the drop on somebody else.

"Hiya!"

Uli made an attacking motion towards the window, with her knife suddenly appearing in her hand.

"Oh!" I said, finishing up my notes. "That reminds me, I have something for you."

I pulled out a small, wrapped box from my knapsack. I handed Uli the box and smiled.

"Happy birthday, Uli! It was kind of a last-minute purchase." I felt like

245

a dork admitting it, but I was a terrible liar. "Sorry I hadn't asked about when yours was before today."

Uli looked at the box with trepidation and slowly took the gift. She opened the box, revealing two tiny pearls of turquoise with copper metal wrapping around them. They had tiny hooks that let you attach them to an object like a piece of wood or leather. The person I bought them from said it'd make for a fantastic charm.

"Earrings?" she asked curiously, gingerly putting them next to her ear.

"Uh, no," I said, a little confused. "I got them as a charm to put on your sheath. Giezha mentioned you liked turquoise, so I got these for you."

She gave me a look that said, "Are you serious?" and used her sleight-of-hand again. A tiny pair of lapis lazuli was in her palm, shaped exactly like the turquoise I'd got her. She quickly put them on her ears, proving that the salesman I bought these from had swindled me. As I hung my head in shame, Uli laughed and patted me on the back.

"It's alright Asher, I prefer them as earrings. Besides," she said as she pulled my chin up with a finger, "I do love turquoise."

Uli got closer to me and moved her hand to my face. Her eyes' shape and even color had changed. Usually, her eyes were like bright copper coins. Now, they were wide and circular and had turned a light shade of pink, illuminated only by the oil lamp.

Slowly, she pressed her hand against my racing chest. "We're not actually on duty, you know..." She whispered in my ear. "The girls are watching from the building next to Rogorm. They said I should enjoy my birthday present."

"Really?" I asked as Uli straddled me. "What would that be?"

Uli looked at me with an evil smile, and snapped her fingers. In the blink of an eye, she was completely naked from head to toe.

"Right..." I laughed a little nervously. "I guess you can do that with sleight of hand as well. Ha..."

With surprising force, Uli shoved me down onto the bed and began to kiss me. Uli grabbed my face and aggressively pressed herself against me, trying to open my mouth. Unable to stop her momentum, her body pressed against mine, continuing her onslaught of physicality. Happy to oblige, I unbuckled my trousers as she ripped my shirt off me. Literally.

"Hey," I said in garbled protest while she kept kissing me. "I liked that

246

shirt."

Finally pulling away from me, Uli wiped her mouth as her chest heaved up and down.

"I'll buy you a new one, Asher," she said hungrily. "I need to go shopping and pick up a new dress anyway. Now let me have my real birthday present."

When I tried to move, I realized that my left hand was cuffed to the edge of the corner post of the bed. Uli's smiled sadistically as she kept staring at me. The sudden turn of events could only make me laugh.

"Haha, ah... I'm in danger."

Uli threw herself onto me and began to kiss my neck, her fangs brushing my artery. "That's right, Asher," she said as she started to stroke my fully erect cock. "The girls knew how often we've been getting interrupted, and got me something for my birthday too. Mmmh. Mmmh. You, all to myself." She held my head with her other hand, cradling it with her arms.

When she started to pick up the pace, I let slip a moan of pleasure as her soft hands stroked the entirety of my member. The roughness of her treatment was offset by the gentle skill of her hands. When I made the noise, she giggled and started to go even faster.

"You like that? Yeah, I bet you do, you little boy toy, ahh!"

As she was starting to take over, I used my free hand to massage her clit. As I did, her small, athletic frame writhed against me, wiggling and pressing her hips into my palm.

I played with her, rubbing in wide circles, applying light pressure around the edges. She was dripping wet and incredibly tight as I slipped in a finger.

"Oh, Gods," she moaned, biting her lip. "You are a bad boy, Asher."

My reward for my act of rebellion was a bite on my neck and faster strokes of my cock. I began to leak precum onto Uli's hand, which, when she noticed, made Uli sit upright. She looked at it dribble on her palm for a moment before slowly licking it off. She stared at me as she moaned in satisfaction, grinding her hips against my hand.

"I think I know what I want next," she whispered.

Dismounting me, she crawled up to my face and stood up. Seeing her body up close was like looking at a master sculpture. Every muscle was delicately carved, creating the surreal feeling of soft marble. As I ran my

247

hands up and down her legs, she stepped closer.

All I could see now was her tight and wet pussy lips in all their dark green glory. I was now directly eye-level with her pretty slit. I sat up straight and looked up. Uli's eyes were directly on me, her chest slowly going up and down as she breathed in and out. Somehow, a girl like Uli being like this in bed made too much sense. I wasn't going to complain, though.

"Eat me out, Asher," she whispered as she began to finger herself in front of me, circling her clit repeatedly. I stroked my cock to the show while she spoke. "And if you do that, I'll ride you. I'll ride you until the morning comes."

"Well..." I said slowly, grinning at her. "That sounds fun."

In a show of non-submission, I used my free hand and grabbed her by her ass, pulling her pussy towards my mouth. She let out a squeal and grabbed the back of my head as I tongued her. I circled around her clit with my tongue, matching how she fingered herself while I squeezed her ass as hard as I could. Her legs trembled, and her hips bucked as I felt her body shake and shudder. Uli also started moaning louder and louder.

"Yes, yes, yes!" she screamed, grabbing the back of my head and pulling at my hair.

Pulling her away for a second, I took a deep breath. I looked at the previously confident and self-assured Uli, now barely able to stand. Her mouth hung open, and her hungry eyes now melted at my gaze.

"Shhhh," I teased. "We can't let the others hear us. It could blow our cover."

Whatever I said relit the fire in her heart-shaped-eyes. She pulled my face back in, burying it against her pussy. Taking the cue to get back to work, I licked her pussy faster and faster. Her cute moans rattled out of her as I suckled on her clit and changed my tempo, going faster and slower. Faster and slower.

The changing in pace was her favorite, and Uli's voice went higher and higher. My heart raced as I felt my left hand beg to join in grabbing her. With a burst of energy and a jerk of my hand, the handcuff links exploded, freeing my hand.

I grabbed her with both hands and rested her legs over my shoulder.

"Yes! Oh fuck, yes!" She screamed, tightening her legs around me as I

248

held her up. "Oh, keep going, Asher! I'm gonna cum! Ah!"

I held her body against mine continuing my worship of her body. With one final flourish and licked her until her hips started shaking uncontrollably. I felt a squirt of liquid against my face. Uli screamed into her arm, and I felt her body slacken against the wall she'd pinned me up against. For a moment, I held her there as she struggled to catch her breath, slowly continuing to circle my tongue. Uli was incredibly light in my arms.

"I... I... Wow," she panted, defenseless, as I lowered her onto my lap. She wiped my mouth with a bedsheet and held my face. "You really know how to treat a girl on her birthday."

Gently, she pulled me closer and kissed me. Our sweaty bodies tightly coiled around each other. As we kissed, I felt her rock her hips back and forth. Soon she was resting her pussy against my cock. I could just barely feel the tip graze up against her. Uli looked at me and silently slid herself back. The both of us shuddered and moaned as I entered her tight body. She squeezed onto me with a grip that threatened to never let go.

"Ah, Gods..." she moaned, slowly pushing the rest in. "It's even better than Mara said..."

"She-she really did talk about it?" I groaned, unable to stop myself.

I couldn't help but blush in embarrassment at her talking about that with the others. Uli noticed this and grinned as she slowly began to move her hips back and forth. She hung onto me, moving back and forth, slowly pumping my cock.

"That's right, Asher," Uli whispered into my ear as she wrapped herself around my shoulders and started bouncing up and down. "She told me all about how you fuck her senseless with that big, thick cock of yours."

I felt my mind go blank as I held onto her ass while she expertly bounced up and down, tightly wrapped around me. She gently nibbled my neck a few times, making my whole body tighten up. Thankfully, Uli was careful not to bite down hard with her fangs though.

"She was certainly right about how big you are... Oh, fuck, Gods, yes! I can see the outline when you go inside my tight pussy. Gah!"

Uli tried her best to whisper this, but she couldn't help but shout as I felt myself beginning to lose the battle. I looked, and she was right. You could see the barest outline of my cock going in and out of her against her toned abs.

249

"She told me how you're like nothing she'd seen… Or felt. How you made her addicted to you." Uli grabbed onto my shoulder blades, and I felt her nails dig into me. Reflexively, I grabbed her by the hips and held her down. When I did, her eyes lit up, and she gasped. "Shit, sorry. I just—I just couldn't help it."

"That's fine," I said, a sadistic grin. "I don't mind a little roughness. Just don't think you're the only one who can deliver it."

I gripped her hips, pulled her up, and yanked her down on my cock. Uli squealed, and I felt her fingers dig further into me as her legs wrapped as tight as possible around my hips. Without thinking, I picked Uli up and put her onto her back, thrusting as hard as possible into her. As I fucked her, Uli bit onto the sheet in an attempt not to scream to high heavens.

"Ahhhhh! Fuck, yes, Asher. Fuck me just like that!"

I kept my tempo up exactly as she asked. The only sounds in the room were our moans for each other and me fucking her. I found the most effective way to keep her from causing a noise violation was to kiss her. She happily entangled with me while I pinned her to the bed and fucked her senseless.

Her voice went higher and higher as I felt a massive surge forming inside me. I went faster and faster as I felt Uli's pussy squeeze and convulse.

Uli's words melted together in rapid fire demands. "Yes, just like that, Asher. Don't stop. You're gonna make me fucking cum. Don't you dare pull out, you hear me? I took a potion already, so just keep going!"

I could feel her pussy squeeze tighter than ever as I kept pumping her relentlessly. She screamed in my ear to cum inside of her as my body seized up.

I held her tight as she kept me wrapped in place while thrusting as hard and as fast as possible. I felt the pressure I'd been holding explode with one final thrust as the levee inside me finally broke.

"Fuck!" I shouted.

"Aaah, mmm!"

Uli's arms wrapped around my neck and her legs around my waist as I flooded her insides. She squeezed all over my cock as I pressed her into the bed. Uli's nails dug into my shoulders, clawing at me, apparently unable to stop. Uli whimpered and moaned as she orgasmed, biting into me.

"Oooooh Asher."

Staying there for a moment, I felt her breathing return to normal. My seed had filled her completely, leaking out of her as we lay breathless on the bed. I saw her looking at me, her eyes gentle and pure.

"That was amazing," I whispered, wrapping an arm around her.

"Yeah," she said, smiling. "And it's just the start."

"What?"

With one final flourish of her sleight of hand, a familiar orange bottle appeared in her hand. She quickly pulled off the stopper and took a swig. As soon as she took the first gulp, I could see her body shudder with newfound energy.

She looked at me, ears flapping, wide-eyed and ready to go, handing me the bottle.

"Stamina potion," I said, nonplussed. "Well, you said it'd be until morning, and it is your birthday."

That night, Uli got precisely what she wanted.

I shifted my attention to the hulking monster as it cocked its head and grinned. Balls of white-hot fire the size of basketballs appeared in its palms.

Chapter 23

Avisday Dawn, 15th of Seeyrn, Year 678, 4th Age

The next day came far too early and far too violently. The sound of an explosion jolted me awake from a deep sleep. Jumping out of bed, I felt blood rush up to my head as I heard screaming outside the building.

I turned around and saw a massive fire burning across the street. Uli was also on her feet, staring at the fire in shock and horror. With a single look, we both sprang into action. We were dressed, running down the street, and heading to the fire within moments.

People screamed as they ran away from the fire engulfing the building Rogorm was in last night. Several people were lying on the ground, with clerics, healers, and others administering medical attention.

The pandemonium of the fire made an endless wave of people run in every direction. Finding a hole, I grabbed Uli, and we ran to a small opening near the center of the street.

Thick, black smoke curled into the air, blocking the sun. People had flooded the street, running away from and towards the flames to gawk at them. Most just looked on in horror at the scene while Uli pulled something from thin air and looked at me.

"Dammit, we need to help!" she shouted. "I'll help with the injured! You help put out the fire."

As Uli ran off, I froze looking around at the carnage unfolding as the heat of the flames made the air like an oven. What was I supposed to do? The only things fighting the flames were people throwing buckets of water or using rudimentary spells.

Water! I could make water!

Cursing myself for my slow thinking, I frantically tried to remember the specific combination for summoning water. As I pulled the rune's order out the deep recesses of my brain, my arm began to glow blue with tiny runes.

Water shot out of my hand like a strong hose. As I shot the water out, I tried to coordinate my stream with the others doing their best to dampen the flames.

Uli, meanwhile, was pulling as many potions as possible out and ran to the impromptu medical teams. Hundreds of people were lying in the street receiving medical attention. Most were covered in soot, struggling to breathe with burns up and down their bodies.

My heart sank as more and more people were covered with sheets and cloaks. A contingency of people carried the most badly burnt off to the side, where a few clerics desperately prayed to their gods and goddesses.

"Where are Giezha and Mara?" I shouted, feeling the drain on my mana. The heat from the flames washed over me, coating me in thick layers of sweat. Uli was getting overwhelmed by the constant requests for potions, but she managed to stay on top.

"I don't know!" Uli shouted while running a set of bandages over to help someone the badly burnt. "They better not have run in there!" She pulled out gauze and salves, handing them to the different groups.

A whooshing sound could be heard up above. It looked like people were flying into the top of the building. Water was jetting from a few figures above as they entered the building from the roof.

"Good, the cavalry is arriving," Uli said, looking up into the sky.

The crowd erupted in cheers as several flew into the building to catch any stragglers. Trying to do my part, I chugged a mana potion Uli'd given to me and continued to spray at the fire.

No matter what we did or how much we coordinated, the flames refused to die down, burning hotter and hotter. Luckily, we saw the reinforcements that flew into the building start to emerge with people.

They flew them out to an area now cordoned off by members of various guilds. There I saw Giezha and Mara helping coordinate the healing and treatment. Giezha assisted in healing spells while Mara ran supplies in and out of the area.

The flying rescuers recovered nearly a hundred bodies, most severely burned and on the brink of death. Despite their robes now covered in ash and smoke, I recognized them as Ivory Forge. One of them saw me and motioned for me to come over.

Running over, I grouped up with her and the others.

The Ivory Forge member, a male elf with long black hair, asked me to give an update on the fire.

"Nothing we're doing is getting the flames to go down," I explained, sweating from all pores. "We've gone for the base of the flames, tried to hit

254

it with a single concentrated water flow, nothing's working."

The Ivory Forge member swore in elvish. "If we can't save the building, let's focus on preventing the fire from spreading. You all coordinate with the other members, I'll get on the horn with—"

Just as he was about to finish giving orders, a half-orc woman tried to run back into the building but was stopped by the mob of people. Her face had a nasty burn on the left side as she shoved and clawed away from people trying to stop her.

"Chima!" she wailed, desperately trying to claw herself free. "Chima! Mommy's coming!" She looked at us desperately, tears stinging her face. "Please! My baby's in there. Let me go, let me get her!"

Ah, fuck.

All four of us looked at each other, torn on what we could do. The Ivory Forge member sensed what we were about to do. Looking at each of us, we could see the pain of leadership on his face as he let out a command to the mages.

"Seal up the building! We need a barrier, now!"

The mother wailed as if her soul were ripped in half. "NOOOO!"

Dozens of mages surrounded the building, and a barrier began to shimmer. A translucent black layer of mana began to form starting from the base. It rose high up into the air, ten, twenty feet high.

The mother desperately broke free, sprinting to the barrier. It rose above her head as she pounded her fists on the barrier. "CHIMA! CHIMA! STOP! MY BABY'S STILL IN THERE!"

Dammit. Now I had to do something really fucking stupid.

The elf grabbed the others and tried to get them to help out with recovery and shielding. Seizing the opportunity, I tried to muster as much energy into myself for a really, really stupid high jump. The heat inside me matched the flames licking the air as I prepared for a one-way trip.

Uli was the first to notice as I started sprinting to the building. "You help me with—Asher!"

By the time they noticed what I was doing, I unleashed the explosion of energy in me, leaping into the air. Hot air blistered my face as I looked down and sailed over the barrier. Climbing higher and higher.

I crashed through one of the exploded windows of the building right as the barrier reached the next story.

255

Throwing out my hand, I let out a jet of water in front of me, trying to blast the flames away. With my hood up and a shirt covering my face, only a tiny slit for my eyes was exposed.

The bright orange and yellow flames mixed with smoke everywhere gave me a fresh view of the bowels of hell. My skin instantly blistered against the heat of the fire. Shooting out torrents of water, I managed to cut through the flames raging around me.

Water continued to jet out of my hand as I felt that drained sensation continue creeping into me. Scanning the floor as best as possible, I didn't see anybody left. The rescue crew didn't even leave corpses. The fire roared into my ears while I searched for a staircase. Making my way into the middle of the room, I saw a large staircase that went up and down.

"Chima!" I shouted, trying to hear the little girl. Dodging flames, I ran up the next level shouting for her. "Chima I'm here to save you!"

Once I was on the next level, I heard the faint sound of a voice screaming above me.

"Help! Mommy! Someone, please!"

Shaking off the drained sensation, I sprinted up the stairs. As I ran, the wooden stairs began to crack and splinter until I felt a stab of pain in my calf. A piece of burning wood fell from the railing onto my leg.

"Shit!" I screamed, feeling it's splintery flame.

Grabbing it, I threw it off my leg before continuing up. Adrenaline coursed through me as my head thundered, forcing me to stay focused. Ignoring it, I ran up several flights listening for the girl.

"Chima!" I screamed, coughing as the smoke slithered into my lungs. "Chima!"

"Help!" the little girl screamed.

Finally, I heard her on the fourth floor and bolted down the hall, shouting for the girl. Debris cracked and fell down from the ceiling as I tried to track Chima's sound. A jet of flames exploded from a room, nearly burning me to a crisp. The jet of water I'd been spewing was quickly becoming a dribble. Without many options, I had to turn off the water and focus on getting to Chima.

"Chima!" I called out, trying to find her in the circular maze of rooms. "Where are you?"

"Monster!"

As she screamed, I could hear a second creature. It growled and shouted before the sounds of crashing rang out. The crash coincided with the entire floor shaking. Chima let out a terrified yelp while my own muscles screamed out in pain and exhaustion.

I was running low on oxygen, and the mana drain only weakened me further. At the corner of the hall was a door ajar. I saw a massive silhouette from the edge, along with the sound of a little girl.

"Ahhh!"

"Chima!"

Running as fast as my legs could carry me, I ran in and kicked the door out of my way. When I looked, I could see a massive brute in the middle of the room. The monster towered over me, with a tiny half-orc child struggling in his grasp. The walls were collapsing on all sides as I stared at the hulking green monster.

"Let her go!" I shouted, trying to douse the flames.

Chima screamed while the monster looked at me and roared. It looked like a giant goblin similar to Rogorm. In fact, its nose was the exact same shape as his. It also had the same facial structure. The only thing that was different besides its now massive size were its eyes. They were milky gray with no iris... Just like the rat-zombie.

"I said drop her, Rogorm!" I shouted, pulling out my sword. "Now!"

The hulked-out Rogorm-Zombie dropped her and lunged at me. Its razor-sharp talons swung down, and I ducked, rolling underneath him to Chima.

I held my sword out in front as I kept between him and Chima, who cowered behind me. When Rogorm lunged, he did it so forcefully he crashed through the wall behind us.

"Chima, there are people coming to get you, okay?" I said to her, trying to calm her down. "I'm gonna get the scary monster and make him go away. The people outside will put out the fires and get you too. It's gonna be okay."

I concentrated, spraying water around us, dousing the flames in the room. The little girl just cried into my cloak, refusing to move. As soon as the fires had been put out, a ball of flames flew into the room, exploding. Chima squealed as I threw myself over her, protecting her from a piece of flaming wood. Luckily, it clashed against the shield on my back.

"Aghhhh," I groaned in pain. "Motherf—"

257

"He started the fire, mister," she whimpered as I saw a pair of gray dots cut through the flames. "He got all crazy and started shooting fire."

Fuck. Sounded like whatever or whoever was behind Rogorm and the other transformations were getting bolder. Or better.

I shifted my attention to the hulking monster as it cocked its head and grinned. Its smile reached much further than its mouth should have been capable of, going all the way to its ears.

Balls of white-hot fire the size of basketballs appeared in its palms. It turned it's head more before bursting forward.

Refusing to let it get to Chima, I threw my shield in front of us and counter-charged. Every bit of me was on fire, inside and out, as I tried to power my way through him. While the fire burned inside, hot ash and cinders flew into my face from the burning fabric and walls.

Rogorm swung again, and I ducked underneath his attack, slashing at his midsection. My sword cut into his abdomen, causing blood to spew like a geyser. Without so much as a flinch, Rogorm front kicked me in the chest. Too fast to block, the kick sent me flying through the air and crashing through a wall.

I crumpled to the floor, lying at the side of a burning cot, looking straight through the hole in the wall I'd made. My vision went blurry, and I could feel something stabbing into my lungs. Unable to sit up, I realized it was my own ribs stabbing into me.

"Broken ribs," I said, coughing a bit of blood up. "Classic."

Flames lashed out at my neck with bits of wood and splinters covering my back. I let out a wheeze for air, but the lack of oxygen, broken ribs, and punctured lung prevented any relief.

I slowly stumbled back to my feet and heard the powerful thuds of Rogorm charging.

"GRAAARGGH!" He smashed through the wall, into the room, swinging wildly.

Unable to dodge, I threw my sword up, slicing at his fingers. He continued to attack as if he didn't even notice he'd had his hand chopped off. All four fingers and part of his palm flopped down past my head.

He sent another kick, nearly impaling me in the chest. I smashed my shield down, knocking his kick out of the way at the last second.

I weaved in and out of his attacks, feeling hot air rush past my face.

I rolled out of the way from his last attack, doubling over as my chest impaled itself. Tiny droplets of blood came up as I hacked and wheezed.

Rogorm growled, tired of my lack of dying. Grabbing a flaming piece of furniture, he flung it at me. I dropped to the ground as it exploded against the wall. A hail of hot cinders and wood rained down on me.

"Fucking hell," I muttered, "Gotta get out of here."

Rogorm's let out an evil chuckle, and he threw a ball of fire at me. Stuck in a corner, I could only throw my shield up. The fireball crashed against my shield, splashing like water as it wrapped around me.

Suddenly, everything went white as my whole body was lit on fire. Every square inch of me was stabbed with a white-hot knife while the fire clung to me like glue. The magic equivalent of napalm.

"GAHHHH!" I screamed out in pain while the globs of fire stuck and burned my skin.

Rogorm grabbed me and threw me back toward Chima. I crashed into a wardrobe while Chima cowered in the corner. My vision was blurry as the white flames covered my body.

"Mister!" the girl screamed out and ran over.

"Chima, get back." I struggled as the flames ate away at me.

Before I could stop her, the little girl touched my shoulder, producing a warm glow. The pain covering the inside and outside of my body dulled, and I was able to open my eyes. Chima's hands were glowing bright blue, and I saw her little necklace glowing.

"You have to get up, mister!" she cried.

"GRAAAAGH!" Rogorm bellowed out, ready to charge again.

This motherfucker.

"Go back to the corner, Chima," I growled as I staggered up, still covered in flames. "I just need a moment."

Needing to end this quickly, I conjured up the fire inside, burning hotter than any of the flames on me. I felt my organs quake and protest as the energy inside tore me up from the inside.

Using every last fiber of my strength, I stared at the hulking brute and charged. Thrusting my sword forward, I let out a war cry, ready to kill this bastard.

"Come on!"

"Graaargh!"

Concentrating the power into my legs, the one part of me that wasn't on fire, I charged. Unleashing the fire inside, an explosion of my 'nova' energy, I rocketed into the air towards Rogorm.

White-hot flames wicked off me as the force of my jump created a pressure wave, blasting the air out from me. The gray eyes of the monster opened wide as I thrust my sword forward and slammed into it.

Shhhk!

My sword plunged right through Rogorm's chest clean to the other side. Blood and viscera exploded as I crashed shoulder-first into it. The beast fell backwards and I pulled my arm up at the last second. Any later and the monster's weight would've snapped my arm.

The monster let out a death rattle with a single shudder, and its gray eyes turned black. Thinking fast, I ran back towards Chima.

As I ran, the building shook, and a jet of flames exploded through the floor, cutting me off from her. Chima screamed as the wall of flames began to engulf the room she was in.

"Chima!" I wheezed at the top of my damaged lungs, jumping over debris and through the holes in the walls.

I tried to concentrate all of my mana into a blast of water with everything inside me. I was able to cut through the fire, but I felt my mana drain faster and faster. I saw Chima in the middle of the room as the walls and floors creaked under pressure.

The building was collapsing. Fast.

Grabbing Chima, I held her to my chest and ran back towards the entrance. Smoke filled my lungs as I worked my legs as hard as possible. My eyes stung from the heat and smoke that penetrated through my eyelids. Chima's tiny body could barely take any more of this.

Before I could get to the stairs, I felt the floor collapse underneath me. There was a hole in the floor where my feet had just been. The building couldn't stand the raging inferno anymore.

"Hang tight," I told Chima as I cradled her. "I'll get us down."

With my path to the stairs blocked, I was forced to climb down the hole and onto the next level. The floor groaned under the sudden weight and splintered under my feet. I kept the stream of water going, but my exhaustion was overwhelming.

I tried to clear a path on the stairs, but the water stopped coming out.

260

Instead, it was turning to steam. No matter what I tried, the fire kept getting bigger and bigger. Hotter and hotter. And I was getting weaker and weaker.

Chima screamed underneath my cloak as I huffed and puffed. "Mommy!"

"It's gonna be okay, sweetie," I whispered, trying to soothe the scared child. I coughed into my hand and turned away, filling it with blood.

We couldn't get through the wall of flames in front of us, and panic was overtaking me. Luckily, I saw a window at the end of what was once a bedroom, facing the Inn I had been in moments before. I ran over and looked out.

The massive crowd of people could see my head poke out, and they screamed. I could just make out Giezha, Mara, and Uli assisting with first-aid. The barrier holding the inferno at bay was covering the entire building.

"Giezha!" I screamed as loud as my smoke-filled lungs would allow. I waved an arm frantically towards her.

She looked and saw me, her mouth agape. I felt the fire getting closer and closer, and I knew I had to act fast. Smashing the window with one hand, I grabbed Chima and held her up out the window. I could hear the people in the crowd scream as I looked for someone to catch her.

Giezha and the other mages blasted at the barrier, creating an opening for me. Mara, Uli, and the others quickly crowded directly underneath the opening as the flames started to burn the back of my neck. A sea of people had their hands up, ready to catch her. Knowing this would be my only chance, I looked at Chima.

Her face was covered in soot, and it looked like she'd been scratched up by Rogorm. But as I held her, she tried to make a brave face.

"It's gonna be okay, Chima. They're gonna catch you, okay?"

The brave little girl covered her eyes as she cried and nodded her head. My hands were shaking like crazy. I did my best to aim directly for the middle of the crowd. I started to hear explosions behind me as the fire burned, and with a heave, I threw Chima to the crowd. She glided through the opening in the barrier straight to the crowd.

The little girl screamed as she flew through the air, but I saw Giezha, cast a spell to catch her as others slowed her momentum.

I exhaled in relief, ready to collapse. That relief, however, was quickly doused. I heard a voice behind me, chanting in an unknown language. A blue light shined behind me, and I turned around, seeing an extremely tall figure in a cloak.

"What the—?"

Before I could react, a blue light enveloped me, and I threw my hands in front of my face. A concussive blast exploded before me, and I was flung backward.

Crashing through the wall, I felt my body become light as a feather. The blast's shockwave was too much, and I faded from consciousness.

The last thing I saw before fading out of consciousness was the hooded figure as I tumbled out the window, and a golden aura surrounding me. After that, I could only hear the crowd's screams as I fell.

And then, everything went silent.

Chapter 24

Avisday Evening, 22nd of Seeyrn, Year 678, 4th Age

Fuck, everything hurt.

A dark purple light penetrated my eyelids as I heard a faint hum. Someone was holding my right hand as another was wrapping something on my leg. The strangest sensation came from my chest. It was as if my chest was... growing.

Not in the muscular sense. It felt as if my skin was growing back. I could hear the distinct voices of Uli, Giezha, and Mara, all muttering. Mara must have been the one who was holding my hand. I could hear her whispering a prayer through sobs. Giezha continued to speak a flow of incantations as the pain in my body cooled and numbed.

Uli sounded like she was trying hard not to lose her cool. "Please, please, please wake up, Asher."

Slowly, my heavy eyelids began to peel open. The light of day poured into my eyes as I softly exhaled.

My vision was blurry, but I could tell I was in a healing room at the guildhall. A few guild members sat in chairs watching me pensively. I breathed in deeply, trying to get the sensation of oxygen in my lungs. To my surprise, I was able to breathe relatively normally.

Blinking a few more times, I managed to wiggle my toes and fingers. As I lifted my head, all three of their faces looked astonished. Giezha's incarnation stopped dead in her tracks as Uli and Mara's jaws dropped.

"Hey," I said as I felt a sudden onset of soreness. "Did Chima make it out okay?"

Ignoring my question, Mara grabbed me by the shoulder and cried as Uli and Giezha looked incapable of words or action.

As Mara squeezed me, I came to the happy conclusion that I managed to

263

avoid another visit to Gathos. That happy thought was quickly replaced by the memory of the last thing I saw when I got blasted out of the building—the cloaked figure.

I sat up, inspecting my body. I was sore, but all the breaks and bruises had recovered. I just felt tired. Really fucking tired.

"How did you not die?" Giezha asked, prodding my chest. "And your armor is still fine for some reason."

"Stubbornness and fantastic healing," I said, only half joking, as I swatted her hand away. I looked down and saw that my clothes had been replaced by a tunic in the guild's red and black colors sporting a patch on the right chest of the official logo. "I'm gonna miss that old shirt, honestly. Red does suit me, though."

Looking at the side of my bed, my armor was still relatively intact. Giezha chalked it up to a self-repairing spell the original tailor had placed on it. Most other guild members gave me slaps on the back for my bravery and jeers for my stupidity.

"Seriously," Giezha huffed. "What in the world could make you survive a fall like that? And what even caused it? We saw you throw the kid out seconds before you were just flying through the air unconscious."

Mara looked at my hand, running hers over the ring she'd given me. The topaz color was now gone and was now clear as glass.

"It was the ring I gave you," Mara said quietly, looking at the ring. "Back in Zizar, I asked the cleric to provide a blessing for you. The ring was imbued by the cleric, and he said that Evlana would watch over you."

I grinned as I thought back about when we went to the churches. "I thought you said the cleric wanted to thank me?"

Mara blushed brightly, and we had a good laugh. It was nothing to be embarrassed about, honestly. Her doing that had literally saved my life.

"Tch." Uli gave me a dark look and walked out of the room.

By the looks of the sun outside, it was only the early afternoon. Plenty of time for more chaos. A few guild members laughed about something amongst themselves while Mara and Giezha looked at each other.

As we left, Brody told us Dawnthorn wanted a meeting with us in a few days. We agreed to meet with her on the condition that she come to us at the Silver Cup Inn so that I could rest.

I felt fine, but the others insisted on this condition.

264

Uli's sour mood did not change for the rest of the day, and she kept shooting me furtive glances while I helped Sal out at the bar. Sal, like the others, insisted I go to bed and rest, but I was brimming with energy. After all, I had gotten a free ticket back to life today.

"What happened up there?" Mara asked as we helped take out the garbage. "There was a blue flash of light, and then you flew out the window. A couple sorcerers from Black Sparrow flew up and caught you."

She grabbed me and held on tight.

"We were really scared we would lose you," she whispered.

"Yeah," came the angry voice of Uli, picking up a box of onions just delivered. "Really worried."

Mara bit her lip and gave a worried look as Uli stomped back in. I just squeezed her and gave her a kiss on the head.

"I appreciate your concern, Mara," I said, holding on tight. "I really do. But I'm too stubborn to die. Plus, I can always count on you and the others to keep me safe."

I spent the next few days recovering, trying not to aggravate my injuries. A few members from the guild came to check on us, while the little girl and her mother from the fire came by to thank me. Chima had a small bandage on her arm from where Rogorm had grabbed her, but she was in high spirits.

She giggled as I put her on my shoulders and pretended she was a dragon. The mother tried to give me a tiny bag of coppers and silvers, which I repeatedly refused to take.

"Just doing what needed to be done," I assured her.

I could hear Uli mutter something under her breath behind me.

All in all, I was the talk of the town. People were shocked that such a young adventurer would do something so risky. Doubly so, since I was a Red Breaker and there was no profit to be had in what I did.

By the day of our meeting with the captain, rumors swirled about the bright blue light from right before I was blown out the building. The main rumor was a Potion of Liquid Thunder boiled over before exploding. I didn't bother to correct them. The fewer people that knew the truth, the better.

The bar was full of well-wishers coming to thank Uli, Giezha, Mara, and me, while Sal made them buy a drink before leaving.

Mara insisted I take a moment in the afternoon with her so that she could show her "appreciation" for my heroics. Thanks to Giezha reluctantly covering our duties like the wingman she was, I enjoyed the fruits of my labor.

I was disheartened when Kiersa didn't show up, but figured she was just too busy.

As evening came, I pushed my luck at closing time by breaking the news of our meeting with the captain to Sal. Sal was ready to send me back to Gathos and stomped off, muttering about ungrateful children.

Uli, Mara, and Giezha looked at me pensively as we all sat down. Despite the cheerful mood I'd been in, the fact I'd come so close to dying hadn't sat well with anyone.

"Sorry for scaring you guys like that," I said, looking at the table. "I-I shouldn't have run in like that, but I just..." I looked up at each of them. "I just acted without thinking. I could have endangered you if you ran in there with me."

"What were you thinking?" Uli shouted. "I looked away for two seconds! And what do I see? You! I see you jumping through a broken window into a massive fire with a barrier locking you inside!"

Mara looked like she wanted to say something, but Giezha spoke up first. She placed a hand on Uli's shoulder.

"Uli, that's enough."

Uli turned to swat Giezha's hand away. "No! It's not enough!" There was a single tear in the corner of an eye as she turned to me. Her face was bright red and her pupils wide as saucers as she bared her fangs.

"I couldn't go in to get you, no matter how much I wanted to. Because I needed to help the others. The people who made it out. I had to sit there. Helping everyone except you. My own teammate! My own friend! My—"

"Enough, Siannodel," came the voice of the captain.

Dwanthorn stood by the door, flanked by three people—Vurshung, along with two others in Ivory Forge uniforms. The four of us got up from our chairs and saluted Dawnthorn.

She motioned for us to sit and brought a set of chairs and an extra table. The captain sat across from us while the Ivory Forge crew flanked her on both sides. I briefly saw Sal walk to the backroom, locking the door behind him.

266

Vurshung said nothing, but his compatriots eyed us with disdain. One was a human female with sallow skin and black hair in a top-knot. The other was a dwarfish man wearing thick golden ear and nose rings with a red buzzcut.

The dwarf whispered something to the woman that made her laugh before turning her nose towards us like we smelled of feces. I rolled my eyes and turned my attention back to Dawnthorn.

Once again, the captain made a point to say as little as possible. She waited until the nerves inside of me were ready to explode. She slowly pulled out paper and a writing utensil before whispering into Vurshung's ear. She thought about her words for a moment before nodding.

"Aye, miss. That'd do," Vurshung said, side-eyeing me while his supposed subordinates glared at us.

Sal kept his eyes on the captain but stayed silent.

"So," the captain said conversationally, looking at us. "I guess it's fair to say… Things have gotten out of hand."

She made a gesture to me, and I flinched. The captain continued.

"I understand that you were hot on the trail of the silver thief. Clues about a courier, random attacks that weren't so random, and you managed to track down a highly valuable person of interest. Thank you for your notes, by the way, Siannodel. Very well written."

Uli simply nodded as the captain pulled out a stack of papers from her notes and put down a wanted poster on crinkly, brown paper. It had a picture of a goblin on it with the name "Rogorm" at the top. The reward wasn't exceptionally high—certainly not enough for anybody to try and catch him. Mara jumped into the conversation as Captain Dawnthorn was about to speak.

"Captain, request for clarification with regards to Vurshung Thansiz and company's participation in official Red Breaker business."

You could just barely see Mara preemptively flinch in case the captain attempted to smack her, but no such strike came. Instead, she just looked at the rest of us with an eyebrow raised. The two from Ivory Forge snickered loudly at Mara before being silenced by Vurshung's glare.

Dwanthorn looked at the Ivory Forge like she'd bitten a lemon. "Vurhsung and company will represent Ivory Forge. It pains me to say this, but the Council has decreed we will jointly investigate because of

267

the convergent nature of our contract and theirs after word of your quest reached The Council."

Oh for fuck's sake Kiersa.

We all looked at each other as Vurshung maintained a calm exterior. His eyes traveled from one person to another as he sized us up. The dwarf had puffed up his chest while the woman was preoccupied with her nails.

"Thank you for the explanation, Madam Dawnthorn," Vurshung said with an exaggerated bow. "As you all may or may not be aware, there has been a decades-long shortage of moonstones in the region. Once, Naled was the center of trade for these stones. Powerful objects, moonstones, especially aginst the undead."

I made a mental note to thank Isaac and the girls for suggesting that I gift such a stone to Kiersa.

"This shortage's origin has been traced to the days following the Undead Incursion. In this day and age, their rarity could rival sapphires." Vurshung tapped the wanted poster of Rogorm. "We believe that he was a key component in the creation of artificial scarcity. An undercover agent in Ivory Forge was set to arrest him in a sting tomorrow evening. However, that is no longer a possibility due to recent circumstances."

"You killed him." The woman behind Vurshung sneered towards me.

The captain ignored her and pulled out a different set of papers and read from them. "While saving the half-orc girl, you found him in a feral state, grown to gigantic proportions. The girl also reported that he was the one who started the fires. Other eyewitnesses corroborated her story of a goblin nearly ten feet tall, with dull grey eyes, throwing fireballs around the building after setting off an explosion."

Giezha's eyes went wide at the description.

"That's sounds just like the rat-undead," she said, looking at me and then the captain.

Dawnthorn closed her eyes and nodded solemnly. "Yes. The silver theft and moonstone trade issue are somehow connected, with the undead brutes linking the two. Hearing of the convergent nature of these quests, the Council decided we must share our investigation. Vurshung has been leading the charge for Ivory Forge and wanted to make sure we were all up to speed."

"There'd be less to get up to speed if not for this lout," the Dwarf shouted, pointing at me. "Killed two fuckin' suspects already! Firs' rat-man and then that green-skinned fuck."

The dwarf let off a series of slurs towards goblins, goliaths, and half-elves. I could feel Uli's fists tremble in her lap as she clenched her jaw not to speak. Mara and Giezha were ready to jump him already.

"So, I was supposed to let them kill me?" I asked as calmly as possible.

"Actually, yes!" the woman said in a tone like a parent explaining something to a toddler. "Would've been easier for everyone. We'd have the leads to our investigation, and your friends would have a higher share of the reward!"

"Watch your tongue," Mara said warningly, leaning over the table.

The woman rolled her eyes and got in Mara's face, whispering, "Try me, halfbreed."

"Moving on," Dawnthorn said, raising her voice. Mara and the woman didn't move as the captain continued. "There was another attack matching the description of these two events this morning. It happened just before the explosion in Iron Court."

"The owners of the Golden Sky Tavern, Kiersa and Aire Denrel, were attacked by a zombie this morning before dawn. It managed to make its way to the top floor of the building, attacking them in their home."

My heart fell out of my chest hearing that. I quickly got up to run and go check on Kiersa. Before I got far, Giezha grabbed my shoulder, gesturing for me to stay.

Vurshung pulled a hand out, producing a small white pebble. "Ms. Kiersa managed to repel it with a spell powered up by a moonstone. This was all that remained."

"What? The moon elfs over yonder?" the Dwarf scoffed. "How'd those beggars get a moonstone? Must've stolen it."

"I gave it to them," I said quietly. "A gift to celebrate the Moon of Tiur."

The dwarf gave me a look of utter confusion. "But why give it to the sludgie? May as' well give them a hunk of granite! You shouldn't bother to waste a stone like that on 'elves' like them."

"Shut the fuck up!" I shouted, pounding a fist on the table and standing up. The others looked on in surprise, while the Dwarf seemed bored by me. "I have had it with your bullshit. You racist, shit-eating, prick!"

The dwarf made a face of mock adoration.

269

"Awwww, widdle rooks got 'is knickers in a twist about me. You fuckin' the beast?" His eyes grew wide, and he let out a disgusting, bellowing laugh. "Look! He's mad 'is whores is gettin' hurt! Ah, heard you were kickin' boots with the sludgie bitch, and this here gree—"

I reached across the table and socked him in the eye, snapping his head back. The woman tried to put a knife on me, but Mara responded by headbutting her in the nose. The woman recoiled and swore to high heaven.

At that point, every one of us had pulled out a weapon except for the captain and Vurshung. The woman's staff was covered in bright golden light, while the dwarf had a pair of spectral daggers in her hands.

"Enough!" Dawnthorn and Vurshung shouted simultaneously.

Vurshung threw a hand up, and the Ivory Forge members lowered their weapons. The dwarf made a face and gestured for me to come closer. Uli and Giezha grabbed me by the shoulder as I took the bait.

Dawnthorn ran over and stuck a finger in my face. "Get your fucking act together, Merrick." She growled. "I don't care about this bullshit. You got that? We have a job. Do the job. Get paid. Fight them later. Or else. And next time you give me a report, make sure you tell me everything."

I just nodded my head and stared forward. My blood was pumping and ready to burn. I'd already died once this week. Why not get a little risky?

"Vurshung!" Sal barked. "Get a handle on your crew or get out of my inn!"

Vurshung grabbed the dwarf and pulled him over for a quick conversation. The dwarf's face remained expressionless, clearly ignoring whatever Vurshung had to say. He simply nodded when Vurshung stopped speaking and made a gesture involving his middle finger towards me.

"Alright," Vurshung said, trying to keep this joint effort from falling apart. "I understand tensions are high. But we need to work together. Put simply, we know there are larger forces at play. Whoever is involved in the silver and moonstone black market is likely trying to tie up loose ends. Although it has not been officially confirmed, there have been other sightings and disappearances in the last few weeks." Vurshung brought out a few missing person signs with their descriptions and drawings. He took a deep breath before continuing. "Based on the evidence at hand, there may be a second incursion on the horizon."

Every single one of us turned and looked at Vurshung. His eyes were deadly serious as the air was sucked out of the room. Everything I had read about the first incursion sounded like a nightmare scenario. Apparently, the streets had been lined with the dead. Bodies had to be burned immediately due to the risk of them coming back as zombies. Almost a tenth of the city's population had been lost.

"And that is why we have to take care of this now," Dawnthorn said, slamming a sack full of gold and platinum on the table. There had to be well over ten thousand coins weighing down the table. "The council has personally guaranteed payment for this quest. No other guilds are to know, and no other members are to know outside of those here, and a small detachment. Any members who assist will do so under the impression that this job is for other purposes."

"We believe we know where the rendezvous for Rogorm and his associates was. It is currently under surveillance by a team of Ivory Forge and Red Breakers as we speak."

"So why not go there now?" Mara asked, still eyeing the elf. "We could catch the thieves on their home turf?"

The captain clenched her fist for a moment before speaking.

"Ivory Forge has been given full control of the investigations at this point. Their stance is to hold back on engagement until we know who is going in and out."

We looked at Vurshung, who made a gesture that said, "Sorry, but it's out of my hands."

The captain gritted her teeth and continued. "They'll likely be laying low for the moment then. Our scout team is on high alert and will warn us of any movement. When the signal arrives, it will be our job to intercept. In the meantime, I suggest we adjourn for the evening."

The captain got up from her seat, and everyone else followed suit. The dwarf and I stared each other down as the other Ivory Forge members left.

Captain Dawnthorn asked me to walk her out, making the others exchange confused looks with me. Sal's dark demeanor only worsened as we were ushered out the door by him. The captain flashed me a smile, which gave me a bad feeling about the rest of my night.

Chapter 25

Avisday Night, 22nd of Seeyrn, Year 678, 4th Age

The captain and I walked out as Sal slammed the door behind us. She gestured for me to walk with her, and I obliged. It was hard to concentrate, thinking about Kiersa and her family being attacked.

The streets near the inn held only a few stragglers for the evening as the sea of stars twinkled above. The nights were getting colder, sometimes threatening to reach freezing temperatures. Tonight was one of those nights. The wind off the lake seemed to bite at your ears and nose.

"I appreciate your restraint with the dwarf," the captain said quietly as Sal slammed the door behind us. "It would have been in bad taste to cave his skull in."

I bit my tongue lest I say something stupid. The captain gave a smile with surprising warmth and pulled out a pipe, lighting a patch of tobacco.

"Keep an eye on Sal for me, Merrick," she said, exhaling a series of smoke rings. "I'm afraid he might disappear."

"Why would he?" I asked, watching the captain's smoke-ship float its way to the Xalia and Avis.

The captain didn't answer and took another long drag.

"Salvatore Yaxel is not the fatherly satyr he presents himself to be. In my time, I knew him as a hard swilling braggart and a sorcerer the likes of which I'd never seen." She paused momentarily as she gathered the words for her following sentence in a puff of tobacco. "He also dabbled in necromancy after the death of his wife and children."

I stopped dead in my tracks and stared at her. She was unsurprised by the look I gave her and simply shrugged. There's no way that could be true.

"Is that why people call Red Breakers turncoats?" I asked the captain. "Because one of the founders studied necromancy?"

272

Dawnthorn shrugged. "More than studied. A lot more. One night, Salvatore accidentally unleashed a small hoard of zombified goats and pigs in the middle of the guildhall. They got out of the hall and into the streets. Needless to say, he put our guild in a sticky situation. We managed to get out from under the controversy, but barely. That was the start of the end for Sal in the guild. The public doesn't know it was him that did it. So now, the whole guild shares his blame."

I wavered and didn't say anything. I simply nodded my head, agreeing to keep an eye on him. As I bid the captain goodnight, I knew I would have a very uncomfortable conversation in the near future.

Arriving at our destination, the captain turned to me one last time. "I'm sure you'd figure this out soon, but I've been asked to relieve myself of involvement." It may have just been the moonlight, but I could've sworn a tear glistening in the corner of her eye. "For the good of the Red Breakers, you cannot risk telling me anything."

Dumbfounded, I just nodded my head.

Man, this guild stuff was messy.

"Captain?" I asked as we turned towards the Guild District. "I'd like to ask you a question."

Dawnthorn looked up at the sky, predicting my question. "You were wondering why Mhurren and Mick didn't come into the conversation."

"Yes," I said.

She waved her hand and laughed. "That's quite simple. It was a matter outside of the scope of the joined contracts." The humor in her voice quickly vanished as she spoke. "Besides, they are likely already investigating it on behalf of the council."

I stumbled over my feet when she said that. "They are?"

"Yep, gotta love politicians." the captain said, puffing away at her pipe. "Good night, Asher."

As concerned as I was about what the captain told me, I had other things on my mind. I sprinted towards the Golden Sky Tavern to see Kiersa.

The tavern was devoid of people in or out when I arrived. A few onlookers whispered as they passed, but none dared go near. The closer I got, the clearer the horror became.

"Oh, no," I whispered to myself.

The front doors of the building were broken in, and as I walked closer, I saw the path of destruction the zombie must have taken. I walked through it all, seeing broken chairs and tables strewn about. The trail went upstairs, and I saw a ragged hallway with scratches and pieces of broken wood everywhere.

"Kiersa!" I called out. "Kiersa! Aire! Are you there?"

Suddenly, two muffled voices arguing could be heard at the end of the hall.

"Kiersa?" I said, quieter this time. "Kiersa, are you okay?"

The door swung open, and I found a familiar knife in my face. Flinching back, I saw Aire scowling at me, and his arm extended. Kiersa was holding a small dagger at her side by a bed. Someone appeared to be sleeping. Aire waggled the knife at my throat, demanding my attention. He growled in his deep, rich voice.

"What trouble are you trying to bring to my family now, boy?" He shot a glare at Kiersa, who was about to speak. Turning back to me, he continued his questioning. "First, you caused a ruckus during our celebration, and now I hear that she was attacked by a foul creature before. Because she was with you!"

"I—"

"Silence!" he shouted, slicing at me again with his knife.

Kiersa stood still at the foot of the bed. Tears streamed down her face as she dared not speak. Looking closer, I could see several scratches on Kiersa's arms and clothes. Aire was sporting a series of cuts on his shoulders and arms. It even looked like a bite mark on his wrist.

As I surveyed the damage, his words made more and more sense. I did bring this on them. I made her a target of whatever bastard was doing this. She was in danger. Her father was in danger. Her mother was in danger.

"Whatever heathen curse you have brought onto this family, you will remove it!" Aire shouted, his eyes narrowed at me. "First, an explosion rocks the entire city. And who is there? You. My daughter is attacked by a monster. Who was there? You. And who was it that likely sent this monster to my beloved this morning, nearly killing us? You!"

"I-I... What happened?" I finally got out.

"A monster attacked us!" Aire said, cutting into the air. "A beast shrouded in darkness attacked Kiersa while she was tending to her mother, my beloved. When I heard their screams, I wrestled the beast, nearly losing

274

my life to it. The Shepherd blessed us, and we managed to drive the beast away."

Kiersa let out a small sob, and I could see a recently healed gash on her shoulder. I trembled, trying to speak, but finding no words.

"You curse us with your false stone, Redbeaker! You curse us!"

"The moonstone?" I asked incredulously. "No, you got it all wrong. The moonstone saved us! It..." I trailed off, looking at Kiersa. "I just wanted to help heal your mother."

Kiersa burst into tears and dropped the dagger, running to me. She ran past Aire and threw herself into my arms. I held her tight, trying to wrap my mind around such a targeted attack.

Aire shook with rage, looking back at his wife, lying still in the bed, fast asleep. His eyes bulged as he stared at us. Kiersa put herself between him and me, her hands outstretched.

"Don't you dare lay a hand on this man," she growled. "He has done more for us than you could imagine."

"He has endangered this family and poisoned your mind with trinkets!" Aire shouted, still trembling with anger.

I gently nudged one of her arms down and stood beside her, staring at her father. I wasn't about to let him endanger his daughter over his grudge with me.

"He is—"

"He lit the Everlasting, Father!" Kiersa shouted, causing Aire to drop his weapon to the floor. His mouth slackened as his rage turned to shock and disbelief. "With the Shepherd guiding my words, Father. Asher was the one who reignited the Everlasting."

"No," he said in disbelief. He looked at me, rage and confusion at war for supremacy in his eyes. "You lie!"

Kiersa muttered an incantation as he shouted this, and a circle traced around the floor, with runes and glowing light. A Truth Circle.

"He lit the Everlasting, Father. He lit it for me, simply because he wanted to make me happy."

Aire looked at his daughter, gobsmacked. His entire life had melted before his eyes as the circle glowed white underneath.

"Kiersa, my daughter," Aire trembled. "How long have you been this way? How much of your mother's magic have you studied?"

275

"Years," Kiersa said, trembling, the white light signifying her truth. "For years I have read Mother's writings and divinations. She was a cleric, wasn't she? Gifted by Ihena? Well, I was too!"

Aire could only nod, too dumbfounded to speak.

"She wanted to be an adventurer, just as I do." Kiersa's eyes burned with passion. "Like I will be someday."

Aire looked at his daughter desperately but said nothing. Instead, he turned to me. "You really revived it? For my daughter?" I'd never have thought a voice so small could come from such a powerful and large man.

"Yes," I said quietly, the circle's white glow as pure as winter's snow.

Aire took a deep breath and looked at his sleeping wife. Walking over to his wife, he placed his knife down on a table and rubbed her head. Kiersa joined by her mother's bedside as I stood by her. Her mother looked so frail.

"Nosha has not woken for months," Aire said softly. "Moonstones have kept her alive while we searched for a cure. We'd hoped a large enough collection could potentially cure her. But it seems her sickness is taking its toll."

He stroked his wife's head as Kiersa leaned by my side. I hated to think that they were so close to finding a potential cure, only to have it ripped away from them.

"I promise I will find more moonstones, Mr. Denrel."

Aire looked at me, not in an adversarial fashion, but as a man.

"I will do everything in my power to make sure that she wakes up." I stuck my hand out to shake his hand. "You have my word."

Aire chuckled for a moment, looking at the circle below us. "I should have suspected you'd be involved somehow. You are an interesting young man, Mr. Merrick."

Aire looked at me and shook my hand. I offered to stay the night and watch over the house for him, which he accepted. Kiersa kissed her father good night and left the room.

For the rest of the night, I sat at the top of the stairs, with my sword by my side. Aire stayed up with me for a little while, bringing me a cup of water. About an hour into my watch, Aire decided to go back to sleep. Before he left, Aire pointed to the room Kiersa slept in.

"Please keep in mind that she is saving herself for marriage and do your best to not defile her, lest you be ready to take responsibility." The way he said it wasn't really a threat but almost a matter-of-fact. Aire was many things, but able to see through his daughter was not one of them.

Later into the night, Aire finally went to sleep and locked the door behind him. As I threatened to nod off myself, I felt a blow of air tickle my ear. Jumping forward, I turned and saw that it was Kiersa. Before I could say anything, I was silenced by her voluptuous figure in nothing but a sheer dressing gown.

"I can't sleep." She whispered.

She took me by the hand, and I saw her breasts jiggle from the side as she walked me downstairs and into a room they usually rented out. It was a typical modest room with a bed, chest, and table. Kiersa locked the door and turned around.

Without saying a word, she walked over and kissed me. When I felt those soft lips against mine, I was surprised. Surprised by how she grabbed me and thrust her tongue into my mouth.

"Kiersa," I said, having to tear myself away. "I need to be on guard, I promised your father..."

Her eyes were soft, and she held my face gently.

"Asher, please." She whispered. "For just a moment, I need to forget about what happened today. Let me be selfish for just a little bit."

I held Kiersa close, looking into her beautiful, beautiful eyes. Her fear, her vulnerability, her desire all weighed on my chest.

I nodded my head and slowly kissed her, wrapping my arms protectively around her. She peeled off my shirt as she sat me down on the bed. I could feel her heart race as our hands explored one another. Her sweet, gentle moans filled the room and I took her gown off, placing it to the side.

"I was so scared," Kiersa whispered as I squeezed her, kissing on her neck.

"You're safe now," I whispered huskily, gently laying her down on the bed. "I promise."

I traced my hands up her legs, kissing her thighs and up to her hips. Kiersa let out an excited moan as I got closer. Kissing the point where thighs met, her legs opened to me. Her hips rocked gently as I tasted her, slowly licking her.

I took my time, slowly arcing up and down, just long enough to feel

Kiersa shiver against me. Her legs trembled as I spread her wider. Her clit was swollen and heaving, begging for attention. Slowly, I traced more circles around her spot, making Kiersa moan into the night. Her hips bucked against me as I felt her hands grasp at my head.

"You'll never be scared like that again," I said, pulling myself away for just a moment. "I promise."

She could only nod rapidly as I stared at her from below.

"Should I continue?"

Kiersa bit her lip, whispering in confirmation. "Yes, please."

I continued to worship Keirsa's wet pussy, extracting as much pleasure from every minute movement. Kiersa's hips began to circle in the opposite direction that I moved my tongue. I felt the gentle press of her thighs turn into a potentially dangerous squeeze the more I licked her.

"Asher," She moaned "More..."

With one last flick of the tongue, I began sucking her clit. I started gently at first, grabbing onto her thighs and spreading her wide open. Her muscles began to tense, and her left leg shook violently as I got more aggressive. My heart raced as I felt her body writhing against my face.

She was getting close. I began flicking my tongue wildly over her clit, pulling it ever so slightly away from her and into my mouth. I was voracious, hungry, and desperate, burying myself in her lap. I pulled her legs up to my face, licking, suckling, and kissing every bit of her.

"Asher!" She squealed, snapping her legs around my head.

At the last second, Kiersa managed to grab a pillow, biting into it as she screamed. I felt her whole body tremble and shudder. Her whimpering screams were muffled by the fabric of the pillow, as Kiersa shook wildly in my arms, unable to control herself.

I slowly knelt her lower half down back onto the bed. Kiersa's chest heaving as she gazed at me . Her lips trembled, mouthing something to herself as I took a drink of water and wiped off my mouth.

I slowly climbed on top of her, running my hand up her leg and along her side. A single tear stung her eyes as she smiled up at me. The whole world dissolved, leaving only us floating along the ether on the bed. I positioned the head of my cock into Kiersa.

"I don't want to take advantage of you, Kiersa." I whispered, needing to give her an out. "I know we've done it plenty, but, I won't do this if you don't want this."

Kiersa put one hand on my member and the other on my cheek as she kissed me.

"Make love to me, Asher," She whispered. "It's all I want."

Kiersa pulled me in to her, sliding in with ease. We both let out a breathless sigh of ecstasy, feeling each other again. Her breasts flattened against my chest as I pressed down, slowly pushing the last bit inside her.

"Oooooh fuck," I grunted.

Kiersa wrapped her legs around me, pushing me in deeper as we kissed. Slowly I rocked back and forth. Moaning into my ears, Kiersa started grinding her hips as I thrust. We kissed, moving in perfect rhythm to each other.

Our arms wrapped tight against each other as I struggled to keep myself from exploding. With every rock of my hips back, her legs forcefully pushed me back in. Every thrust felt like my last as my abdominal muscles contracted, and I slowed my breathing.

"Kiersa," I whispered, feeling her squeeze around me. "I'm getting close. It's too good."

She tightened around me even more as Kiersa clawed at my shoulders. I kept going, maintaining our gentle pace. I kissed her neck feeling her curls tickle me as I buried myself into her. Her body shook and shuddered as I felt the crescendo come closer.

"Come with me, Asher," She moaned as I nibbled at her nape, "I'm so close. Kiss me while you do it."

Unable to contain myself and my lust I began to speed up. I couldn't help myself as I began to thrust harder and harder. Kiersa moaned into my ear, begging me to keep going. I felt a warm splatter against my cock as Kiersa let out a long warbly moan.

Feeling it, I kissed Kiersa deeply and passionately. With a final thrust into her tight, shaking pussy, I came deep inside of her. We both moaned, trembling and hugging tightly as the wave of pleasure crashed over top us.

We laid there for a while, unable to remove ourselves from each other. I could feel the temptation of sleep grip around me, as I felt Kiersa's breasts slowly rising and falling beneath me. I kissed Kiersa again and whispered into her ear.

"You'll always be safe, Kiersa. I promise."

279

After helping clean her up, Kiersa and I got dressed. Her legs were shaky, so I carried her up the stairs with ease. Setting her back on her feet by her bedroom, Kiersa gave me a kiss on the cheek.

"I wish you could come in," She whispered. "But I think I'll be able to sleep just fine now."

I smiled as she giggled, closing the door. I returned to my post, making sure to keep my promise with Aire. When dawn approached, he saw me sitting there, exhausted and holding my sword.

He tried to shake my hand, but I just gave him a thumbs up. Aire gave me a curious glance, but his ignorance of his daughter's true nature proved too great. I saluted him and stumbled home as the sun crested over the horizon to greet me.

When I finally made it home, Uli was at the door waiting for me. She still looked unhappy with me, but her expression was much kinder than before. Mara and Giezha weren't the early riser types, so they were still asleep. Sal waved a hand at me as he walked toward the stock room.

Unpleasant thoughts swirled through my head as I remembered what the captain had told me. I shook it off and looked at Uli.

"I take it Kiersa's okay," she said.

"Yup..."

As I spoke, I walked up the stairs while Uli followed me. "Aire threatened to gut me like a fish. Then he found out I lit the Everlasting. Then I promised to save his wife. After that, I stayed up all night and guarded the house for them! Then Kiersa and I... comforted each other. Then the sun came up. Now I'm tired. So, I'm going to bed."

Uli just stopped and stared at me before cracking a smile.

"You are so full of surprises, Asher Merrick. Good night."

Uli quickly swept in and kissed me on the cheek before leaving me to rest. I shut the door behind me and collapsed on the bed, asleep before my head hit the pillow.

280

Chapter 26

Evlanday, 23rd of Seeyrn, Year 678, 4th Age

I decided to sleep in, not waking up until the sun was already beginning to set. All things considered, nobody minded me taking a day off. That evening, we went to check on the Rendel family. They were hard at work repairing the lower floors, they were thrilled to see us.

Aire took the time to thank me again for last night and ask if I had any trouble. Kiersa gave me a wink behind his back, and I smiled and assured him it had been uneventful.

We offered to help repair the broken furniture and clean everything. We were quickly waved off as a congregation of followers of Ihena came, bearing gifts and labor to assist their brothers and sisters in faith.

"Well, I guess we aren't needed," I said, dodging a pair of halflings carrying brand new tables for the tavern.

"Agreed," said Mara. "Let's go to the guildhall and prepare for the mission."

So far, the scout team, which included Valdir of all people, reported a series of high-level magical traps and enchantments preventing entry. The captain and Vurshung were convinced the smuggler was still in the city. Eventually, they would need to return to that safe house.

"But why can't we just go in and turn the place upside down?" I asked, going over the captain's notes with everyone in one of the guild offices for the third time. "What's stopping us?"

"Vurshung's orders," Uli said, rubbing her temple as she tried to find something we may have missed. "Like Captain said, Ivory Forge owns this thing now."

"Something about this is a little fishy," Mara said, bringing in some food and drink to keep us going. "I'm sure that the Ivory Forge bastards know

281

more than they are telling us."

"Probably because they are investigating us," I said, which frustrated Mara further.

Mara shook her fists angrily as she tried not to break something. "Why are they doing that?"

Giezha shot a thumb in my direction. "Because of dumbass over there, and probably because they're suspicious of the guild. Especially considering someone left an 'anonymous' tip."

I knew that I would be eating crow for having Kiersa give a message to the council for a while. Luckily, everyone but Giezha stopped browbeating me about it so much.

I'm sure this was because I nearly died a few days ago. But hey, anything to keep them off my back.

Uli's icy treatment of me had finally warmed over, and things were back to normal. The rest of the night was spent going over our notes on the two investigations into the silver disappearance and moonstone shortage.

The sheer density of the Ivory Forge's investigation into the moonstones was staggering. There were massive stacks of papers and notes going back at least three years to be read through.

Most of these were Vurshung's, which, as time went on, descended into rambling. He was obsessed with the case. By the time I made it three months into the investigation, it was far past midnight, and we were the alone in the guildhall, save for a few stragglers.

After a few more hours, we needed to head home, which meant seeing Sal. My stomach churned at the thought of him being potentially involved in this.

The captain basically said he was a prime suspect, and it was my job to investigate him. However, there was no way I could keep this from the others.

This cloak and dagger secret investigation stuff had us all at our wit's end. They needed to know.

Stifling a yawn, I twisted and popped my back while the others poured over the reports of the three undead attacks that had occurred in the past few weeks. The council had covered all of them up, saying they were random attacks.

Uli looked ready to down an energy potion while Mara sipped green tea

282

in the hopes of staying up. Giezha was already snoozing with her witch's hat as a makeshift pillow. I tapped her shoulder to wake her up.

"It's getting late, guys, we should be heading home."

The others nodded their heads sleepily and began to pack things up. Uli muttered something about stashing her notes in her chest as I awkwardly tried to get their attention.

"Listen, I really need to talk to you all. It's about Sal." The others dropped their notes and turned to me.

"What's up with Sal?" Mara asked first.

I swallowed and chewed on my lip, trying to spit it out. "It's about his time with the Red Breakers. Specifically, what the captain told me when she had me walk back to the guild with her. According to her... According to her, the Sal she knew was very different than the one we know. Does he ever talk about what it was like in the guild? What he did there?"

All of them shook their heads, making what I had to say all the more uncomfortable.

"Dawnthorn was one of the founders with him, right? And there's hardly anything of him in the historical records or by the guild's record-keeping. According to the captain, he fell out with the guild mostly because of what he did after the Incursion."

"Like what?" Giezha said skeptically.

I breathed in deep, trying to muster the courage to rip off the bandage. "Sal was a sorcerer for the guild. And a few years after the Incursion, he was found studying necromancy. Practicing, actually."

"Sal?!" they shouted in unison.

"Apparently, there was a huge commotion when he accidentally lost control of animals that he had been practicing necromancy with. The guild took the blame without giving him up, which is how we got the reputation that we have."

"The Dead Stampede?" Mara asked, pulling out an old report she'd read earlier. "This report from the Red Breaker logs says that they couldn't find out who was responsible. There's no way that Sal did it!"

Uli looked at the report and swore under her breath. "The dates match up with when he left. If he didn't leave because of disgust at the guild's failure to uncover the culprit, then that's one hell of a coincidence."

"That has to be it!" Mara said, yanking the paper back into her pile. "Sal

283

lost his family in the Incursion. There's no way he would have sullied their memory like that."

"Desperate times..." Giezha said sadly.

"Call for desperate measures," I said, nodding. "Look, I'm not saying that I believe her. I'm just saying that they think there's something there. We won't find anything in the logs, but we might find something by talking to Sal."

Mara absolutely refused to entertain the notion that Sal had anything to do with this investigation. Giezha and Uli seemed to take the idea more seriously. Not wanting to argue any longer with sunrise only a few hours away, we called it a night and headed back home.

Mara quickly rushed ahead of us, carrying a massive stack of papers in her arms. Giezha made a sleepy promise to calm her down, leaving Uli and me to lock up the office.

Apart from her goodnight kiss the other day, Uli had still been avoiding me. As we walked back to the Inn, an awkward bubble of silence wedged itself between us. I felt awful for making her worry so much, but it was also out of character for her. Perhaps, she was also feeling a bit awkward after the other night.

"So..." I said, trying to break the ice. "Busy couple of days, right?"

Uli looked at me and gave an awkward nod.

"Read any good books lately?"

Nothing. I was starting to flounder as we headed the corner towards home.

"Steal anything cool recently?" I immediately regretted the question, afraid she would be offended, but she burst out laughing. She clutched her belly, laughing as her ears wiggled.

"Oh, my goodness, Asher, you can be downright awkward at the best of times." She flashed her trademark grin, and I felt a weight come off my chest. "No, I haven't stolen anything too interesting lately. I was too busy worrying you might die."

She punched me in the shoulder lightly. We joked about the whole affair as we walked and compared notes one last time before heading in. Sal was fast asleep in his room while Mara and Giezha waited up for us. I bade the girls goodnight, but Uli grabbed my hand before I left.

"Need something—oh!"

284

Uli pulled me over and gave me a kiss, holding my face. She winked and ran off to bed while Mara and Giezha snickered and teased me. I laughed them off and laid down for a proper rest.

The next few days rolled by in relative peace. None of us dared to interrogate Sal, but we spent each day delving into the cases' notes and researching the Incursion. Even the less sensationalized writings described the events as hell brought straight to Echo Veil.

Entire families were destroyed with destruction at every level of society, before the Empire eventually sent a garrison of troops to support the removal of the zombies.

There were rumblings that this was politically motivated by the Nulgat Kingdom during a brief skirmish near the southeastern border by the Iron Forest. However, the Nulgati never used the widely reported Incursion as an opportunity to attack.

This provided a critical opportunity to push back the horde and eventually became a crucial part of peace negotiations.

Besides our joint investigation with Ivory Forge, we were still chasing down leads to the location of Mhurren and Mick and Uli's scouting mission.

Unfortunately, a side effect of the building catching fire and Rogorm's death was a lot of people suddenly going blind, deaf, and mute.

The only ones who knew the truth about it were Ivory Forge, who found the body while putting out the fires, and a few of us Red Breakers. Despite devoting nearly every hour to these quests, neither investigation had any meat to it. We were trying to paddle a canoe with one oar, spinning in a circle.

As for Uli's scouting mission, there was nothing out of the ordinary. The mountain blocked off any trade routes, and all roads were north of the mountain chain.

The only thing even remotely interesting in the records was about the area being where a lieutenant to the Dragon Khorba, named Zhol, died hundreds of years ago. This dragon apparently did a lot of damage, but I had to focus for now on researching the mission.

The Ivory Forge crew regularly demanded long-winded meetings, producing nothing of substance. These were simply opportunities to sneer at us and stroke their egos. Any time that stupid dwarf named Kasuc let

285

out a racial remark, Vurshung had to quickly jump in between us while the woman Agostina threatened us. He was powerless to stop them and frequently ignored him.

This came to a head during an investigation with Vurshung and Mara. We were going around town to re-interview some of the last contacts of Mhurren and Mick. Giezha and Uli were forced to tag along with Kasuc and Agostina in The Docks as we headed for that hobgoblin Towser. Mara and I were steaming at an objection the two Ivory Forge members had towards Uli interviewing Towser.

"And what the hell does 'preference towards similar species' even mean? Uli doesn't even know him!" I demanded, stomping up the stairs to Towser.

"It means that they are lay about racists whose only contributions so far have been distracting you from doing your job right," he snapped as we got to Towser's floor.

I was taken aback by the typically regal Vurshung snapping like that. Mara was quick to place a reassuring hand on his shoulder. She managed to put his fiery temper on ice without a word, and he exhaled painfully.

"Ah, I'm sorry, young Asher, my stress has been getting the better of me." He looked at the entrance and an evil grin spread across his scaly mouth. "Would you mind if I kicked the door in? I've wanted to do that for a long time now."

"Go right ahead!" Mara said brightly while giving me a wink.

Mara and I sorely needed some entertainment compared to the days of research and dead ends. We watched as Vurshung pulled out a longsword he carried with an ornamental hilt and quickly inspected it. Motioning for us to get in position, he readied himself in front of the door. Right when Vurshung was about to kick the door in, it opened, and Towser's head poked out. Vurshung quickly recovered from his surprise while Towser gave us a sour look.

"What do you want? Buying or selling?" he grumbled, holding a cold spell on a busted lip.

Vurshung pushed his way in, which Mara and I followed. Towser swore in Goblin and rushed behind his counter. Towser noticed the Ivory Forge insignia on Vurshung's cloak.

Towser drummed his fingers on the table. "If you're buying, hurry up. Gotta close early."

We looked around the shop casually as Towser watched us with impatient eyes. They quickly snapped from each of us as Mara, and I talked about the different varieties of potions. Vurshung inspected the halberd on display in a large glass case.

"Interesting," Vurshung said, checking the bottom of a green potion with a chunky texture. "This potion seems to be similar a batch of potions stolen during import last week." He pulled out a journal and began writing inside of it. Towser's eyes bugged out of his skull watching Vurshung.

"Dammit, whaddaya want!?" He shouted, pointing to Mara and me.

"Information regarding misters Mhurren and Mick." Vurshung said, taking charge.

"Told those two, I ain't seen those two nitwits!" he shouted.

Vurshung stared at him unblinkingly. As Mara and I brought our purchases to the counter, Vurshung kept up the glare. Towser began to really sweat as we applied the invisible pressure. He sold us the potions for thirty gold without even noticing that, mixed in with the stamina, mana, and healing potions, was a Potion of Fire Breath.

That was fine with us, though. It had a different magic shop's name on the seal, meaning it'd been stolen as well.

"Alright!" Towser finally shouted, banging his fists on the table. "I didn't tell you everything the last time you were here, all right?"

"How'd you do that when Giezha had a Truth Circle on you?" I asked suspiciously.

Vurshung leaned in and cocked his head. Towser bent under Vurshung's gaze but shot me an evil look. "Strong enough will can break even the mightiest spells, boy."

Glancing at Vurshung, whose hand had drifted to his sidearm, Towser wiped the grin off his face. "I was telling the truth about the potion. I don't know what it was was. I don't know what happened to it. But you weren't the only ones asking."

"Who else was?" Mara asked, putting the potions we bought in her bag.

"Was getting there!" Towser shouted. "It was some old goat. A satyr with those stupid little glasses."

Ah, shit. Sal. Vurshung didn't move, but Mara and I exchanged nervous glances.

"Anyways, he came in a couple days ago. Seemed to know more than he

287

was letting on. Really shifty."

"Ask any questions we didn't?"

Towser stopped and thought for a moment as Vurshung towered over the hobgoblin. Steam could be visibly seen coming from Vurshung's nostrils. If Towser didn't tell the truth, he was toast. Literally. The heat melted whatever bits of a tough guy act Towser had left. It was something to behold.

"In Dusyr, I'm getting there! He asked if the city Midmanch ever came up in conversation. I said it might've, and he got all jittery 'n such. Then he asks about some 'Red Ledger' they were carrying. Like I saw what was in they's bags!" Towser gave a final look to Vurshung and puffed up. "I told him to go check with the guild, and he ran out without buyin' a thing. That's all! Swear on my mum's grave if she were dead."

Vurshung's gaze squeezed the gumption out of Towser, and all that was left was the quivering truth. Without saying a word, Vurshung nodded and smiled.

We walked out of the store as Towser shouted idle threats. The fact that Sal was the one who came to Towser and didn't mention it was terrible. The crosshairs were starting to align around the old goat's head.

We waited for the others in our agreed-upon meeting place: the abandoned remains of Rogorm's hideout. The bottom floor was the least badly damaged, and it was easy enough to get in unseen. Sitting in a back room on damaged boxes, we waited for the others.

Vurshung had another stack of notes he'd been adding to at every stop. He certainly had a way of filling up the page with verbosity. As we waited, I broached the uncomfortable subject.

"Not looking good for Sal, is it?" I asked.

Vurshung and Mara shook their heads.

"Aye, it's not." Vurshung looked up, scowling. "Agh! I hate withholding information." He looked at the both of us and took a deep breath. "Promise me that you will not repeat what I say except to your compatriots Ms. Uli and Ms. Giezha."

Mara and I nodded, exchanging nervous glances.

"The truth is that the council assigned us an additional special quest."

"You mean the one besides the moonstone quest," I said, to which Vurshung nodded.

288

"That is correct. Our real aim is to investigate the Red Breakers." Vurshung said, which made Mara place a hand on my elbow.

"Mr. Salvatore was already the main suspect of the investigation. Were it not for young Asher's tip about the zombie rat, we would not have included you in this investigation. However, being key witnesses to such events necessitated your involvement. I thank you for your hard work through all of this."

Mara and I nodded as she squeezed my arm tighter. It was insulting that we had produced just as much good work as they had, but Ivory Forge had no intention of including us from the beginning.

They really were a bunch of elitist pricks.

Right on cue, Uli and Giezha walked in with scowls plastered across their faces. Kasuc and Agostina followed shortly thereafter, sitting beside Vurshung with their noses turned up.

"Find anything good?" Uli asked, whispering in my ear.

"Sal's the main suspect, and we got some evidence to back it up. I'll fill you in later," I whispered back.

"Sal is a suspect, but not the only suspect," Vurshung said, looking around the group. "We have reason to believe that Mhurren Aleslock and Mick Setirg were his accomplices."

I did a double-take. "What? He loathed those two. They were never allowed in his bar. Hell, last time I saw them, he was cracking their skulls."

Kasuc rolled his eyes and jumped in. "We know. We had agents watching as you snapped Murphy or whatever's arm. We also know that he was seeing them regularly for the past five months in secret."

"Where?" Uli demanded, trying to make sense of such a ludicrous accusation.

"Deep in Iron Court," Vurshung said ominously. "He would spend the days at a time in the slums, leaving his bar completely unattended. He was in contact with Rogorm, whom he first became acquainted with through Mhurren and Mick."

"Shit," Mara said under her breath.

Now he was connected to the zombies, the silver issue, and Mhurren and Mick. The missing piece this entire time was Sal. And it was right under our nose. Turns out, that wasn't the only thing under our nose.

"How'd you manage to keep this under wraps without getting found out?" Giezha asked. "Ivory Forge operatives are known entities because of their close ties to the council."

"Like this, newbie."

Agostina flourished her staff and smacked its bottom on the ground. She and Kasuc were enveloped in a black shadow before their outlines began to morph. Kasuc shot up into the air while Agostina's ears shrank and hair grew. As the shadow faded and they came back into the light, they had transformed their appearance. Kasuc was now a tattoo-laden goliath, while Agostina was a half-elf with a scar across her nose.

Those motherfuckers.

"Oh, fuck you." I groaned. "You've been tailing us the entire time? Why didn't you grab the courier for the silver?"

Kasuc rolled his eyes. "We weren't concerned with the silver, you dolt. We thought he was working for you Breaker lot. Little bastard slipped through our fingers."

"And now you're stuck with us," Giezha noted. "Great work."

Both of them decided they were too good to talk to us. Again. Like every other time we spoke. Because they're assholes.

With a casual snap of the sorceress's fingers, they transformed back into Kasuc and Agostina. The last shred of trust I had in Ivory Forge burned into cinders, was stomped into the ground, frozen over, and thrown into a volcano.

Vurshung simply hung his head in defeat before continuing.

"We need to confirm the possibility of a connection with the city of Midmanch and our joint investigations. Towser also mentioned another possible clue during interrogation." He turned to us. "Are you all aware of something called the 'Red Ledger' in your guild?"

Giezha was the first to speak up. "The captain's personal ledger. Includes pieces of information no other guild members have. It's likely heavily guarded."

"Great!" I said, happy for an easy follow-up for once. "We can ask Dawnthorn for it so we can confirm all this."

Everybody looked at me like an idiot. I was probably an idiot for thinking it would be easy.

"I'll take that as a no."

"There's no way Captain hands something like that over," Uli said,

290

pinching her temples.

"It would probably implicate your guild in enough shit to throw you all in jail for life a hundred times over!" Agostina laughed. "Maybe the gallows if we're lucky."

Just as I was ready to carve her like a Thanksgiving turkey, Uli stood up.

"Fine. We'll get the Red Ledger."

She walked over to Vurshung, who towered over her even while sitting. "You don't see what's inside the book. We copy down only what's relevant. Write it down word for word and show it to you."

Kasuc and Agostina were about to protest, but Vurshung had finally had enough and shot a warning look at them. Neither would admit to being intimidated, but they shut their traps for once.

"Deal," Vurshung said before standing up. "You bring us the information, and we will continue from there. Hopefully, nothing happens between now and then." He got up and left with the others. "I suggest you move quickly, Ms. Siannodel."

Uli sighed and turned to us, producing a torn piece of paper with a Red Breaker seal.

"Who's ready to steal from the guild?"

291

Chapter 27

Xaliasday, 7th of Tavlin, Year 678, 4th Age

A tense air filled the team everywhere we went knowing we had to break into the guildhall. Weeks crawled by as we continued to look over our shoulders.

Vurshung took the liberty of telling the captain we'd hit a dead end but expected a big break soon. She groused about wasting time and money but was held powerless by Ivory Forge's control over the investigation.

Regarding Ivory Forge, there was no telling if Kasuc and Agostina would tip off the guild to mess with us.

We hoped that there would be some information coming from the scouting teams. Still, every day, Valdir's paper crane messengers would contain a whole lot of nothing. Most worrying, we were forced to take turns keeping an eye on the number one suspect, Sal. Our suspicions only grew because he never left the bar. At all. From morning until night, he was in the Silver Cup Tavern.

As a team, we tried to stay busy. Uli spent nearly every waking hour she could in the guildhall, trying to find ways to get to the Red Ledger. It was apparently moved recently to a hidden section of the guild. She pinged ideas off me on nights she was home early while teaching me the basics of lock picking, hiding in plain sight, and general sneaking.

Giezha and Mara would split time helping me train while also finding some time for pleasurable activities.

For Giezha, that meant bird watching from the top of the library. I'd join her up on one of the spires, watching finches, seagulls, and other winged creatures stretch their wings to the horizon. Occasionally, I'd pull Mara along, and we'd combine birdwatching with watercolor landscapes.

As I continued my training, I was getting the hang of the more esoteric parts of magic. Using portions of the fire and wind runes in combination with others to create a basic sound that could be used as a method of illusion.

"Good," Giezha said, uncovering her ears from my latest attempt. "You can mimic a bird song. Now try to get the volume to a realistic level." An

292

elvish wizard came into our study room to scold me for being too loud in the library.

As soon as I drained my mana and finished observing the daily migration patterns of robins, finches, and swallows, I'd head out to The Warren.

The recent lessons with Mara there turned out to be part academics and part practical. We would go over basic stances and formations with different weapons before trying them out, step-by-step. The purpose was to learn quick and non-lethal takedowns in the event we get caught.

Unfortunately, the lessons now included guest-instructor Vurshung.

Although his plethora of knowledge was helpful, I missed having alone time with Mara. Around the time she started teaching me to use a bow, Mara finally had enough. Vurshung had the grace to not teach over her, but Mara was tired of his constant tangents.

"Now remember, young Asher," Vurshung blustered, holding four different types of arrows. "You will never know what type of ammunition you have available to you. You could run out of your standard-issue iron arrows and be left with nothing but flint and sticks." He showed off an arrow I had made under his tutelage no less than ten minutes ago. "Or you could discover a magical set of arrows in a treasure hoard."

"But there would be no guarantee that the arrows are in working order or even safe," I said, reading off the notes he'd given me. "Vurshung, I really appreciate the lesson, but I'm currently training with Mara."

Mara was tapping her foot impatiently by the shooting line. There were three targets set up fifty yards out at the edge of the Warren's walls. Vurshung had elected to go deaf to my complaints, and I looked to Mara for help. Rolling her eyes, she whistled loudly with her index finger and thumb.

"Vurshung!" she shouted, causing his head to snap to her mid-sentence. "We're still going over the basics. If you want, stay for the lesson. Otherwise, you can skedaddle!"

Vurshung apologized, and I went to my red-headed sensei for my lesson. "Alright, so these different bows have what's called different weights to them..."

By the time I would arrive back home, I'd be too exhausted to do much. Which was a shame because there was still plenty left to do. Every night, Kiersa would come and visit us, carrying a platter of whatever extra food she and her father had made. Aire had finally relaxed after the zombie attack, and Kiersa joined us playing cards, listening to music at the tavern, and trying and failing to beat Mara in backgammon.

"How is she this good?" Kiersa demanded after losing the tenth game in a row for our side.

Mara simply stuck a tongue out and collected the ten copper I'd bet on Kiersa winning.

Whenever we asked Kiersa about her magical training, she'd get misty-eyed and trail off. She alluded to wanting to escape the life of cooking and cleaning for patrons at her father's tavern several times.

"I just want to go on an adventure!" she shouted one night, several shots of firewater in. "I'm tired of hacking pork and bubbling stews. I want to go out and get my hands dirty! Dive into some dungeons! Fight some dragons!"

She was sorely disappointed to hear that we had not crawled through any dungeons nor fought any dragons. Whenever she demanded to hear about whatever quests we were on, we'd tell her escorting missions, city detail, or "can't say, too classified." The more we said the last, the more she wanted to know.

Who could blame her?

At the end of every night, I'd walk Kiersa home, and she'd ask if I wanted to stay. Tempting me with delicious breakfast, endless stories of her customers in the night, and a body I could only assume Ihena herself thought of in a dream. I turned her down. Usually.

This night was different, however. The night of the heist. Each of us spent the night on the town creating alibis.

Uli and Mara decided to paint Iron Court red, while Giezha went for an all-night study in the library. I spent my night with Kiersa, waiting for when I finally got the call. We were lying in bed, cuddling our naked bodies together.

"So, you think Giezha's going to try and join the fun?" Kiersa asked, rubbing a hand over my chest.

"What?" I said, turning and looking at her body glisten in the moonlight. "No way, Giezha doesn't strike me as the type to want to get involved with me. She's way too serious."

"Oh, she's serious, alright," Kiersa teased, drifting her hand down my abdomen. "She's seriously thinking about jumping you every time your back is turned."

She pouted when I looked unconvinced. "It's true! She's the quiet type, but you know what they say about them. Plus, I know what it looks like when a girl is staring at you with hungry eyes." Her hands drifted lower, and I smirked, returning the favor. She gave out a soft gasp and bit her lip.

"And what do you mean by joining the fun?" I whispered into her ear as I got on top of her. As I started to play with her clit, she got me raring to go for round three. "You make me sound like I'm just some kind of toy."

"No, ah!" She moved her hips, begging for more of my hand. "It's just clear that we don't mind sharing you is all. Oh!"

"You don't mind?"

"N-No, oh fuck. We l-l-like it,!"

Right as I was about to seal the deal, I heard a soft knock at the door.

"Don't worry," came the whisper of Uli. "Aire is still fast asleep somehow. Now hurry up, and get your gear, Asher! We've got to go." I looked at Kiersa and smiled sadly. "Duty calls."

Kiersa gave a salute and kissed me. "Go on, Mr. Adventurer. I'll be waiting for you when you get back." With one last protracted kiss, I put my clothes back on and opened the door.

Uli, Mara, and Giezha were all standing in the hallway with my gear in tow. Uli was totally straight-faced, while Giezha was more than a little impatient. Mara, on the other hand, looked quite pleased as she pulled her ear off the door.

Quietly exiting the Denrel residence, we made our way to the guildhall. By this point, it was extremely late, and nobody was out and about. Even the vermin had gone to sleep.

"How Mr. Denrel doesn't get woken up by all that noise Kiersa makes, I'll never know," Giezha said, rolling her eyes.

"She casts silence on his room," I said nonchalantly. "He never even knows I'm there half the time. Other times, Kiersa just tells him that I've come to see her after renting one of their rooms downstairs."

Bragging about my sexual relationship aside, we switched gears and prepared for our break-in. The front door was out of the question, but Uli's research gave us another path. The Ledger was kept hidden in a remote area under the guild, which meant we could get to it through the sewers.

295

"These should protect our identities and our sense of smell in the sewers," Uli instructed, handing us all black bandannas and cloaks to cover our faces. "We'll need to be ready for patrols, and if one of us gets found, we get out ASAP. Stay hidden, stay out of sight. Guild has no way of knowing about the mission. They'll be going for the kill."

We found an old entrance to the sewer outside the city in a blind spot of the city guards. The sun would not be up for at least three more hours, and the night watch was lazy with their patrol route.

A particularly lazy guard's hourly stop for a bathroom break provided the perfect opportunity to slip into the sewers completely unseen. I smiled wryly at how many days I'd spent watching them go through the motions, night after night.

"Blegh!" Mara hissed, plugging her nose.

"Blegh" was right. I don't exactly want to detail all the nasty specifics of what the sewer smells like. But whatever you think it smells like is probably accurate. Just multiply your worst nightmare by ten or twenty.

Raw sewage flowed through its river of muck as we crept through the sewer's dingy, wet walkways. Occasionally, we would bump into the occasional giant rat, which Mara quickly dispatched.

Uli carried a map of the sewers she got from Gathos-knows-where, while Giezha kept a small bullseye lantern trained on it. The sewer was a maze underneath the city streets above. At times, I could just barely see moonlight through a grate. Other times, it sounded like a building creaking above. However, they'd designed this city, the sewers did not match the roads.

Eventually, we got to our destination. At an intersection of two canals, we could see a wall section with slightly discolored stones. We crossed the canal over a small stone bridge and waited for Uli's signal. She studied her notes one last time before looking back at the stones. Breathing deeply, she tapped parts of the wall in a specific pattern. On the last tap, the stones dissolved into a wooden door with a large iron handle.

"Locked," she said, clicking her tongue. With a flourish of her hands, she summoned a set of lockpicks and quickly got to work. Less than a minute later, we heard a loud thunk.

"Shit!" she hissed. "Remind me to have you cast silence on that next time," she whispered to Giezha.

The door pushed open, and we all slunk in. Inside the door was a small room with boxes, a wooden chair, and a messy desk. Mara swooped in and checked the table for any clues. The other door was unlocked from the other side. As Uli began to work on that lock, I saw a shadow move behind a small seam in the wooden door. Grabbing Uli, I pulled her and Mara back behind a set of boxes.

"Get down!" I said, stuck between whispering and trying to alert them.

A voice on the other side went, "Huh?"

Giezha was too tall to hide behind the boxes and dashed into a corner behind the door. As the door creaked open, I felt something slide across my legs.

I was horrified by a long piece of twisted red ropes slithering from Uli's hand. It made the sound of a hissing snake as it slithered across the floor. My attention quickly snapped to the door opening, revealing a half-elf Red Breaker member I'd seen a few times around the hall.

I think his name was Pilock.

"Who's there?" he asked, with a knife drawn. Walking into the room, he turned and quickly spotted Giezha.

Before he could shout, the serpentine rope uncoiled and struck at the guard. He gave a muffled shout as Giezha threw a powder in his face, causing him to fall to the ground. I jumped out and caught him so he wouldn't crack his skull. He was fast asleep in my arms as the rope coiled around his mouth tied his arms. Giezha picked him up and threw him under the desk.

"Sleeping powder and boa's rope," I noted, remembering Giezha's lessons on magical items. "Effective."

Giezha gave a proud nod while Uli rushed us into the other room. With the guard's key in my possession, we were now in the inner sanctum under the guild. This appeared to be more storage, filled with extra weapons, some food supplies for long-haul quests, and a selection of wine.

"At this point, we're flying blind," Uli said, huddling us together. "Let's split up and look for the Red Ledger. It's probably going to be hidden in a locked bookshelf. I'll go with Giezha. You two meet us here in twenty minutes."

"What if we find something?" I asked, looking around in paranoia.

"Use a bird call," Giezha said, summoning a pair of songbirds. "Just don't turn everyone deaf with the signal."

I didn't like the idea of splitting up. It meant more chances to get caught. But the four of us together would be mighty obvious if we were seen. This way, we'd have some plausible deniability. Mara looked just as unhappy with the idea as I was but nodded her head. Uli quietly opened the other door and checked outside.

"There's a hall up ahead—probably leads to a bigger room. We'll go ahead and let the birds out. When you hear three chirps, that's us." Mara and I nodded, and Giezha and Uli gave us the thumbs up.

Giezha looked at us and spoke before leaving the room. "I'll have silence up at all times when not giving a signal."

With that, they left. There was no sound aside from occasional muffled footsteps. Every second stretched into hours waiting for the signal. My heart screamed in fear as it battered the inside of my ribs, coursing adrenaline through me. My mind raced through the different ways this could all go to hell.

Pilock could wake up and set off alarms. Uli and Giezha could be seen by someone in a spot of bad luck. Traps could be around every corner for all we knew!

Like Uli said, we were flying blind.

But we had to press on. Dawnthorn would never risk the guild by handing over the notes of her own volition.

Mara sensed my fear and gently squeezed my shoulder.

"It's gonna be alright," Mara whispered gently. "They've got this."

I slowly breathed out. "We've got this."

Suddenly, we heard a commotion outside. Birds frantically chirped as several pairs of footsteps rushed to the sound. It sounded like at least three pairs of feet.

"What was that?" shouted a voice. It sounded like Brody.

"No idea," came another. "Birds must have gotten down here, again. Probably one of Pilock's pets."

"Bah," came an angry third voice. "Let them rot in the manhole for a little while, then. I'm not sitting in that musty old room."

The three voices trailed off and could be heard walking their separate ways. The distraction had worked, and we needed to wait for the signal.

"Chrip. Chirp. Chirp!"

298

Showtime.

Checking that the coast was clear first, I gently pushed the door open. The hall was a short passageway lit by a set of torches in dire need of oil. The other side was an open area with a few wooden tables filled with documents and a set of stone pillars holding up the ceiling. One of the birds curiously picked at the paper on the ground before fluttering off.

"Sound came from that way," I said, pointing to a door across from us on the short side of the rectangular room. I poked my head around the corner, looking the other way. "Shit."

The only other way out was a large archway that opened up to an even bigger open area. I motioned for Mara to follow me and hugged the wall to my left as we slowly snuck through the room. Mara kept her short bow in hand while I had a knife to jimmy a lock open. We stayed low and slow as we moved

Fighting my base instincts, I slowly made my way with Mara towards the arch. Checking the corner, I saw Brody walk into a room and shut the door on the other side. With a quick check, the coast was clear. We dashed in the opposite direction and into a room with the door open. Inside the small room were a bunk and an open chest.

"Sheets are messed up," I noted, rifling through the chest. "Probably where the guards sleep after their shift." Looking under the bed, I noticed a key on the ground and pocketed it.

"Coast is clear, Asher," Mara said, checking outside. "Let's hurry up."

We quickly slipped out of the room and into the main area. It was a large and wide space with a recessed floor. Torches ran shadows along the walls. My eyes struggled to adjust to the dimness. The songbird from earlier twittered along a rafter up above, and we made our way to the next room.

"Haven't heard from the others," Mara said quietly, a tremor in her voice belying her calm demeanor. "Should we send our location?"

I looked around at the room, which was a total bust. Nothing but broken daggers, torn leather armor, and slashed potion glasses. A veritable junk room with no discernible hidden passages or storage units.

I spent an extra-long time looking to avoid going with her suggestion. I was terrified by the prospect of casting out a bird's call loud enough to wake the dead. But the look on Mara's face agreed with my gut feeling. They needed to have an idea of where we were.

I grabbed a collection of the torn leather and wrapped it around my hands. Concentrating every bit of willpower into the spell, I tried to summon a sound illusion of the birds chirping.

I watched the runes travel from my arm towards my ring wrapped in torn leather as I tried to keep the volume in check.

Tweet... Tweet... TWEET!

The last chirp of my fake bird blasted out with the force of a car alarm. I quickly pulled off my ring and held it to my stomach, trying to end the spell as quickly as possible. The echoes of the screeching bird out of the room and throughout the halls. The songbird outside went into a fit of chirping and audible fluttering.

"Damn," Mara hissed, throwing open the door with her bow out. "Follow me!"

Mara and I rolled out of the room and behind a pillar. The songbird was having a meltdown of sorts up in the rafters, kicking up dust and zooming in a bright yellow blur. The sound of guards clattering their way towards the source of the screech filled the air.

My heart raced as I looked at the two ways out of the large room. Both of them involved fighting. As panic gripped my throat, Mara let an arrow loose towards the ceiling.

Shhk!

With a final chirp, the bird's twittering was cut short by the barely audible sound of the arrowhead piercing into the wooden ceiling. The yellow finch hit the ground like a tiny meteor and exploded into a puff of feathers. The dead bird lay there motionless as we hid behind the pillar. A moment later, Brody ran into the room, looking every way.

"Hey, Iji!" he called out, looking towards the archway.

We froze underneath the table we were hiding under. If this Iji were to walk in, they'd see us plain as day. For a tense moment, we waited. Brody continued searching for the noise source as we heard three chirps behind us.

Relief washed over my body; they hadn't been caught yet, and probably took out the other guard. Brody knelt at the sight of the dead bird and shook his head.

"Coast is clear, Iji! Just those damn birds."

Brody walked towards the area we'd just been in. We rotated back to the archway, staying out of sight as Brody shouted.

He muttered to himself as the telltale three chirps rang out again.

We quickly dashed back to the door Uli and Giezha had gone through and shut it behind us. Giezha's signal rang out again on the left side of the hall, and we ran past whom I presumed to be Iji, knocked out and in the corner.

Hopefully, she'd just been put to sleep.

We followed the sound of songbirds to a large, circular room. The room was lined with tables of magic items encased in crystal.

Cards were set inside the crystal, providing descriptions of the magical item's effects, location of discovery, and estimated value. The walls were covered in glowing pink crystals, which gave the room an ethereal feeling.

I much preferred this over torture-room-chic everywhere else. Crouching at the opposite end were the silhouettes of Giezha and Uli.

Mara's tense expression eased slightly at the sight of them being in one piece. Brody could be heard off in the distance laughing about suicidal songbirds. Uli had a glint in her eye as she looked at me with that trademark grin.

"Ready for the big show?"

The stones disappeared with a series of taps on the blank wall, revealing a large wooden door with three locks. Several lock picks were already strewn on the ground, which I quickly picked up.

"The locks need to be opened simultaneously, and I can't pick them," Uli said as they looked at me and held up an ornate key. "Did you find the other keys?" My eyes lit up as I pulled out Pilock's key and the one I'd found in the guard's room. They were perfect matches for each other. Uli and Mara gave a fist pump while Giezha stayed on the lookout. Handing a key to Mara, we put the keys in the locks and prepared to turn.

"Count of three," Uli said, trying to contain her excitement. "One...Two... Three."

The locks clicked open, and the door silently opened. Inside the threshold was a large room, mostly empty, except for the back wall with silver shelves. We all dashed into the room, leaving the door ajar. Before we stepped too far, Giezha cast a detection spell for traps and magical effects.

"Coast is clear," she muttered, looking around. "I'd have hoped for more security."

We ran up to the shelves, scanning for the Red Ledger. The previous room had been a decoy, making it look like the goods were all encased in the crystal, while the most valuable stuff was just beyond their reach in a hidden area. My eyes glazed over the super valuable items while scanning until I found the Red Ledger.

"Bingo," I said, pulling the red book off the wall.

It was a hefty book with thick beige pages bound in what felt like red alligator skin. The cover had the logo of the Red Breakers on it. I handed it to Uli, who summoned a set of quills and sheets of paper. We read together, flipping through the pages of the massive book while Giezha shone her lantern on it. At that moment, Mara threw something down on the ground.

"Look!" she hissed, opening an identical book. "There are two ledgers! I'll copy down this one, you two copy that one. Giezha, speed up our reading." My eyes began to move rapidly through the pages as blue swirling lines danced from Giezha's staff to my head.

I was reading the book ten times as fast as I normally could. The parts that I could read told incredible and detailed stories of heroism and terrifying danger. Glancing at the pages, they were written in at least a half-dozen languages. Others hinted at illegal activities. The guild's leaders also made multiple mentions of the Undead Incursion. Nearing the end of the Red Ledger, she stopped.

"This is the latest Red Ledger," Uli said, rapidly copying everything down. "I caught a glimpse at the page while the captain was writing in this thing during my mission briefing." Her eyes slowly grew wider and wider as she copied everything down. "What the fuck?" she whispered to herself, reading a section I didn't understand.

The voice of Brody could be heard off in the distance. "Hey, Iji, go tell Pilock he can take a break, okay?"

Uli continued to copy everything she could down, but her hand had started shaking violently. She nearly spilled ink all over the page before she snapped out.

Giezha and I exchanged confused looks while Mara focused on writing in the older version. It was out of character for Uli to be this out of sorts. My stomach sank as I thought about what she might be writing down.

Uli started muttering to herself as she turned the page. "Alright, next is..."

302

"Hey, Iji!" Brody called out again. "Status?"

"Fuck," I said. "Hurry up and get what you can, Uli!"

Uli's eyes were welling up in tears as they zoomed through the pages. A look of shock and horror grew and grew on her face. The sound of Brody running towards our direction echoed through the halls. Mara and Giezha shared my look of worry as things were going south very quickly. Giezha tossed me a bag and started an incarnation. A light shadow cascaded over me, and I went deaf. Just before I lost all hearing, I could hear Brody's voice.

"Iji!"

Swearing to myself, I ran out of the room to try and ambush Brody. I liked the guy, but there was no doubt he'd be trouble. Dashing out of the room, I couldn't hear anything, giving me the impression that the silence surrounded me.

I saw Brody at the end of the hall, standing over Iji's body. His face, illuminated by a torch, displayed horror and confusion. I pulled the hood over my face and pulled my knife out, ready to fight.

He shouted something that probably amounted to, "Who the fuck are you?" at me.

Brody pulled out a magic wand that glowed bright red, aiming for me. But, before he could say another word, I threw my knife at his face. As the knife flew, I ran straight for him.

He dodged the knife as it embedded itself in the wall and let off a blast of arcane energy. The blast came in fast, but I managed to duck underneath. Right on top of him, I attempted a silent takedown.

With his free hand, Brody slashed at me with a knife. I batted his attack away and shoved the palm of my hand under his chin. His head snapped back, and he stumbled into the wall. Grabbing a fistful of the sleeping powder, I tried to shove it in his face.

Brody recovered and dodged the dust before trying again with the knife. Blocking my face, he dug the knife into my left shoulder. I let out a scream of pain that would have rung out were it not for the silence spell.

Brody tackled me onto the ground screaming at the top of his lungs. Preoccupied with the sound that didn't come out of his mouth, he didn't notice my hood fall for a split second. When Brody looked back, I pulled the hood back down.

303

Before he could slash my throat, I unleashed the half-dose of sleeping powder still in my hand, slamming it into his face. The powder clung to him as it forced its way up in his nose. I pushed him off me, and Brody passed out, fighting the effects of the powder.

Just as I picked myself up and found my knife, the others caught up with me. Their faces made it clear that whatever was in the ledger was terrible news. The silence spell wore off, giving me a chance to speak.

"Healing potion, anybody?" I grunted, holding my shoulder.

"Later," Uli said, clearly disturbed. "Wrap it up with this and hurry. We need to go. Now."

With a tense nod, I bandaged myself and ran as we left the scene. Iji and Brody were passed out on top of one another, and as we dashed out the building, Pilock had slumped onto the ground. Our footsteps rang out into the sewers as we made our way to freedom. None of them said a word as we followed Uli. Mara was sniffling to herself, while Giezha's face was more stoic than that of a statue.

By the time we made it back to the sewer entrance, daylight was poking out of the horizon. There was a light frost on the ground as songbirds welcomed the new morning. The others didn't even bother checking for guards as they quickly ran out of the sewer. I followed suit, thanking my good luck for not there being a guard on duty at that moment.

Rather than turn around back to the city, we ran out into the woods. We needed a place to dispose of our clothes and for me to heal without anybody seeing. After running for ten minutes, we made it to a small clearing in the woods.

One of the creeks that fed off Lake Shabba bubbled under our feet as I finally sat down. My arm felt like it was moments away from falling off as Giezha undid my bandages and healed me. As I regained feeling, I saw all the others sitting around looking defeated.

"Guys?" I grunted, feeling the wound close. "What was it?

"Not what, Asher," Uli said through gritted teeth. "Who." She picked up a rock and threw it into the creek, splashing icy water everywhere. "There's no more doubt about it. No other suspects."

Fuck.

"Sal did it."

304

Chapter 28

Avisday, 8th of Tavlin, Year 678, 4th Age

It took a while for the girls to calm down and explain everything. The sun had finally risen over the frosty horizon before we began to make our way back.

The Red Ledgers were filled with writings from the captain and several past captains and high-rankers. Details about missions, important treasure, political intrigue, the works. Sal was only at the beginning of the first ledger and the end of the second.

He was listed as a founding member as "An Unspecialized Sorcerer." Outside of the initial roster, Sal was mentioned with connection to a few important missions, reports, commendations, etc. Nothing stood out to implicate him in anything suspicious, except for the last three entries.

The first entry was by the captain herself. It was during the Undead Incursion and about funerals. There were many, and they were frequent. However, the entire guild's roster attended a funeral for two people—Isabella and Igitha Yaxel—Sal's daughter and his wife.

The second entry mentioned Sal's item report missing several books from a successful bust on a necromancer hideout.

The third... The third confirmed that he was behind the zombie pigs and goats. Statements were signed by the captain and three more founders' names. The issue went all the way to the council.

After that, his name was conspicuously left off the roll call on the next page. The only roll call in the entire book.

Sal didn't show up until the last few pages in Mara's Ledger writings. The captain mentioned Mhurren and Mick noticing him in Iron Court about two months before they disappeared. They saw him searching for something in the library. He had a picture of a square war hammer covered

305

in spikes on the ends and with a skull in the middle.

"When Mara showed me this note, I went back and looked at the first few pages," Uli said, flipping through her notes. She pointed at a drawing just like the one described. "It's called the Smite of the Dead Giant. That was what Mhurren and Mick were looking for—a war hammer that could turn the undead into these brutish monsters."

Mara continued the story. "The Red Breakers found it during a scouting mission deep into the country of Nara on behalf of the Empire. It was right before the Undead Incursion," Mara said, pointing to another set of notes. "Only problem is, it never made it to the city. Disappeared along with the team sent to find it. Rescue teams searched for weeks in the mountains, but only found a shredded camp and a ripped journal."

"What about Sal?" I asked, looking for the connection.

Uli sighed and flipped to the next page. "He was assigned to a mission three hundred miles east in the Nara Peninsula. But there's no log of him entering or exiting Nara. Three weeks he was basically unaccounted for. Asher, this thing was lost less than fifty miles from where I was scouting."

Walking back through the city, we tried to theorize different ways Sal could be innocent. Mistaken identity? Coincidences? Evil twin? There was another option we considered too…

"Perhaps he's being framed," Mara suggested desperately. "What if it's that hobgoblin? He saw Mhurren and Mick too! Sleazeball loves to sell illicit goods."

"Maybe," I said while Uli shook her head.

"He's not the type to get his hands dirty," Uli said. "He's just a grifter."

"Makes quality potions though," Giezha said. "What about Ivory Forge?"

That suggestion gave us all pause for thought, but seemed outlandish. Why have us be the ones to investigate? However, once we made it back to the Inn, all those thoughts were put on the backburner.

Kiersa was waiting for us outside the door, and glass littered the street. Looking up, we saw a window had been smashed.

"That's Sal's room," Uli said ominously.

Kiersa ran to us when she saw us, jumping into my arms. "Something happened!" Kiersa said, hugging me tightly. She pulled back and looked at me, eyes watering as her hands shook like leaves in the wind. "I tried to keep my distance and keep an eye on the Inn from across the street. But

306

then it sounded like an explosion went off from the Inn! I saw somebody fly out of the window and out of sight."

A few people on the street looked around and talked amongst themselves. Whatever happened had a lot of eyewitnesses. We split up to hear accounts and check Sal's room. Mara and Uli stayed to talk while Giezha and I went upstairs.

The building was empty but looked totally unharmed. A faint smokey and gunpowder smell wafted in from the room. As I was about to kick the door in, Giezha stopped and checked for magical traps. Sure enough, there was some kind of trap magically attached to the door.

Giezha pulled out her book of spells and read from a trap-breaking incantation. As she spoke, a wave of pink energy enveloped the door breaking a previously invisible chain.

"I should have that memorized by now," Giezha said in annoyance with herself. Opening the door, we were surprised to see the cold room was completely covered in white fire. "Mage's Fire!" Giezha shouted. Slamming the door shut, she gave me a look of horror.

"That sounds bad," I said, slow on the uptake.

"Very bad." Giezha said before rifling through her book of spells again. "Here, read this with me so we can get the fires out. On the count of three."

On three, Giezha opened the door, and we both read through a long and complex set of incantations that were written in common, elvish, and treespeak. As the runes lifted off the pages and into our magical items, a misty grey cone appeared out of them.

Giezha pointed the cone at the white flames, causing them to slowly disappear. I followed suit as I felt my temperature drop down to zero. The room was beyond freezing. It was as if the air had been misted with liquid nitrogen. It hurt just to breathe inside it.

"Don't leave a single spot," Giezha said, covering her face with a scarf. "Try not to let the fire touch you either."

The temperature in the room slowly rose as we put out the icy fires. The tiny embers elicited no sound and produced no smoke either. Were it not for the flames' scent, you would have never known that this room was on fire.

Whatever the fire touched didn't burn away either. It made things... evaporate. Like hot water on snow, it was as if it melted away. The remains

307

were a sandy dust that was cool to the touch.

"How bad of a sign is this, Giezha?" I asked, looking around the room for clues.

"Very much so." Giezha said, unlocking a cabinet. "Look at this." Giezha ripped a trunk in the cabinet off its hinges with her bare hands. Inside the trunk was a gigantic pile of moonstones. That trunk had to be worth thousands, potentially tens of thousands of gold. "See anything else?"

Right as she said that, I looked underneath Sal's bed. Underneath that bed was a tiny glittering bar wrapped in paper. When I pulled it out, I saw that it was a bar of silver stamped with the Church of Sylo's seal: two trapezoids stacked on top of each other, depicting silver and gold. The paper had a drawing on the inside of the paper. A drawing of a hammer with a skull on it. Just like the Smite of the Dead Giant.

"Fuck," I murmured to myself.

"Yeah," Giezha agreed. "C'mon. We need to tell someone about this." She grabbed the giant collection of moonstones and walked out the door.

"The captain or Ivory?" I asked, pocketing the silver bar.

"I don't fucking know. Just somebody."

Fair enough. We brought the others into the Inn to show them what we found. They took it a lot better than I expected to. Perhaps they'd prepared for the worst after hearing the witnesses' testimonies.

"At least three people saw a hooded figure leaping out of the window as it exploded," Mara told us, clutching one of the moonstones. "The description matched what you told us about the guy in the fire, Asher."

"Oh," I said, not understanding for a half-second. "Oh... shit."

"Yeah," Uli said, rubbing a second silver bar that we found inside the moonstones wrapped in crinkled parchment. "Two witnesses said they saw goat hooves from underneath. Jumped to the building across the street and disappeared into the ether."

"Sal's fucked." I said, holding a particularly large moonstone in my hand, enjoying its impossible softness in my hands.

The door to the Inn suddenly burst open, revealing the captain, flanked by Ivory Forge. I quickly pocketed the moonstone as the captain moved her eyes across the room. She looked positively livid while Vurshung and company had a strong poker face.

The heels of her boots clicked against the wood floor as she walked

308

over to the table. Without saying a word, she looked at the evidence we had collected. The silver, the moonstones, the notes from the Red Ledger. Shit, the notes. I locked my gaze with Uli, feeling abject horror as she read through the notes, murmuring to herself. After finishing her reading, she clicked her tongue in disgust.

She threw the collected evidence in a bag much too small to hold everything and shoved it in my lap.

We knew that Sal wasn't the only one in trouble with that single look. She motioned for us to follow, which we obeyed silently.

Ivory Forge split apart for us to go directly behind her. As we walked, I felt the noose tighten around my neck. Despite our best efforts, we had been caught stealing from the guild.

I struggled to think about how we could have been caught, frantically retracing my steps in my head. We didn't take anything, nobody saw our faces, and they didn't have fingerprints on us. Or did they?

As the four of us made our way to the gallows, I couldn't help but wonder if we had been betrayed. Perhaps, Ivory Forge simply needed somebody to do the dirty work for them. Then they could demand the notes and let the captain do whatever she felt like with us. The same thought was painted on the faces of the others. The cold wind bit at my nose and ears but still felt warm compared to the fires we had just put out.

"We've much to discuss," the captain said airily as we passed the street the guild was on. "You've had a busy few days."

Mara's cheeks trembled as she struggled to not speak. "Captain! If I could just—"

Dawnthorn cut her off. "Shhh. Just walk, don't talk." The underlying threat in her superficially sweet voice chilled my heart.

Eventually, she took us to a cafe at the edge of The Docks and Iron Court. She had us sit down with her and the Ivory Forge crew, ordering a round of coffees and hardy breakfasts for everyone.

Giezha's massive leg bounced up and down next to me, threatening to shake the whole table. Ivory Forge whispered amongst themselves but said nothing. The captain's face had switched from blind rage to a tranquil fury.

Our food arrived, and Dawnthorn made an excited "ahhh" before digging in. She motioned for us to eat as she chewed a mouthful of potatoes and meat. The massive collection of moonstones and silver sat atop the table

309

covered in a rag, just begging to be seen.

I nibbled on bits of food, watching the captain eat breakfast as if none of us were even there. The Ivory Forge crew looked almost as pensive as us, but they simply ate their meals and stayed quiet.

"I love breakfast," the captain said, smiling at us. "No greater pleasure than starting the day right with a hearty meal." She placed her cutlery on the empty plate, letting out a satisfied belch. "Ahhh, that was nice."

After that, she just stared at us, motioning for us to eat. None of us moved. Eventually, silence in the entire situation became too much.

"For fuck's sake, Captain!" I pleaded. "Just say it already."

The captain just smiled and shrugged. "Alright." She peeked through the rag at the moonstones and laughed. "Ivory Forge told me about your little trip underground. What'd you find out?"

Uli jumped across the table, slashing at Vurshung with a knife. Mara managed to stop her blade at the last second as Uli tried to jump onto the table. Several patrons looked at us in curiosity before returning to their meals. I guess this was a regular occurrence.

"Sit," the captain said sweetly. "Or else."

Uli sat down but kept the knife firmly in hand. Gritting her teeth, she took a deep breath before speaking. "We found... information that corroborates with the theory that Salvatore Yaxel was behind the silver theft and most likely connected to the moonstone shortage."

"I can see that!" Dawnthorn laughed, rooting her hand around the box of stones.

Uli continued, still staring daggers at the lying bastards in Ivory Forge. "We also found a strong link to Mhurren and Mick's disappearance in accordance with a search mission they were on. Salvatore had a drawing that matched the description of the object of their search in the southern region where I worked as a scout."

"The Smite of the Dead Giant," Vurshung said quietly.

Son of a bitch.

"Yes..." Uli said, breaking under the smile of the captain. "In short, it was Sal. All of it. He's the thing that connects the silver, the moonstones, Mhurren, Mick, and the mission you were assigned previously. Sal was most likely part of the Undead Incursion. And he is looking for the Smite of the Dead Giant as we speak."

310

The captain sat and absorbed our story. She clearly knew most of it already and was just giving us the chance to tell it ourselves. Nobody said anything as she silently spoke to herself, looking up at the cloudy sky. After a few minutes, she nodded her head and looked at us.

"Well, you did it," she said with a shrug. "You found out who did it, found out what their angle is, wrapped it all up in a bow, and presented it to me. Good job." The short moment of hope was quickly dashed away with her next words. "All it took was betraying every single member of the guild. You ripped apart any shred of confidence, respect, or trust that I could have ever had in you."

I jumped to my feet. "But—"

She threw a hand up and continued speaking. "You did your job to the letter of the agreement. You did what you were asked. By Ivory Forge. When they asked you to shut me out, you did it without a second thought. Congratulations! You did it." She picked up the box along and stood up with Ivory Forge. Dawnthorn placed a hand on my shoulder to sit back down.

"You are officially no longer a part of this quest. Payment will be given at the end of the week. Go pack up your stuff from the Inn and find somewhere else to sleep. We'll need to pick through there with a fine-toothed comb." She dropped the happy facade for a moment, revealing a look of utter disappointment and disgust. "Now if you will excuse me, I have a report to write to the council."

We sat there in stunned silence for almost an hour. The captain never mentioned the words "fired" or "get out," but we could tell that we had just done irreparable damage. We left the uneaten food at the table and walked away.

We had done everything we were asked and could do and got the results we wanted. But why did it feel like we made everything worse?

"What now?" I asked.

"Sleep," Uli said, which the girls silently nodded too. "Hope Kiersa's got some rooms available."

The Inn was empty, with a few curious patrons waiting outside for the place to open . We pushed past them and locked the door behind us. It didn't take long to pack. Everything fit inside the trunk, and I figured Sal wouldn't miss it.

Once I got everything together, I walked downstairs to help the girls. They were a lot messier with everything and needed help sorting stuff out. At least, it seemed that way.

Uli was folding the same robe over and over again. Giezha couldn't decide which witch hat to bring and which witch hat to wear. Mara, meanwhile, kept loading and unloading everything in rapid order, trying to find any inefficiencies in her method.

I quietly helped them get their things, and we went to the Golden Sky Tavern. The angry crowd demanded an explanation that we were too drained to provide as we walked away.

Kiersa, Ihena bless her, took us in on the spot. She and Aire assured us there'd be no charge. Each of the girls got their own room, fully furnished and right next to each other. I was given a small half-room in the corner that barely fit the bed, my trunk, and myself.

"Asher," Kiersa said, hugging me from behind as I unpacked. "If you need anything, just let me know."

I turned around and hugged her tightly. I pressed myself into her and buried my face in her shoulder. I wanted to cry. Cry my eyes out until there was not a single tear left. But I couldn't do it.

I just held onto her, feeling a deep, heavy pit in my chest. Kiersa held me tight and rubbed my back, whispering words of encouragement in her sweet, sweet voice. Just the sound of her soothed me.

My body ached, and it felt like I had been run over and thrown into a pit of spikes.

Kiersa's hand grazed against my wounded shoulder, and she gasped. Kiersa healed my wound a little more, taking away the pain more than the injury. It felt much better. As I laid down to rest, I felt something in my pocket. A moonstone.

"Oh Ihena!" Kiersa gasped, "It's... it's so big."

I chuckled. "Thanks. I like it when you say that." I tossed it up and down a few times before handing it to her. "Here."

Kiersa went bugged-eyed, making her beautiful irises pop out even more. Even as my eyelids threatened to shut themselves permanently, I couldn't take my eyes off her. She really was so beautiful.

"Payment for the rooms," I said, pressing it into her unsuspecting hands. Before she could protest, I fell asleep as the lunch rush came in.

Chapter 29

Klinesday, 5th of Extrin, Year 678, 4th Age

"Asher!"

I bolted upward from a nightmare and stared at a wooden wall. My breathing was ragged and uneven, every gulp of air threatening to make me sick.

"Uli?" I croaked. "Giezha, Mara?"

My hands jittered around, feeling for something. I was on something soft. A bed. The room was small. Very small. That's right, I was at the Golden Sky Tavern.

It was night, and the evening rush was in full effect. It'd been a month since we were kicked out of the guild and took up residence with the Golden Sky Tavern.

Aire was running the show solo while Kiersa attended church this evening. The girls were all probably out right now. Since getting the boot, they'd thrown themselves into practice.

Giezha and Mara spent every last copper they had getting reps in at the Warren and studying in the Library. When they weren't sharpening their blades or minds, they'd take shifts at the Tavern. Uli would disappear for long periods, coming home with fistfuls of silver she'd gotten doing who-knows-what.

I threw on my sailor's uniform after calming down.

Meanwhile, I'd gotten home from doing a freelance mission with a local guild named Bronze Fish. They specialized in fishing expeditions and hung around the markets near The Docks. I'd been brought on as extra muscle to move cargo.

I'd just gotten done working two successive weeks of fourteen-hour nights, and was happy the contract ended. Instead of delving into dungeons and saving damsels, I was a glorified fishmonger, moving barrels of

313

whatever the fisherman caught in the middle of the night.

I'd hoped Uli would join me on the fishing contract, but she rebuffed the idea and stormed off when I suggested it.

After ordering "breakfast," I milled around for a while before I decided to clear my head with a walk. My head needed the cool air. I told Aire to let the girls know I'd gotten off work, and he patted me on the back as I left.

The air outside was crisp, and autumn was already battling an early winter. The threat of snow hung heavy in the cold night air as the barest slips of sunlight peeked out through the horizon.

Without anywhere in particular to go, I walked past the Silver Cup Inn. Ivory Forge members were still guarding the entrance as I kept walking. The sight of those bastards made me sick.

"Cocksuckers," I muttered, stifling a yawn.

One of the guards took objection to my words, but I paid him no mind. Without anywhere else in my mind, I found myself along the beach, walking to the Everlasting.

Its light cut through the fog from this distance, providing a guiding light for the ships out at sea. There was nobody to bother me as I walked along the shores of Shabba Lake, feeling its icy spray tickle my ankles.

I breathed the cold air, filling my lungs and expelling the last remnants of mucky heat from the summer. The cold air shocked my insides and woke up all the bits and pieces of me still clinging to slumber. I felt invigorated by the chilly water and crisp air.

The Everlasting was only a stone's throw away now. It's restored firestone burned brightly, warming the area around the lighthouse. I laid my back to it as I felt the mist of the lake's gentle waves on my face.

"What am I gonna do now?" I asked myself, knowing damn well I had no answer.

"That's a good question," came a familiar voice from behind me. I turned and saw Brody. He gave me a wave and sidled up next to me. "Enjoying the view?"

I didn't say anything and just nodded. As he approached, I noticed that Brody's nose was off-center. No doubt broken in our scuffle.

I quickly looked away as he twiddled his thumbs. He didn't say anything. Instead, he just chuckled to himself. I did my best to maintain a poker face.

"Captain would like to see you," he said, slapping me on the back. "Said to look for you and deliver a message about an important mission. Wants me to bring you to her."

I looked at him, confused. Mission? We were all but expelled from the guild, according to her. Now she wanted to have us in for a mission?

Brody read me like a book and nodded. He pulled something out from his robe and handed it to me. It was a small envelope with the guild's official wax seal.

Brody got up to stretch and spoke, "Don't worry about the uh... incident, Asher." I looked up, and he gave me a good-natured smile. "Nobody else in the guild knows except the captain and me. She's mad, but she understands your motivation."

"Yeah?"

"Yeah."

With that, Brody walked off, leaving me to watch the moons peaking their way through the dense fog and clouds, illuminating my letter. I pulled out the small parchment, peeling off its back and unfolding the ruddy thing. It was the captain's handwriting.

Let's finish this.

It was past midnight when Brody left me alone with the captain. Her piercing white eyes cut through me like a sword through a straw dummy. She'd certainly had her pleasure making us feel like dummies lately.

As per usual, she didn't say anything for the longest while. She kept that neutral expression on her face as we stared each other down. This time though, it felt different... This time, she wasn't intimidating me. It was an offer.

"We're in," I said loudly and clearly. "I don't care what is next, but we're in."

Dawnthorn continued to stare at me, so I stood up and leaned over the table.

"I want to see this mission through to the end, Captain. I'm tired of all the cloak-and-dagger bullshit. All the secrecy will just come to bite you in the ass if we aren't able to prevent a second Incursion."

Faced with her continued silence, I felt my rage at the situation overflow.

"There are innocent lives at stake! You are going to let the crew and I put a stop to this violence and find the culprit. Do you hear me?"

315

Without realizing it, I had stuck my finger in her face. I was afraid she'd swipe it with a knife, but instead, she blinked slowly. I felt my hand vibrate, and I wanted to pull it away. But I knew I couldn't. This was no time for cowardice and no time for backing down.

After a minute, she finally spoke.

"Deal," she said simply.

I was so taken aback I pulled my hand away and backed up a few steps. "What?"

"Deal," she said again. "You fucked up the break-in, but you're right. It's your mission. If you want to see it through, fine. Join me. I'm going to bust down the hideout whether those Ivory fuckers like it or not."

"Really?" I couldn't help but show excitement at the notion.

The captain gave me another surprisingly kind smile. "Really."

She tossed me a rolled-up piece of paper with the seal in black wax. "Top secret. Only for you and the crew. Read it when you get home, and don't let anybody know. Be there in three days."

I stuffed the paper in my inner jacket pocket and saluted the captain. She saluted me back, and I ran from the building, skipping along with hope in my soul and a song in my heart. Or something like that. The point was: this was it. We were going to get back at those Ivory Forge bastards. My sense of justice battled with my overwhelming competitiveness.

On the way back, I decided to go pick some stuff up to celebrate. I stopped by Ms. Rosria's Shop of Knickknacks and Whatnots. The elderly gnomish lady had the strangest hours that luckily coincided with mine. Her cat streaked across the floor when it saw me and hopped on my shoulder as I shopped.

"Let's see, flowers for Mara to use for her pigments... A 'Never Sweater Better' headband for Giezha's workouts, and what do you think we should get Uli, Ambrose?"

The chubby calico meowed a suggestion I couldn't decipher.

"She'd love this necklace to go with those earrings you got," Ms. Rosria said, appearing behind a stack of old books. "She wears them everywhere, Asher. Ambrose, why don't you go pick up the number 41 perfume for Ms. Kiersa, eh?"

Ambrose jumped off my shoulders and sauntered his big furry butt to the back rooms.

"You keep quite the company, Mr. Merrick," Ms. Rosria said with a wink. "What's the occasion?"

I took my purchases and brought them to the counter. She had a nice collection of necklaces, and I picked out a turquoise clover as Ambrose brought a small perfume bottle in his mouth. It smelled like cinnamon and cardamom with some peachy notes.

"Excellent choice, Ambrose." I smiled and looked down at the broken rings. "Ms. Rosria, how much would it be to fit a gemstone in a ring?"

When I got back to the tavern, the girls were finally home and eating dinner at one of the tables. Before any of them could say a word, I slammed down the sheet of paper. They all looked at the black seal, and then up at me in horror.

"What'd you do?" Mara asked, a bit of lamb hanging out the side of her mouth.

"Asher?" Uli said, her voice rising dangerously. "You didn't go back to the cookie jar, did you?"

I grinned and ordered a chef's choice platter and a casket of ale. We would be rich, and I needed a damn good meal while explaining everything.

Kiersa had just gotten back from church and desperately wanted to listen in, but Aire saw to it she was too busy with the other late-night tables to stick around.

The girls' mood improved by the feast and excitement plastered all over my face. Mara greedily tore into the second meal while I explained Brody coming to find me and the discussion with Captain Dawnthorn.

I tried to play down my talk with the captain, but they were impressed I'd kept my finger in her face at the risk of losing my finger. After telling them everything, I downed a whole mug of beer that was surprisingly strong.

"We're back in?" Mara asked, bouncing up and down, sloshing her drink on her shirt. "For real?"

"For real," I said, feeling a fire in my belly from Orc's Tusk Ale. "We got three days to prepare."

"That's not a lot of time," Giezha said, worried. "We're low on supplies, and even if this payout is what we're hoping for, we'll need it to last."

"Not with this credit from the guild," Uli said, reading the sealed paper with bug eyes. "We've got a five hundred gold credit on behalf of the captain."

Mara and I both choked on our drinks at the announcement.

"Get some good gear; get some good food, and get a lot of it. Time for the long haul..."

"Long haul?" Giezha asked, her face reddening from a few sips of brew.

"Sounds like she wants us to help her find the Smite of the Dead Giant," I surmised. "Where it was lost."

"How long should we pack for?" Mara asked, finishing off the last of the lamb chops. "Long haul isn't very specific."

"It says here the mission's expected to be from two weeks to a month." Uli pulled out a ripped half of an incredibly mangled piece of parchment. Its sides were crusted with age, and the paper was obnoxiously crinkled. "This map I pulled from the box shows we're going straight into the mountains that I uh... went to before. Captain says to expect rough terrain, bring lots of warm clothes, potions, and healing supplies."

"Food?" Mara asked, grabbing a few bits of bread.

"Basic rations and hunting gear. Save the rations for when food gets scarce up at the top," Uli said, flitting her eyes to Mara.

I stopped listening for a moment when I noticed that look. It was weird but, I could have sworn Uli was blushing for some reason.

Not the regular blush Uli had when she got embarrassed, but a... different kind. I shook my head and got back to the conversation.

Mara grumbled, but I promised her I'd share some of my credits for her gluttony. How she managed to stay so trim, I didn't understand.

Before the evening went on too long, I gave everyone the gifts I'd picked up, and received glowing reviews. Kiersa and Uli immediately tried on their gifts, exchanging excited squeals. It was interesting seeing Uli's more girlish tendencies appear.

Meanwhile, Mara went off to try out her new pigment sources. A small part of me just wanted her to have the pretty flowers, but oh well. Giezha just looked at her gift before silently putting it on under her hat and blushing furiously.

That's a win for Asher.

Soon the last patrons had left the tavern, and it was only us and the Denrel family. Aire had already turned in and was fast asleep upstairs. Kiersa gave me a kiss on the cheek and headed upstairs.

318

Mara gave me a devilish grin, goading me to try my luck for the evening with Kiersa. But when I tried to follow her, Kiersa stopped me from coming in.

She smiled and touched my face. "Sorry, Asher, but I'm gonna need to sleep alone tonight."

Before I could say anything, she shut the door and locked it. Odd. I was bummed out since I'd be up for a while as I tried to correct my sleep schedule. I decided to go do some watercolors out by the Everlasting using Mara's techniques.

I slipped into my room to grab some supplies but was surprised when I saw both Mara and Uli waiting for me on my bed. They stared at me with hungry looks in their eyes.

"Hello, ladies," I said, feeling the intensity in their stares. "Unfortunately, I have a rule about when you've been drinking."

Mara and Uli looked at each other and grinned. Mara and Uli produced tiny vials with a sparkling blue liquid in them. With a clink of their glasses, Uli and Mara downed their drinks.

Mara savored the potion, licking her lips. "Sobriety potions, Asher. Kiersa's church was brewing them to help with the local drunks."

Uli walked over to me in nothing but a black chemise cut above her waist. I swallowed the drink she handed me and felt my head instantly clear up. Uli gently grasped my hand and led me to the bed. I watched as Mara rubbed herself while beckoning me, making my heart hammer out of my chest.

My clothes were stripped off me in the blink of an eye. Shoving me onto the edge of the bed, Mara straddled me while Uli lay next to me.

"We've missed you, Asher," Mara whispered huskily, holding my face as she kissed me. "Haven't we, Uli?"

"So, so much," Uli said, gently caressing my chest.

Uli reached down and enveloped my throbbing cock with one of her delicate hands. She stroked up and down firmly, making me groan. Mara wrapped her arms around me, kissing me more deeply. My head began to spin as I tried to absorb and appreciate all the stimulation.

"We think it's time to give Mara what she wants," Uli said softly. "She's wanted this for so long."

The lips of Mara's pussy rubbed against my thigh as she straddled it

319

while Uli got down on her knees and proceeded to suck me off.

"Fuuuuck," I groaned.

"It's so hot seeing you like this, Asher." Mara cooed, her voice dripping with pleasure. She started to kiss and gently bite the side of my neck as she talked.

Uli stopped for a second, grinning. "Mara's been dreaming of this, you know. Watching me suck you off."

Mara bit her lip and smiled, rocking herself back and forth. Uli's face had turned beet red, but her pupils were heart-shaped and bright pink. Mara put her hand around my throat and pushed me down to the bed.

"I think it's time to let you two have your fun," Mara said to Uli, dismounting me.

"Mmmm…" Uli bit her lip excitedly as Mara sat down next to the bed and touched herself as she watched us.

Uli stared at my rock-hard erection and started fingering herself. "You ready?" Uli asked me with a lascivious grin.

I let out a groan as Uli slowly slid my cock down her throat. She licked along the bottom as she held me in the palm of her hands.

"How good is it, Asher?" Mara asked me, getting lost in her pleasure.

I could only nod as Uli inhaled almost my entire cock. She moaned around my length while continuing to tease and toy with her pussy. I felt like I would explode at any minute as I stared at Uli heart-eyes. Her fangs gently grazing the edges.

"Fuck," I grunted.

Uli slowly pulled her head back, taking a long deep breath before climbing on top of me.

"Now for the real fun," She whispered into my ears. She turned back around to Mara, who was still trembling with pleasure. "You getting a good view of this? I'm about to rock his fucking world."

"You haven't already?" I joked, lining myself up for Uli.

Uli and I locked eyes, dropping the flirtation and games. Uli's trademark grin replaced by a small smile. I tightened my grip around her waist.

"Give it to me, Asher," Uli whispered, reaching up and caressing my chin.

Without a word, I slowly pressed my cock inside. Uli let out a whimper and wrapped her legs around me as I pulled her down. As Uli wrapped her legs around me, I couldn't help but gasp as I slid in the rest of the way. Uli started spasming and wildly grabbed for me, pulling me closer for a long, sloppy kiss.

"God, you're so good," I whispered into Uli's ear before nibbling on it.

"Ahhhh! Asher, that's so sensitive!"

"Good."

I continued pumping Uli up and down, as she began to dig her nails into me, moving herself up and down to match my rhythm. Her ears wiggled in protest, trying to break free from my bite.

Uli's moans and squeals of pleasure were only broken by Mara's voice.

"Oh, fuck yes," Mara said lustfully. "Give it to her, Asher."

Uli bit her lip as I watched a plan hatch in her mind.

'Yeah, Asher," Uli moaned, moving herself faster and faster. "Give it to me. Make her really watch it and turn me around."

Following her lead, I helped twist Uli around so we both faced Mara. I held her up by her thighs spreading her legs while Uli and I stared at Mara. It felt a little embarrassing at first, but the way Uli tightened as Mara watched told me everything I needed to know.

"It's so good, Mara," Uli teased, wrapping her arms around my shoulder as she laid back. "The way he's fucking me... nice and rough. Ah!"

Uli let out another moan as I held her up and down, pushing my cock in and out. Mara was biting her finger as she rubbed herself, leaking all over the chair as she watched Uli and me fuck.

I picked up the pace and started hammering Uli. I felt a wave pouring over me, getting close to washing over.

"You like watching, don't you?" I said, locking eyes with Mara over Uli's squeals. "You like watching me fuck Uli while you sit there?"

"Yes," Mara moaned, speeding up her own self-pleasure. "It's so hot. Keep fucking her, Asher!"

One of her legs started to vibrate as she sped up.

"Ohhh fuck, Mara. He's gonna cum inside me." Uli giggled, grinding herself down on me. "You wanna see him do it?"

Unable to speak, Mara nodded her head rapidly. Seeing how much she got off on all of this, it was my turn to change things up. Holding Uli up in the air, I held her knees to her chest and slowly pulled out.

"Don't stop!" Mara said desperately, edging herself on the finale.

321

"God, I love doing this with you, Uli," I whispered, kissing her as that wave was ready to burst. "You're so beautiful." I kissed her again. "So tough and smart. So sexy."

Uli screamed out my name as I kissed her neck. "Asher! Oh, Gods, show me! Show me how much you love it! Faster! Fuck me harder than you ever have before!"

Uli continued talking, but she switched to Goblin, which she spoke much more rapidly.

I looked over at Mara. I could see her red hair sticking to her skin as she was already cumming her brains out. Her breasts jiggled in the air, begging to be grabbed and squeezed. I'd get there later, but for now, I shifted my attention back to Uli.

"Cum insider her, Asher." Mara begged as I kissed Uli's neck. "Do it!"

Hugging Uli tightly to my chest, grabbing her by the left breast and her waist. We could both feel my cock swelling inside, begging to cum. Uli's screams and Mara's moaning were drowned out by the wet sounds Uli and I made as I fucked her with everything I had.

Uli's nails dug in my shoulder while her toes curled. I squeezed Uli tight and felt myself orgasm harder than I ever had before. I did my best to stare Mara down, despite my foggy vision.

Cum spurted out of me, filling Uli. I could feel Uli's whole body vibrate as our orgasms clashed. Mara kept switching between staring at Uli and me as Uli squeezed her legs tighter around me while her convulsing pussy squeezed every bit of cum out of me. Holding Uli tight, I did what she had asked and continued thrusting after I'd cum.

"Asher," Uli whispered. "You're amazing."

Breathing raggedly, I laughed. My cock was still harder than steel. "Hah, I'm just getting started. Are you still up for another round?"

Uli giggled breathlessly.

"Why don't you take care of that with Mara?"

Laying Uli down, I turned my attention to Mara, splayed out on the chair. Neither of us said anything, but Mara spread open her pussy and mouthed the words "fuck me."

I picked Mara up and thrust into her in one continuous motion, my path lubricated by how turned on she was. She gasped, wrapping her legs tightly around my waist as I pushed her back up against the wall.

The thick wooden walls shook as I thrust as hard and fast as I could into Mara. I grabbed onto Mara's plump ass, pinning her securely. Mara's arms wrapped around me, and she kissed me while bobbing up and down with each thrust.

"God, you're fucking tight," I grunted. "How'd you like our little show?"

Mara leaned in, placing her head on my shoulders as I rocked her back and forth. She bit down on my shoulder, licking and kissing along my neck.

"It was so good, Asher. It was so good. It was really...really..."

Before she could finish, Mara started crying into my shoulder. I froze up, not sure of what to do. Mara looked up to me and smiled. She squeezed me with her arms, hugging me, tears streaming down her face.

"I was so afraid when I asked Uli to do this with me, Asher. I was afraid you'd realize you hated the idea. That you'd think less of me."

"No," I said quietly. "Never."

Walking us back to the end of the bed, I sat us down. Mara stayed wrapped up tight, leaning her head into mine. Neither of us said anything. Mara and I just held onto each other and stayed as one.

"I'll only ever see you for what you are, Mara," I whispered into her ear.

"What am I?"

"Perfect."

Mara gently pushed me down and began to bounce up and down. Her whole body glowed like an angel in the dim candlelight. Her breasts swung up and down, enticing me once more.

Sensing exactly what I wanted, Mara took one of my hands and brought it up to squeeze her soft, heavy breasts.

Mara continued to ride me, squeezing me tightly with her warm pussy, as she leaned closer to kiss me. She moaned into my ear as the sounds of our bodies connecting echoed in the room.

"Do it, Asher," she whispered into my ear. "Cum inside me. Give it to me."

My toes curled, and I could feel Mara's body convulse with mine in simultaneous orgasm. This wasn't as powerful as the one before, but it provided me with a feeling of a kind of weightlessness. I felt my entire spirit lift as Mara and I rode the high together.

I held her face as we looked into each other's eyes. Our shuddered breaths slowly returning to normal.

323

Uli broke the silence, clapping slowly. "Whew. That was intense."

Mara and I both laughed in agreement. I realized now that Uli was under the covers of my bed. Mara climbed off and joined her.

"Thanks again, Uli..." she said with an embarrassed smile.

Uli gave Mara a hug and laughed. Unable to say no to a good time, I slipped into bed between them. We spent the rest of the night joking and talking about how we'd probably be dealing with noise complaints. Little did they know about Kiersa's sound dampening spell she used whenever I came up to visit.

After a quick wash, we decided to get back in bed and the girls slowly nodded off. As they snuggled up to me, I said a quick prayer thanking Gathos before closing my eyes to nap, hoping to get back on a regular sleep schedule.

Chapter 30

Xaliasday, 7th of Extrin, Year 678, 4th Age

The next few days were gone in a blur. We spent the first day comparing armor and weaponry to equip ourselves with. I bought a vial oil of sharpness for my blade, extra cushioning for my shield, and plenty of options to keep me up and at it. As tempted as I was to visit ol' Towser, I felt he'd use the opportunity to finally poison me.

Giezha purchased a few spell scrolls for spells she wasn't familiar with yet. One made climbing easier for us, which she spent most of her time studying in the library, and another to understand languages more easily.

"If there's a warning carved in the mountainside in some language we've never run into, I want to know about it" she explained while hurriedly snatching the last potion from the alchemist.

Uli bought Forget-Me-Please instant darkness powder which chewed almost all her credit. Mara was tempted to buy a full-sized hog in a butcher's window, but she decided against it at the last moment.

"I'll just go buy jerky instead. Besides, I need some arrows and to trade for those gauntlets from that elf Brinzhe at the guild house," she sighed sadly.

On the meet-up day, we split a whole hog courtesy of Aire. With our bellies full and a rare warm autumn wind at our backs, we made our way out of the city to meet with the captain.

Despite the sun fading into the horizon, the rings of Echo Veil's neighboring planet were glowed dimly in the sky. Trying to ignore the butterflies going to town in my stomach, I asked about its name.

"Ourilia," Uli said, clearly focused on the mission as we walked.

We all shared an uneasy feeling as we marched.

This was really it.

After so much time, effort, and frustration, we were ready to end this. Even if it meant confronting Sal. The safehouse was hidden in the forest, and we were set to meet with the captain. It was the perfect chance to entice Sal into making a move.

"I really hope we don't have to fight him," Mara whispered while holding her bow. "Sal's our friend."

"Yeah," Giezha scoffed. "A friend who betrayed the city and raised an army of the undead."

"Quiet!" Uli hissed, giving them both a deadly glare. "We have our orders, now let's execute them. To the letter."

I took rear guard, but couldn't shake my uneasiness.

I wasn't as close to Sal as the others, but I still felt bad about what we'd have to do. Every bit of evidence pointed to him. Every investigation led to him. And on top of that, Sal fled the city the moment everything began to click into place.

Pushing those uncomfortable thoughts away, I tried to focus on the mission. Unsure of what to bring, I had my sword, shield, dagger, and casting ring at hand. I carried Mara's extra bow and quiver on my back with a backpack of camping equipment.

After nearly an hour of walking through the forest, Uli threw a hand up. "Shh! I think I see the captain."

She pulled out a torch and lit the flame. Covering and uncovering the flame in a specific pattern, we waited for the captain to return the secret code from the letter.

Once we saw the other figure's torch flicker in the correct fashion, we put the torch out and made our way up to her. The captain was out of her regular uniform and wearing blood-red leather armor filled to the brim with potions, wands, and daggers.

She had a slightly wild look in her eyes as we made the rendezvous.

"Was getting worried about you showing up." She grinned. "We go in, get the info, and if Sal's there, take him out."

"Scout team?" Uli asked, settling next to her.

Captain Dawnthorn shrugged. "Ivory Forge finished their shift, and I told ours to stay home. Have a drink. Go see a whore." With a deep breath she looked at all of us. "So, we ready?"

Dawnthorn darted forward before we could answer. We swiftly followed suit as Dawnthorn elegantly floated between the branches, trees, and fauna. Mara and Uli stayed right up on her tail while Giezha and I lagged behind.

After running a mile deeper into the woods, we made it to our destination. We could see a slanted wooden structure surrounded by the thicket of ash trees. It was once a shack, but the tree growing through the roof and dead vines made its carcass gave it a more... dead appearance.

Dawnthorn held her hand up and hid behind a tree, directing us to follow suit. "Stay frosty," she said, throwing up her hood and sneaking forward.

She motioned for Uli to follow her and the rest of us to go around the back. We crept closer and a putrid smell punctured my nostrils, making me gag. It smelled like rotting flesh mixed with something... something sinister.

The others caught a whiff and nearly gagged as well. We all readied our weapons as we made it to the back. There were no windows, no doors, no hidden compartments, so we circled back and entered the shack.

The inside was more telling.

The wood floor had rotted away, covered in dirt, dust, and... I didn't want to think about what else. Death's festering smell emanated from all surfaces. A table ran along one side filled with books written in sharp and aggressive lettering.

"Abyssal," Giezha muttered to me.

While looking around, Mara discovered something along the floorboards.

"Guys!" She hissed, swinging open a trap door. A reeking stench blew into the room as dozens of moaning voices could be heard from below.

"Fucking—" The smell was so violent and offensive, Giezha and I doubled over and vomited outside the door. "Holy fuck, that's bad."

Giezha said nothing as we returned to the others, trying to ignore the festering odor. Walking down the rickety stairs revealed a basement larger than the shack above it. Lighting up torches, we illuminated a house of horrors.

Most of the basement was taken up by a large jail cell with dozens of shambling bodies behind a set of rusted bars. They all had the same gray eyes as the rat zombie and Rogorm had. They turned their heads in unison at our presence, trying to charge down cell door.

"Back!" the captain shouted as we ran up the stairs, pushing her through and shutting the trap door behind us.

The muffled sounds of the rusted bars breaking down could be heard underneath us. I frantically did a headcount to make sure that nobody was

327

left behind.

Counting everybody present, I threw as much weight on the trap door as possible as zombies clawed and scraped at it from below. The stairs were too narrow to hold so many at a time, and the sound of the stairs crumbling was followed by the thuds of the undead bodies.

We all looked at each other wide-eyed about what to do. Even the captain was at a loss for words. Mouth agape, she took a moment to speak, pacing back and forth, failing to come up with the words. I tentatively looked around for more information and clues. Perhaps there was a log of where the undead came from.

"Why weren't the undead larger?" Giezha asked while we tore apart the shack, looking for clues to where Sal went.

"Maybe he doesn't have the hammer," the captain suggested, rummaging through a pile of rags.

"How do you explain the rat and Rogorm?" I asked.

"Maybe he knew how to enlarge them already, simply wants the hammer to help out. After all, why didn't he just kill Asher in the fire?" Her voice was odd when she spoke. She almost sounded... bitter.

That made me stop what I was doing and turn around.

"What do you mean?"

The captain turned and gave me a funny look. "When you got blown out of that building, it was Sal. Right? Probably thought you found the map to the hammer or something."

"No, that's impossible," I said, shaking my head. "Whoever did that was at least a foot taller than me. Sal barely comes to my chest."

The captain gave me a look and spoke impatiently, "No... the eyewitnesses said they saw Sal with a cloak on as he left the building."

"No, they didn't." Uli said, picking up on the strange vibe. "I interviewed them myself. Said they just saw Sal in his regular clothes. Nothing about a cloak."

"Besides," I said, pulling out the ripped bit of map Mara found in the box. "I don't remember telling you about a map."

Alarm bells were starting to go off in my head. Off in the distance, I could hear people approaching the shack. It was hard to tell how many, but the distinct sound of multiple voices trudging through the thicket could be heard.

Something was starting to smell fishy, and my mind was thinking very unpleasant thoughts. I stared at the captain, and surprisingly, she blinked first.

Ah, fuck.

"Captain..." I said slowly. "Can I ask you something?"

"I don't see why you'd want to," the captain said, her eyes darting everywhere. "We've got to catch Sal! We're wasting time."

"Why didn't you do something about Sal earlier?"

"What?"

Mara tilted her head, thinking about what I said. "Well, if you knew about him being potentially involved, why not bring him to the council? Why wait so long?"

"W-we were secret lovers," the captain stammered.

"No way," Giezha growled. "Sal would never cheat on his wife. Especially with you."

Uli gave a signal behind her back, and Mara and Giezha got beside Uli and me, surrounding the captain. I saw Dawnthorn's right finger drumming against her pocket, itching to pull something. I felt something in my palm. Uli had pressed one of her instant darkness powders into my hand.

"You had all of the information," I stated. "Hell, everything we know, is what you were telling us. Who had access to the logs in the Red Ledgers? You. Plus, you said you've been investigating this stuff for years, but you didn't notice how perfectly Sal fit into the Smite of the Dead Giant going missing? How?"

"Why not investigate?" Uli prodded.

"Why let him go?" Giezha asked, her staff starting to glow.

Mara's eyes lit up like fireworks in realization. She shrieked and pointed her finger at the captain. "YOU FRAMED HI—"

BOOM!

A gigantic fireball flew in through the window and exploded right in front of us. The force of the explosion knocked me off my feet, and the dry wood lit up instantaneously.

As I flew through the air, I grabbed Uli and tried to roll when we landed. I hit the ground hard, slamming into the front wall of the shack.

I stumbled up, sporting a heavy bruise under my right shoulder. The white-hot flames licked the air, filling the room with smoke. Giezha and I

329

blasted the walls with water from our staff and ring.

"Mara!" I shouted, getting a lung full of smoke.

She coughed several times, crawling on the ground. "I'm good! Took a bookshelf to the back."

"You stupid fucks!" Dawnthorn shouted, unleashing a torrent of deadly light beams through the smoke. "I said wait for my signal!"

Right on cue, I could hear another stream of hissing fire from outside.

"Hit the deck!"

It was like a bomb went off next to me, which would have done serious damage if I hadn't hidden behind my shield and the upturned table.

"Die!"

Dawnthorn let out a torrent of explosive spells from her position, forcing us out of the burning pile of the shack. Outside, three figures were illuminated by the raging inferno. Vurshung, Kasuc, and Agostina.

Well...until they transformed into Mhurren and Mick.

"Mother. Fuckers."

Before I could say anything, all three of them jumped at the opportunity to get into the fray. Vurshung leaped into the air for a massive slash, which I barely managed to avoid.

Mhurren started chanting as the soil around me shifted before hands began to claw their way up.

"On your six, Asher!" Uli jumped from behind me and made a stab at Mhurren, only to be parried by Mick's greatsword.

Mara quickly joined into the fray, going one-on-one with Vurshung. I heard Giezha going up against our now-former Captain.

Mhurren's cocky look slipped into a scowl as I thrust my blade toward him and Mick. Uli flanked them from behind. Her moves were fast and precise, instantly appearing behind them as I pulled their attention.

Before she could land a blow, a zombie popped out of the ground, grabbing her by the ankle.

She let out a shriek, slashing at its arm. Her knife easily cut through the sinew and bone, leaving only a stump at the zombie's wrist.

I slashed at Mick, only for him to grab my sword with his hand and shove me back. Simultaneously, Uli's undead assailant ignored its injury, biting into her arm.

"Ahhh!"

"Uli!" I shouted, throwing up my hand. I let off a blast of fire, which Mick dodged, blasting the zombie's head clean off.

Before I could recover, Mara shouted out in pain. Vurshung's blade was buried into her shoulder as it began to glow bright white.

He was going to smite her from the inside. I tried to unleash another torrent of flame, but the fire fizzled out in my palm. Looking back, Mhurren cackled with his hands glowing bright green.

"Nice try, rookie!" Mhurren goaded. "But you'll need to step your game up against a real spellcaster!"

Desperately, I slung my shield at Vurshung like a frisbee. His eyes flitted over, and he dodged the attack with ease, but Mara made the most of the opportunity. Pulling out a knife, she slashed upwards at Vurshung.

Unable to dodge two attacks and keep hold of his sword, he let go and dodged backward. Mara pulled the sword out and let off a warrior's cry before slashing forward.

"RRRAARGH!"

Mick slashed at me with his massive sword, missing me by inches. "C'mere!" he shouted, slinging the greatsword like a plaything.

Heaving the sword into the air, he tried to slam it down and bisect me vertically. I rolled forward, missing the blade. I got in close, trying to take away his space.

There was no room for him to swing the greatsword, and I pulled out the knife Uli had given me. I stabbed at his throat, but he managed to block with his gigantic forearms.

This was bad. Any minute Mhurren, Vurshung, or even Dawnthorn could pop up. I started churning a fire in my belly, feeling the heat radiate cross my body. I needed to end this quick.

"Kasuc!" Mick shouted, getting overwhelmed. "Help!"

"My hands are full, you idiot!" Mhurren shouted, sending undead after Uli, who dipped and dodged her way through them. "And it's Mhurren, you fucking moron!"

I gritted my teeth and pressed Mick, repeatedly slashing with my knife. I slipped under his attacks, avoiding his wild flailing.

As strong as he was, he was twice as dumb. I connected with his groin with a push kick, doubling him over. I went in for the kill, but he pulled a club from his back and swung hard.

331

Muscle memory kicked in, and I tried blocking his attack with my knife. All that did was redirect the blow slightly from my stomach to my busted shoulder.

"Fuck!"

I flew back, rolling into the ground. Another quick glance showed Uli getting surrounded by skeletons and undead as Mara and Giezha tried to fend off Vurshung and Dawnthorn. The raging inferno behind us was had caught in the trees, lighting up the area.

With nothing left but my fists, I decided now or never. Concentrating, my fists started to glow a golden aura as I put myself in a boxer's stance, bouncing on my feet. Mick snarled and slobbered as he held the tree-sized club like a baseball bat in his hands.

With a roar, he swung at me wildly.

"Stay tight, slip the attacker," I mumbled, thinking of Mara's training. Mick sliced upwards with a huge uppercut, where my head had just been. "Use momentum against them." I advanced, trying to grab the bat. Mick doubled back at the last second, losing his footing. He struggled to stay up as I advanced on him. He swung once, twice, three times. I managed to avoid each attack.

"Dip... Parry... Counter!" With one last swing for the fences, he aimed for my head. Turning my hips, I exploded forward with a right cross.

BOOM!

My fist connected, shattering his club. My attack continued forward into Mick, hitting him in the chest. On impact, Mick flew backward, landing ten yards away, clutching his chest.

Mhurren turned in horror. "Mick!" He looked at me, baring his teeth and shouting. "You! Shoulda killed you back at the bar!"

"Bring it!" I snarled, rushing forward.

Rearing back for a punch, I saw Uli covered in scrapes appear from behind. Mhurren unleashed a wave of black haze right at my face, hitting me square on.

My muscles contracted, and I felt my whole body try to seize up. It was like every muscle cramped as horribly tight as possible. I cranked the gears through sheer willpower, putting my muscles to work. These fuckers were moving, no matter how much they wanted to grind to a halt. With one last push, I managed to break free of whatever Mhurren splashed me with and

332

bull-rushed into him.

Mhurren tried to strike me with his magic staff, but I blocked it with an upward palm strike.

With a quick turn of the hips, I swung forward with a right uppercut, trying to knock his head off. At the same time, Uli went for a slice at his neck. As my fist was set to connect with his throat, the universe stopped.

"Counter," Mhurren whispered.

I heard the distant sound of bells, and the world started back up. My punch died on impact, but a glowing white light flashed from my fist. The light turned and zipped towards me up my right arm. At the last second, I recoiled, putting up my arms in front of my face. The ensuing explosion would have killed me if I hadn't done that.

Instead, the explosion threw me into the air, sending me flying like a cannonball shot with too much gunpowder.

As if the universe wanted to send me a handwritten letter with the words 'fuck you' on it, I crashed into the fiery inferno that had enveloped the shed.

Even better, the barrage of fireballs had destroyed the floor, leaving a massive hole in the basement. I landed on the pile of undead, crushing at least one of them under my weight.

"Graaagh!" They all began to scratch and claw at me, even from underneath.

Scrambling, I rolled off the pile of bodies and ran from the swarm. Thanks to the fire above, the undead's rotting flesh and exposed innards were on clear display. They gnashed and gnawed with their hands outstretched, slowly giving chase. Almost all of them were in a clump I ran from, but a few stragglers were closer.

"Hey!" I shouted up top. "Anybody got a ladder!?"

Either they couldn't hear me, were preoccupied, or...

I ran to the corner of the room, trying to keep as much distance as possible. When they got too close, I could try and run around them and climb up what was left of the stairs.

My vision was patchy, and it was hard to lift my arms higher than my stomach. As I backed into the corner, I pulled out a health potion and downed it. I smashed the bottle against the wall, producing a large shard of glass I could use as a weapon. I had to make the best of what little I had.

333

The undead began to close in on me locking any hope of running around. I felt the chill of failure run down the back of my neck as I swung the glass in front of me. The potion had numbed the pain, but my shoulders weren't working well.

I backed up against the wall behind me, hopelessly trying to avoid the undead's extended hands. I was only prolonging the inevitable, but the prospect of being torn up by undead entirely consumed any rationality.

To my surprise, I fell backwards, as the wall appeared to give out behind me. I turned around to see a tunnel that extended into darkness. At any other time, it would not have been a particularly inviting sight, but now I had an escape route.

A voice came from above, piercing through all other noise.

"Asher!"

It was Mara.

Fuck.

The undead continued to close in, and I knew I had to make a choice. Run, or help. Well, not really. It wasn't a choice at all. It was the most obvious decision in my life.

I gritted my teeth and ran straight forward. "Alright, you stupid nova bullshit, I'm gonna need another hit."

I directed every ember of fire into my legs and feet. I ran straight into the zombies and kicked off the ground, shielding my face with both arms.

Several undead bit and scratched me as I leaped into the air, clinging on for a ride. My jump was nowhere near as powerful as the ship jump, but I didn't need it to be. Sailing about fifteen feet up, I aimed myself forward as the hungry undead clung onto me.

One bit onto my wrist, and I punched it off, leaving its teeth behind as a souvenir. The others fell back to the ground with a crunch as I landed topside.

Looking around, I saw those four motherfuckers closing in on everyone they'd managed to corner. I sprinted back into the fight, and I could see at least one of them was down.

It was Mara.

Chapter 31

"Get away from them!" I screamed at the top of my lungs, launching a wall of flames from my ring at full force.

With a wave of his staff, Mhurren negated my spell again. Dawnthorn launched a counterattack of lightning my way. The smell of ozone penetrated my nostrils as I sprinted forward, missing the blasts by inches. With no weapons, no mana, and stamina fading fast, I decided to pull out an ace up my sleeve.

"Blackout incoming!" I shouted, throwing the Forget-Me-Please at the group. A large sphere of pure darkness enveloped everyone in a ten-foot radius.

Jumping in, all sound died, leaving me devoid of sight and sound—a sensation I was intimately acquainted with. Grabbing for Giezha and Uli, I threw them out of the sphere and felt on the ground for Mara. The sphere started to fade away as sound slowly returned to my ears.

"Mara!" I screamed, barely audible to myself. I looked down in horror, seeing her covered in wounds. She had a nasty gash across her stomach and her eyes were fading fast.

I picked her up and sprinted back towards the fire. It sounded like Dawnthorn was starting to recover from the reverse-flashbang.

"Uli! Throw the other one at me!" I screamed, trying my best to carry Mara as carefully as possible. "Follow me! I got a plan!"

Uli pelted the other black stone past my head without a second thought, hitting the discombobulated traitors behind us. I ran straight past them toward the pit filled with undead.

Running around the giant hole, I climbed down into the nest of the undead, holding Mara tight with one free arm.

"There's a secret passageway!" I shouted to the others, whose shocked expressions were appropriate. I screamed at them as I ran to the corner.

"Hurry up, or we'll get separated!"

That got their tails in gear. I ran into the corner, seeing the small passageway's entrance. Ducking inside, the others were behind me a few seconds later. And so were the zombies.

Giezha shut the door behind us and pointed to the ground.

"Lay her down here!"

I knelt and placed Mara on the ground. Her face was pale, and she felt cold as ice. I held her hand while Giezha performed healing spells on her. Mara coughed up blood, and the wounds Giezha healed opened back up the second she turned her attention elsewhere. Mara strained her eyes to look at me, squeezing gently.

"Hey, stranger," she said softly.

She was dying. As Giezha tried in vain to heal her, Uli's eyes went wide. She snapped her hand out, and a moonstone appeared. She shoved it into Giezha's hand.

"Use it!" she commanded. Uli did her sleight of hand a few more times, making bandages and a white bottle appear. From the other side of the stone wall was the sound of zombies shuffling. Hopefully, they didn't know we were here.

"Asher," Uli whispered to me, handing over the bottle. "Rub this salve in her wounds."

I nodded and opened the bottle, pouring its contents onto a set of bandages. The salve was a thick green sludge that smelled like pine tar. I spread it on the bandages and rubbed it over the deepest gash going up to her side along her ribs and stomach. The salve hissed against the wound, and her blood vessels turned dark before releasing a black gas into the air.

"Cursed weapons," Giezha said quietly, swearing in a different language. "Prevents healing. You keep rubbing that stuff in and I'll heal."

Slowly, Mara's breathing returned to normal. She wasn't on death's door anymore, but she had lost consciousness. We took that as a blessing as our attention snapped to the noises outside.

It was the others, and they were arguing.

"Where'd those fuckers go?" Dawnthorn shouted before presumably blasting an undead.

"Stop killing the specimen!" Vurhsung shouted, his voice much harsher than ever before. "It's bad enough that bastard stole them and hid them in

336

this gods-forsaken-shed."

"Where are they?" Dawnthorn shouted again, her voice much closer now. "I finally got them here to take the rap and you idiots blow the entire plan to smithereens! Literally! You fucking blew it up!"

A sickening thunk of metal against skulls came next. "We'll make more zombies, boss." It was Mick. The bastard had somehow lived. "We can jus' go'in and get 'em!"

More bones were crushed rapidly, much to Vurshung's protestations.

"Dammit, stop!" Vurshung screamed before letting off a spell of some sort. "I could have used them! Discovered more about the process!"

A slap rang out through the air as the sound of zombie moans disappeared. "Your little experiments nearly blew this whole operation, you second-rate sorcerer! Leave the necromancy to me! We're leaving. I copied the map down and hoped that these two would properly dispose of the original."

Mick sounded hurt as he mumbled. "I ripped it up and hid it."

Mhurren smashed a skull on the ground and spat. "Those fuckers got ate by the looks of it. Let's get moving."

We held our breath as they continued to argue. The sounds of their argument slowly drifted further and further away. We sat there in the darkness, illuminated only by a single torch.

I looked at the others, and they weren't much better than Mara. Giezha had a nasty cut from her chin to her cheek and a burn on her shoulder. Uli was so covered in so many shallow cuts and scrapes, it was a wonder she was even held together.

After several minutes, I peeked outside. Snow had begun to fall, sapping the fire of the heat necessary to burn. The wind howled as the dark sky swallowed the world around. The whole world looked like a snowy blur, wrapped in darkness. I closed the door and walked back to the others.

"How is she?" I asked, looking over Mara while Giezha healed Uli.

"She'll live," Mara whispered, half coughing, half laughing.

A wave of relief washed over my body as Mara opened her eyes. She looked at us and smiled weakly, holding her hands over her stomach.

She looked up and asked us, "What's the plan, guys?"

None of us said anything. We were still reeling from the total defeat we had just been handed. Looking back, our chances had been slim. We'd

337

faced skilled opponents with decades of experience while being ambushed.

Survival was a victory. However small.

Uli's eyes burned red hot with rage while her pupils shifted and shook, but her face stayed as tranquil. She pulled out a piece of parchment and matched it up with the piece Mara had lifted from the box earlier. They fit together perfectly. On the map was a pass through the mountains with instructions for finding a secret cave. Next to the 'X' that marked the spot was a hammer with a zombie in the middle.

"We're going to that dungeon and we're going to get that hammer," Uli said, her voice heavy.

Giezha nodded. "Agreed."

I bent down and knelt beside a pile of charcoal powder. I grabbed my old bandanna from my pocket, shoved it in the powder, and smeared it all over until my blood-red bandanna became matte black. Affixing it back on my forehead, I pulled out my last health potions and gave them to Uli and Giezha to top off.

"Count me in. But this is far from the last thing any of us are doing."

Giezha and Uli took their bandannas and recolored them, using the charcoal from the fiery remains of the shack. Readorning the bandannas in our new colors, we cut the last ties to the Red Breakers, leaving us alone as our own group.

Alone, but not defeated.

Mara lifted her hand up, taking out her bandanna to recolor as well. "Yeah..." she said with a cough. "We're just getting started."

Chapter 32

Avisday, 8th of Extrin, Year 678, 4th Age

As much as we wanted to get moving that night, we needed to wait for Mara's condition to improve. With the snowstorm raging outside, we decided to hole up in the entrance of this tunnel for the night.

None got much sleep, but the rest was necessary. Uli looked over the map and pointed out that the map only took you as far as Midmanch; however, we could find more directions at the "Black Bird."

We figured it was unlikely Dawnthorn's crew would get a head start on us in the snowy weather. We'd lost the battle, but they were licking wounds of their own.

I took the first watch and spent the night pondering what I could have done differently. Mhurren somehow managed to completely reverse whatever damage I was about to do. That was the only thing that surprised me more than him being a sorcerer.

According to Uli, he didn't have much magic left after that, but he was still packing plenty of dirty tricks. Mick was just a tough son of a bitch to soak up damage and demand attention. Next time, I'd make sure he didn't get up.

"Dawnthorn fights like a maniac," Giezha grunted, going over her notes for the tenth time that evening. "Half her spells hit the undead chasing us. She seemed rusty. Like a champion fighter who'd been out of the ring too long."

So, Mick was the muscle, and Mhurren and Dawnthorn were the casters. Vurshung was no slouch either. Despite his age, Vurshung was the definite threat at the top. Whatever he had on that sword cursed you worse than it'd cut you. And even without it, he could hit you like a truck.

After I finished torturing myself going over what I could have done better, I woke up Uli for her shift of the watch. I laid down next to Mara, who'd been sound asleep, and held her hand. She smiled and turned to me, mumbling my name before returning to her slumber. I followed suit in record time.

I was getting old in my early twenties.

Surprisingly, or perhaps unsurprisingly, Mara was the one who woke me up. She had a fresh scar on her stomach, and her armor needed to be fixed or replaced.

Uli was failing to summon the materials to repair the leather hide. Her face twisted and soured.

"That ain't good," she grumbled, trying over and over to summon. "Someone cleaned me out! All my other spots are empty!"

Dawnthorn or the Ivory Fucks must have done it.

"If that's happened, do we even want to bother going back to the city?" I asked, fishing for some spare leather in my backpack. While looking, I gave Mara some chainmail to put over the empty area. "I vote we just head straight down to Midmanch and try to beat them there. How long will it take?"

Uli opened the entrance, and the ground was immediately inundated with snow as heavy winds whipped through the air. It was a whiteout outside. Uli brushed the snow off her head. "In this weather? At least four days, assuming we start now and don't stop until nightfall."

So much for warm autumn weather.

I shrugged and picked up my gear. "Sounds fine with me. If Mara's ready, I'm ready."

Mara jumped up with the midriff of her leather armor jingling with chainmail. "Mara's ready, so let's go kick some ass!"

Before we left, we all scrapped together a set of furs from the bodies of the zombies. It disgusted me to do so, but I couldn't argue with a life or death situation.

We decided to check where the tunnel led to in case it shortened our trip in the snowstorm. We also were afraid Dawnthorn might send somebody to clean up the mess.

Being thought dead had its uses.

The underground walkway bent and turned, with the occasional rat skittering underneath. Eventually, it spat us out in a collection of rocks hiding in a tiny hill. The sun fought valiantly against the blizzard that had beset us earlier.

We managed to catch a peek at its morning position during a temporary respite from the snow. There were at least three inches of heavy powder on the ground, chilling my feet as we turned south.

We were going to travel right between Gamunz and Gakinbhar the entire time, hopefully avoiding all humanoid contact.

My teeth chattered, and I pinched my fingers under my arms as we trudged through the snowy forest. I kept the rear guard while Uli was upfront. Mara struggled to keep pace, so Giezha tried her best to keep her buffed up with stamina spells. Mara kept assuring us over and over that the injury wasn't the problem, that it was just a cold.

Winter's surprise attack left most of the wildlife reeling. Foxes and hares still not out of their summer furs stuck out like little red, orange, and brown flames darting across the snow-covered maples and birch trees.

Despite the miserable conditions, I marveled at the flaming red leaves holding on to the snow above my head. The occasional squirrel or jerebo darted across the branches, knocking the snow off.

"I hate jerebos." Giezha grumbled as the snow drifted into her face. "Little ring-tailed monsters."

"I like them," I said as a curious jerebo followed us along the trees.

Jerebos were like a mix between a grey squirrel, red panda, and an ocelot. Grey and red fur with tiny white spots and a ringed bushy tail made for an adorable little critter.

"They seem to like me too."

The curious fellow jumped on my shoulder and chattered in my ear. I fumbled around for a bit of food in my pocket, and handed the little jerebo a bit of jerky. It munched up the food quickly and hopped up to the trees off my head.

"See?" Giezha said huffily. "They're selfish creatures."

I laughed. "Clearly, you never owned a cat."

After a short break for a meal and warming up, the snow fell again. I always considered myself a bit of a penguin, but the others, Mara especially, didn't seem to enjoy it. However, I helped improve the situation when Giezha and I fire blasted some stones before putting them in sets of spare socks. A very nice way to warm the hands in the cold.

The sun began its all-to-early descent, and we stopped and built a pair of lean-tos with the available wood and materials. Our fire managed to keep us from freezing to death overnight. Mara snuggled up to me so that we could share body heat.

We spent the next two days trudging through the snow in near-total silence. The cold choked the land, absorbing all sound in every direction. A whisper turned into a shout, speaking became a maelstrom. The only persistent sounds were our feet grinding through the increasingly heavy snow.

Each day the temperature would just peak above freezing, and each night it crashed far below, refreezing a new layer of ice. We had our heading and decided not to waste our time or precious energy with speaking.

We simply trudged along, taking turns to assist Mara in the travel. The walking was difficult on her scar, and we frequently stopped to give her time to rest, fussing over her injury while assuring her it was fine.

"Enough!" Mara shouted the night before our expected arrival. I had offered to reapply the healing cream after Giezha ran out of mana. "My wound is completely healed! I don't need you three treating me like a child!"

She stormed off to her tent, which we put up for her while gathering firewood. The three of us sat lamely by the fire, looking to see which would make the mistake of trying to talk to her. Mara was never angry like this. We decided to leave her be and not force the issue.

Electing to take the first watch, I sat out in the frigid dark, scanning for enemies after the others headed to bed. The fire burned and crackled at my heels while I struggled to discern whether the shadows were friend, foe, or neither.

After about an hour, I decided to be chivalrous and stupid. Ain't that just like me? I went to Mara's tent and gently tapped her foot.

"Psst." I said, tapping her foot again. "You awake?"

Mara turned onto her back and glared at me. "I never went to sleep, dummy." She grabbed her sword and got up with difficulty. "What's wrong?" She looked around outside the tent, trying to see if there were any enemies. When she saw there was nothing there, she gave me another look. "If you came to apologize..."

I stuck my hand out for her. "I came to see if you wanted to join me on

342

the watch." She looked at me skeptically but accepted the gesture. I pulled her up and continued. "I'm still getting used to this keeping watch thing and thought I could use some help."

Mara looked at me sullenly, but I could swear I saw a smile hidden underneath her frown. While huddled next to the fire, I tried to ask her for pointers on what to look out for.

Partially because I knew Mara preferred to help than be helped, but mostly because Mara just knew what I needed to learn. The icy exterior she'd built up slowly melted away as she answered my questions.

"I always try to ask myself how I'd try to ambush the camp while I'm doing my shift," Mara explained while looking out towards a thicker section of trees. "I know Uli and Giehza have the brains, but I've got them beat in battle wit."

She took a few swings with her sword. She was slower, but still quick and precise. Like how a professional athlete is still light years ahead of you even when they're only at fifty percent. She stopped for a second on her swing and looked out to a hill. I just managed to catch a few small shadows pop under the hilly spot. She said nothing and sat next to me. Right next to me.

She walked her fingers up my chest and whispered into my ears. "Three bandits up the hill. Two goblins, one humanoid. Most likely from a bandit nest closer to the roads." She pulled me in for a kiss. "It's also good to trick them into thinking they're ambushing if you've seen them. They'll come in with their guard down."

She suddenly pushed me onto the snowy ground, grinding her hips on me. She certainly knew how to get my guard down too. After a second, she gave me that predatory look she saved for battle. "I'm going to go into the tent to grab my bow. Make it look like we're going in to have sex."

Mara threw her head up and moaned loudly. Off in the far distance, I heard the bandits' approach. To add to the bit, Mara pulled off her winter jacket, revealing her beautiful breasts, instantly perked up in the cold. She winked at me as she sauntered into her tent.

"Focus, dumbass!" I thought to myself. "Get in there and make it look convincing."

I scrambled into the tent, grabbing her coat. Mara had her bow ready and her armor on, aimed straight out. I smacked my head, realizing I'd left my sword outside. Mara laughed and smiled at me.

"Rookie move Asher. But don't worry. It just makes it look all more realistic." Mara stopped to make more sounds of rhythmic lovemaking, pulling me down with her. She fixed her bow over my back, pointing it towards the hill. "Now start thrusting, but not too hard. I need a clean shot."

I looked at her in disbelief. "You sure?"

Mara looked up quickly and smiled brightly. "Gods damn right. Now fuck me!"

I felt a little silly but started slowly moving my hips. Mara kept her eyes on the sliver of an opening outside to look for the enemies. After about a minute, her eyes lit up, and she pulled an arrow back. She whispered into my ear.

"There is a knife at my side. When I shoot the arrow, jump up and start swinging at them. They're by the fire"

I nodded and made a sound like I was about to finish. Mara had to suppress a laugh while I did my best not to distract myself with the feeling of her body next to mine. When she gave the signal, I grabbed the knife by her bedroll, and she let loose an arrow.

Thwip!

"Ghhk!"

A gurgled death rattle came from the camp center, and I jumped into action. It was just like she said—three bandits, all wearing mismatched clothes and random broken weapons. The human toppled over the log with an arrow buried deep in their chest.

"Geh!" one of the goblins shouted.

With the knife in hand, I grabbed the closer goblin and stuck him in the gut with the knife. His eyes went wide before I pulled out the knife and buried it in his chest.

He let out a gurgle as steam rose from the puncture in his chest. Blood dripped onto the snow in thick dark red globs.

The other goblin didn't spare his compatriot a second glance before charging. A second arrow sailed through the air, piercing the goblin in the head and pinning him to the ground. In a matter of moments, the three bandits were dead. I looked at my hands, which were shaking violently.

Mara emerged with the bow in her hand, looking at her handiwork. She gave a proud nod and scanned the horizon. It seemed they had been alone. My heart was racing as I buried my hands in the snow, trying to get the blood off.

"Shit," I muttered to myself. "Shit shit shit shit shit shit."

Mara helped move the bodies away from camp. Apparently, the wildlife would take care of the rest.

Once I cleaned my hands with some soap and warmed-over water, I sat back down by the fire.

"Fuck." I muttered, my knee bouncing up and down rapidly.

I kept looking back where we put the bodies away from camp over and over again. My heart was racing as I tried to shake off the adrenaline.

"Hey," Mara said gently, sitting next to me.

I flinched away from her, my breathing ragged. Mara gently pulled my head to her shoulder, and stroked her fingers through my hair.

"First kill?"

My throat was dry, and I felt a tightness in my chest. "Yeah," I whispered. I hadn't realized it, but it was the first time I had done that. With the zombies, it was different, there was a disconnect between their body and their soul. But this?

"It all happened so fast," I muttered, trying not to hyperventilate.

It had also been so... easy. In the five seconds that I knew that bandit, I killed him. Stabbed him in the gut and then shredded his heart with a single stab of the knife. My mind was filled with thoughts about who they were, what they wanted in life, who they left behind.

Mara and I had a long talk after that. We talked about the realities of this life. About how a split second can be the difference between life and death for you and for your loved ones. I talked about how I wasn't the one who killed the snake woman.

How Uli saved my hide.

I had every intention of killing Dawnthorn and the others, of course. That was personal. A vendetta. But this? This was impersonal, a chance encounter that could have been avoided. But it hadn't been, and now they were dead. And it could have just easily been us.

Mara looked at me with an emotionless expression I'd never seen on her before.

"I know this is scary for you, Asher. But you need to understand this: I

345

will not endanger Uli and Giezha's lives for your sake." She said it with such weight and seriousness, never once blinking. "We are all each other's responsibilities, and if you cannot handle that..."

She took a moment and looked straight through my eyes and into the depths of my soul.

"If you cannot handle that, then you aren't cut out for this. I'm serious, Asher."

I didn't really have the words to say anything, so I just nodded. Mara gave me an unsure look before bidding me goodnight. I woke up Giezha for her shift and explained what had happened.

She didn't say anything but handed me a calming potion for my nerves. I gratefully downed it and headed back to my tent.

That night I dreamed about what would have happened if I didn't kill the goblin and what could have happened to the others.

The next day, Mara's condition improved to the point that she could keep up with us. The weather also improved, cresting comfortably above the freezing point and beginning the slow melt of the autumn snowstorm. This last leg of the journey was about twenty miles through flat plains before entering the hilly valley at the foot of the Boshead Mountains around Midmanch.

We'd probably get there a few hours after nightfall if we hurried. And hurry, we did. The calluses on my feet got a few new friends by the time we arrived.

Arriving, we saw that Midmach was no city, and barely constituted a village. A single road went east-west through it, and farmland dominated the landscape. We emerged from the forested hills above the village long after nightfall.

Sneaking into the village, we made our way to the Village Square. The square was lush, with the mostly human and dwarf residents singing and dancing as a giant bonfire burned. The people all carried balls of snow that they threw into the fires to much hoopla and applause. Music thumped as a collection of drums and cymbals clanged and banged rhythmically with a pair of woodwinds made from large horns and a single-stringed instrument.

Many partygoers wore masks covering their noses and cheekbones in blues, golds, and greens. A preacher was chanting about how the goddess

346

of the harvest, Seeyr, brought the first freeze early so that the crops would be of firm root and ripe fruit.

"Don't you just love when they throw a rhyme in the sermons?" I whispered to Giezha, who cracked a grin.

We used the distraction to sneak around the congregation and slip into the Beaten Mule's empty tavern.

The owner was a short male human kissing his dwarven wife and children goodbye while they went to the celebration. He quickly rushed his wife and children out the door upon seeing us.

Our haggard appearance mixed with dark cloaks to hide our identities made for an intimidating picture. It looked like he was about to make an excuse to leave, but I raised my hand, holding a couple of gold coins in it.

"We'd like a room, sir," I said in a voice not entirely my own. "The festival outside drew our attention on our travels."

The man gulped and accepted the coins, telling us there was a single room available for the four of us. He studied each of us a little too long for someone apparently terrified by our presence. His eyes darted over to a set of posters lined up on a wall filled with news and the goings-on around town.

Plastered at the top were four wanted posters featuring each of us with eight hundred gold bounties on our heads. When I saw him make the connection, I casually reached for my sword.

"I assure you," I said, taking another step forward to the counter. "We are not who you think we are. And if we were?" I turned my voice into an angry growl and squinted my eyes at him. "I'd suggest you forget seeing us. Unless you want our bounties to get exponentially higher."

The poor guy looked like he was about to piss himself. I barely had a finger on my sword, but he held his throat like I'd already sliced him.

He nodded his head, threw a key my way, and we quietly marched into the room to the right of the bar counter. Before shutting the door behind me, I gave him the "I'm watching you" gesture.

The second that door shut, we all let out a collective sigh of relief, shedding our winter clothes.

"Finally!" Uli sighed, throwing herself onto the only bed available. "I thought I'd never feel a warm bed again in my life."

Unpacking amounted to throwing everything on the floor and bed,

347

including our bodies. Uli pulled out the map and double-checked that we hadn't missed anything.

Now that we were in the city, we had to decipher what was meant by saying we could find the answers at the "Black Bird." Blackbirds weren't exactly rare here! We had spent the last four days ruminating about what it could be, coming up with zilch.

I rubbed the soles of my feet as I thought of a terrible, no-good, unfairly realistic idea. "Hate to suggest we start walking already, but maybe we should talk to the locals while they're in one place. Maybe we grab some masks and keep our identities hidden."

Giezha laughed sarcastically while cleaning her glasses. "Good luck getting these bumpkins to not assume every goblin and goliath they meet isn't the one with the fat bounty on their head. Uli nodded her head in agreement.

"Well, Mara could pass for human, and Asher's well... Asher." Uli pointed to the two of us. "You two go on and find the information. Gi and I will search for clues in the map. We can also keep an eye on tavern boy."

"Works for me," I said, shrugging and turning to Mara. "It's a date?"

Mara's cheeks burned bright red and she gave me a flirtatious look. We had our heading. Now we just needed to cover our heads.

After a short conversation with the barkeep, he was thrilled to provide some masks his kids had made. We assured him two of our compatriots would be staying and observing from the tavern.

Just to be safe.

I switched to my regular clothes while Mara apparently kept a dress tucked away in her bag for emergency dances, balls, and festivals.

I didn't have anything to wear outside of my regular clothes, so I was underdressed, just like every other date in my life. I winked at the barkeep as we walked outside and into the festival.

Most of the festival condensed closely around the band playing live music. The holy man had stepped down and started enjoying the wine. A lot of the wine.

Children frolicked about while we did our best to blend into the crowd. Mara turned left, looking for symbols and signs, while I staked out the preacher.

The preacher raised a large tankard with wine, smiling at the people

348

walking around. "Ah, yes, blessings to you and to you." He tipped back the wine and downed over half in a single gulp. "Ehehehe, may our bounties be as filling and robust as the wine we have been given!"

Sensing an opportunity, I sat beside the rosy-cheeked man. Up close, he appeared frail and thin, a state which previously hidden by his magnanimous robes. His eyes lit up at my joining him.

"Welcome!" he shouted, raising his drink. "A traveler may always find home in the church that is life. Here." The man poured me a drink and toasted me before I had finished gripping the cup.

"Thanks," I said, sipping the exceptionally average wine. "I appreciate the hospitality."

The preacher winked and let out a contented sigh. "Like I said, those weary from travel can always find a home here in the village of Midmanch. The bounties of Seeyr are great, and it is our sworn duty to be kind and hospitable. Why, there's no greater honor or pleasure!"

The old man laughed a belly laugh while topping off his drink with one of several empty bottles at his feet. Several townsfolk looked at the preacher and either laughed or looked away.

"I appreciate it, Father, really."

The preacher looked at me funny. "Who says I'm your daddy?"

"Oh! Sorry, sir," I said, realizing my faux pas. "It's what I called holy men growing up in my church. It's meant as a sign of respect, rather than parentage."

The preacher looked at me hard before taking a drink. He licked his lips and burst out laughing. "Well, I ain't your daddy, boy! Ha!" He slapped his knees and held his stomach, laughing at my unintentional zinger. "Why, I'm only that girl's granddaddy. The one that your wife is talking to."

He pointed over to Mara, speaking with a young dwarven woman with long silver hair braided past her waist. They were very deep in conversation, and it took me a minute to comprehend what he said.

I did a double-take and took a long drink. A very long drink. After a tiny bit got down the wrong pipe, I coughed, sputtering over my words.

"She's uh, not my wife," I said, trying to wash down the choking on wine. "She and I are friends."

The old man laughed and patted me on the back. A knowing smile crossed the geezer's face as he shook his head. "No," he said quietly.

"You're not married yet. But you will be. Call it an old man's intuition, call it spiritual divination, but it'll come. When you're an ol' fart like me, you figure this stuff out quick."

I suddenly grew very uncomfortable next to this strange old man. I decided to try and push forward with questioning for answers and skip the smooth transitions.

"Thanks for the heads up, sir. I was going to ask you something." I ingratiated myself by pouring him a nice tall drink of wine. "Are there any kind of blackbirds that come around here often?"

The old man scratched his bumpy chin and sipped his drink. "Well, the ravens stopped comin' a few months ago. Rooks been headin' out since the freeze few days ago."

"Rooks?" I asked, confused. "Like the chess piece?"

"Nah, the birds. Little buggers they are. Stole my lucky pendant a few weeks ago, so I prayed that they get on out." The preacher laughed and took another drink. "Wished I didn't know that we got an early winter to deal with." The man nudged me and pointed back to the girls while the band whipped up some new music. "Quit talking to an old fool like me and go dance with your not-yet-wife."

The old man practically shoved me at Mara. Stumbling forward, I made a cordial introduction to the preacher's granddaughter before walking away with Mara.

Her face was deep in concentration, looking toward the mountains off in the distance. As a woman started singing in a deep, rich voice that flowed like the river, Mara snapped out of the spell she was under.

She looked at the band, who were playing a soft tune dancing along with the air. Speaking of dancing, many of the partygoers had split off into pairs, and were dancing intimately.

The preacher gave me a thumbs up out of the corner of my eye while his granddaughter sat next to him, looking dejected. I looked back to Mara, surprised to see a single tear rolling down her cheek.

"It's Uesis' ode to Azira," Mara said, clutching my arm. "This was the song my father always played for my mother."

It was a beautifully composed tune. Its tempo was slow and deliberate, like a stroll through the forest on a breezy day. Each instrument layered atop one another, weaving in and out of prominence as if the instruments themselves were dancing.

As I started to sway to and fro with Mara, I picked up on the song's time signature as three-fourths. An idea crossed my mind, and I pulled Mara closer, placing one hand around her waist and holding her right hand.

"Asher?" Mara asked, confused by the position I held her in.

I looked at her and smiled as my heart far outpaced the music. "It's just a dance I picked up from back home," I explained as I did my best to remember the waltz. "Just mirror my movements and follow my lead," I whispered as the music wrapped itself around us.

Mara's eyes twinkled, and she nodded her head. As the music twirled through the air, lifting the spirits of everyone there, I stepped forward, and Mara stepped back, flowing through the steps with grace like she'd been doing this her whole life. The world around me blurred as I fell deeper and deeper into Mara's emerald green eyes. I felt her heart race with mine as I held her close.

"What were we here for?" I joked.

"The blackbird," Mara said softly.

"Right. I guess I had something more important on my mind."

"Oh?" Mara asked as I dipped her into my arms. "What's that?"

I held Mara for a moment, almost weightless in my arms.

"You."

We swayed and flowed, twisting and turning like two leaves twirling in the wind. Mara's hand was light in mine, and she moved with such grace. I couldn't help but laugh at how she outstripped my own abilities at the dance in her first moments of trying it.

As the music faded out and the world faded in, I slowly became cognizant of the people around us. Many stopped their dancing to watch us instead. As the band played its final note, much of the crowd, mostly the women, burst into applause.

We both gave a quick nod before quickly returning to the crowd. Several people asked about the type of dance we did, while we tried our best to ignore and deflect.

When we managed to get a moment to ourselves, we fell silent for a second. I lifted her hand to me and kissed her fingers.

"Thank you for the dance, Mara."

Her cheeks gave her flaming red hair a run for their money. I'm sure I wasn't far behind.

"So," I said, breaking the silence. "What'd you find out?"

Mara's expression changed back to business mode. "Well, according to the people I talked to, there's been no sign of the four anywhere. We might have got ahead of them, so that's good." Mara paused to think for a moment. "Or they changed to look like other people and are ahead of us. Which is bad. Other than that, she said all the blackbirds are gone."

"That's what the preacher told me too," I said, frustrated by our lack of progress. "Said the ravens are gone and the rooks have migrated."

"Oh, I hope Giezha doesn't get sad! She loves rooks," Mara said, looking back to the tavern. "Hate that they're stuck in there. Uli will probably see if there's a chessboard to play Gi with."

A light bulb appeared over my head. Rooks... Chess... Forts...

"I got it!" I shouted, grabbing Mara. "Did they mention a fort to you?"

Mara thought about it for a moment. "Yes. It used to be a three-tower fortress."

"But?"

Mara's eyes lit up. "But two were destroyed! And now it's just the one tower."

I grinned and we both spoke at the same time.

"Like a rook."

Chapter 33

Klinesday, 12th of Extrin, Year 678, 4th Age

We found the castle ruins outside of town near the mountains. It was a crumbling structure with several pieces of rotted wood jutting out towards the other towers' previous locations.

Now, only this corpse of a defensive architecture was left to reach into the morning sky. We'd managed to get out of town unharmed thanks to the barkeep playing nice. We had no doubt he'd tell someone as soon as possible, so we made our departure before the sun rose.

We entered the tower through a hole blown into the wall. Ancient arrows and a few rusted blades were scattered about the mossy stone floor. There were holes in the walls and marks where bodies had been burned by intense heat everywhere you looked.

Rummaging around, the only thing we could find was broken junk from the tower's ancient history. While Giezha and I looked for a way up the broken stairs, Uli kicked over a pile of rubbish.

"Guys!" she shouted while pointing at a previously hidden trap door.

Grabbing the handle, the door swung open quickly. In fact, the metal of the handle was freshly oiled. Pointing this out, we all assumed a defensive position.

A ladder hung down from the side of the door into the dark abyss. Staring down the vast darkness, I smelled something disgusting—akin to rotten eggs. Before anyone could jump down, I threw my hand out.

"Wait." I pulled out a spark stick I'd traded for from a sailor and grabbed a piece of wood on the ground. Lighting the torch, I aimed down the hole. "Everyone be sure to duck away."

Everyone cleared the way as I took a few steps back and tossed the torch into the trap door. It fell for a moment before igniting.

FWOOSH!

A massive fireball exploded out of the mouth of the trapdoor. An anguished scream of pain could be heard from something down there.

As the flame died down, we all gingerly peeked over the door. Several torches were now lit by the fire and the charred remains of a purplish-blue creature with very long limbs. It wasn't moving, and when I threw a rock at it, it didn't budge.

"Nailed it." I grinned. "Well, that's a good sign, I suppose. Nothing like a death trap to say we're going the right way."

Pulling out some spare rope, Mara and I fastened it to the stone wall. Giezha cast some dancing lights down while Uli took point. The room was a cavernous circle with a single hallway. The stink of rotten eggs was replaced by charred flesh and hair. The room was at least twenty feet high and wide enough to fill an Olympic swimming pool in any direction.

I wondered if there was an equivalent of the Olympics in Echo Veil as I discovered a collection of shredded wood formed in a large circle. Looking over to investigate, I realized it was shaped like a bird's nest. Inside the nest was a collection of shattered eggshells and bones, which Uli examined.

My eyes were more focused on the bones. Some of them were roughly human-sized. There was also a blood trail in the nest that looked fresh. Giezha looked over the body burnt to a crisp while Mara kept her bow at the ready towards the hallway.

"Looks like a Plogwyst," Giezha said while stomping the creature's head in for precaution. "Anything in the nest?"

"About three broken egg shells." I said, checking around the room for any sign of them. "What're Ploggywasts?"

"Plogwysts," Giezha corrected, waving me over. "A horrible aberration of vulture, humanoid, and crazed violence." She pointed to the serrated beak on the fleshy creature. "They permanently molt their feathers upon maturity. The beaks are excellent at shredding wood for nests and bodies for feeding what's in the nests."

"Think the four of them set this up here?" I asked, eyeing the beast. It was larger than Giezha! "Or did we make their journey easier?"

"Maybe, and maybe," Giezha mumbled, grabbing the beak and snapping it off the mouth. "Either way, their beaks are valuable in some potions."

"Company!" Mara suddenly shouted accompanied with a volley of arrows down the hall. Several painful and angry screams could be heard racing their way towards us. "I think the kids came to check on mommy!"

354

Horrible screeching filled the air as three black-feathered creatures rocketed into the room. Mara ducked out of the way as their razor-sharp talons snapped at where her head was moments ago.

They cawed and screeched, flying around the room, aiming for targets. One that had an arrow snapped off in its chest dove at Mara while Uli fought the smallest of the three. That left the largest and nastiest looking Plogwyst for Giezha and me.

"I really should have bought a bow," I muttered as the bird flew well out of my reach.

"Yes, you should have." Giezha charged her staff and unleashed a bolt of lightning at the beast.

The Plogwyst squawked angrily and dove straight for me. Swinging my sword, I got the Plogwyst with a glancing blow. I sliced at its leg, causing it to let out a howl of pain and drop to the ground.

I charged in for a quick kill but nearly lost my head. The monstrous bird snapped forward, its legs tripling in size as it sprung forward.

"Shit!"

Throwing my shield up in the nick of time, I blocked its chomp. The serrated beak shredded the tip of my shield, tearing the banded metal like it was tin foil. Unable to get a clean shot with my sword, I opened the palm of my hand. After a quick memorization of runes I'd studied for hours, and...

BAM!

A searing bolt of fire slammed into the Plogwyst's chest. The monster let go of my shield and stumbled back, slapping itself with its feathers.

Giezha's voice came from behind. "Asher, duck!"

I hit the dirt, and a second later, a giant knife attached to a spectral green chain pierced through the air and into the Plogwyst. The knife sank to the hilt inside the monster.

Its eyes bulged, and it pecked at the chain, trying to get free. I saw the spectral chain wrapped around Giezha's massive forearms. She snarled and gritted her teeth as she tightened her grip on the chains.

"Hah!"

The knife sliced across the Plogwyst's chest with a single pull, dropping the beast to the ground.

Mara had turned her opponent into a pincushion while Uli pelted hers with a rock and sling. Sensing a chance, I sprinted in her direction. She dodged a strike at the last second, causing the monster to smash headfirst into a wall.

I let out a shout before it could shake off the blow and pierced it with my sword, pinning it against the stone. Red ichor flowed down the hilt of my sword, staining my gloves as the last Plogwyst slumped onto the ground. I huffed and puffed while wiping my blade clean.

We had all managed to escape relatively unscathed. The most significant damage was to my shield and a small cut on Uli's cheek. I dressed her cut and dabbed on some healing salve, sealing it.

Grabbing the torches off the walls, we made our way down the hall. Uli's eyes were best suited for darker environments, so she went up front with Giezha in the back.

I noticed how cold the hall was as we snaked our way through the long tunnel out of the heat of battle. We walked in silence for several minutes, walking up a gentle incline.

"Think it's the right call to go this way?" I asked, warming up another set of rocks in socks.

"Yeah," Uli muttered, lost in thought. "There was a rumor about a sneak attack by the Zala Kingdom back during the Sun's War that cut through the mountains. I get the feeling their attack on the fort came from underneath instead of outside."

"How long did it take?" I asked, imagining a regiment of fifteen hundred soldiers tunneling their way through.

"Almost a year," Uli said. "It was the deepest Zala ever made it into the Kingdom, almost two hundred miles deep. Got some nice leverage during peace talks."

"Half the mountain chain and an order of protection," Giezha said, yawning at the topic. "And now we're going right up to the border."

We walked for hours, slowly gaining in elevation the longer we went. Our feet ached as the cold grew more and more biting. Wind slipped through minuscule cracks in the rock and down the shaft, blasting us with the cold. We all took a break to bundle up before continuing.

My legs were the only warm part of my body. They were absolutely on fire trying to push up the incline.

As we continued to push ourselves through the dark and desolate hall, my mind wandered to the poor bastards who had to carve their way

356

through this mountain.

Day after day, week after week, digging deeper and deeper through a mountain with nothing to look forward to except the next shift. How many went insane chipping away at the layers of stone for months on end?

My own mind twisted and stretched to its limits, just imagining the endless monotony. Unable to move any further, we made camp in a widened section of the tunnel. No doubt an area carved out by the original sculptors as a place of rest.

"If I never see rocks after this it'll be too soon." I muttered while chomping a slab of hardtack.

"Don't say that," Uli joked while massaging her feet. "Dungeon diving involves a lot of this. Searching through mountains and caves for the secret spot."

"Any ideas on what that might be?" I asked, drinking from my waterskin.

Mara looked at the paper and tapped the bottom corner. "I do. Look at this symbol." Turning the map over, I saw that a symbol appeared in the middle where it had been previously ripped. "I thought it was just some spilled ink or something at first, but look." Mara held the map over the small fire, and ink from the other side created a skeleton on top of a temple.

I looked at it and marveled. "Ten silver says that's the key to finding the entrance." I looked at the location of the skeleton and pointed at it. "And if you looked at where it is on the other side... aha!" The skeleton's head was nestled on the other side of the mountain from where we were.

We were on the right track and a few days at most from getting there. With nothing left to do, we decided to make camp and set up our tents. The combat from this morning, mixed with the hours of walking we'd done, left everybody exhausted and ready for sleep.

We all ate some rations and used sharpening oil on our weapons before setting up our tents for sleep. In these conditions, even a semblance of normalcy kept us sane.

After an uneventful first watch, I walked over to wake up Mara, but my hand was grabbed before I could open her tent cover.

My head snapped over, and I saw Giezha staring at me. I felt a chill run down my spine when I looked at her expression. It was... intense, to say the least.

Her staff lit up, and a sphere cascaded on top of Mara and Uli's tents.

357

The sounds of Mara's snoring were silenced. With another few muttered incantations, I saw arcs of light go in both directions of the cave. I tried to wrench my hand free, but Giezha's grip was like iron.

"Giezha!" I hissed. "What's wrong!? Did you see someth—" She placed one of her gigantic fingers over my mouth and made a gesture for me to be quiet.

"I need to talk to you in my tent," she said, her voice cracking at the end. I could only make out her form from the gentle glow of the small light orbs she had summoned. "I managed to copy some alarm spells down to protect us. Come."

"Okay, but can't this—whoa!"

Giezha picked me up by the arm and walked over to her tent. It was nearly as tall as the cave because of her massive stature, and inside was a lit oil lamp, her bedroll, and a large stone she'd used as a makeshift table.

"Sit." She said this while placing me onto the table, knocking over a few books.

"Look, Giezha," I said, making sense of her weird behavior. She hurried over to her bag and started ruffling around, pulling potions and bottles out. "If this is about where I'm from and everything, I don't think this is the best time." She ignored me and rubbed oil on her neck and arms. "If that's not what it is, then I'd like to know what's bothering you."

She looked at me before turning back around and grabbing her staff. She poked her head out of the tent before casting silence located in this tent. I was starting to get really frustrated. "Giezha!" I shouted, standing up. "What is going on?"

Giezha looked at the entrance flap of the tent and bowed her head. "This."

Giezha's robes dropped to the ground, revealing her bare physique as she kept turning away from me. She turned around with a deep breath, revealing a pair of massive breasts wrapped in cloth. Her whole body, save for her breasts and her crotch, was exposed.

She walked over to me, her incredible muscular and toned physique coming into harsh shadows. The heavy lighting made every muscle pop as her chest heaved up and down above my head. Faint lines traveling in every direction moved up and down her body. The only imperfection in her grey skin was a long scar that traveled across her ribcage and down her right side.

"Does my scar bother you?" she asked quietly. "The mark of my clan's shame?"

I shook my head, enraptured by her boldness. The scar must have been related to the incident at the shop in Iron Court.

"There's nothing in the world that could get my eyes off of you right now."

She unwrapped herself with a small gulp, the long white cloth cascading onto my face. When she finished, her breasts were freed from their bondage. Giezha knelt, pushing her breasts against my face.

"I spent the last hour masturbating to the thought of this, Asher," she said, breathing heavily as she pulled my shirt off.

"You have?" I asked, still in awe at her body.

"I need this right now, Asher." She whispered to me. "I need this because I don't know what tomorrow holds."

Before I could respond, she pulled me over to her bedroll and kissed me, burying her tongue against mine. After pulling back, she looked down at me, her chest rising and falling with her ragged breaths. Being this close for the first time, I truly appreciated how fierce and beautiful Giezha was.

"I've been masturbating like this since you tackled me into that wall. I may be a wizard and a scholar, but I'm a goliath. We're very proud of our strength and our bodies. And you charged headlong into it. Into my pride."

She pulled my pants off in one fell swoop, revealing my throbbing erection. She looked down at it and licked her lips.

"You do that with everything, Asher Merrick, and I find that extremely attractive. I appreciate how you rush into every opportunity, tackle every obstacle like a beast."

"Do I?" I said, watching as she placed her breasts around my cock, making it disappear entirely. "Because I'm happy to charge into this as well, I just didn't think you were interested."

As she massaged my member with her breasts, she looked at me, raising an eyebrow. "Did you think I preferred a meek sorcerer who would stimulate me mentally? Somebody I could match wits with, perhaps?"

She picked up the pace, and I felt the lubrication she applied to her breasts. It was warm and tingled as she moved up and down. I felt my body tighten, ready to burst at any moment.

"Men like that bore me," Giezha said, sticking her tongue out and swirling it around the head. "They are intimidated by me. They pigeonhole me as an oddity." She opened her mouth and started sucking my cock, taking it straight down to the base with ease. As I was about to blow my load, she looked at me and came back up. "But you, Asher Merrick, are exciting. You challenge me. And when I'm challenged, I improve. I become greater. Stronger. More capable. You're going to make me unleash my potential."

It took every ounce of my control to not explode up to this point. Breathing in and out as deeply as possible, I looked at Giezha. "Glad you feel that way. I like you too, Giezha. You're—" Before I could say anything, Giezha stood up and squatted right over my cock—now inches away from her dripping pussy.

"I'm going to fuck you now, Asher," she informed me, putting her hands on the ground by my head. "You're going to cum very soon. So am I."

Before I could say anything, she lowered herself, and I felt my cock slide into her with the greatest of ease. My whole brain started firing off signals as I felt the inside of Giezha wrap tightly around me. It was like her insides were vibrating.

We let out moans of pleasure as she pressed down, taking me in entirely. She lowered herself onto me, pressing me down into the bedroll and smothering me with her breasts. I felt her heartbeat as she raised her hips before slamming down into me.

"Giezh—!" That was all I got out with one of her tits pressed into my mouth.

"Ohhh, fuck." Giezha moaned, her voice rising in pitch. "Oh, Gods!"

Sucking and licking her tits while she continued to ride me, I knew that I had no chance of escape. She started going up and down faster and faster, bouncing her ass up and down. The vibrating sensation I felt in her vagina became too much until my body, mind, and soul could no longer bear it.

My hands reflexively grabbed onto her rear, and I spanked her ass as cum exploded out of me. As I did, she stopped, sitting upright while I painted her insides. My vision went foggy, but I could see her eyes roll upwards as she bit her lip, slowly grinding into me.

"Oh, that feels so good, Asher," she whispered, her abdominal muscles flexing out as she ground herself against me. "I'm sorry if you were hoping

360

for sleep, I won't let you." When she said that, I noticed I had not softened one bit. If anything, I was even harder. "I used a special gel I bought in Zizar to keep you hard long after your first orgasm. It feels really nice with the one I used for masturbating. According to Uli, you won't need it, but..."

She looked down at me, rubbing one of her breasts as she started to ride me again. "I wanted to make sure." Pressing her weight onto my hips, a grin appeared. "And don't worry about any injuries... I'll heal you."

With that, she jumped down and started kissing me ferociously. Her pussy tightened more and more as she fucked me, slamming herself down onto my cock. Sweat started to roll down her body, mixing with mine like our saliva.

As she kept me pinned, her voice kept going higher and higher the longer we went. Using all my strength, I matched her fast and hard rhythm, thrusting up with all my might. I felt her gasp, and I wrapped my arms around her, kissing her deeply.

"Ah!" She started slowing down until she stopped moving entirely, letting me take over momentarily.

I ran my hand through her hair and kissed her again.

"Fuck, Giezha," I said out of breath, looking at her flushed face. "You really are beautiful. Like really, really beautiful." I moved my right hand to her cheek and my left down her muscular arm and onto her back. "God damn."

I slithered my left hand further down and toyed with her clit, rubbing up and down as I thrusted. Giezha's voice broke for a second, and she threw her head back.

The faster I went, the more she moaned. I rubbed my hands over her abs and felt her taut muscles contract and her body shake. Giezha's eyes rolled back as her wet pussy convulsed in orgasm.

"Oh, yes, Asher. Yes, do that more," she whimpered as I felt another load blast out. "Fuck, when you cum like that it just makes me start to cum all over again. More! More!"

She fell on top of me, and a primal hunger growled deep inside. I flipped her onto her back and looked her in the eyes. Her eyes wavered as she breathed in and out, slowly coming down from the high of her orgasm.

Her heartbeat echoed inside of me, and it was like I truly saw Giezha for the first time. Her beauty, her fire, her gentleness. My heart fluttered, and my stomach did backflips, seeing her and feeling her. But something in my mind rattled around uncomfortably.

I cupped her face and looked at her. "Giezha, I need to know something. Why me? Really. And why now?"

Giezha looked at me, her eyes locked onto mine. "Because I wanted it to be with you. A friend, someone I cared about. Someone I could trust. Like I said, it could be now, or it could be never."

That thought had not crossed my mind yet. It was true. Tomorrow we would be descending into the dungeon. And after that, there might not be another tomorrow. The thought weighed heavy on my mind, but when I looked at Giezha... it was okay. It was going to be okay. Because no matter what, I got to have tonight.

"Good answer," I joked.

She giggled before pulling me back in for another go-round. My head swirled with only one thing on my mind. Fucking Giezha until the both of us lost sensation in our legs.

Despite orgasming in rapid succession, whatever magical sex gel Giezha got her hands on was working. I was just as hard as when we started, and I couldn't help but wonder if I should call a doctor if it lasted longer than four hours.

"Asher, it's amazing," Giezha moaned, wrapping her massive legs around my waist. I tried to continue the rapid pace of our fucking while fighting the raw power in her legs.

"Choke me, Asher." As Giezha said that, she grabbed the hand I had on her ass and planted it on her throat.

Careful not to crush her esophagus, I lightly wrapped my fingers around the sides of her neck. I pressed against her neck gently and continued to violently fuck her.

Her face was bright pink, but she didn't have any trouble breathing. She still moaned and gasped and giggled as her pussy vibrated along with my thrusts.

Giezha had long ago lost her voice and could only squeal and yip in pleasure. I could feel her tighten up as my cock throbbed more and more, her juices smothering my cock.

With the last bits of energy in my legs fading, I ramped up the pace for one final push. Grabbing her neck with one hand and her breast with the other, I looked at her and gritted my teeth.

"Fuck!" I grunted, shooting out the very last of my sperm inside Giezha's convulsing, trembling pussy.

Giezha grabbed me by the shoulders and buried me into her chest one last time as she rode the high of her orgasm. I felt her heartbeat humming rapidly as my cock finally threw in the towel and gave up.

We laid there for several moments, huffing and puffing, trying to get our breath. Everything beneath my legs felt fuzzy, and I couldn't wiggle my toes.

When I finally rolled off her, Giezha's flushed expression and askew glasses told me it was the same for her. I held her hand, and we lay together, basking in the afterglow of a violent supernova of passion and lust. It was a perfectly romantic moment. Until Mara started clapping.

We both bolted upright and saw Mara giving us a round of applause. Her face was bright red, and she had probably been listening for a while. Uli wandered into the tent bleary-eyed and gave us an annoyed look.

"About time you made it three for three," Uli grumbled, carrying a nightcap out with a mug of what smelled like coffee. "Now catch some shut eye and don't you dare think about starting back up again." She grumbled as she walked away.

"Damn near caused the place to cave in."

Mara bit her lip and winked at us before leaving us alone. I got up to look for something to clean Giezha and the mess we had made. She was positively overflowing with cum, and it had stained onto the bedroll.

She simply grabbed her staff, and with a tap of her finger, she cleaned herself, me, and the bedroll. I gave her a look, wondering why she decided to keep her room with the girls such a pigsty. She read my mind and pouted.

"Just get over here and cuddle me, dammit."

Limping over, I got under cover of the bedroll next to Giezha. As we lay next to each other, her breasts pressed against my head like the world's most perfect pillows.

363

The statues depicted heroes and adventurers in combat. Their weapons were drawn, and their bodies frozen in action.

Chapter 34

Tavilday, 13th of Extrin, Year 678, 4th Age

The next day, Giezha and I both woke up feeling refreshed. As we packed, Giezha acted almost as nothing had happened. Almost. As we walked to the other side of the mountain, she was much closer to me as the rear guard. Uli and Mara said nothing, but Uli gave me a sporting smack on the ass as encouragement to hustle up with packing. A feat I returned in kind.

"How much longer?" Mara complained a few hours after we had begun. "This is driving me crazy!"

"I'm sure it is, Mara," Uli said, staring at the map, her teeth clenched. "But this map only tells me where we are going, not where we are!" I thought that even a GPS would be useless buried under a mile of rock and stone. Mara stuck her tongue out and bit into a bar of hardtack.

Morale continued to dip as we trudged along the dark, silent, unyielding corridor. I grew convinced we weren't even moving anymore and started throwing rocks I'd find on the ground ahead. Luckily for my sanity, the

364

rocks I threw appeared a short while later as we marched forward.

We rested once to soothe our aching feet, shovel food in our mouths, and push on. We elected to drink a few bits of some stamina potion I'd saved for the occasion to keep ourselves alert and ready—a fantastical version of coffee or energy drinks.

Maybe it was the stamina potion. Perhaps we were going crazy. Or maybe it was a sixth sense. But we could feel it. Indescribable energy tickled the hairs on our necks and grabbed at our throats. A dangerous percolation exposed our nerve endings and rang in our ears.

The feeling of getting close.

The first actual warning was the temperature. It was comfortably cool in the mountain tunnel during our journey. But the temperature had started to sink lower and lower as we marched further and further. No light appeared at the end of the tunnel, but howling, hissing, screaming winds announced it.

"Fuck, that's cold," Giezha chattered, reheating the stone and sock hand warmers for us. "Let's turn around."

All three of us gave her an evil eye, fully aware of her terrible attempt at humor. Clad in our winter clothes, we marched forward into the stinging wind of the tunnel. The ringing in my ears grew louder and louder, stinging my eardrums with its incessant pitch. My only respite was grinding my teeth loud enough to drown the noise as my muscles burned and ached for relief.

"Oi," Uli said, pointing forward at something. The first something in nearly two full days of walking. "Look!"

A light. It took everything in our power not to sprint towards the light regardless of its potential danger. Pulling out our weapons, we walked towards the light. It wasn't like the burning whiteness of the sun flooding into a darkened room. It was a bright pink dot that faded in and out off in the distance.

Slowly, we approached. Mara's bow was ready to pierce whatever monster provided the illumination. The cold sank deeper and deeper into our skin as we heard the howling winds grow louder and louder. Snow started to drift into the tunnel until it accumulated several inches deep.

"Look," Uli said, pointing to the ground. "Tracks."

The tracks looked like deer hooves. Or, more accurately, a satyr's. We looked at each other before continuing. Sal had come this way before, and we were catching up. Tiny stones poked holes through the snowdrift as we walked further and further. Making our way to the light source, we saw a bright pink symbol carved into the wall.

Checking the back of the map, it was a perfect match. Off to our left, we could see the light of the outside beckoning and goading us to walk away. Under the light, Sal's footprints disappeared. Instead, there was a large circular carving in the ground with arcane symbols and runes written in Giant, according to Giezha.

"It's the entrance," I surmised, "The question is how we get in."

Giezha studied the carvings for a moment, nodding her head.

"It's instructions written in Giant, It requires a spell," she said, lifting her staff as runes began to swirl around the air.

Giezha spoke in a tongue I'd never heard before. Her words echoed through the hall in a deep and spectral pattern. As her words reverberated in my chest, a blue light began to flow around the symbol's outline. It snaked its way up and down the patterns of the stone. The floor began to shake with the thuds and sounds of massive stones shifting in the mountain.

"Stop!" Uli shouted as rocks began to fall from the ceiling. Giezha's eyes began to glow the same color as the stone.

I grabbed Giezha, trying to shake her out of it. "Giezha!"

A stone narrowly avoided my skull as the cacophony grew louder and louder. The ground felt like an earthquake, and we were underneath a fucking mountain! Giezha's words echoed louder and louder, battling the mountain's roar.

Mara grabbed a handaxe, ready to smash the glowing symbol. But, right as she wound up her attack, there was a flash of brilliant light, and the shaking stopped instantly.

The glowing dimmed to a faint hum, and Giezha's expression returned to normal. Everybody looked at her while the symbol slowly moved backward. A massive seamless door shifted open, spanning at least twenty feet up. A bead of sweat rolled down Giezha's forehead as she sipped a mana potion.

"They came through this way earlier," she said, out of breath. "Their incantation caused the rocks to fall from the ceiling and onto the ground before the fresh snowdrift blew in."

Stones had fallen on top of the snow, forming tiny mountains along the ground. A faint green glow illuminated the deep chasm looking out into the door. Giezha picked up a large boulder with one hand and tossed it down. After several seconds, I heard a loud splash. Giezha turned to us, determination sprawled across her face. "We'll have to jump."

Mara shook her head, looking down. "That's insane."

"Yes, it is," Giezha deadpanned.

Uli gave her a look as well. "Are you crazy?"

"Probably."

"How do we know it's safe to jump down there?"

"We don't."

Mara tried to reason with Giezha. "There has to be another way."

"She could slow our fall down." I suggested, estimating the drop to be about a hundred feet. Give or take another fifty. Probably giving.

Giezha nodded her head. "We'll need to jump together then."

I walked over to the edge of the sheer drop, looking down. A wobbling sensation formed in my stomach as I stared into the abyss—the kind where your body is telling you to jump, but not really. My legs wobbled and swayed, and I felt lunch returning from my stomach. Uli and Mara both looked unconvinced, but I was confident. Mara and Uli argued with Giezha about what to do.

"H-Hey, Uli," I said, my voice catching my throat. "Is there any way to convince you?"

Uli slowly crept over, looking down at the drop. Her eyes widened in horror the longer she looked. She shook her head vigorously.

"No way," she said. "Not happening. Can't convince me this is the way to go."

When I looked back down into the chasm, I agreed. It was a terrible idea.

I gulped and gave a nervous laugh. "Well, I'm gonna go." Before anybody could do anything, I jumped down into the cave.

I could hear Mara scream out to me as I sprung forward. "Asher!"

Darkness quickly surrounded me in every direction. The tiny blip of light above me faded fast. This was a more considerable drop than just 150 feet. It was all up to them trusting in Giezha now. I floated in the air, my legs walking in place. The wind rushed through my ears, deafening me to the

367

world as I flew blind.

"I wonder if I die like this?" I shouted out to myself, trying to contort my body to have my legs hit the water first.

Oh shit, what if there was no water? What if they knew we were coming and saw the rock we threw, making an auditory illusion of water. A sickening knot tied itself in my stomach as I realized this could all be a trap. I was about to die to a fucking cartoon gag. All the work I put into this, all of this effort for nothing. As I pondered this, I heard a noise above me.

Wait. I heard a noise above me. I saw the girls floating towards me as Uli was unleashing a torrent of what I could only assume were vicious threats and swear words in Goblin. Giezha's staff glowed a feathery white that wrapped around our ankles.

Giezha and Mara were pale-faced, while Uli's was flushed red as she screamed up and down before we gently fell into the water. We quickly swam forward to the water's edge, Uli still punctuating every word with a menagerie of colorful language. Drying ourselves off, Mara gestured for her to quiet down.

"We don't know where the captain and the others are," Mara warned. "We need to be careful."

Looking up, we got the first full glimpse of the area: a massive system of caves carved out of jagged rocks. The floor was a tiled pattern beaten, weathered, and covered in dust.

Dim, yellow mushrooms glowed along the walls. The air was musty and thick with the damp smell of mold and decay. The crumbled remains of giant stone statues and columns littered the floor as we walked through the room. Our footsteps should have echoed in this cavernous room, but they were muffled. In fact, it was quiet. Scarily quiet.

We drew our weapons, looking for a clue as to where the four we chased had gone. Footprints went off in every direction of the large room. At the center were several steps up where one of the four had walked toward. The steps lead up to a weathered throne made of stone.

Uli called us over, having found a passage out after checking along the walls. A large passageway led out, where the wind could be felt blowing out toward us. We reported our findings to each other, and it seems like whatever they were looking for was on that throne.

368

"Let's go," Uli said, leading the way. As we walked, she hung back with me, having the others walk ahead. Uli looked at me with a steel-eyed gaze. "I'm going to keep this simple, Asher. You ever do that again, and I will castrate you."

I felt my lower half tighten at the notion. Nevertheless, I looked back at Uli, furrowing my brow. "All I did was trust Giezha's idea. That's not a crime."

"It was stupid!" she hissed.

"It worked."

With that, I walked ahead to catch up with the others. Uli shot me a dirty look as she passed by, taking the front scout position. We found a smaller area with a tile mosaic motif walking into the next room.

Along the walls, arcane patterns were scattered, with runes written in Giant. Giezha studied them intently, her face darkening the longer she read from them. I was preoccupied looking around at the piles of bones belonging to creatures near Giezha's size.

"I don't like the looks of these bones," I warned, keeping my sword at the ready.

"I don't like these runes," Giezha said, finishing her translations. "Someone set a boobytrap in here." She turned and looked at the pile of bones. "They were supposed to attack us when we got in here. However, it looks like that already happened."

One of the eye sockets began to glow, and quick as a flash, two arrows buried into each socket. Retrieving her arrows, Mara noticed something underneath the skull.

"I think it's hiding something," Mara said, pushing the piles of bones out of the way.

I helped move the bones over, revealing a chest hidden under the piles. The lock was already broken, and the inside of the chest was empty. A silk fabric lay with a heavy indent in a straight line. It looked like it was for a rod or something.

"Any ideas?" I asked, finding nothing underneath the cloth but old cork.

"Could be a staff," Mara guessed. "Or a handle for something."

"Handle?"

"Yeah, it was common in the Second Age for ceremonial weapons used in formal declarations of war to be kept in separate pieces in accordance

369

with Extris' Laws of War."

"Think that could be for Smite of the Dead Giant?" I asked, hoping she disagreed.

"I think you're right on the money," Mara concurred, her face taking on her blank, predatory expression. "If it's in pieces, they might still be searching the caverns. Maybe we can beat them to it."

Scouring through the cave, we learned that this was likely an underground cathedral at some point. Scriptures, murals, and dedications to Zhol and Adar, the Gods of Death and Life, littered the walls and were found in every room.

However, what was peculiar was just how large all the rooms were. They were all twice as tall as Giezha at the smallest and more often stretched far past any light could reach. The occasional bat's wings could be heard flapping overhead.

After searching for several hours, the only evidence we found was the other for having already been here. Upturned tables, shredded papers, and freshly kicked up dust were everywhere we looked.

Uli demanded that we stay as a group, with her on the lookout and Giezha casting spells to detect traps or secrets. Despite our heavy precautions, we saw neither hide nor hair of anyone.

"She gonna be alright?" I whispered to Mara, looking through some texts describing a giant's ascent to the top of the mountains in the early Second Age.

"Hard to say," Mara said, only half-reading some of the texts. "She's nervous. Paranoid."

Uli threw a book near my head, missing and smashing into the stone walls. "I heard that!

The further we delved into the abandoned church of life and death, the thicker the air felt. Spores began to float visibly in the air, forcing Giezha to cast a protective bubble on us. Eventually, we made it to a large stone wall with smoothly hewn inscribed in giant runes. We looked to Giezha for a translation of the monumental inscription.

"Abandon hope to all the heathens defiant," Giezha said, struggling to breathe right. Pausing, she popped open a mana potion and gulped it down. "Come t-to Zhol, or taste our Smite of the Dead Giant."

Giezha collapsed onto her bottom, dangerously low on mana. She

370

needed time to let the potion take effect before moving on. Uli looked over the door, checking for themes in the wall and feeling for a hidden compartment.

I checked Giezha's notes on giant runes while Mara rummaged around for stamina potions she could safely give to Giezha. Mixing potions was a tricky business.

"That rune is wrong," I told Uli, pointing to a two-part rune. "'Hammer' and 'God' in Giant combines for the word 'Smite', but that hammer rune is wrong."

Uli looked at the rune and then Giezha's notes. Checking back and forth several times, she nodded her head, concurring with what I noticed. The 'hammer' rune was supposed to be a square with a long line down the middle. However, the rune on the wall had a hook attached to the bottom of the line.

"Giezha!" I called over to our resting sorceress. "What's a hook at the bottom of the hammer rune mean?"

Giezha thought for a minute, looking up in the air. "Key."

Uli and I looked at the 'key' rune and gently pressed it. The rune turned dark brown before fading into nothing, revealing a keyhole and a handle. I took a step back, giving Uli room to work.

She fidgeted with a pair of lockpicks in her hands and bent over to inspect the lock. It looked like a regular lock to me. Still, Uli studied it for several minutes, raising her lock picks and lowering them several times. After fifteen minutes of her staring at the keyhole, I tapped Uli's shoulder.

"What's wrong with it?" I asked.

"It's too easy," Uli said, gulping. "What if there's a trap?"

"We disable it." I said simply.

"What if it kills us?"

"It won't."

"How do you know that!?" Uli snapped at me. "How could you possibly know that?"

Mara watched over Giezha, who was taking a breather, trying to focus her mana. She just looked at me and shrugged.

I turned back and looked at Uli. I tried to reassure her. "Because you're here Uli. Because if there's anybody who can unlock this thing, it's you. I know you won't let me get hurt. You won't let anybody get hurt. I trust

371

you."

Uli clicked her tongue at my pep talk. "Fat load of good that is! What's it matter if you trust me? I don't trust you!"

That one knocked me for a loop. Mara jumped up to my defense, putting a hand between Uli and me.

"What's wrong with you Uli?" Mara demanded, her eyes narrowing. "Asher is trying to help you!"

Uli threw down the picks and stuck a finger in my nose. "I don't know who the fuck you are, Asher Merrick. I'm in a life or death situation with someone who doesn't even have the balls to say where they're from." Her eyes had changed a dangerous shade of red. "I don't like it. And I don't trust it! And I'm tired of you hiding behind some bullshit excuse."

A subtle flash of white in her other hand tipped off her signature knife. Without thinking, I drew my sword, jumping back. Uli's knife was now firmly in front of her, while Mara tried to stay between us. I planted my feet hard into the ground, waiting for Uli to make her move. I didn't want to hurt her, but she was acting crazy.

"What the hell is wrong with you!?" I shouted, my muscles tensed in anticipation. "I already told you, it's complicated. Giezha and Mara can both vouch for me!"

Uli threw the knife past Mara's head straight towards my skull. With a quick parry, I knocked her weapon airborne. As the knife sailed upward, I felt a gentle breeze under me.

"Shit!" I cursed.

A second knife missed my stomach by inches, putting me on my heels. Uli's golden eyes flashed in the dark as she swiped. I parried her strikes while trying to regain my footing.

The wet stone underneath made me slip on my back. My shoulder slammed into the ground as I tucked my head to avoid a concussion. My sword clattered to the ground, and I saw another flash of white. Uli was on top of me, driving the knife at my throat.

I heard Mara scream out, "Uli, no!"

With a desperate grab, I snatched her arm. Flicking her wrist, she tossed the knife to the other hand. Uli slashed downward, only to be caught by my left hand. Uli was fast, but she wasn't nearly as strong as me. My body sensed danger, and a poorly timed supernova could snap her arm like a twig.

"Stop it!" I shouted, trying to shove Uli off me. "Get off!"

I threw Uli off me with a final shove and scrambled to my feet. She grabbed her knives, huffing, and puffing, only to be grabbed from behind by Mara. I rubbed my shoulder and holstered my sword, heart pounding in my chest.

My ears burned bright red, and I scowled at our diminutive leader. She struggled to get free, but Mara had her in a full nelson off the ground.

"Enough!" I shouted at the top of my lungs. My eyes popped out in rage as Uli looked at me scornfully. "You want the truth, huh?!"

Giezha jumped up, her feet wobbling beneath her. "Asher! Don't!"

Anger boiled over inside me. Fuck it. No more games. "I'm not fucking from here!" I said shouted, my eyes bulging.

"Wow," Uli said sarcastically. "Shocker"

I gritted my teeth. "No. I'm not from this world. From Echo Veil. I'm from a different world entirely."

You could hear a pin drop. Uli was shocked as Mara and Giezha stared in horror. My heart began to slow down, and I processed what I said. I touched where I'd been shot and killed, taking a deep breath.

"I was killed, Uli. Murdered. And then I was brought here by some fucking god named Gathos."

Nobody said anything, processing my words. Uli looked at me and over to Giezha repeatedly. Giezha shambled over and placed a hand on my shoulder, staring at Uli. Her expression was grim but determined.

"It's true, Uli. Asher's an Otherworlder." Giezha looked from me to the still stunned Uli. "I put him under a Truth Circle when we first met. As far as I can tell, it's the real deal. Mara was there too, she saw it."

"You're crazy," Uli said, looking at me. "That's impossible!"

"No," Giezha corrected her. "It's not unheard of for Otherworlders to appear in the first millennium of an Age."

Uli's terrified expression gave me a sick feeling. "Why is it so bad that I'm not from this world? Why does it matter that I came when I came?"

Mara looked at me gently while Uli stepped closer like I was a wild animal. "Asher, an Otherworlder's arrivals usually signify a great conflict or upheaval."

I looked at them confused. "What?"

Giezha started talking again."Many Otherworlders became great heroes and villains of Echo Veil. Some led armies, moved mountains and changed the world around them. And they almost always came when the End of an Age was upon us."

"End of an Age?"

"Armageddon," Mara continued. "The end of the world as we know it. My elven ancestors still remember the world coming out of The Arrival of Khorba, The Eternal."

"The Dragon?" I asked, recalling the name but nothing else. "How bad could he be?"

Uli's eyes widened in horror at my comment.

"You really don't know..." She took a deep breath before speaking. "Khorba was a dragon the size of a mountain. He created the Wall Eternal and split the world in two. He now rests in the mountains of his island."

"So, what, I'm a harbinger of another Dragon descending from the heavens and destroying the world?" None of them said anything, which only terrified me further. "Giezha, you said you didn't know who Gathos is, right?"

Giezha shook her head, and the others didn't seem to know who he was either. "It's not unheard of for gods to become forgotten or lost to time. Others are overshadowed. As for being a harbinger... we have no way of knowing."

Uli had a far-off look on her face, looking at the stone wall. "He sounds familiar, but I can't place it." Uli's eyes shifted to me, her expression still blank. "One more question," she said, gripping her weapon. "And be honest."

I nodded my head, desperate to get this all over with.

"Annie, the girl you mentioned in the bathhouse." Uli said, her words knocking the wind out of me. "Is she the one that killed you?"

As she said those words, I could tell Uli already knew. Mara and Giezha both looked confused. When Uli said her name, Anastasia appeared before me, her gun smoking as it pointed at me. I felt the sting in my chest under my armor, remembering the scars she'd left.

"Yeah..." I said, looking away from the illusory Annie and at the ground. "She did. When you... attacked me that night we were ambushed, I thought I saw her instead of you."

Digesting my words, Uli nodded her head. "Did you love her?"

Fucking hell, Uli.

All eyes were on me while a single tear welled up in my eyes. The pain of it all still stung deep in my soul. Dying was painful. Remembering who killed me and why she did it was so much worse.

Oh, well. Fuck it. Might as well own it.

"Yeah." I sighed. "I loved her."

Nobody said anything for a while. My words hung heavy in the air. Mara and Giezha both looked incredibly uncomfortable, but Mara came over and patted me on the shoulder. Uli didn't say anything, turning away.

"We should get moving. I'll pick the lock, and we can get out of here."

Uli calmly walked over to the lock and picked it up in a flash. She didn't say anything as she picked up her gear, walking through the massive gate. Turning her head to us, she motioned for us to follow.

Giezha took a deep breath and walked over to Uli while Mara bit her thumbnail and looked at me. I was just as dumbstruck as they must have been. I started to walk up to Uli with a deep sigh, but Mara grabbed my sleeve.

"Asher," she said quietly, giving me a sad look, "I just want you to know, none of this stuff matters to me." She pulled me in for a hug, squeezing tightly. "I know you're a good man, and a better friend."

Mara let me go and gave me a peck on the cheek before turning to join the others. As they disappeared into the darkness, I heard Uli call out to me.

"Hurry up, Merrick!"

The next area was as quiet as the rest of the cavern. However, along both sides of the vast hall were a series of stone statues. The statues depicted heroes and adventurers in combat. Their weapons were drawn, and their bodies frozen in action. I walked up to a statue of a man with a large, curved sword, inspecting the stone.

"This looks brand new," I said, noticing the bright white of the marble. "No dust, no cracks, nothing."

The center of the room was a complex pattern of intertwined vines, going in every direction. A few torches were already lit, and the smell of burning oil tickled our noses.

Another indication of someone being here before us. The eerie quiet of

375

the room broken only by the gentle crackle of torches was unsettling. Once again, the room was large and filled with stones. There was no reason our voices did not echo ad infinitum.

I walked over to Uli, inspecting the statue of a goblin casting a spell from a book. Her eyes turned to me before quickly darting back to the statue. I stood awkwardly behind her, looking at the goblin statue.

The work on the statues was genuinely marvelous. They felt alive and expressive. Their eyes almost moved along with you as you walked around it. Mara and Giezha walked up ahead, leaving only myself and Uli.

"I'm sorry about earlier," Uli said, looking away. "I didn't mean it when I said I couldn't trust you."

"It's fine," I said, feeling a dry itch in my throat. "Just taking care of the team, didn't want anyone getting hurt."

Uli turned around and held my hand. Her golden eyes warbled as she pulled me in for a hug. "I was also afraid of getting heartbroken," She muttered, her cheeks burning bright red.

I bent over slightly and squeezed Uli reassuringly. I really couldn't blame her. Breaking away, Uli's face held a look of relief as she looked closer at the statue.

"It's funny," she said, pointing her finger at the eyes of the goblin. "You could almost swear it's ali—ouch!"

A sizzling pop was heard as the white marble eyes of the goblin oozed out, snapping at Uli.

A bit of her finger touched the white muck, and the acrid smell of burning flesh filled my nostrils.

Grabbing Uli, I jumped back as the statue began to dissolve. I turned around, seeing the other statues following suit. The statues melted into masses of white and grey blobs, hissing as organic material was swallowed by these formless masses. Unleashing a blast of fire, the oozes lurched away, creating a path.

"Let's go!" I shouted, grabbing Uli and running. "Giezha! Mara!"

Dozens of the statues previously depicting warriors now coalesced into a wave of muck, burning through the marble flooring. Noxious fumes spewed from the reaction as we sprinted towards where Mara and Giezha went.

Without turning around, I unleashed another blast of fire out of my hand.

376

The flames sizzled against the monstrous ooze, but I could hear it gaining on us. A low timber of rushing fluid thundered behind us, like a lava flow rushing down the mountainside.

"Faster!" I urged Uli, who began to lag behind. Uli was swinging her legs as hard and fast as possible, but she was just too damn small.

Looking back, the oozes had combined into a veritable tidal wave. Shit. Running out of options, I grabbed Uli and turned on my afterburners. With a sweltering heat in my legs, I started to burn on the insides.

Uli clung to me as I carried her in my arms, building up the energy in my legs. The way forward was nothing but a dark hallway, closing in as more and more statues melted into the oozing muck. The wave began to close in from all sides, trapping us to drowning in a burning, acidic death.

"Uli!" I shouted, getting ready for a hail mary. "Got any of that darkness powder stuff?"

Uli ruffled around her satchel, potions bouncing out and instantly disappearing in the ooze. She pulled out her last use of it. The oozes started to close in on all sides as my vision became nothing but the bubbling mass. My legs ached for relief as the tension coiled tighter.

"On the count of three, throw it at my feet!"

"What!?" Uli shrieked, unable to process my idea.

"One."

"Hold on, Asher!"

"Two!"

"I'm serious!"

I looked at her as the oozes began to cast a heavy shadow over us. "Trust me!"

She looked at me, her mouth open in horror.

"Three!"

Uli threw down a charge of the darkness powder, completely blinding us for a moment.

BAM!

With a blast of power, my feed exploded off the ground. I felt the wind of the oozes rushing around me as they pounced where I had just been. Tiny flecks of the muck landed on my ankles, burning into my skin like sparks off a welding machine. Soaring through the air, I wondered if we would hit the ceiling and get turned into a paste on the wall.

"Hey!" came a familiar voice from below.

Suddenly, a feathery white ethereal force wrapped around me, and I gently floated to the ground. Giezha and Mara were below, surrounded by a massive wall of flames, keeping the oozes at bay. Giezha guided us to the other side of the fire, and we landed gently. The killer tidal wave rushed towards us before stopping at the sight of the flaming wall.

"Oozes are afraid of fire." Mara said, checking over Uli and me for injuries. "And they hate the smell of oil."

Giezha smashed a decanter of oil onto the flames, causing the fire to grow and the ooze to gurgle angrily. Uli and I quickly turned and ran from the oozes, grabbing Mara and Giezha. The ooze didn't seem to chase us, unable to leap over the towering inferno.

"How'd you get away from it?" Uli asked.

"It went back towards you guys all of a sudden," Mara explained, looking at Giezha angrily. "Giezha said to set up a perimeter and wait for you guys."

Giezha turned up her nose and huffed. "I trusted they could handle themselves."

"Not the trust I was hoping to earn today," I joked.

Eventually, we completely separated ourselves from the oozes of the room the false statues were in. We walked down the hall, which opened up into another cave system.

The same symbols and religious paraphernalia followed as we went, but the aura changed. Instead of glowing mushrooms and silent halls, glowing crystals started to poke out of the walls as echoes bounced across the cavern.

Symbols of runes and pictures of death and destruction also began to litter the stone walls. The well-manicured floors shifted to cobblestone and bare ground, but most sinister was the feeling running up my back. The feeling of electricity zipping through the air and up my spine.

"I think we're getting close," Mara whispered.

There was a hum off in the distance down the cave. It was deep and heavy. Pounding at your chest as its vibrations were so low it almost sounded like nothing. A chill went down my spine, and I shuddered. The hum was reminiscent of my time in the void. It sounded like death.

"Yeah." I gulped. "We are."

Exhaustion seeped into our bodies, and we rationed out our last stamina potion. My muscles begged for the sweet release of sleep. Or death. It was clear on everybody's face just how tired we all were. But as we shook ourselves awake, the hum grew louder. The vibrations started to replace our heartbeats. I felt the cave's cold be replaced with the frigid touch of death.

A green light appeared as the system widened out. The violent mosaics reappeared with depictions of giants slaughtering masses of people.

The light hummed with the same frequency as the near-silent noise, vibrating rapidly. A single figure was shrouded in a literal cloak of shadows in the middle of the open area.

The circular floor was easily the size of a football stadium, with rows of stone steps curving inwardly. The rows all pointed toward the figure and gigantic mosaic. The humming noise now sounded like it came from everywhere.

The figure stood, hands stretched out to the mosaic, holding several items and shooting lights out at the wall. The light seeped into the artwork, making its finer details glow the same sickly green as the light we saw earlier. The image on the walls became clearer and more refined, revealing that this mosaic was the center point from which the others emanated.

In this massive painting and stonework glowed the dragon Khorba, The Eternal. Khorba's figure loomed over a mountain burning the world below. Next to the terrible dragon was a massive person, wielding a war hammer picture with spikes on the ends and a skull in its middle. The hammer pointed down the mountainside as a swarm of bodies and skeletons moved where the hammer pointed. The four of us all thought the same thing."

"Shit."

The figure in the center of the amphitheater-like structure stopped for a moment. The glowing light became solid, and they slowly turned. The objects in the person's hand matched the hammer on the wall. The figure clicked the handle together with the face of the hammer. The shadows began to fade as a pair of horns appeared from the figure's head.

"Come on down, girls," an all-too-familiar voice said. "It's time."

We all slowly walked down the steps, down to the humming stage. There was no way. The figure stood there, hammer in both hands, his head hung low. I looked at him and knew it was impossible. It couldn't be! We stopped about ten feet short; our legs were frozen in fear. The goat-man looked up, his eyes empty and soulless.

"I'm sorry about the statues, girls. I was told they would kill you quickly and painlessly.

Chapter 35

Tavilday, 13th of Extrin, Year 678, 4th Age

Sal looked at us, his eyes gray and foggy, matching his withered skin. "You shouldn't be here."

"No," I said as the girls were too stunned to speak. Sal's eyes drifted over to me listlessly.

"This is impossible, Sal. It was Dawnthorn and the Ivory Forge crew after the hammer! We caught her lying about your involvement! She framed you, Sal!"

An echoing clap emerged from the shadows. Slowly walking forward was Dawnthorn. Vurshung and the others appeared from the shadows behind her. They were adorned in the same silver and white robes as Salvatore, marked in the same repeated pattern as on the stones. Vurshung and the two Ivory Forge crew members scowled at us.

None of us moved at the sight of them, too stunned to move a muscle. Dawnthorn smirked and threw her hands up in mock defeat.

"Guess I'll be the one to say it," she said with a chuckle. "You are right, we did frame Salvatore for everything."

"Why!?" I demanded

"Because you lot were smarter and more stubborn than we bargained for." She scowled. "We were planning on framing you all, luring you in with the silver bars." Her voice became singsong and mockingly dramatic. "A young set of heroes on a search for the missing silver!" Her eyes turned to slits as she looked back at us. "You'd be lead here and framed, while Mhurren and Mick picked up the pieces. And once we were done? We'd make the Undead Insurrection look like nothing. But you had too many questions."

"You were too stubborn to die when I blasted ye offa that building too,"

381

Mhurren added.

"Then ol' Sal came poking around and stole the silver bars. Had to think on our feet, we did." As he spoke, the image of the sorcerer blasting me off the building flashed through my mind. It was Mhurren who'd nearly killed me.

Vurshung snarled. "Just needed to get rid of you first."

Dawnthorn was about to say something before closing her mouth and turning to Sal with a smile. "You may have the honors."

The satyr scowled at Dawnthorn, his eyes glinting in the sickly green light. "It's true. I told them to frame me for everything. The past, the attacks and transformations in the city...all of it."

"Why?" Mara whispered, her hand trembling next to her sword. "Why, Sal?"

His dull eyes floated over to Mara, his shoulders dipping lower. "I didn't have a choice. They said they would do unspeakable things. They said they would bring my family back as undead, just to have them kill you. You need to leave! Run away! Get out of here!"

Mhurren and Mick clicked their tongues, drawing their weapons. "Enough talk. We shoulda jus' killed 'em already!"

Before either of them good move a muscle, Salvatore's eyes went bloodred. Shoving his hands towards them, a set of zombified hands burst out of around, grabbing and clawing at their feet.

Mhurren swore loudly as he tried to disintegrate the undead hands while Mick swung his weapon wildly. He was now carrying an excessively large battle-ax.

"Don't you dare," Salvatore said quietly as the undead rose from their grave.

Vurshung's eye flitted over to Sal, and he growled, pulling his gnarled sword out. With a single slice, a giant black wave erupted from the tip, blasting away the undead hands into nothingness.

Sal and Vurshung both stared at each other, taking steps forward. As they did, Dawnthorn snapped her fingers, and a metallic rope snaked around Salvatore, binding him.

"Enough!" She looked at Salvatore, her head moving around him like a snake examining an egg. "You're coming with me, Yaxel. I've got an army to raise for Khorba." Her wrists and neck clattered as a soft white glow

382

covered her. She was covered in jewelry made of moonstones.

Sal stood down and turned back to us, still frozen in shock.

"After I lost my wife and daughter, my life fell apart. The light left my eyes. Music never touched my ears. My heart grew cold and I did not know the goodness of life. For decades, I was nothing. A husk. An undead drifting through life—no goals, no hopes, no dreams." Sal looked at each of us, the weight of the world on his shoulders. "It's true, I did study necromancy in desperate hope of bringing back my love and my daughter. But I realized what that meant. What giving myself to the... the darkness and villainy of necromancy meant."

He turned and faced Dawnthorn, tears streaming down his battered face. "I should have always known it was you. You killed them! YOU KILLED THEM!"

Dawnthorn rolled her eyes at Sal. "Cry me a river, Yaxel." Dawnthorn's eyes began to glow, and she pulled out her magic wand, pointing to the ground underneath us.

Hands shot out of the stonework as undead and skeletons grabbed at us. We all jumped back, slashing, stabbing, and bashing the undead away. The first few undead collapsed to our attacks, but almost a dozen more quickly climbed out of the ground. They gnashed their teeth and slowly advanced on us as we were forced backward.

Sal shouted out to us. "No! Let them go! You got what you wanted!"

Dawnthorn grabbed Sal by the collar of his cloak and threw him towards the glowing mosaic. "Shut up! We've got a hammer to unlock and an army of the dead to raise. The job's not done until Zhol is standing in front of us." She turned back to Vurshung, Mhurren, and Mick. "Kill 'em."

Dawnthorn pointed her wand at the ground, and a massive wall of glass erupted from the ground up to the ceiling.

At her words, the trio of Vurshung, Mick, and Mhurren pounced. Mhurren took control of the zombies that Vurshung had not killed, pointing them in our direction. At the same time, Vurshung and Mick leaped forward, slashing their weapons down at Uli and me. I dodged at the last second while Micks' ax split the ground and launched debris everywhere.

"Oops," Mick said, looking up from the crater he caused. "Missed ya."

Out of the corner of my eye, Giezha tried to stop the zombies from attacking us, casting shielding and protective spells. Looking back at Mick, I saw that his movements were just as slow and clumsy as before. Mara launched a volley of arrows at him, and I stabbed forward with both hands.

Mick's pupils dilated right as my sword was ready to plunge into his sockets. A moment before my sword and the arrows were about to turn him into a pincushion, a bright green light erupted and our attacks were stopped just short.

"What the—?" Before I could finish my sentence, the green sparks latched onto me, erupting in flames. "Whoa!"

Mick gave a crooked smile. "Thanks for the counter, Mhurren."

The sticky green fire burned my skin spreading until my whole body caught fire. Trying to pat the flames out only burned my hands. The fire stuck to my fingers, and I screamed out in pain.

Dropping my sword, I could feel every inch of my body crying for mercy. Undead and skeletons surrounded me as Mick let out an evil laugh before jumping up to strike. His ax smashed down, and I jumped away just before he could bisect me.

Mick's ax smashed down on the ground, shattering the undead and skeletons. Still on fire, I tried to roll and snuff out the fire, but it raged hotter and hotter. Fire roared in my ears as I heard Giezha scream out, "Asher!" A torrent of water blasted me with the force of a firehose.

The torrential water managed to put me out, but it went straight up my nose. I hacked and coughed as water rushed into my throat and lungs. On landing, I felt my left ankle bend backward.

A bolt of pain raced up my brain from my ankle and back again. Blinking rapidly, I tried to work out what was going on through my double vision—two Micks were charging right at me.

Jumping back up, I tried to dodge his attacks. The zombies and skeletons scratched and grabbed at me, desperate for flesh. Unable to jump or run, I grabbed a skeleton by its ribs and flung it at Mick.

"Nice try, idiot!" Mick slammed the skeleton, shattering it to a thousand fragments. "These won't protect you!"

Using the undead as shields, I avoided his onslaught while thinning out the hordes with Mick's wanton destruction. One attacked Mick, only to be immolated by his fiery protection. I continued backing up, caught in the momentum of the fight.

"Get back here weakling!" Mick taunted, beginning to slice through the undead deliberately.

Mhurren caught on as he battled Uli and Giezha, dodging fireballs and Uli's fire breath. "Quit attacking them, Mick! He's using you!"

Mick either didn't hear him or didn't care. Keeping his eyes trained on me, he sliced through an entire swath, cackling madly. Cutting his way through, he stopped and grinned.

"Gotcha."

With a final step backward, I fell back into the lowered portion of the stairs. Mick burst into a run, ready to turn me me into paste on the ground.

Desperately, I flung my shield off my back at his face. With a single swing, he knocked the shield away. Mick swung his ax high into the air, ready for the coup degras. I couldn't dodge out of the way. I was a sitting duck, and the cacophony around me had my head spinning. I had no sword, no shield, my muscles were on the brink of failure.

Mick roared in sadistic laughter. "Hahahaa! Gonna kill you and go find your little moonie girl back in town. Maybe I'll have Mhurren turn me into you like he did with the beggar."

"You stay away from Kiersa!" I shouted.

The star inside me was fading, and I didn't have much left. I was grasping at straws. Grasping for something to save me. Grasping at... my hip!

As a tiny ember bubbled inside, I waited. There was zero room for error. His ax was a half moment from beheading me as I held onto the knife at my hip.

Wait for it...

"Die!" Mick screamed, swinging his ax straight down.

Putting every bit of power into my right arm, I threw the knife end over end. Simultaneously, I kicked myself to the side with my left hand and foot. Tumbling end over end, the knife whistled for a half-second. The ax came down, slicing a few strands of my hair. In a blink, the knife disappeared, covered by Mick's arm.

Tumbling to the ground, I scrambled to stand up.

"Mick!" Mhurren roared furiously.

Charging, I saw the knife buried deep into Mick's chest. The protective green bubble shattered around him as ethereal wisps of green floated into the air. Mick's face was pale, and his eyes wide, staring at the knife plunged into him.

"Whuh?" he mumbled.

Rushing over, I grabbed at the knife. Gritting my teeth, I looked the sorry bastard in the eyes. With a twist, I felt the warm gush of blood splatter over my arm.

His firey shield snapped at me, dying as Mick let out a death rattle. The life quickly left his body and he went limp.

The fiery shield continued lashing out, so I kicked his body away from me. Wiping the knife off, I looked over the battlefield, seeing Uli slashing at the glass dome. Giezha fought off Mhurren while Mara tried to keep her distance from Vurshung's constant advance.

Mhurren's eyes filled with rage as he screamed out. "You bastard!" Ignoring the others, he pointed his staff at me as it started to glow bright red.

Sensing danger, I ran up the stairs, and located my bow and shield. A red shadow started to glow over me as a whistling sound appeared. I saw a tsunami of red arrows cresting downward over me.

"Shit."

Grabbing my shield, I jumped behind a large boulder, broken from the steps. Several bolts whistled past my head as I hunkered down. A split second later, the spot I was just in exploded with arrows.

A few dozen smashed into the boulder, slamming the rock into me. After nearly getting pulverized by the rock, I pulled out two of the few arrows that didn't fall out of my quiver.

Knocking an arrow back, I jumped up, aiming where Mhurren and company were fighting. The glowing green light grew brighter, and I could see the finer details in Mhurren's face. His face was contorted with rage as Uli's rocks pinged off his flaming sphere of protection.

Giezha's chain and sword combination whipped against the shield repeatedly, only to be sent back at her. Angry flames joined in Mhurren's counter, but Giezha nimbly dodged out of the way.

An explosion rocked the arena from the side. Vurshung's body was wrapped in black flames, chasing Mara. She quickly bounced up the stairs, avoiding Vurshung's slashes through the air. More of the black flames accelerated from his sword as he swung, exploding on contact with the first

386

thing they touched.

I shot one of the arrows at him. The shot sailed wide right, but Vurshung's attention was momentarily averted. Mara twisted around and shot a half-dozen arrows she'd clutched with her bow. All six shots whizzed through the air, puncturing Vurshung's flaming exterior in a tight grouping. Vurshung stumbled back, and Mara looked at me from the top of the stairs. She furrowed her brows, shouting at me.

"For Evlana, relax your grip!" Mara looked back to Vurshung and pulled something from her pocket. "I'll be right back!" Mara dodged another explosive slash and disappeared into the cave system. Vurshung followed her in hot pursuit.

"Get back here, you harlot!"

I took a deep breath and aimed my shot at Vurshung. Releasing the tension in my hand, I felt my bow slacken, held my breath, and exhaled.

THWIP!

The bolt soared through the air towards the back of the bastard's head. Vurshunng's head snapped forward as my arrow hit the mark on the back of his now flaming skull. Vurshung let out a deathly growl, and I quickly jumped down the stairs out of sight.

"Where are you, you cowardly—"

BOOM! An explosion rocked the top of the staircase.

Vurshung let out a roar of anger as black smoke erupted from where he stood. Mara had thrown one of Uli's vanishing powder bombs mixed with something nasty.

"I'M GOING TO FUCKING SLAUGHTER YOU, MARA!" He screamed, running out of the dark. "I'M GOING TO FIND YOUR PATHETIC FAMILY AND FORCE-FEED THEM YOUR ENTRAILS!"

Vurshung ran off into the caves, forcing me to stay behind and help Uli and Giezha finish off Mhurren. As I clutched my last five arrows, Mhurren's flaming shield orb cracked and splintered, with tiny spouts of flames dancing across its surface. Uli and Giezha kept pelting him with attacks, dodging his blasts of fire from the shield.

"Hurry up with the fucking ritual!" Mhurren shouted. "Mick's down! Dragon's gone off the deep end! Come get these stupid brats off me!"

The ground trembled at his words as the green light grew brighter and brighter. Fucking hell, Salvatore and Dawnthorn! Their ritual was making

387

the ground shake! The patterns on the mural start to move and warp like a living painting.

Mhurren, ignored by the others, screamed in frustration. Giezha's chain attack continued to batter the orb as she strained her face in concentration. She had to be running low on mana.

"What the hell," I grunted, torn between helping them finish Mhurren and getting to the ritual. As I struggled, a spectral anaconda the size of a bus appeared behind Mhurren.

"Kill them, dammit!" he shrieked. "Kill them, kill them, kill them!"

The snake hissed and lashed out, chopping at Giezha. With a flash, her summoned weapon disappeared, and her own protective orb encased her.

Boom!

The fangs of the anaconda slammed into Giezha's shield, instantly smashing it to pieces.

As it bit down again to eat her, Giezha's staff erupted in flames. The snake threw its head up in the air, spitting and hissing in rage.

"Answers that," I mumbled, knocking my arrow back.

I aimed for the weak spot Uli and Giezha had created in Mhurren's shield. My heart hammered in my chest as I struggled to steady myself. The gigantic serpent's ethereal tail slammed on the ground, sending debris into the air. I coiled to strike, and I could just barely see Uli disappear behind Mhurren.

"Hey!" I screamed at Mhurren, desperate to get his attention. "Taste this!"

With an exhale, I shot the arrow at Mhurren. Walking forward, I pulled back again and shot a second time. A third time. A fourth. Each shot followed in a tight pattern. The snake's attention shifted over to me, its eyes narrowing.

Thwip! Thwip! Thwip! Thwip!

The shots sank into the orb, sending spurts of flame into the air and ricocheting back towards me. The snake blocked my view, flicking its tongue out.

"HISS!" The snake struck as I jumped back.

Too slow.

The snake's massive head slammed into me, launching me upward. Cracking against the stone wall, I felt the air get sucked out of my body.

With a wheeze, I crumpled to the floor, smacking my head against the ground. My vision blurred, and it felt like I was swimming.

The hit locked my body up, freezing all my muscles. The cold stone floor was the only sensation I was vaguely aware of.

I could sense the giant snake looming over me. Looking for its minuscule prey. A bit of blood trickled out my mouth as I groaned.

"Come on, legs," I urged. "Work!"

"Hisssss..."

Tensing what little bit of strength I had in my legs, I waited for the bitter release of death. The ground trembled, and I felt a giant lurch. The snake's shadow disappeared, and I knew I was about to die. I closed my eyes.

"Asher!" screamed Giezha's hoarse voice.

"Huh?" I managed to mumble.

A warm sensation washed over me, and I felt my body return under my control. Flexing my fingers a few times, I got the feeling in my arms back and pushed off the ground. Giezha stood over me, her staff glowing bright gold as she struggled to breathe.

"Don't you dare die on me," Giezha struggled to say. "Don't you—" Giezha stopped, pulled out three health potions, and started slugging them.

"Uli?" I asked, wobbling to my feet. Looking over to Mhurren, I saw the snake was gone and Uli standing over Mhurren's corpse with his neck opened up.

I fumbled around, looking for a health potion on my hip. My finger recoiled at the painful slice of broken glass. The rest of my potions had been crushed in the fight. Giezha quickly shoved one in my hand.

"Gotta stop Dawnthorn." I grunted.

The ground continued to shake as Giezha and I lumbered over to Uli, who was clutching her stomach. A shallow cut on her side bled out, and I pulled some wrap out from her pack, quickly dressing the wound. Uli hissed in pain as I tried to stem the bleeding.

"Invisibility potion got me close enough to finish him." Uli grimaced. "But his counter still got me."

As the glowing from the mosaic grew brighter and brighter, we ran to the barrier and tried to beat it down with our weapons. I swung down with all my might, feeling it glance off.

My sword ineffectively slashed at the thick glass, while Mara's knife did just as little. Giezha chose to forgo weapons or magic and punched the glass.

The ground beneath us continued to shake rapidly while our feeble attacks did nothing. Nearly washed out by the green light, Dawnthorn had one hand pointed to the mosaic. Her other hand was cinched into Salvatore's head, forcing his participation. Her moonstones glowed in the darkness, augmenting her power. He struggled against her, trying to knock her away.

"Sal!" Uli screamed, stabbing at the microscopic scratch she'd created. "Sal! You don't have to do this!"

Nothing we did could damage the glass wall, which had to be at least a half-foot thick. Giezha could no longer punch the glass and resorted to bashing it with rocks from the ground. Flecks of blood flew from her battered knuckles.

"What do we do?" I shouted as the magical roar became deafening. Before either could say anything, Vurshung's manic rage came over the din.

"YOU HEAR ME, YOU BITCH!? I'M GOING TO USE YOUR ROTTED FLESH AS FERTILIZER!"

Mara appeared from the shadows, jumping down the stairs. Just behind her were the constant attacks from Vurshung. Blasts of deadly black energy exploded on contact with the stairs as Mara weaved in and out of his attacks. Massive chunks of rocks flew in every direction, forcing us to duck from the debris.

Completely ignoring us, Mara ran straight to the barrier Dawnthorn had constructed. As she ran, Mara grabbed the last few arrows in her quiver and shot all of them in rapid succession.

The arrows headed straight for me, causing me to duck. They landed next to another, against the glass structure next to the scuffed-up area I had slashed. Mara motioned for us to get out of the way. Two massive dark waves appeared behind her, shimmering like the void I'd seen in death.

All three of us ran to the side, trying to avoid Vurhsung's attack. Mara grabbed her shield and slid down, covering her face.

As Mara slid, Vurshung came back into view. His face was scarred even heavier, with dozens of tiny slices across his mug. He was utterly lost to the madness and rage as his reptilian face glowed with hatred.

"DIE!"

The two beams of black energy flew almost in slow motion to the glass, causing Vurshung's rage to turn into instant terror. Sensing what was happening, I exploded with a tiny burst of nova-speed, grabbing Mara by the arm and yanking her out of the way.

"Asher! What are you doi-"

BOOOOOOOM!

Vurshung's cursed sword bursts exploded against the glass. The detonation knocked all of us off our feet as glass showered in every direction. Shielding Mara behind my battered shield, several pieces flew by while a chunk implanted itself in the shield. Mara was covered in cuts and scrapes, and it looked like her right arm was burned.

"What happened?" I asked, getting back up.

Mara's eyes were fixed toward the glass shield and mosaic, her hunter expression glued in place. "Lead him around the cave and used his attack to give us an opening. Let's move!"

Her plan had certainly worked; the blast from Vurshung's attack had made a gaping hole nearly ten feet across. Vurshung was too slow to dodge the fallout, and a giant piece of glass was embedded in his chest. With a terrified look, Vurshung dropped his weapon and fell to the ground.

He didn't stir.

We ran to the hole, and inside we saw both Salvatore and Dawnthorn lying on the ground, covered in shards of glass. Dawnthorn's body was pincushioned with glass, looking much worse off than Salvatore. The old goat had managed to avoid some damage.

"Sal!" Mara screamed, running over to him. Giezha tried to grab her, but Mara slipped out and knelt beside Salvatore. He moaned and rolled to his side, bits of glass falling off him.

"Girls..." he whispered. "Run."

The ground began to shudder as the mosaic crumbled. Its massive stone sections crumbled into a black void behind it.

A guttural roar echoed through the chambers as we felt locked in place. Pair of gigantic red eyes appeared in the void as the mosaic crumbled away to nothing. Green vascular lines trickled towards bright white pupils.

Its stare paralyzed us.

Dawnthorn's body began to shudder as she started laughing. Cackling,

391

more accurately.

"You're too late!" she shrieked, turning her bloody face to us. "We did it, Sal! The world will know the Smite of the Dead Giant! This will make that little Incursion of mine look like child's play! Rise oh mighty Zhol! Rise!"

The two giant eyes grew larger and larger as a sick and twisted smile grew from the void. Grabbing Sal and Mara, I sprinted away with the others. The ground shook as the owner of the red eyes appeared from the void.

We saw a giant skeletal figure with bits of flesh hanging off its bones and a massive hammer in his hands. The monster was impossibly tall, and its hammer was just as large, crackling with green energy. Its posture was the same as the giant standing on top of the mountain in the mosaic. It stood there silently, while its head crested up against the top of the cavern.

Dawnthorn cackled madly as the giant monster observed us placidly. Rusted metal armor and leather banding swayed from its body. Most of the flesh on his body was dissolved but bits and pieces remained.

"It's a shame you stopped us when you did!" Dawnthorn screamed, "We were almost done with the resurrection. A few more minutes, and I could have had him at full strength and the hammer ready to resurrect an endless sea of the undead! But no matter! Khorba will still reward me for my service! Mountains of gold! Continents of coin!" Her arms began to glow green, and the cuts on her body sealed with a hiss.

"After he destroys you, I'll use your souls and an endless horde of moonstones to return him and the hammer to their full strength! And the Great Dragon, Khorba, the Eternal, will complete his mission to destroy the world with his lieutenant at his side! And I'll be rich beyond my wildest dreams! The Incursion is just the beginning!"

As Dawnthorn shrieked, Sal stirred again, moaning in pain. "I'm so sorry."

The giant skeleton made a sound akin to laughter, and I gritted my teeth. "Bit late for apologies, Sal," I growled. "Time for action."

The giant heard what I said, and its hammer slowly rose up into the dark with a massive swing. Glancing around at the others, I noticed that we all had the same expression on our faces. Anger in the face of the impossible. The boss fight was finally here, but instead of getting a bunch of health packs and ammunition before the fight, we got to face all the sub-bosses simultaneously. And now we were totally drained.

"Got any potions?" I asked Giezha, who simply shook her head. "Any tricks, Uli?"

"Nope."

Mara checked her quiver. "I scrounged up some arrows."

I would have laughed at the ridiculousness of it all if it didn't hurt to laugh. "Well, I guess it's time to end this."

Right as the monster began to swing, a bright silver barrier erupted in front of us. The hammer swung down with impossible speed, connecting with the shield, and causing an explosion of light. As we shielded our faces, the bright light sent a shockwave outward, making the whole cavern tremble.

"We're not dead yet," Sal said, gritting his teeth and stretching out his arms. Silvery light emanated from his fingertips, moving towards the shield. Sal looked at me, blood trickling down his nose. "Time for action, Asher. When I release this shield, you and the girls need to fight. You need to win!"

This old goat had some spunk I'll give him that. We nodded as the giant smashed down again.

"On three," I told everyone.

"One...two..." The giant splintered the magical shield with its last swing. "Three!"

I tried to gather every bit of energy I had and burst forward into a sprint. I charged straight at the skeleton, aware that I only had one chance. One chance. I needed to kill this thing before Dawnthorn could make it any stronger.

"Oh no, you don't!"

A bolt of green energy appeared in my periphery, and connected with my shield, exploding it into nothing. Dawnthorn's face was contorted in rage as green cracks of energy splintered down her face and arms. She snarled at me and threw out more disintegration spells.

"You are not ruining my plan, you filthy human!"

Several rocks, arrows, and spells all converged on her as she said that. She nimbly avoided every attack with extreme dexterity while keeping the pressure on me. I ran around, dodging each attack by inches. The giant swung down again, but Sal managed to catch it with his massive shield.

393

"I need to get close!" I shouted, weaving towards the giant whose eyes were trying to follow all of us running in multiple directions.

"Got it!" Uli was right behind me, able to dodge the attacks more easily. Giezha and Mara split apart, trying to keep the giant from attacking all of us at once.

"I'll distract Dawnthorn!"

Sal took on Dawnthorn, his eyes glowing bright green as black spirits swirled around him. Everything inside me wanted to run towards them, but I knew this was our only chance. Sal couldn't hold the giant back forever.

"Whoa!" The giants strike smashed down in front of Uli and me. Jumping out of the way at the last second, I tumbled under the giant's nose. "Uli!" I shouted, looking frantically for her.

I saw Uli clutching onto the top of the hammer Zhol wielded. She balanced on it, unseen by the monster, whose attention was fixed on me.

I could just make out the glint of her white dagger as Uli stared at the giant's face. She was either going for the kill or distracting. Either way, I needed to get up there quick.

"Come on," I growled to myself. "Just a little more!" I stood under the giant, and tried to well up every last bit of energy I had inside of me.

Embers, sparks, kindling, I needed something! I'd never used my nova this many times in a day. Let alone this many times in a single fight.

The tiny flame trickled down my legs and into my aching feet. I wasn't sure I'd ever walk again, but it was too late to worry about that.

The giant looked down at me, and I saw Uli crawling on a bony bit of its wrist. It opened its skeletal jaw several times before making a sound. It almost sounded like a voice. A voice made from rusted metal and sulfur. Its sound stung my ears with a rancid evil that sent a deathly chill down my spine.

"Die..." It spoke, raising its hammer.

As its hand came down, I saw Uli jump off the giant's arm onto its shoulder. Zhol froze in place, its red eyes turning to look at Uli. I needed to jump. Now.

"COME ON!" I screamed, unleashing the last gasp of energy I had.

Unlike my typical explosions of energy, I didn't rocket upward instantaneously. Instead, I felt my body float upwards higher and higher, picking up speed as I went. I felt myself accelerate up into the air, right at the beast's eyeballs. Its attention focused on Uli. I saw the glint of white metal in the air before disappearing into the beast's eye.

"GRAAAAGH!" The monster bellowed out in pain, throwing its head back.

Gripping my sword, I swung down and connected into its skull, dragging along its crown for several feet. It paid no attention to the shallow cut as it dropped the hammer onto the ground. The earth quaked underneath as it grabbed at Uli with its free hand.

Uli jumped up to avoid the swipe. In midair, she pulled out a length of rope and used it to hook onto the finger bone of the monster, going along for a ride.

"Asher!" I heard her scream. "Kill it!"

I stood up, ready to pull the sword out, but the giant yanked its head back, causing me to fall. Desperately, I grabbed onto a crack in the giant's skull, hanging on with a single hand. Uli floated up along the rope and saw me barely hanging on. Her eyes went wide in horror as the giant made an evil chuckle.

"Uli!" I shouted, seeing her fly into the air.

"Die..."

With its other hand, the giant swatted down on Uli, who was helpless, floating in the air. I screamed out wordlessly as the giant's hand cast a shadow over her. She closed her eyes, and time slowed down to a torturous crawl.

No. No. No. No! This couldn't happen! No!

With my left hand, I stretched out to her desperately.

"Shield!" I screamed, flooding my arm with all the mana I could muster. The specific rune sequence was fuzzy, but it didn't fucking matter! I had to remember. I HAD TO!

"SHIELD! SHIELD! SHIELD!"

For a single moment, for a single, glorious moment, the exact runes needed for the shield spell appeared in my mind. As I let out a final guttural scream, every drop of mana in my body came racing out of my hand to Uli.

Blood poured down my nose as I squeezed the magic out of my body. The giant's hand descended upon her as my protective red bubble flew through the air.

SMACK!

Uli rocketed to the ground like a meteor, crashing into the ground. When I looked down, I lost all feeling in my arms. She was crumpled in a heap. The translucent, red shield chipped and cracked all around her. When I looked down, I also saw Giezha and Mara flanking Sal, splitting their attacks between Dawnthorn and the giant.

Sal was locked in combat with Dawnthorn in front of where Uli had crashed. The giant's eyes glazed over to the battle, and grabbed for the hammer,

"Hey, ugly!" I screamed down towards its ear canal. "I'm right here!"

Pulling with all my might, I yanked myself up and pulled the sword out of the giant's skull. I felt its big bony head shift as I ran towards its eye socket. Uli managed to severely piss that thing off with her dagger. I wondered what a thrust with my sword would do to it.

"Pest..."

Jumping down, I landed on the bottom of its nasal cavity. Its massive eyes stared at me emotionlessly. The more I stared into its eyes, the angrier I got.

All this death, destruction, and treachery were committed for him. Resurrecting this stupid lieutenant to some asshole dragon trying to take over the world.

Fuck that dragon! Fuck this giant!

"Fuck you!" I screamed, charging towards the same eye Uli had attacked.

I slashed at its eyeball with a swing, connecting right where the pupil met the iris. And I went straight through it. As I completed the arc of my slash, it felt like I had gone through nothing and fell into its eye socket. Turning around, I couldn't stand up inside the socket and had to crouch. I suddenly realized red-eye wasn't there. It was just an illusion.

A false weak point.

"Fool..."

Before I could grab onto anything, the giant skeleton leaned its head forward, and I started to fall. And fall. Looking down, I saw the others, pinched into a tight group as Dawnthorn sent blast after blast of magic. Unable to stop my fall, I watched as the ground raced towards me. I could only close my eyes.

Crunch.

Crunching, snapping, and breaking filled my ears as I bounced like a rock hitting the ground. My vision went to total fuzz, and I felt blood trickle out the side of my ear.

My arms and legs broke the fall, and I managed to tuck my head in at the last moment.

"Fuckin' hell," I managed to groan

I was in so much pain that my brain didn't know what to do. Shock I think they call it.

"Giezha! Asher's down! We need a shield!" Mara called out, lights flashing all around us. "Guys, we—Argh!"

Something heavy hit Mara, and I heard her hit the ground beside me. "Mara!"

I needed to get up.

I managed to open my eyes. Mara and Uli were both on the ground, barely holding onto consciousness. Sal and Giezha were overwhelmed by Dawnthorn's relentless barrage of spells and attacks.

As I pushed myself up with my unbroken left arm, Dawnthorn summoned a giant hammer in the air. It smashed through Giezha's shield with a single swing. Giezha landed on her head while Sal was knocked on his back.

"What a pathetic scroll, Nightstride," Dawnthorn taunted. "You were a third-rate sorceress with fourth-rate talent," Dawnthorn said as she walked away. "All the potential in the world... wasted. Kill them, Zhol, oh Great One! And I shall complete your resurrection."

The giant looked at me as I struggled to stand, pushing up with my chipped and broken sword. It cocked its head curiously.

Uli, Mara, and Giezha groaned in pain as I limped forward. None of them were able to get up. I looked at them all.

Broken. Defeated. Completely defenseless. Scowling, I turned back to the giant and Dawnthorn.

"Her name's Giezha Nightstrike," I grunted, coughing up blood. "And you haven't won yet, you stupid bitch."

My sword dragged against the broken stone floor, sparking and crackling as I struggled to carry it. My right arm and leg were deadweight, completely broken beyond hope. Dawnthorn looked at me, shocked I was breathing. Let alone standing. The green lines on her face arched with

397

magical energy as she eyed me up and down.

"You refuse to quit, Merrick," she said, nonplussed. "I'll give you that. Of course, the second I sent some of my experiments to attack your little moon elf girlfriend, I suppose that guaranteed you wouldn't stop until you killed me."

I coughed up blood, which cleared my throat enough to speak again. "That was you, eh? I guess I'll let Kiersa know after I cut your fucking head off."

The giant looked at me, moving its head to the other side.

"Stubborn..."

"Asher," Sal struggled. "Please, don't."

I gripped my sword with one hand and put it before me, beckoning Dawnthorn to duel me.

"Mara, Uli, Giezha..." I said, seeing them all struggling to stand and fight. Each holding onto their weapons stubbornly. When I looked at them, their eyes were stung with tears, unable to hold their fearsome expressions. "I just... I wish I..." My voice caught in my throat.

No time for long speeches.

"Thanks."

"Asher!"

"Stop!"

"Don't!"

Ignoring them, I turned back to Dawnthorn and the giant. She had a sadistic smile tracing across her lips.

"Not backing down?" she asked.

Shifting my stance, I smiled. Waiting for oblivion. "I'm just getting started."

I charged, and Dawnthorn killed me in a flash of brilliant, purple light.

Chapter 36

Everything was pitch black. Silent. It was a familiar sensation.

I was back in that infinite void of nothingness. The non-existence that haunted me whenever it was too quiet for too long. I floated in nothing as nothing. At least, I was doing that until I opened my eyes. A person was standing over me with their hand stretched out. They had a familiar face, narrow and wrinkled, surrounding a pair of rainbow-colored eyes and golden pupils.

"Gathos," I murmured. He had a sad smile on his face. I accepted his helping hand and stood up, facing him. "What's going..."

Next to him was a large oval cut into the infinite void. On the other side, I could see the girls. They were beaten, bruised, and crying their eyes out. All of them huddled over someone lying on the ground.

"No," I groaned as Uli pounded her fist on my chest inside the portal. I turned to Gathos, my eyes pleading. "Come on!"

Gathos sighed and clapped my shoulder. "I suppose those who hold a light for the lost will sometimes be the first snuffed out."

I felt a lump in my chest, seeing my corpse on the ground. My skin was ghostly white, and there was a hole in my chest the size of a ping-pong ball.

"I thought I did it right this time," I said, tears streaming down my face. "I really did."

Gathos squeezed my shoulders again and turned me to him. His face was plastered with worry. "You did do it right, Asher! You really did. You fought for what you believed in. Fought for what was right. Fought for the people you cared for. It just..."

"Wasn't enough." I hung my head in shame as the giant skeleton lifted its hand, ready to smash my crew to bits. I looked on in horror as Sal, barely held together in a single piece at this point, threw every bit of mana he had into a shield spell. "They're going to die, Gathos!"

Gathos closed the portal with a gesture from his hand and frowned. "They are already dead, Asher. I'm sorry." He gestured for me to walk with him along the void's invisible path. "In the void, time does not exist. Whatever has happened, is happening, or will happen, does not matter here. We are outside of this thing you call time."

My stomach turned itself into a knot so tight it was about to split. "They're already gone?"

Gathos looked at me and nodded. I instantly fell to my knees, my legs buckling beneath me. I felt numb. Numb to everything around me. Noises faded into the back of my head, high-pitched and so impossibly faint they could not be real.

I balled up my fists so tight they began to bleed. This could not be real. This could not be real! Tears streamed down my eyes as I cried into my bleeding palms.

"It's not true!" I screamed at Gathos, my eyes blinded in a fury. "You plucked me from another world after I died to save the lost!" I got up in Gathos' face and pointed in the direction of where the portal had been. "I was supposed to save them!"

"Asher, please."

"No!" I screamed, shoving away the hand he tried to place on me. "No! I refuse to accept this! I can't fucking die right now. Fuck that, fuck this, and fuck you!"

I ran back towards where the portal had been, falling into the void. When I landed, I was next to Gathos again. He gave me a look of concern, which I returned with a glower. I shook with rage as I looked at this so-called god. This bastard had plucked me from my afterlife only to have my heart broken again! Fuck him!

"Take. Me. Back." I said, trembling. "You said I needed to achieve my potential, so let me do it!"

Gathos gave me a look of pity.

"I'm sorry, Asher, but I can't. It is time for your soul to return to where I borrowed you from."

"Why?" I screamed. "Why can't you just take me back!? You already did it!"

"Asher, it doesn't work like that. There are so many differ—"

WHACK!

400

Before he could finish speaking, I socked him in the eye as hard as possible.

Gathos stumbled back, clutching the left side of his face. His eyes burned like fiery suns for a moment as he rubbed his face.

"You punched me."

I ran up and tried to punch him again. My fist made contact with his face, but the momentum stopped immediately. He brushed my hand away and looked at me, nonplussed. So, I punched him again. And again. And again. Each blow landed with absolutely zero impact.

"Asher," he said, again brushing my punches away. "I'm sorry, but I can't take you back."

"Fuck that!" I screamed, desperately. "You're a fucking god, Gathos! You already did it!"

"Asher!" Gathos shouted, grabbing me by the shoulders. He did not squeeze me, but it was impossible to move. He looked me in the eyes, the rainbow of color swirling around, his golden irises wobbling. "I. Can't. It was different when I brought you to Echo Veil."

I struggled but couldn't move at all.

"I'm truly sorry, Asher, but I can't! Your soul has already traveled from one world to another. And besides, you came here through a conduit in this world. You crossed from one world to another. You must cross over to another world for your soul to stay intact."

"Intact?"

He let me go and looked at me sadly. "Asher, what you're asking for is not a miracle. It is a miracle of miracles. If I failed, your soul would be ripped to shreds. No ocean to return to."

I arched my eyebrow and gave him a look of disbelief.

"And? If you're telling me it's possible, I'll do it!"

Gathos furrowed his brow and snapped his fingers, reopening the portal. I looked and saw the shield cracking under the weight of Zhol's attacks.

"Your soul will have to cross over into its own world, essentially inverting. If this fails, you will not only not exist, but you will also have NEVER existed. Your life, your accomplishments, your relationships, all of them, gone."

I looked at the girls and Sal, all of them trying to protect my corpse, unleashing the last of their strength in their final stand. Dawnthorn lazily

401

flicked her wrist, absorbing their desperate spells and attacks.

As I looked at them, my mind raced with everything we'd been through in the short time I'd known them. When I thought of them dying here, it made me sick. As for the risks involved...

"Do it," I said calmly. "You want me to be a hero? You want me to reach that potential? Save the lost for you? I can't do it standing here. Bring me back and I'll help you guide the lost."

Gathos looked on at the scene and shook his head, sighing. "Even if your soul isn't shredded into oblivion, your soul will likely become damaged beyond repair. The soul ocean may not accept you. Reincarnation would be impossible."

I shrugged indifferently.

He chuckled and raised his hands in the air with one last look.

"Alrighty, one last piece of advice though..."

Suddenly, a hurricane-force gale started blowing in my face. My equilibrium started going haywire as I felt the world tilt upwards. I looked down, and suddenly the portal back was underneath me. I stood frozen in the air as the wind whipped against my face.

"Asher!" Gathos shouted, his face a mixture of worry and bravado. "I didn't give you the power of super strength. I gave you the ability to unleash your potential! You decide what your potential is! Your possibilities are limitless!"

I looked at Gathos, covering my face with my arms. His words clicked something in my mind, and I nodded, understanding what he meant.

I hurtled down toward the portal, directly over my dead body. Hurtling towards my second-second chance, I remembered my life before coming here. The life I failed to live. The life I'd never live again.

As I crossed the portal, I felt myself become incorporeal, flying straight into my body. Reaching my hand out, I touched my chest, suddenly blind. I couldn't move anything. My body felt like absolute hell. Blood was pouring out of me, and I heard voices. Far away voices that echoed in my head.

"Asher!" It was Uli. I could feel her bent over on my chest, sobbing as she tried to do something for me. "Asher, please don't die!"

"Uli, it's too late!" Mara screamed, miles away. "We can't save him!"

Giezha's frustrated grunts came next as the sound of magic colliding in the air pinged off in the distance. "A little help here!"

Uli pressed something into my chest, sobbing away. She was trying to stop the bleeding from the hole in my chest. Her trembling hands clumsily as she tried to stitch me up in the pandemonium going on around her.

"She's failing," came the voice of Gathos, clear as day. "She's going to keep trying to save you, and it'll cost the girl her life."

"No." My voice came from somewhere outside of my body. It was floating somewhere while I was locked in my body.

"Here's your chance Asher," Gathos informed me. "Your chance to put your soul back in your body and save the day. But if you can't do it, that's it. Now open your eyes."

Following his command, my eyes shot open. I looked up at Uli, staring at me with tears flowing down her scarred and bleeding face. She didn't react to my eyes opening and kept trying to perform medicine. Her confidence and thirst for life replaced by terror and woe.

"Please, please, please."

I couldn't move any of my limbs or say anything. It was like I was being held in place by something. I tried to move my body, but I was locked in place. As I struggled, a crash rang out.

"Sal!"

The top of the shield had been pierced by the giant's hammer, knocking Sal to the ground. Mara ran over to him, shouting something indistinct. As she did, a magical bolt hit her in the arm, sending her spinning to the ground.

"No!" I screamed from my place of nothingness.

Uli's eyes shot up as I screamed, and I looked around.

"Asher?" she whispered.

Another bolt of light, and I saw Giezha go down.

"No!"

"Asher?"

Suddenly, everything was on fire. I felt my essence forcing itself into contact with my corpse. It was like two magnets of the same pole trying to push themselves together.

"Come on!" I screamed, looking at my stubborn body in a blind fury. "I'm not fucking done yet!"

I lurched towards my body with all my willpower, imagining myself clawing into my own skin. As I did, I felt a shooting pain in my arms.

Claw marks appeared on my body as I tried to will myself back to life. Gripping even harder, I tried to pull my soul back to the body, feeling my hands, arms, and everything around me vibrate.

"What the—"

Light began to pour from the slices in my body, and the harder I pulled, the slices and cracks in my skin grow deeper. My skin turned bright orange, and the golden light had bits of glitter floating up into the air.

I could hear Dawnthorn's disgusting voice off to the side. "What's going on? Why is his body doing that?"

Her existence infuriated me, and I pulled harder and harder, sinking my grip as tight as possible.

"FUCK!" I screamed in agony as I stubbornly ripped into my body, feeling my soul shred and tear. I'd have doubled over if I had been in my actual body, vomiting in agony.

But I wasn't. I wasn't in my body. I wasn't doubled over in pain.

I was a stubborn son of a bitch willing to risk his entire existence for one last chance. So, fuck it.

What's pain beyond recognition to someone who already floated in the abyss of death?

What's the possibility of never existing to somebody who didn't exist when they were alive?

What's the fucking point of any of this shit if you're not going to risk it all?

"COME ON!"

The entire arena shook as everybody looked up and around, hearing a furious ghostly wail from all directions. My body glowed brilliantly with golden light and searing heat. With one final scream, I threw my soul into my body with a furious roar.

"GRAAARRGH!" I screamed, jumping up from the ground as the ground instantly became still.

Still holding onto my sword, my chest heaved as I looked around at the shocked expressions of everyone still conscious. My body was covered in long splintering cracks that glowed gold and orange.

The sensation I had in my body was something far beyond adrenaline. Far beyond the sensation I usually got when I unleashed my nova ability.

I felt dangerous and all-powerful.

404

I felt like a god.

Looking down, I saw Uli's shocked expression.

"Asher," she said, almost too stunned to speak. "You—"

I gently placed a finger on her lips and shushed her. As I touched her face, her wounds instantly began to heal. The others stirred awake, joining Uli in looks of shock and awe at my resurrection.

"Let's get you all healed up," I said, remembering the healing spell from Giezha's book a few months ago.

The runes danced off my hand, and a massive stream of energy flowed into the girls and Sal. All their wounds closed, and they looked as good as new.

"What are you?"

I turned around and saw Dawnthorn looking at me in horror. Her eyes were wide, and her teeth bared, revealing a chipped incisor.

"Me?" I asked, sizing up her and the giant skeleton whose red eyes could only show a look of mild interest. "I'm Asher fucking Merrick. I've died twice because of greedy bastards like yourself."

Dawnthorn sneered but didn't move.

I gripped my sword and imagined it covered in a golden flame as the blade ignited. With everything I was capable of now, I could make happen. I was tasting my potential like never before. I looked at Dawnthorn, my eyes wide and my muscles tense.

"I've been sent on a mission from the Gathos, the King of the Lost. A mission to save people like my crew and destroy people like you!"

The lines on my body glowed brighter as I felt a surge of energy through my entire body. Before, it'd felt like an explosion propelling out of my body. But now, I was the explosion.

Like the inside of a star, producing infinite amounts of energy in a ball of nuclear fusion. It was amazing! It was maddening.

"And I'm the motherfucker you couldn't kill!" I screamed as the ground beneath me began to crumble. "You think I'm just gonna roll over and die because you want to work for some limp-dicked dragon sleeping on a pile of gold!?"

Dawnthorn recoiled at my words, and the skeleton growled.

"Die..."

I looked at the skeleton and motioned for him to bring it on!

"Fuck you! You think I'm gonna die for them?" I frothed, pointing to my compatriots. "No, I'm gonna live for them! With them! You hear me?"

My sword exploded in a burst of power, and the golden flames turned into a brilliant golden light of pure energy. A star molded into a blade. I looked at it and knew: I was gonna fuck them up.

"I'm just getting started, mother fuckers!" I spat, pointing to the ground in front of me. "Get your ass over here! I'm gonna fuck you up!"

The skeleton let out another growl and began to swing right as I reached my zenith.

Chapter 37

Xaliasday Dawn, 14th of Extrin, Year 678, 4th Age

I felt the wind rush as the giant's swing careened toward me. Time slowed to a crawl as I watched its attack. The beams of light shifted and danced along the cracks of my skin, and I felt it all rush up my arm. The unfathomable depths of my energy churned in desperate desire to unleash itself.

"Finally," I whispered.

The giant hammer swung down, the air current pitching a deathly whistle.

"Die..."

The attack smacked straight at me, crushing the ground to a fine powder. I heard the girls scream in terror while Dawnthorn let out a deathly cackle.

"Fool! You fool! What idiot bastard comes back to life with such bravado, only to die just as quick? Ha! You spoke so high and mighty for yourself, only to..."

The ground shook underneath my feet. I looked up at the hammer, stopped by my outstretched right hand. My sword had instantly crumbled under the impact.

Slowly, the hammer rose in the air as I cast a flying spell on myself. I remembered seeing it in a scroll Giezha was studying several months ago and figured I could remember the runes if I tried hard enough.

Pushing the hammer up with my hand, I felt a tiny trickle of resistance from the skeleton's shaky grip. My eyes glowed bright gold with malice as I rose out of the crater and into the air; fingers sunk deep into the face of the hammer.

"You were saying?" I said, staring at Dawnthorn's shocked face.

"Impossible..."

407

"For you."

With a brilliant flash, the energy in my hand exploded out in an actual supernova of flames.

BOOOOOM!

I felt the stone turn into glass before shattering in a thousand shards. The skeleton stumbled back, and its red eyes widened as it began to fall.

"That was for my sword."

I needed a sword with mine gone. But how could I? Wait! Giezha summoned a sword! I floated in the air, feeling my mind run a thousand times more efficiently, remembering the sequence of runes Giezha had used to summon her weapon. A detail so miniscule, it was like remembering the individual grains of sand from the beach with Kiersa.

"Summon!" I screamed, the overflowing in my body exploding like a web around me.

"Bastard..."

The mana congealed into a gigantic chain, with links the size of my sword's pommel. Good enough. I whipped the chain link around the skeleton's skull. Its metal links dug into the thick bone, crackling and splintering. I pulled myself toward the skeleton with a yank, jerking its head toward me.

The giant was much faster than it had any right to be. I felt another rush of air. Underneath me, its clenched fist flew up. I didn't have enough time to adjust, and it made contact.

FWOOSH!

I was flying in the air, straight into the ceiling. Rocketing into the ceiling, I crashed into the rock, burrowing my body several feet into the ground. The mountain shook as I felt the hundreds of thousands of tons of granite shudder above me.

The warm flow of blood trickled along the back of my head. I was as durable as I'd ever been right now, but even that had limits.

"Fucker."

Clenching my fist, I popped the fractured bones in my fingers in place. The sickening crack and pop of their resetting sounded like the rocks grinding against each other around me. Shoving my elbow out, I smashed a section of the rocks out. I wasn't letting go of this fucking chain.

With a yank, I dislodged myself and kicked off the ceiling, right above that stupid skeleton. Its red eyes glowed, and the light trailed its movement.

The fucker was bobbing and weaving. With another massive punch, it was ready to do some more damage to the fly buzzing around it.

"Not this time, fucker!" I shouted, unsummoning the chain.

My acceleration continued in a straight line. What the little bit of momentum I lost, I had a perfect trajectory. I flew right through the giant's fingers.

FWOOSH!

The giant's left hand tried to block but only managed to shield a small portion of its face. Another blast of fire from my hand exploded at full force. The flames lit the room up like a sun, vaporizing the dust in the air around me.

My skin stung at the conflicting forces of flames cut against my skin. The bright golden flows of light began to dim as I unleashed a torrent of flames larger than the first. But that was fine. I didn't need this to last forever. Just long enough.

"HAAAH!"

Throwing my fist forward, I punched the same eye of the giant I had mistakenly climbed into before. I flew right through the illusory red eye into the back of its socket, glowing like a firefly in the starless sky.

My fist connected with the decayed and rotted bone. And it shattered.

Exploding out the back, I flew out in a hail of bone and the few remainders of its brain matter. I impacted the ground like a meteor. I turned my head to the side and watched as the skeleton fell to the ground, its arms stretched to the sky it never saw.

The final words of the giant were much softer than expected.

"Impressive..."

Zhol fell to the ground, hitting the mosaic it had first climbed from.

The sheer force of the monstrous skeleton's fall was the first note in a crescendo. The ground quaked again, slow and softly at first. But then it grew stronger. It grew faster. It grew louder.

"We need to go!" I shouted to the girls, dodging the stalactites falling from the ceiling.

The girls' faces all wore the shock as Dawnthorn, but they quickly shook it off as the ground underneath crumbled. Grabbing Sal, I healed him up, getting him off his feet and out of the other's hair. Mara led us up the stairs, weaving in and out of the falling debris.

"Asher!"

An arc of green light flew past my face, exploding the stairs before us. Dawnthorn's wand was outstretched in her shaking hand—blood vessels popping like red vines in her pure white eyes.

Dawnthorn gritted her teeth as she scowled at us. "You fuckers! You motherfuckers! How dare you! Khorba shall rule all! And you will not stop me!"

Uli turned, holding her knife out at Dawnthorn. "Yes, we will." She looked at Mara, Giezha, and me. In unison, we nodded, ready to end this.

Once and for all.

I looked down at Sal's body, and he whispered softly. "Go on Asher, this old goat'll be fine."

I placed Sal down behind a fallen piece of debris and took my place with the girls. Dawnthorn stood there, coiled like a snake, cornered by four enemies. But there's a saying about a cornered animal.

"Die!"

Dawnthorn tried to feign attacking me by looking in my direction while attacking Mara. The spell zipped over to her, but Giezha caught it with a last-second shield spell. At the same time, Uli charged forward with her white dagger.

Uli sliced at Dawnthorn from underneath while I shot a firebolt at her. Giezha followed up with a fireball of her own behind Dawnthorn. As Dawnthorn jumped back, deftly dodging Uli's attack, she threw her hands out, sending two spectral walls in front and behind her.

The spells exploded in massive Fireballs against the shield, forcing Uli to jump away. We leapt forward, charging at Dawnthorn through the rain of debris. Mara was the first to arrive, dodging under a spell and slicing up at Dawnthorn.

"Shit!" Dawnthorn swore as she caught the sword with a pair of glowing blue hands. "Been a while since I had to use these," she mocked. With a flick of her wrist, Mara went flying backward.

I grabbed Mara and spun her in the air, throwing her momentum back at Dawnthorn.

Uli threw a series of daggers at Dawnthorn, which she swatted out of the air. Running around, I tried to flank Dawnthorn and slashed downward

410

with my sword. Dawnthorn hissed as she threw out another shield, but my attack crashed right through the shield. Despite this, Dawnthorn's expression didn't change.

"Pissant," she mocked, pushing my sword away with the palm of her protected hands.

The force of my attack threw me into the ground, burying my sword into the stone.

I felt Dawnthorn's presence behind me, but before she could stab me in the back of the head, she was forced back on the defensive.

With a single mighty grab, I yanked the glowing sword out of the ground, which had turned to molten magma around the blade.

"Come on!" Mara shouted, slicing and dicing after Dawnthorn.

I watched as Uli and Mara failed to touch Dawnthorn. Phantom versions of her appeared as Uli and Mara repeatedly swung, hitting nothing but air.

Giezha was trying to aim a spell in all of the chaos. "Asher!" she called out to me. "Throw me in the air!"

I looked at her like she was crazy but didn't argue. Rushing over, I grabbed Giezha by the waist, careful not to throw her through the ceiling.

"Nice change of pace," Giezha said with a wink. "We should try something like this again."

I just grinned as I threw her directly over others. Giezha soared into the air, and I readied myself for a burst. Seeing Giezha reach the apex of her flight, I exploded into a blur of speed. Before anyone could notice, I grabbed Uli and Mara.

"What the?"

BOOOM!

Giezha unleashed a massive blast of lightning and ice shards the size of tree trunks. Dawnthorn disappeared under the deluge as the light flashed from the electric shocks. Mara and Uli both jumped off my shoulders.

"Hot, hot, hot!" Mara hissed.

As Giezha floated down, the rumbling of the cave stopped. The last few crackles of electricity arced around the ice shards, and everything fell still.

Our haggard breathing slowed, and we looked at each other. The cavern had turned into a gory battlefield strewn with the bodies of the bastards who had betrayed us. The only visible evidence of the giant skeleton were its hand and part of its arms sticking out of the hole it had fallen into.

411

The world became silent around us. No scurrying rats. No drips of water from below. Only the sounds of our breathing as we stood there, staring at the column of ice shards. However, something didn't feel right.

Something felt off. We could sense Dawnthorn. And just as I was about to open my mouth, she confirmed our suspicions with a massive explosion.

"I will not be stopped by whelps like you!" Dawnthorn shrieked in a red shroud of magical energy. "You will never again feel the warmth of the sun! The light of day will never touch your cursed skin! I will bury you in this tomb of your own creation!"

Beams of bubbling red magic shot off in every direction. The second it made contact with anything, chain explosions rattled off. The entire mountain was going to collapse under the collective force of her desperate attack. She wasn't trying to attack us anymore. She was simply going to bury us with the mountain. Even if it meant she was going down too.

Suddenly, the god-like energy I felt coursing in my veins didn't feel as god-like anymore.

I strained, feeling the energy seep out of me. "We need to get out of here!" I threw up a shield around us, blocking Dawnthorn's explosive beams.

Mara hunkered behind the shield, picking up a few loose arrows. "Nobody's arguing, but how do you plan to do that?"

Red light streaked past my face, blasting my shield and one of my hands. The shield cracked and splintered, leaving a hole in our defense. Concentrating my dimming flow of mana, I repaired my shield. My hand was surprisingly okay.

"I have a plan," I said, staring at the dying red star in front of me. "Attack."

Pushing the shield ahead of me, I charged at Dawnthorn. Explosions rattled around as her last frantic attack battered my shield. I saw the light grow dimmer and dimmer as I expanded my shield wider and taller.

Soon, almost all of Dawnthorn's red beams were hitting my shield as the lights faded in my arms and legs. The overflowing mana closed, and I began to feel my body drain.

Every step felt harder and harder as I pushed the shield forward. Before, it was weightless. But now, it felt like I was pushing an elephant.

"I'll take the front!" I shouted, feeling my shield turn brittle. "When you see an opening, hit her with everything you've got!"

The girls had fallen behind, but Mara could almost keep pace. I gave her one last look and a devilish grin.

"Asher, if you die on me twice in one day, I'll kill you!"

Boom! Boom! BOOM!

Snapping my attention back to Dawnthorn, I saw my shield crumble to the ground. Almost all of my mana was gone as I absorbed everything I could.

The telltale fatigue seeped into my muscles. Ignoring it, I grasped for my sword, which was still a bright energy beam. At least I had that going for me. When the final piece of the shield crumbled in front of me, I gripped with both hands and attacked.

"Raaargh!" I swung downward at the bubbling mass of magic surrounding Dawnthorn.

The concentrated beam of energy sliced through like a hot knife through butter. I saw Dawnthorn's hand reach up and push against the blade as it cascaded downward. As she did, the explosive red energy melted around Dawnthorn. Her whole body was singed and covered in scars and fresh cuts.

"Giezha did a number on you," I mocked as I went for a horizontal slice at her head.

Dawnthorn said nothing as she dodged in and out of my attacks. In a flash, she punched me in the solar plexus. It felt like she hit me with a baseball bat, and all the wind got sucked out of me.

Gritting my teeth, I held my ground and swung again. And again. And again. Every single attack missed, and was followed by a devastating counterattack. A throat punch. A blast of fire to my arm. An icicle in my shoulder.

No matter how much damage she did, I stood there. Defiant. The last bit of the gift that Gathos' gave me swirled around in my core. And I wasn't going to use it for one big punch or flashy attack. No, I was going to use it to stand in front of this stupid bitch and take whatever she could dish out.

Swing. Counter. Kick. Counter. Every single blow hit harder than the last, tempting me to quit.

"Fuck you." I spat out, blood spewing from my busted lip. "I'm right here, bitch."

413

As I said that, a giant boulder fell from the ceiling cracking right over my skull. My vision went blurry for a second, but I shook it off. Dawnthorn stared at me in terrified bewilderment before turning back to her boiling hatred.

"Die already!" she screamed, her red aura glowing.

Jackpot.

"No."

Gripping my sword like a baseball bat, I swung at her from the side. The opaque red light obscured her vision, and she hissed in pain as my attack missed its mark. Explosive beams shot in every direction, battering my body like magical grenades. The skin on my body peeled and cracked as blisters of blood exploded. Although I tapped into every bit of my gift, it was barely enough to hold on.

With one final swing, I twisted and swung down like I was chopping wood. A beam connected with my chest, eviscerating my remnants of armor. My skin was singed, and I felt the muscle and sinew bubble up from the intense heat.

"Finally," Dawnthorn breathed, holding my sword with both hands in the air.

"It's over," I finished for her, coughing blood.

"What?"

THWIP! THWIP! THWIP!

A trio of arrows pierced through her throat from behind.

SHINK!

A knife pierced through her chest from behind.

Zap!

A finely tuned bolt of electricity hit her in the head.

I looked around and saw each of the girls in their positions. Mara had her bow outstretched as she appeared from behind the giant's hand. Giezha stood from atop the stairs, her staff still crackling with electricity. And Uli, with her dagger piercing Dawnthorn, stood right behind her.

Dawnthorn's hands went slack, and the bright white of her eyes dulled. A last desperate gurgle of life breathed out. Unable to resist, I flourished my fading sword.

Shhk!

Dawnthorn's head fell to the ground, sizzling from instant cauterization.

With that final attack, my blade faded away into nothing. I felt the familiar grip of the pommel filled my hand. Uli gave me a crooked look and a smile.

"Seriously?"

My breathing was deep and ragged. "Yeah... No way I'm letting her come back."

Falling onto my butt, I groaned as a lifetime of soreness instantly washed over me. The others ran over, along with Sal following behind. I laid my head on the ground, past caring about any potential betrayals or last-second enemies. I'd come back from the dead, endured near-fatal wounds, and got the killing blow.

"If Sal starts to betray us, please just shoot him," I mumbled, closing my eyes.

The familiar sound of Sal's hooves on the ground grew louder and louder. I sensed his presence and opened my eyes. He simply smiled and extended a hand to me. Unsure at first, I grasped it, and I felt a powerful surge of mana.

"Whoa!" I shouted.

Energy surged through me, and the drained sensation left my body. I was still incredibly sore and tired, but I didn't have the nauseous fatigue anymore.

I stood up and looked around at the others. We looked around with stupid grins plastered on our faces. We had done it. We won!

"So, now what?"

That question lingered on everybody's face as we sat down by the stairs. None of us said anything for several minutes as we struggled to process everything. Finally, it was Uli who spoke up first.

"Sal, they didn't happen to have a hoard of treasure down here, did they?"

I couldn't help but laugh at the hopeful tone in her voice. She stuck her tongue out at me while Sal thought.

"You know..." he said, twirling his beard, "They did! And I know where it is."

Chapter 38

Xaliasday Morning, 14th of Extrin, Year 678, 4th Age

After resting for a little bit longer, we followed Sal up the stairs and down a passageway. It was thin and narrow, forcing Giezha to do a squat sidestep the whole way. I doubt anybody but Dawnthorn had access to it.

"When they caught me, they used their treasure room as a makeshift prison. They'd been skimming off the top of the guilds for years, hording wealth." Sal explained.

Eventually, we found ourselves in a small circular room with white spires reaching up to the ceiling. The room was roughly the size of the main room of the Silver Cup Inn.

Tables overflowed with scattered papers and melted wax candle; chests filled with various pieces of gold and silver littered the floor. And in the very center of the room was a silver and black chest.

"Ten gold to the person that opens the chest," I joked, sure that it'd be booby-trapped.

Sal fished around one of his robe pockets. "As it just so happens—"

"Got it!" Uli said, kicking open the chest. To my surprise, nothing happened, and the beautiful half-goblin smirked, blowing me a kiss. "I'll just take that out of your split."

We spent the next several hours combing through the hoard of treasure. Altogether there was about fifteen thousand gold in coins and a few scrolls and potions inside the room.

Giezha and Sal were able to identify a few of the potions of giant strength and fire breath—perfect for imbuing those abilities into a gigantic undead skeleton.

Inside the chest was a couple of other items. One was a bag that managed to hold an incredible amount of stuff inside it. We managed to fill the entire bag with all the coins we had found in the room.

"Dibs on the coin purse," Uli said triumphantly, holding more money than any of us had ever seen in our lives.

"Fine," Mara said, holding a bright green chainmail shirt. "Dibs on the Fadril armor."

"Fadril?" I asked, looking over a broken glass ball.

"Super durable but light armor," Mara explained, slipping it on. "Fits like a glove!"

"How about you, Giezha?" I asked, picking over the items. "Safe to assume you'll be taking all of the magic scrolls and potions?"

The clatter of glass against each other told me everything I needed to know as Giezha filled her backpack with an endless stream of funky-colored potions.

When I got to the bottom of the chest, there was a handle. The wall next to me shuddered when I pulled it, before sliding away. Everybody looked at me and then into the hole in the wall. Upon inspection, we found a massive horde of silver bars stamped with the symbol of Sylo on them. It was the missing silver from our original mission.

The next discovery made me let out a low whistle.

"I think we found the missing moonstone, guys." A seemingly endless supply of moonstones filled the cave. Their pearlescent white glow dimly lit the room. I shuddered as I stared at what could have been millions of gold worth of moonstone.

Even a single moonstone was powerful enough to augment magic to unbridled levels. I'd experienced this first-hand when fighting Dawnthorn. She was virtually unstoppable one-on-one.

In the wrong hands, this could create an army that could take over the continent. Maybe even the world? I shook my head, tossing those thoughts away. It wasn't my place to judge or to ponder. Frankly, I didn't care about any of that.

The final item that we found while cleaning out the treasure hoard was a piece of rope. At first, I figured it was just a discarded piece of equipment, but everyone's eyes shined like diamonds at its silver and brown threads.

"I never thought I'd see one in real life!" Mara exclaimed.

"I'd give my staff for the chance to make my own," Giezhaa mumbled, caressing the rope. "Homeland Rope." Without even looking for me to

417

prompt her, Giezha explained, "This can take you home and back from anywhere in the world. A single thread can take a month to produce."

"Any idea on where it'll take us?" I asked, fearing the possibility of winding up at a different cult's hideout."

"I do," Sal said, putting it back in his hands. "It's what they used to kidnap me. I'd been tracking Mhurren and Mick on and off for the past few months, but every time I was about to find them, they wound up back in Naled. It should take us right home."

Not bad for a bit of rope. "What do we do with the stuff we can't bring with us?" I asked, pointing to the horde of moonstones.

Uli was the first to answer. "We bring back as much as we can and show it to the council. If we can show proof that we returned the silver and the moonstones, they'll have to believe us."

"Especially if we can point them to where it had been hiding all this time," Giezha added.

When she said that, I couldn't help but laugh. I had forgotten we were wanted criminals.

We gathered everything into Uli's Space Bag and still had enough room to carry a substantial amount of moonstones and silver bars. Now that we had the items and a way to get home, we had to figure out what to do once we got there.

There was no telling how long we had been in the caves, and just appearing in the middle of the night wasn't a great idea. Especially if that rope transported us to the guildhall.

Even if Dawnthorn was dead, she was sure to have warned the whole guild about us. They would think that we broke in trying to kill her or something.

"We need a plan," I said, racking my brain. "But what do we do?"

"Can't walk through the front gate," Uli yawned, flipping a coin. "I guarantee that it's kill on sight with all of us. Especially you, Sal."

Sal pursed his lips, thinking of an idea of his own. "I don't suppose we could show them the bodies. No, they would just think we killed them and that was that."

"Be hard to plead our case of innocence with a bunch of bodies," Giezha said, threatening to doze off on the floor. Her mana had been completely drained several times, and it was a miracle she was even awake. Goliath

418

women were just built differently, I guess. "Realistically, we don't have anything to prove that we didn't just kill them and steal everything."

Mara's eyes lit up, and she slammed her fist into her palm. "I've got it!" She looked at us with a giant smile, bouncing up and down. "We take the skeleton!"

I looked at her, shocked. "Wait what."

"What?"

"Do what now?"

Sal's eyes went wide behind his broken pince-nez, and he opened his mouth before closing it. We all just looked at her, shocked at the absolute audacity. That thing was a hundred feet tall at minimum. How were we going to bring it into the city?

There was also another problem.

"Mara, if we teleport that thing to the city, it'll crush whatever's underneath it. We could destroy an entire section of the city with that thing."

Mara's excitement faded, and she slumped her shoulders. "Oh..." I hated to burst her bubble like that, but there was no way we could move that whole thing with us.

"However, we could maybe take just the skull." I suggested. "Would it be possible for the scholars to identify this guy was that dragon asshole's lackey or whatever?"

Giezha was taken aback by the flippancy with which I spoke about Khorba at first but nodded her head. "Yes, that would certainly be possible. Not to mention, they would be able to identify the magical signatures left on the skull." She made an uncomfortable face. "That might make things worse for you, Sal."

He shrugged and waved his hand.

"I'll be fine. Let's just get you all home. I should have just enough mana left to levitate the skull back up to us and we'll be able to go."

As we walked back to the skull with our loot in tow, I mentioned a slight problem with the plan.

"This could still destroy a good portion of the guildhall," I warned the others.

Uli blew a raspberry. "Fuck 'em. We'll pay the damages and then it can be their problem. I'm done with that fucking guild."

419

Giezha nodded her head. "Agreed. I will be quite happy to be out from under the some of the guild."

"Freedom." Mara sighed. "We'll just need to figure out what to do after that."

I laughed as Sal levitated the skull up and placed it next to all of us. "I think this should be enough to make us all sought after free agents."

None of the girls laughed at what I said, and instead, their eyes grew larger and larger. Mara let out a shriek of excitement while Uli and Giezha looked at each other, shaking their hands wildly. Giezha let out an excited shriek of her own which was much higher pitched than it had any right to be.

"We're gonna be so fucking rich!" Uli shouted, doing a little happy dance. "Every guild in the city will want us!"

"Forget the city, Uli!" Giezha said, bouncing up and down. "We'll be able to move to one of the larger cities! We'll have enough to go all the way to Midania! We'll be rubbing elbows with diplomats, scholars, and the Emperor himself!"

It warmed my heart seeing them so excited about what was possible now. All their struggles would finally be recognized. Their hopes to break out on their own had finally come true. It was a whole new chapter coming up.

"Well," Sal said, dusting off his hands. "Shall we head home?"

"Let's do that," I invited.

Holding on to the skull, all of us gathered around Sal. He lit a small flame and started to burn the rope as we all waited to be teleported. At first, only silver and copper smoke floated up into the air, covering us in a thick fog. Despite the smoke's thickness, it didn't choke me or take my breath. It just blinded me to the world around us.

"When the smoke clears, we'll be home," Sal told us as the dripping of the cave faded from earshot.

Replacing it was a howling wind as a sudden burst of gale chilled me to the bone. Blowing the smoke away, saw that the rope had not taken us to the guildhall. Instead, we were in the remnants of the old shack that they had ambushed us in.

There was at least a foot of snow on the ground and a thick sheet of ice from melting and refreezing several times. We all quickly looked for our coats and winter gear, donning as many layers as possible. The sun

420

was barely visible, rising from the eastern horizon. A thin layer of clouds covered the sky in blinding light. After such an extended time in the mountain, even dawn's early light was blinding.

The skull stood almost as high as the shack was before blowing up. We ran to the basement level and hunkered down in the small alcove we hid in previously. Disturbingly, the zombies were still underneath the thick snowfall, causing us to nearly trip over them several times. On the one hand, it was disgusting, but on the other, that meant nobody knew this place was here.

Once inside, we built a fire to warm ourselves up. The smoke drifted out the door, which we left open. The heat of the fire battled the frigid temperatures to a comfortable stalemate. Despite this, none of us dared take our clothes off, lest we invite a sudden gust of freezing wind. Uli sat next to me as we huddled together, rummaging through her bag.

"Aha!"

Uli's trademark grin etched onto her tired face as she held the scroll. Unfurling, it revealed a series of runes. She handed it to Giezha, who'd already laid on the ground, ready to doze off.

"Hey," Uli said, nudging Giezha's hat. "What's this one do?"

She bonked Giezha on the head with the scroll several times. Giezha pretended to be asleep before finally losing her patience.

"Alright! I'll read it!" Giezha snapped, taking the scroll and furtively reading it. She looked at Uli suspiciously. "Where did you get a scroll of disguise?"

Uli made an innocent face and stuck her tongue out. "It was in the treasure room, those two pricks had a stockpile for their little body changes."

I rubbed Uli's head and reached out for the scroll.

"I can go and find Kiersa to get us an audience with the council."

Before I could get the scroll, Sal grabbed it.

"You all are tired, and I have some direct contacts with the council. We will be able to skip most of the formalities if I go."

I looked at him suspiciously when he started reading from the scroll. I still didn't have all the answers to why he was there. Sensing my distrust, Sal looked at me with a sigh.

"I understand your trepidation, Asher," he said, putting the scroll down.

I raised an eyebrow at him. "You do? Because I'm pretty sure I'm the one that died back there."

Tension filled the air, and everybody looked between Sal and me. The others had a long history with him, but I didn't.

"Remind me what you've done to earn my trust."

"Asher," Mara said, reaching for my shoulder. "He was trying to protect his family and their memory. Would you have done the same?"

I couldn't speak of family matters, but her words did ring true. After all, I literally just got done pulling my soul back into my dead body for the slim chance of saving them.

"Why don't we both go?" Sal offered. "That way I'm not left with them, and you can keep an eye on me. It's a chance for me to earn the trust that you have rightfully withheld from me."

"I didn't withhold it, Sal," I countered. "You shredded it to pieces when you got me killed." I wanted to say more, but I stopped myself, not for his benefit or mine, but for the girls'. They've been through enough. "That being said... I'm fine with it. Who gets the disguise?"

Sal smiled and handed it to me. "You can have it."

I took the scroll and looked it over. The mana was already supplied in the scroll, and I just needed to activate the first few runes to use it. What I'd look like, I had no clue. The girls gave me the thumbs up, and I just shrugged. Why not, right?

Once we made our way through the caves, it took us about an hour to get back to Naled.

Sal instructed me not to activate the scroll until we were outside the city. The usual caravan of traders, adventurers, and lay folk were making their way in and out of the city. Tossing on a cloak and mask, Sal instructed me to use the scroll while we hid from sight.

The scroll glowed a faint blue before I felt myself begin to shimmer. I felt the exact same, but when I looked down, I saw a faint wobble around my skin. It was like the haze in the air on a hot day. I looked to Sal, who looked at me funny.

"What are you looking at?" I hissed.

"A half-elf with long red hair."

"What, like Mara?"

He sniggered. "Maybe Mara as a man."

"Whatever, let's just get this over with."

Joining the queue of entrants was an easy task and slipping by with a few coins pressed into the right guard's hands. We were back home for the first time in what felt like forever. Almost.

Sal made a beeline for the Fortress. The old bastard was surprisingly spry, and I had to push my way through the crowd, struggling to keep up. Rather than walking up to the entrance, he walked to the side of the castle wall. There was a gap between the usual perimeter of armed guards, and in that gap was a halfling carving an ivory tusk.

I nearly ran into Sal when he stopped. He stared at the halfling from under his hood for several moments. I didn't say anything, while the halfling mostly ignored us.

After several minutes, the halfling spoke without looking up. "Patience?"

Sal whispered so only the three of us could hear him. "Is for those who have time to waste."

The halfling placed the ivory down and looked up. His wrinkled face sagged and flopped as he moved. His eyes glowed bright green, staring at me. He was using magic to see through my disguise. Once he finished looking me up and down, he turned to Sal.

"I suppose there's no time for cribbage," the halfling wheezed.

"Afraid not, old friend."

"That's a shame," the old man said, standing up and turning to the wall. "I was hoping I'd get my win back." He turned back to me and snapped his fingers. "Look sharp, dear boy!" In a small 'poof!' I was transformed into my regular self.

The stone melted away into nothing with a few precise taps on the wall. A few people stopped to look but kept on walking.

Inside the wall, we made our way across a vast courtyard before walking to a portcullis. With a few snaps of his fingers, the chains cranked the door up, and we made our way in.

Inside the castle was a giant maze of grey and purple stone. There were few windows, and the little light they supplied was supplemented by large glowing crystals.

Figureheads of all shapes, sizes, and species walked around with long white robes, conversing in hushed tones. Once or twice, somebody stopped and looked at us suspiciously, clearly preparing to sound an alarm.

The halfling simply flicked his wrist, and they were instantly silenced before walking in the opposite direction. We were led into a large open room after walking through several halls, gates, and doorways.

"Well, this had better be good, Salvatore."

Sal lifted his hood and bowed slightly. "Yes, Councilman Alouit."

Several lights started glowing around us. Giant pillars of light illuminated the edges of the vast room. In each pillar stood a large white marble throne. Atop each throne was a stern-faced councilman, wearing purple and gold robes. The halfling lit a pipe and walked up the puffs of smoke he created, completing the thirteen-person circle surrounding us.

"The trial of Salvatore Yaxel and Asher Merrick will now commence," said a dark elf woman with a deep voice. Her face was square and angular, with piercing red eyes. "The trials of Mara Brightwood, Ulilee Siannodel, and Giezha Nightstrike will be held at a later date, dependent on the events of this trial."

All thirteen members of the council stood up and held out their hands. Some held wands, rods, and or staff, while the halfling pointed the smoking end of his pipe.

"The truth," they chanted together, "and only the truth."

Below us, thirteen large white circles overlapped each other with arcane symbols. The floor vibrated from the mass of magical power, and my chest felt tight. Thirteen Circles of Truth felt like overkill. Then again, I couldn't think of any way of getting around thirteen at once.

All eyes descended on me. I felt their stares burning enough holes in me to make Swiss cheese. Under normal circumstances, I'd be very intimidated. I would feel like this was a step too far. Like I had been unfairly plucked out of a terrible situation and plopped into more bullshit. Luckily, I was too tired and exhausted.

"Mr. Merrick, we are here to inform you that—"

"Look," I sighed, cutting the dark elf woman off, too tired and exhausted to listen to their spiel. "I literally just got done defeating the skeletal remains of some giant named Zhol that was the lieutenant of Khorba, The Asshole, or whatever. Not to mention walking through a mountain for days on end, death traps aplenty, and a ton of other shit I don't feel like getting into. At this point, I'm too tired. I'm going to skip all the unimportant stuff and tell you what you need to know."

Everyone's expression was priceless. Jaws dropped in every direction while Sal just laughed. Once they were done staring in disbelief at my audacity, they turned their attention to the Circles of Truth. Every single one of them stayed pure white. Several started talking amongst themselves in hushed tones. I decided to just plow through.

I explained the conspiracy, and how Dawnthorn was behind everything with Mhurren, Mick, and Vurshung. I went through the entire process of events from beginning to end. They took particular interest when I mentioned Sal had helped us thwart their plan.

The halfling that brought us in spoke up. "How exactly did he help?"

I stopped to think for a moment. Everything got so convoluted that it was hard to keep track of everything. After a moment's contemplation, I continued while Sal just let me roll with it.

"Those four were behind the moonstone shortage as well as the theft of the silver bars."

They were hanging onto every word, so I continued.

"They stole the silver and created a fake quest to bring me and the others to their secret lair in the southern mountains. Turns out, the Smite of the Dead Giant wasn't just the hammer. It was the giant skeleton dude too. They used the moonstones to power their spells up and summon the giant skeleton dude. Sal was forced to help them after getting caught investigating them."

There was a long pause as I stopped speaking. I gave the Council a minute to catch up to everything, and one of the councilmen spoke up. It was a yellow dragonborn who bore a striking resemblance to Vurshung.

"You mentioned Salvatore Yaxel's investigation. Why did he not warn you?"

Sal spoke up before I could answer. "I held suspicions about Dawnthorn and the others for some time, but did not think I could tell any others. My personal history would have made it difficult for anybody to believe me. Immediately after I found the silver and realized my suspicions were correct, they attacked me. I fled with the intention of finding Councilmen Aloiut, but was captured before that was possible."

The halfling stood up and stared at the dark elf that had been speaking earlier.

"Dawnthorn brought the idea of Mr. Yaxel's involvement forward and had him labelled as public enemy number one before any deliberation could occur. Soon after, Mr. Merrick and company were also wanted people. I believe that we, as a council, owe them all an apology."

A new councilman spoke up; it was a female moon-elf who bore a striking resemblance to Aire Denrel. She looked at me and smiled.

"We also received a warning from an anonymous source about this ordeal," she said, speaking in the exact same accent as Aire. "The source specifically mentioned Asher's gallantry and bravery in the face of the monsters he was accused of creating."

God, Kiersa was amazing. When I saw her, the first thing I'd do was sweep her off her feet and kiss her.

The dark elf scowled at Councilmen Aloiut and the moon elf. "We have no proof that they haven't just made this up! We still do not have any physical proof of this giant, or of the moonstone's whereabouts."

"We got the skeleton's skull if that helps." I said, pointing my thumb behind me. "Plus, like, a ton of those moonstones. We can take you with the magic rope thingy that Sal found. It teleported us to Dawnthorn's hideout. After that we can show you where to find the moonstones and stuff. And then maybe I could get some shut eye?" I asked longingly. "Like I said, came back from the dead, been up a long time, really need some sleep."

I felt my body begin to sway as unholy exhaustion gripped my body. It was a miracle I hadn't already passed out, and I was beginning to run low on miracles. After chewing on my words for several minutes, the entire Council stood up. They started chanting in languages I couldn't recognize as the Circles of Truth faded out.

"You have been granted a temporary leave under the consideration of evidence presented. If your evidence is confirmed, you will be cleared of all charges and receive a formal letter of apology. Mr. Merrick and Mr. Yaxel, please escort myself and Mr. Alouit to the evidence."

It was hard to pay attention as the other members of the Council all began to leave. The dark elf and Councilman Alouit floated over to Sal and me. Sal shook their hands while I gave both a short bow.

Sal showed them the rope and began the process of teleporting us. As the thick smoke enveloped me once more, I couldn't help but wonder how much longer I had until I passed out.

Once the smoke cleared, we were back at the hideout, and the girls had started a large fire to keep warm. Their chattering teeth and scornful looks let me know that we took far too long.

Those angry looks did not last when they saw two members of The Council behind us. Paying us no mind, the dark elf and Alouit inspected the skull with Sal. I walked over and filled them in on everything I knew, which wasn't much.

"What if they decide it's fake?" Mara asked fearfully. "What then?"

"They'll try to execute us," Giezha said, her nose dripping from the cold. "And then we run for our lives. Besides, there's that massive stack of moonstones we stuck inside the skull while you were gone. They'll be happy enough with that."

Uli stood there, silently watching the two of them speak with Sal. I was too tired to be afraid at this point.

If the fates decided we needed to be on the run, I would probably just try and kill these two at this point. I really didn't care. I was too exhausted to care.

"Hey Giezha, how difficult would a weather spell be?" I asked, feeling the snow pelt my face. "Ball park range."

Giezha looked at me funny. "I do not know what this 'ball park' is, but spells of such scale are known by few and practiced by even fewer."

I just gave her the thumbs up and plopped down on the ground. My legs refused to hold my stupid body up any longer. They were done. And so was I.

"If any one of you puts a stamina potion anywhere near my lips, I swear I will get physical," I said, crossing my arms behind my head.

"That won't be necessary, Asher," Sal called out. "We're good to go."

I picked my head up from the ground and saw the skull was getting covered in silver and copper smoke. With a burst of wind, it disappeared, and so did the two members of the Council. The girls all jumped for joy and started screaming in excitement, but I couldn't join in.

I felt my eyelids begin to weigh a thousand pounds, and my whole body felt heavy. The kind of heavy where your limbs are attached to sandbags. As much as I wanted to be a part of the celebration, there was no way I would make it home under my own power.

"Hey Asher," Mara whispered while she wrapped her arms around me.

"The girls and I wanted to know if you were down for a fiveway with Kiersa when we get home."

"Whelp!" I said, jumping to my feet. "I think it's about time we head home, don't you guys? It's time to celebrate!"

The jerebo's eyes were much more intelligent than a regular animal's. It continued knocking on the door, its face looking impatient.

Chapter 39

Xaliasday Afternoon, 18th of Extrin, Year 678, 4th Age

I would love to tell you that I rocked their world the second I got home. I would love to tell you that my most shining achievement of that entire affair was managing to have a fiveway with the most gorgeous women I had met in that world. Nothing would make me happier than telling you that day will live on in memory for myself and Kiersa, Mara, Giezha, and Uli.

But that didn't happen.

Unfortunately, after coming back from the dead, defeating the bad guys, and blowing the minds of a shadowy government organization, I had reached my limit.

However, I did manage one last audacious moment.

"You think Kiersa will be surprised when she sees us?" I asked the others. "Because we kind of just left one day with no explanation." I chattered along, trying to prevent my more lascivious thoughts from bubbling to the surface.

"We just disappeared and then we were suddenly the most wanted in the entire city. You know, Dawnthorn and the others must have had some plan in place to frame us the second we left."

Giezha's shoulders were slumped over as Uli snoozed away on top of her. Mara was barely able to keep herself up as well. Mara's sensuous offer was far from her mind as she trudged along.

Sal stayed back to finish work with the Council while we rested up. Since the Silver Cup Inn was still destroyed, we decided to head to the Denrel's and the Golden Sky Tavern.

It was midday, so the lunch rush should've been out the door. Curiously though, I couldn't see anybody eating inside.

Turning, I grabbed the door handle and pulled it open. It was completely empty, save for three figures by the fireplace. Kiersa and Aire spoke with a tall figure who had their back turned. Both Kiersa and her father listened intently and didn't see us when we entered. We all stopped in our tracks, awkwardly waiting for them to notice us.

"I'm sorry to say that your warning about the undead fell on deaf ears, Kiersa." I recognized the voice as the moon elf woman from the council.

"My daughter nearly died, Ghilanna!" Aire growled, pointing his finger in the woman's face. "They attacked my wife! They came for us here!"

The woman sighed. "I know, brother, but I was up against a hostile Council. They knew I was speaking on Kiersa's behalf and believed I was lying. It wasn't until Mr. Asher and everyone returned with proof that they b—"

Kiersa grabbed her by the arm. "He's back?" She shook the councilwoman violently. "They're back?"

Smiling at the opportunity, I cut in. "We're back!" I said with a wave. The girls awkwardly joined me, waving at the Denrel family.

Their heads turned in unison, and Kiersa let go of her aunt. Her mouth slackened, and she blinked several times.

"Asher," she said quietly. Kiersa walked up, blinking rapidly and looking me up and down. She raised a hand to her mouth and stopped right in front of me. "You're covered in blood. And scars."

Oh, fuck. We hadn't cleaned up yet. I hadn't thought about it, but Kiersa had to be right. I'd been beaten, bashed, burned, and pummeled like a piece of meat. "I am?" I asked curiously.

Kiersa looked at me and slowly placed her hands on the sides of my head. "What happened?"

I looked at the girls who showed zero interest in answering the question. A quick glance to Aire showed a look of general disbelief. I looked at her and saw tears forming. Looked like I was going to get myself out of this mess.

I sighed. "I'm going to give you the basic version for now, if that's fine."

She just looked at me, waiting for me to explain. I took a deep breath and launched into the story of what had happened with Dawnthorn, her minions, and the giant again.

"You killed them?" Kiersa asked, still in disbelief.

"Yeah, but not before they killed Asher," Mara added. I tensed up and turned around, giving her the stink eye. I'd left that part out for a reason.

"You died?" Kiersa asked, tears flowing even harder. "How'd you come

431

back?"

"I'd like to know as well," Ghilanna said calmly. "You failed to mention the specifics during your trial."

Giezha and Uli were both making gestures, desperately pleading I don't say anything, but I ignored them. Fuck it.

"The God of the Lost, Gathos brought me back to life and I had to pull my soul back into my body," I said, rolling my eyes. "I'm actually from a different world and was killed there before being brought back to life here."

"You're an Otherworlder!" Aire exclaimed.

"Yes," I said with annoyance before turning back to Kiersa. "Anyways! Yes, I died. And then I came here to Echo Veil. And yes, I died again. But I got better! And we beat the bad guys." I clasped Keira's shoulders gently. "So, it's all good! Right?"

Kiersa just shook her head, her face cracking into an odd smile. "You're an Otherworlder," she said with a laugh. "You? And you died. And you came back?"

The temperature in the room dropped to minus twenty. I couldn't let Kiersa go, but I was afraid she could snap at any moment.

Unable to think of anything else to say, I nodded my head. "Yeah."

"And you saved the day."

"I think so."

"And the secret mission you had, and the moonstones?"

Uli spoke up, opening her bag, and pulling out a mass of moonstones. "Taken care of."

Ghilanna gave us a raised eyebrow, but I just gave her a look back. So, fucking what if we took moonstones back? We found them, for fuck's sake!

I could feel Kiersa's breathing speed up, turning my attention back to her. Her eyes looked dangerous as she huffed and puffed.

"I would like to reiterate that we will be able to cure your mother, and that I really don't want to die twice in one day," I quickly added, terrified of what she'd do.

Kiersa just gritted her teeth. "You...!"

"I'm sorry! I just—"

Kiersa pulled me in for a deep, long kiss in front of everyone. She held me tight, kissing me more passionately and sensuously than ever before. And let me say, that woman didn't need to improve. She broke away from me for a minute, huffing and puffing.

"I was so worried you might have died. And I was right," she said, her voice struggling to keep even. "And you're telling me everything's fine."

I noticed that some blood had gotten on her cheek, so I gently rubbed it off. "Only because I came back."

Kiersa scrunched up her face and pulled me in for a tight hug, which I reciprocated. As she squeezed me, she whispered in my ear.

"I'm going to fuck your gods damn brains out, Asher."

I looked at her, suddenly wobbly in the knees. "That sounds fantastic..." That last bit of energy I was saving up, finally gave out. "But I'm going to bed now."

Kiersa grinned, ready to say something flirty. However, I passed out in her arms before she got the chance.

The last thing that I remembered hearing was everybody screaming my name in terror. But having already experienced death once today, I knew for certain that I wasn't dying. I was just dead tired.

I slept a long and dreamless sleep. I didn't dream about the mission. I didn't have any nightmares about my death in the mountains. My brain was too tired to even come up with a depiction of that fiveway Mara had put in my head.

No, I just slept and slept as if I were in a coma...

Looking back on it, I was probably in a coma.

There were a few times when I regained a little consciousness. I would hear people talking around me in hushed tones. I could tell when it was Kiersa, Uli, Mara, or Giezha. Occasionally, I'd hear Sal and Aire as well, discussing something.

It was weird. I could tell they were talking and speaking normally, but I couldn't understand what was said.

Finally, I woke up to the sound of a new voice. It was a woman's voice, soft and sweet, almost like a deeper version of Kiersa. She sounded middle-aged and fatigued. As she spoke to me, it felt like my whole body was regaining feeling.

I went from feeling so heavy I was sinking into the bed to as light as a feather. The pitch black of sleep was replaced by light seeping through my eyelids, and I could see the little swirlies and dots that float in my vision.

"You'd better wake up soon, Mr. Merrick," the voice lightly chided me.

433

"The girls are getting worried."

Struggling to rejoin the conscious world, I murmured. "Huh?"

The woman smiled, seemingly unsurprised I spoke. "You've been talking in your sleep lately. You've been saying some very interesting things. Putting ideas in their heads."

"Ideas?"

"Yes, they're under the impression that you care for them more than they thought."

My body regained movement, and I felt my arms and legs twitch. I scrunched my face, thinking about what she'd said. "I came back from the dead to save them. Of course, I care."

The woman chuckled, and I felt a frail hand on my forehead. "You've done more than that, Asher."

I finally managed to open my eyes, slowly blinking several times. When I opened my eyes, the bright light from the window blinded me for a moment.

As they adjusted, I saw a figure looking over me. She was gorgeous with a pointed chin and bright yellow-brown eyes. The sunlight kissed her tanned skin, shining like the sunset on a summer's day.

"Good morning, Asher." She smiled. "It's great to finally meet you."

I blinked my eyes open several times before sitting up straight. This woman looked familiar, but I had a hard time placing her. I saw that I was in the bedroom I'd stayed at in the Golden Sky Tavern. The woman removed her hand from my head and got up.

"They're waiting, you know," she said at the door. "My daughter has been extremely worried about you.

Daughter? I looked at her short, copper hair, and it hit me like a freight train.

"Mrs. Denrel?" I said in disbelief. "You're awake?"

Kiersa's mother smiled and bowed her head. "And feeling better than ever, thanks to the efforts of you all." She stopped and listened as a rumble drew close. "I suggest you brace for impact, dear."

She opened the door right as the thunderous noise rolled in. Kiersa, Uli, Giezha, and Mara all shot into the room, but before they could jump me, Nosha stopped them.

"Now, girls, he's been asleep for a few days, give him some room to

434

breathe." She laughed and left the room as all four of them stared at me nervously.

The room I'd been sleeping in was small enough as it was, but having the four of them in there left it claustrophobic. Sitting upright, I turned my back, popping every joint from my hip to my shoulders, sounding like crushed gravel.

I looked down at my arms, seeing tiny scars trailing up and down my arm like bolts of lightning. They perfectly traced where the mana had literally spilled out of me during the fight with Dawnthorn and the giant.

"Glad to see you're finally up," Uli said in a facsimile of her usual airy tone. "We'd been wondering how long you'd be out."

"Yeah," Mara said uncomfortably. "It's been pretty nerve-wracking."

Giezha handed me a cup of water which I gratefully gulped down. As I drank, Giezha smirked.

"Uli's been crying almost the entire time you were unconscious."

Uli made a sour face and elbowed Giezha in the side of her thigh.

"You were worried too. I wasn't the only one who cried." She pointed to Mara and Kiersa. "So did you, and so did you! We all cried! We thought you'd kicked the bucket the way you just dropped midway through a conversation."

"Right," I said, jumping out of bed. "Well, I'm conscious now, and extremely hungry. So how about we grab some breakfast, or lunch... or dinner?"

As I spoke, everyone's eyes trailed down to my waist, clearly not listening to me. I looked down and saw I was now completely naked and fully erect.

Gotta love morning wood. Or, in this case, post-coma wood, I guess.

Kiersa handed me a fresh set of clothes, which I quickly put on. None of the girls bothered looking away, making a point of watching me dress instead.

"Glad you all are doing alright," I said, pulling the tunic over my head. "How've things been while I was out?"

Uli looked at Giezha and laughed. "They've been busy. We're getting moved into our new home right now."

"New home?"

"Yeah," Mara answered. "Sal's decided not to reopen the Inn. Plus, we

435

can finally afford a place to ourselves."

Oh damn. That's right! Between the reward for the missions and getting out of debt, they were sure to be on to the next big thing.

"Congrats!" I hugged each of them individually, grinning from ear to ear. I also gave Kiersa a hug to ensure she didn't feel left out.

"So where are you guys moving?"

Giezha made a gesture with her head pointing backward. "Over by the Docks. Figured it's best to save up."

Mara picked up on the subtext of my question. "You're coming with us, right?"

I scratched the back of my head, feeling bashful. "If you'll have me."

We all laughed and decided to go out for lunch. Kiersa joined us while her parents stayed behind to take care of the restaurant and celebrate their reunion.

It turned out I'd been asleep for three days. We wound up grabbing fried fish and bread near the new building. While I feasted on enough fish to feed an entire crew at sea, they filled me in on the fate of the Red Breaker Guild.

"Sal, of all people, had stepped up to take over and lead the guild!" Mara said excitedly. "He's gonna try and repair the guild's reputation. Plus, he wants to prevent others from going down the same path as Dawnthorn."

Brody had been his most vocal supporter during a hearing with the council that had been called to determine whether to allow the Red Breaker Guild to remain or permanently disband it.

"They decided to sweep the whole affair under the rug," Mara continued, keeping pace with my voracious eating. "But that meant Dawnthorn couldn't be officially recognized as the mastermind."

"So what? She gets off scot-free?" I asked, finishing off my third salmon.

Uli shrugged while nibbling on a bread loaf. "They paid us a lot of money to keep our traps shut. Besides, the bitch is dead. Fuck her."

We all raised a glass to Dawnthorn and the other's deaths. The surrounding tables misheard us and toasted to the memory of Dawnthorn and the others.

"The Council's hands are tied though." Kiersa added. "Once the Emperor caught wind of a Zala tunnel in the report, he had all subsequent investigations handled by his personal team, The Anointed. The Council was given a story and told to stick with it or else."

"Ivory Forge got off scot free too," Giezha added bitterly.

I could only laugh at our mysterious government getting muscled out of position by an even more mysterious government organization.

Once we got our fill, Uli paid the bill with her endless satchel, making a point to reach down until her entire arm disappeared in the bag. After eating, they lead me down a series of twisting roads. Eventually, we wound up crossing over to Iron Court's waterfront. It was a run-down section of the city where most of the illegal trade went down.

"I thought you said you were living in The Docks?" I asked, more surprised than concerned.

"Nearby The Docks," Mara corrected me. "It's hard to rent this many rooms at once."

After walking the complicated series of twists and turns, I was presented with a dilapidated narrow wooden building stuck between two more significant stone buildings in disrepair. Walking up a series of rickety steps, we reached the top. As we ascended, the building swayed back and forth while spiders dropped around us, filling their nasty webs.

"Please, tell me there are no giant spiders here."

Kiersa smiled brightly. "Nope! Got rid of those first."

I didn't dare ask for more details. Exposed beams hung overhead as we opened a large set of double doors. We entered a large room with a small fireplace beside an uneven dining table with mismatched chairs.

"This is the main room!" Mara announced proudly. "It's great for just milling about and stuff. There's a kitchen, bathroom, and rooms for the five of us."

"Five?" I turned and counted heads quickly. It was five, but... "Kiersa?" I asked, turning to a very proud-looking half-elf.

Kiersa grinned and puffed out her chest. "That's right! You're looking at the newest member of the team! Now that Mother's health has returned, she's insisted that I move out and begin my own adventures."

Kiersa began to excitedly regale me with her ideas for what she could do as a team member and how she'd been dreaming of this day for a long time.

The others all held the same look of nervous excitement while I tried to imagine what type of armor she'd be wearing. And the type that would be able to properly account for her... assets. Once things settled down, I excused myself to check out my new room and have a moment alone.

I'd wound up with the last room on the right beside the kitchen. It reminded me of the room I had in college. A wardrobe, bed, and desk, all crammed together in the corner, so the rest of the room could be free and empty.

After finding the remainder of my possessions inside the wardrobe, I pulled out my shield and the ring Ms. Rosria affixed with my ruby. The ring went on my middle finger on my left hand. I decided to place the shield by my bed with for my now-broken sword by the bed. Looking around, there was plenty of space to adorn with whatever treasures I found in the future.

Sitting down, I looked out the single window in my room beside my desk. It pointed toward Lake Shabba. Several ships arrived and left the port as I watched. I sat down at the desk with a sigh, wanting to decompress.

This narrow stick of a building jutted higher than those surrounding it, giving an unrestricted view of the city and far off to the horizon. All the people out at the harbor and walking around the streets looked like tiny ants, piddling about. I took a deep breath and watched the icy sheets on top of the lake overlap each other for a while. A tiny jerebo ran along several buildings before heading in my direction.

"What're you doing, little guy?" I asked.

The jerebo leaped from a building much too short before gliding up into the air. It rose on a current, landing softly at my window. It held a scroll in its mouth as it knocked on the window with its paw.

I looked around, trying to make sure I wasn't crazy. The jerebo's eyes were much more intelligent than a regular animal's. It continued knocking on the door, its face looking impatient.

"Sorry," I apologized, opening the window.

The critter squeezed its chubby belly under the opening, tapping its paws to push through. Once it did, it let out a trill of excitement, spinning around on the desk. It sat upright and wagged its tail, scroll still in the mouth.

"Is that for me?" I asked.

The jerebo bobbed its head up and down several times, trilling more. I scratched the top of its head, which the jerebo leaned into. As it rolled around on my hand, I noticed it had odd markings on its back.

438

I slowly grabbed the scroll, and the jerebo let go of it. The scroll was a thick, yellowed paper with a gold wax seal.

At first, I was worried this could be some maniac's act of terrorism, but then I noticed the wax seal.

A crescent moon and three stars, silver glitter mixed with the gold. Looking back, the jerebo's markings were just the same.

"Gathos," I breathed. "What'd you do now?"

I opened the letter, prepared for the latest round of ungodly/godly bullshit. The outer layers were covered in runes, while the middle contained a short letter. I focused on the golden ink, reading the letter aloud to myself.

Asher,

Congratulations on proving my intuition about you. Your actions today will change the world for centuries to come.

Best of luck in your new life, and don't forget to take time to enjoy yourself. You've got a lifetime ahead of you, and when the time comes, you'll think about the roses you never stopped to smell.

Gathos

P.S. A friend of mine wanted to thank you for helping some of her followers and insisted on gifting you something. She's always been a sweetheart.

"Gift?" I asked, looking at the jerebo.

As I said that, an ethereal voice whispered in my ear. It was a woman's voice, deep and echoing. She spoke in a language I couldn't comprehend, but it was almost like singing. My eyes drooped from this lullaby for a moment before a bright light began shining in my right hand. The woman's voice grew louder and louder, and the whole room shook, knocking the dust from the exposed ceiling onto my head.

Just as suddenly as it started, the light disappeared without a sound. Replacing it was a longsword with a straight edge, ending in a long point at the end. I turned it over a few times and noticed something peculiar about the blade.

It was snow-white on one side and a coppery-gold on the other. The pommel was also split on each side. Gathos' symbol was on the gold side, while the other was white and purple, with three moons forming a triangle.

"Ihena?" I whispered.

Footsteps thundered towards me, and everyone burst into my room with their weapons drawn. Kiersa was holding an old warhammer that was chipped on the edges. They all looked around frantically before noticing me with the jerebo now sitting on my head.

"Uh, Asher?" Mara asked, noticing the sword as well. "What was that?"

I smiled and gestured with my new sword.

"A gift." I smiled, feeling the sword's power radiate in my hands. "Looks like we're just getting started."

About the Author

Solomon Ignis is an anxious "wizard" who got tired of getting ganked by raiders because the paladin refused to tank while the cleric hated healing. After nearly dying to his own fireball, Solomon packed up his tomes and decided to hit the road once more as a struggling artist. Because at least then he could struggle to survive without zombies chomping his hat.

Want to stay up to date and get free stories, offers, and more? Sign up for my mailing list.

www.SolomonIgnis.com

FOLLOW ME IF YOU DARE:

@SolomonIgnis

/r/Solomon_Ignis

@SolomonIgnis

443